THE TELLING TOUCH

Keira Dominguez

Praise for *Her Caprice*

"It has been a long time since I have stayed up to the wee hours of the morning with a book I couldn't put down. This book was totally worth the groggy sleepy day I had today. I won't give away any of the details but it was a really great read. I can hardly wait to read Keira's next novel. I hope I don't have wait too long." ~a Girl and a Boy

"I loved this book! I stayed up entirely too late at night reading and I have no reservations in saying that I couldn't put it down. One of my favorite parts were a few end of chapter sentences...they were so good that I often read them twice. In truth, my only complaint was that I wanted more." ~Carrie

"I'm an avid reader, so being surprised by "newness" is a delight to me. The time period was obviously thoroughly researched, and the book was free of the glaring cultural inconsistencies so often found in Regency romance. The author stayed firmly within the bounds of the time period.

I truly enjoyed this book and look forward to more offerings from this author! Write quickly, Keira!" ~The Book Gramma

"This book is absolutely wonderful. Almost like a thriller, a regency romance with lots of wit and gutsiness. The secret is surprising and totally original (have never read it anywhere else, fact or fiction!). The hero and heroine seem very real and totally lovable. The other characters largely likeable. The villain is more villainous as the book progresses, so the danger increases to a gripping finale. I finished reading it on a flight and didn't notice that the plane landed or that hours had passed, so absorbed was I in this book. Highly recommend." ~AM

"I love finding an author who has done something a bit different with the Regency romance, while still maintaining its best traditions. The characters in 'Her Caprice' are delightful, the writing is excellent and the tension was at times so great that I had to stop

reading to catch my breath. I'm really looking forward to reading more from this author." ~Lian Tanner

"What a unique and interesting fairy tale Beatrice has a secret and feels it will stop her from normal life. This story deals with parents fear and how they plan to hide the issue. No matter what happens fate has another plan. I loved the beautiful twists and it was written brilliantly too. Keira Dominguez is a new author for me and I enjoyed her story will be on the lookout for other works by her." ~VineVoice

www.BOROUGHSPUBLISHINGGROUP.com

PUBLISHER'S NOTE: This is a work of fiction. Names, characters, places and incidents either are the product of the author's imagination or are used fictitiously. Any resemblance to actual events, locales, business establishments or persons, living or dead, is coincidental. Boroughs Publishing Group does not have any control over and does not assume responsibility for author or third-party websites, blogs or critiques or their content.

ISBN 978-1-951055-56-1

To Frankie Hanna who does this little dance every time she describes the Springfield, Oregon singles scene, circa 1985, which perfectly illustrates why she accepted a marriage proposal from a dashing widower with 25 children. As one of those children, I thank her down to my toes.

ACKNOWLEDGMENTS

I would like to thank the Klickitat Writers--Christine Sandgren, Afton Nelson and Marianne Monson--for mixing "Oh honey, no" with equal parts of "Yes! This!" You are the best and I love you. I would also like to thank my heroic beta readers Donna Lessard, PAULA THACKER (who gets all caps because I forgot her last time), Julie Melanson, Kylene Grell, Debbie West and Stephanie McRae. Thanks to Eliza Wu for popping by my house just when I was looking for Cantonese curse words. Finally, I offer my undying gratitude to my husband Nathan who has taken to being an author's husband (an era known as *Now Costco Feeds Our Children*) like a duck to water.

THE TELLING TOUCH

Prologue

June 1807

Meg poked her head around the front door of Blythe House. The sun had not yet broken the horizon, though the sky was lit with the promise of it. She spied a delicate bundle of wildflowers—devil's bit and common eyebright—tied up in a piece of twine, left conspicuously in the middle of the porch.

A grin spread across her face as she stepped over it to crouch beside the column, running quick, searching fingers around the base until her hand closed on a bit of green sea glass no larger than the end of her thumb. The irregular crescent shape had been softened from endless tumbling in tide and surf until its sharp edges echoed the verdant downs of East Sussex rolling back from the cliffs.

"He's back." Meg laughed. Then she shouted it as she ran through the hall and down to the kitchens. "He's back."

The two housemaids looked up from their breakfast as she raced by, and Mrs Jolly, Grandfather's housekeeper, raised a brow. Meg paid them no mind and her long hair, tied off in a ribbon, rolled against her shoulder blades as she rummaged through a cupboard for a knapsack. "What will you give me, Jolly?" she asked, her voice muffled as she backed out of the space.

Mrs Jolly frowned. "You've not had your breakfast yet."

Meg reached for an apple in the center of the long scrubbed table, took a huge bite, and gave Jolly a look that asked if she was happy now.

"Well?" Meg wheedled with a waggle of her brows.

Jolly laughed, a sure sign of surrender. "You bring me enough trout for our dinner," she said, "and you may have some cheese and a loaf of bread and a few of those pickled cucumbers. Not all of them, mind. You'll be wanting a flask of tea too, I expect." Meg nodded, gripping her unfinished apple in her teeth and shoveling her spoils into a large sack as she slurped the juice.

Jolly removed the apple, scrubbing Meg's mouth with a corner of her apron. "But it's the last time. I don't like to see you running after those young men."

A hunk of cheese slipped from Meg's fingers and rolled across the floor. She grabbed it up again and gave it the merest dusting of her hands before shoving it in the bag. "*Those young men?* Henry, Fox, and Nick?"

"Mr Gracechurch, Lord Fox, and Mr Ainsley, yes," came Jolly's unhurried correction. She corked the flask of tea and wrapped it in a piece of linen. She dropped the apple into Meg's hand. "You're not a little girl anymore, Miss Margaret. Almost fifteen now, which is much too old to be keeping company with boys of nineteen. Things have changed."

Meg shook her head and gave an unladylike snort. "I've been waiting since Christmas for Nick to come home from school and he finally has. We're going fishing." She cinched the sack and stepped through the garden door. The newly risen sun bathed her bare head and she turned her face east, blinded in the sudden light. "Same as always. Nothing's changed."

She gave a laugh made of joy and anticipation, and was away in a flash, running toward the bottom of the garden, and through the gate. If Jolly called more dire warnings after her, she didn't hear them—only the sound of her slippers hitting the soft turf verging the road. Her path took her to the woods, following some familiar, unseen trail, and she pushed her way through the undergrowth, shifting the weight of the satchel, adjusting the awkwardness of her rod.

Her haste made her careless and a thin, springy branch whipped her cheek when she broke through to the clearing. Batting it away, she slid down a short, rocky riverbank and swatted her dusty skirts as she jogged up to two young men.

"Where's Nick?" she asked, hating the breathlessness that betrayed her struggle to keep up with these long-limbed boys.

"Did you bring food?" Fox asked, knotting a fly to his line, not sparing her a look.

She lifted her load.

Henry answered her. "Nick is sure to be late. He arrived home only last night."

Nevertheless, he had stopped at Blythe House to leave a piece of smooth green sea glass on the manor steps. For her. Meg's insides did a little jig.

"Your turn to lay the fire, Fox," Henry said, bumping him in the arm.

"Meg?" Fox asked, looking as helpless as possible.

She wasn't fooled. "It'll cost you a bob."

Henry hooted with laughter as Fox dug into his waistcoat for a coin. "For a fire? You're no better than a highwayman."

She tucked the coin away to rattle in her pocket with the pebble and her knife. "It's a cruel world, Fox. A poor orphan girl must look to her future."

Fox shook his head and ran off with Henry at his heels. The cousins fought for a position farther down the bank, and Meg began to lay out the fire. Deft fingers plucked apart the tinder and shoved it deep inside the heap of sticks. She struck the flint and, as the wad of cotton and beeswax caught, Meg bent low to blow the flame into something stronger, feeding it more wood as it grew.

"You have an hour," she shouted and heard an answering call. She splayed her hands in front of the fire, banishing the chill of the cool summer morning.

"Still bellowing like an ox, Meg Summers?" came a familiar voice.

Her mouth curved into a slow grin as she watched the dancing flames. "Still a mannerless clod, Nick Ainsley?" She glanced up and her breath caught in her throat.

It was Nick—only Nick—but he'd changed in the months he'd been at school. He stood at the top of the bank and she wrinkled her brow, noticing that his careless grooming and ready smiles had not altered a whit. What was it then? A light breeze ruffled his unruly brown hair. It was longer now.

He jogged down to the clearing and dumped his pack and pole. "Did you break up a fight?" At her look of confusion he stepped close and began trailing his finger across her cheekbone. "There's blood there."

She tipped her face up to him as her magic lit the ends of her nerves, the sparking energy skimming the thoughts in his head, telling herself all the while that it was an accident, this touching. She hadn't sought it out. Grandfather could not scold her if he knew she was reading minds without permission.

Poor Meg. What have you done to yourself?

Tenderness trained his fingers to be gentle as he touched her. Affection suffused through him, guiding every muscle and limb.

Little sister.

She jerked at that, frowning. But he had a handkerchief out before she could speak, cupping her chin in his large hands as he dabbed along the cut.

Little sister.

Meg broke loose of his grip, gave a wobbly, uncertain smile, and batted his hand away. "It was only a tree."

"Would you like me to fell it?" he said, posing like a cavalier, sword in hand. An old game.

She laughed.

The cheerful mayhem of Fox and Henry echoed in the clearing and Nick cocked his head, stuffing his handkerchief away as he turned to prepare his gear. "They got here early."

Meg retreated to familiar ground—a refuge from this unaccountable awareness of him. "Elephants crashing through a forest would make less noise. Even you could beat them to the fish today."

"Even me?" He grinned, rising to her bait like one of the sleek speckled trout that ran the stream. "Do you still think you're better?"

Meg sat back on her heels and flashed a wicked smile. She reached for her rod. "I know I am."

She cast her line into a shadowy pool, calming her emotions. *Little sister.* She gave a grunt as she pulled on the line, teasing it out. What good was her magic when she had to read things she didn't want to?

A few minutes later, she was pulling the barbed hook from a fish's mouth and stood, wiping a wet, scaly hand on her skirts. Her shoulders were taken by a shudder of revulsion, hastily suppressed, as her hand slipped into her pocket for her knife.

She looked up to find Nick watching her.

"Want me to clean it?"

She nodded and a flush travelled up her cheeks. Nick beckoned for the fish, not making a fuss about it, not treating her like a child. Instead, he tucked his own knife behind the gills, giving the head a clean slice. Another cut went up the belly and Nick rinsed the entrails in the shallows of the stream. Meg's eyes were fastened to him, though this scene had played out any number of times.

Did Isabelle ever see him like this? Open-necked shirt, hair rumpled from sleep, and a stubble on his chin that told her he was shaving as often as a man now. Not this morning, though. Meg's eyes travelled from his deft hands to his broad shoulders and she turned away as she felt a wish form, right in the pit of her stomach.

The truth of Jolly's words caught up to her all the way from Blythe House, tugging on her hair, shaking her by the shoulder, kicking her on the backside. Things *had* changed.

Nick tucked the fish into a basket and took up his pole again, turning a pleasant smile on her as she shuttered her expression. The first time she had ever done so.

They fished in silence for a long while, until, casting the line in a long, elegant arc and landing the fly in the middle of a quiet pool, he asked, "I've missed all the news from home. Tell me what's new." His voice was casual, but his lithe form tightened.

He wanted to know about Isabelle. Meg would rather speak about a malarial plague. "Henry's sister Susan has fallen in love with a curate. His neck is as long as a giraffe." She grinned. "And Lord Ainsley is courting Mrs Nelson."

Nick rolled his eyes. "My uncle is most certainly not. He is merely the executor of her husband's estate."

"It looks like courting to me," she said. "He's wearing out the track between the Abbey and her house. All those whispered conversations in the churchyard. I told Isabelle and she said—"

His eyes gleamed. "What does a grubby halfling know about courting?"

It was a piece of their usual sparring, but it stung this time. She shook it away, refusing to let this sudden feeling for Nick turn her into a nit. "As much as a landless yokel with straw for brains."

Nick gave an amused grunt and flicked the line for another cast. "And your sister?" he asked, finally coming around to it. "What of her?"

"Isabelle spent a month in Town with Aunt Olympia," Meg said, her throat closing on the words that would tell him of how Isabelle had gotten her way in spite of Grandfather's objections: words that would tell him of how her sister seemed to burn with a new intensity since her return.

"Has it spoiled her for home?" Nick asked, and in that question Meg saw all of him. All his longing for Isabelle. All his impatience. All his dignity in the attempts to hide it. She didn't need to read his mind to know.

Meg shrugged in answer to his question. Yes, Isabelle was spoiled for home. But she had been for years, and you couldn't tell that to someone so determined to be stupid with love as Nick was.

He nodded. "And you? What has changed for you since I went up to school?"

"Nothing," she replied quickly, not telling him about how she'd grown out of her old gowns and how she tried to put her hair up when no one would see her. "I'm the same as always."

"Let's see," he said, stepping close enough to sweep his hand across the crown of her head and run it into his chest, right about the level of his collarbone. "Not quite the same," he said, giving her hair a teasing tug when she didn't laugh.

Meg smiled as he went back to his task. With a controlled snap of her forearm, she flicked the rod back then forward, unfurling the line and dropping it into the stream. Nick had shown her the proper way to do it, patiently teaching until her mastery matched his own. Now he grinned back at her and she checked, mid-cast, at the heart-stopping beauty of it.

"Quick," he called, jerking her loose from her reverie. "Get the net. I've got one on the line. Move," he roared, laughing.

Instinct propelled her as she rushed for the net. He gave a grunt, drawing in the line, and the rod bent sharply as the fish thrashed in the shallows. "Hurry. So help me, Meg—"

Meg kicked off her shoes and yanked off her stockings, leaving them in an untidy pile. She gathered up her skirts in one hand. "Hold on to your garters," she shot back, striding into the bracing water and shrieking as she chased his catch. After a few fumbling attempts, she scooped the fish up in her net and held it aloft. "Got it."

Triumphant, she turned and froze at his expression. The struggle for her prize had destroyed any accidental elegance she had managed to achieve that morning. She was half soaked and fabric clung to her petite frame. Fat droplets of water beaded against the flesh of her arms and the lazy current swirled around her calves. Her skirts, lifted above the stream, were a good deal higher than that.

Meg's eyes held Nick's and, even in her inexperience, she saw warmth, interest. The space between them thickened with possibility.

They balanced like that on a knife's point for the space of three heartbeats—no more—before his eyes widened a fraction and he dropped his rod.

Breath seemed to rush into her lungs. "Is this your catch or mine?" she asked, heart pounding as she scrambled for familiar footing. But there was no answering laughter in his eyes.

"Yours." And then a deep line settled between his brows. "How old are you now, Meg?"

She could hear herself breathing, and the silty river, gin-clear before she had leaped about in it, began to settle. *How old are you now, Meg?* She sent up a silent prayer that Jolly was wrong. She prayed that she was still young enough to scold about a soaking skirt, to ignore propriety, to tag along after him anywhere he went.

She waded out of the stream, pushing the net into his hands.

He took his time, bending over the fish, gutting and cleaning it, intent on his task. "Fourteen," he said finally, glancing up at her.

Meg's cheeks stained crimson and she sent another prayer to heaven that he would never guess that she had spent the last half hour trying out Mrs Nicholas Ainsley under her breath like a half-witted mooncalf.

Her mouth was dry when she answered, though she gave him a teasing curtsey. "How gallant of you to remember."

"And in September you'll be fifteen," he continued, laying bare the bald facts like a fishmonger setting out his catch. Nick went a little white under his tan and shook his head. "Fifteen," he repeated. "Some girls are married at fifteen."

Meg went pale too. This was the end of pickled cucumbers and the mornings spent fly-casting and watching him without Isabelle knowing. He thought her too old. And too young. Hilarious.

A muscle worked in his jaw and he nodded his head at the fire. "Do we have coals yet?"

"Of course," she snapped, silently adding, "you idiot."

He lifted his chin and gave a sharp, piercing whistle, which brought Henry and Fox with their brain-numbing clamor, counting up fish and whacking each other for no good reason. Nick was silent as Meg arranged her own fish on sticks set over the coals, finding a relief in the simple task.

Only when she moved away did Nick come forward to prepare his own meal, crouching on the balls of his feet at the fireside. He looked ready to run.

Henry and Fox talked of nothings, blind to the undercurrents as young men always seemed to be, then Henry wiped his chin with the back of his hand and tossed his fish bones toward the water. “How did you manage to get the biggest fish, Nick? Tell me your tactics.”

“Tactics,” Nick grunted. “It’s not a battle.” His youthful face was strangely hard as he stirred the coals with a long stick, weaving in and out and turning the gray ash into glowing orange. And what was going on in that mind of his? For the first time, she didn’t know.

Light dappled the clearing as a gentle breeze shifted the shadows on the ground, the peace of it at odds with a storm of feelings beneath her skin. It was supposed to be a simple fishing trip, dash it, but confusion ran like a steady stream in her mind. Confusion and longing and anger.

Was he feeling the same?

Meg looked down at her hand and ran a thumb across the pads of her fingers as an idea forced its way to the front of her consciousness. She could use her magic. Even the thought of using her powers on purpose made her cheeks burn hot with guilt. That commandment had been drummed into her from the time she came to Blythe House as a little girl: Never read a mind without permission. Not even Grandfather’s or Jolly’s, who, at least, would know what she was up to.

Easier said than done. When she touched people, their lightest thoughts clung to her mind like burrs on a skirt, whether she wished it or not. But to do it on purpose?

Meg turned over her hands, tracing her eyes along her fingers. Again came a voice in her head, sounding like Grandfather.

Don’t.

But Grandfather couldn’t know what it was like having this magic. He was a man, and a Ross besides. It meant that Meg knew thousands of things she didn’t care about: how Mr Thackery worried about his wife’s cough, or how Esther Gracechurch thought she’d never find a beau after her foot was crushed. Serious things. Silly things. Inconsequential things. Hundreds of them from Nick himself.

Surely it wouldn't hurt to discover something she actually wanted to know.

She gave a frustrated sigh. The extent of Grandfather's guidance on the subject had only ever been that the girls would be dishonorable cheats if they ever tried to touch a person out of curiosity.

Well, she was more than curious. She was really, really curious.

She looked at Nick again, his face turned away from her as though she had done something shameful in coming to the river to fish with old friends. She let the injustice catch fire within her, dragging a few logs onto the blaze in case it threatened to go out, finding her justifications growing each second.

"Talk Henry out of this madness of his, Nick," Fox said. "This running off to war."

Nick tossed the stick into the flames. "He knows his own mind."

"A grand concession," Henry jibed, tipping a flask to his lips.

Meg started with Henry. It seemed less underhanded somehow to read them all. She cut a hunk of cheese and handed it to him, her cool fingertips lightly brushing his. It was enough to feel soft sparks striking the flesh of her hand, winding up her arm, and leaving a trail of warmth along her veins. Once his thoughts reached her mind, her own were brushed aside like a carpenter clearing a table of sawdust curls. In her mind's eye, she saw bright gold buttons on a sharp red uniform and heard his pounding heart beat in time with the drums of battle.

"There will be action in Portugal this fall," Henry said, his tone more casual than the burning wish he felt inside. "Spain, possibly. I don't want to miss it."

His thoughts burned away like the seaside mist.

"You'll miss your head, Henry," Fox said, "when Napoleon blows it off."

Henry shrugged. "Better than lazing about Town."

Meg offered Fox the pickle jar, steadying it and touching his hand.

"There you are wrong," he answered.

Meg slipped into the inky blackness of his mind, disoriented as she read what was uppermost in his thoughts. Gaming hells and rotting taverns sitting on the edge of the dockyards. The bright flick of a golden guinea.

She shook off the image, confused by it and instinctively turning from the dark.

"Would you like something more to eat, Nick?" she asked, cold with fear that he would discover her magic, demanding to know why she wanted to go pawing through his private thoughts. No. These boys might tease her for being fey: for being a white witch who seemed to guess things with unusual accuracy. But they didn't really believe it.

"Nothing more, Miss Margaret," Nick said, exaggerating his formality, making it sound like one more piece of teasing. He wiped his hands on a handkerchief and stuffed it into his pocket. "It's long past time for us to deliver you to your grandfather." He turned to the others. "I want to stop in at Blythe House."

"Still determined to win the fair Isabelle?" Fox asked as they gathered their things. "The lady won't go to any but the highest bidder, I warn you. Your chances are good, however," he added, a calculating gleam in his eye. "It must be nice being the heir to an earldom."

Nick poured a hatful of water over the fire. Smoke hissed from the ground and he kicked dirt over the remaining embers, turning the scene into a wreckage.

Henry cuffed Fox on the shoulder. "Nick's uncle could have a son. Then where would he be?"

Fox laughed. "Lord Ainsley is a confirmed old bachelor. I doubt he could find his own belly button, much less—"

"Fox." Nick's tone was commanding, and he jerked his head toward Meg, who burbled with laughter.

Fox gave Meg a mocking salute and continued in a tamer way. "In any case, I wager that we'll all be bowing and scraping to Isabelle someday, whether it's Nick at her side or no." With that, Fox shouldered his satchel and clambered up the bank after Henry, the sound of their teasing echoing through the quiet woods.

"Ready?" Nick asked, putting his pack on his shoulder as well as hers.

"I forgot," she said, reaching into her pocket to fumble past the coin and the knife for the green stone. She held it out to him with a hand that was as bare as his own.

He stared down at it and for a moment she feared he would refuse to take it. She was certain she would not find it on the porch again. Today was the last time.

Finally, he reached for it, dragging his fingertips across the flat of her palm. It was a touch that was as correct as Mrs Jolly could wish, but underneath Meg's serenity every nerve prickled in awareness of him.

His thoughts went blazing up her neck like a white-hot ember sparking from a fire. There was nothing of the soft constancy in Henry's reflections or the spreading slickness in Fox.

She saw a field of wildflowers, petals upturned in the warm air. Isabelle waiting for him in the rigid French garden at Blythe House, walking and walking the circumscribed gravel path.

The thoughts crashed into one another, joined like mismatched puzzle pieces, and Meg blinked up at him, keeping the tears back. If he had deliberately tried to show her that she had no right to dream of him, even for a little while, he could not have been more clear. All his thoughts were for Isabelle.

Idiot, she thought, shoving her feelings ruthlessly back.

"Come along," Nick said, his voice rough with some emotion she could not understand. He tucked the rock into his waistcoat pocket. "We have to go."

She was bundled back home like a wayward parcel, jogging briskly between Henry and Fox.

Blythe House was lovely in the morning sun, but Grandfather's mount waited on the drive, prancing with anxious feet as a stable boy held the reins. Meg's brow wrinkled. It was too early for Grandfather to tour the fields. Meg skipped up the steps and saw Nick's quick frown as he bent to scoop his posy, wilting in the bright morning sun, and tuck it out of sight.

She turned back to the door and was almost knocked off her feet by Grandfather charging from the house, calling orders behind him. "Send the rider to London at once, I—" When he saw them, his pale face turned ashen. "Meg."

"Where are you off to in such crashing haste?" she asked.

He threw a saddlebag over the back of his horse, checking straps and cinches.

"I'm for Scotland, little magpie," he said when he finished his task. He reached a hand to smooth her hair, surely warmed by the sunlight. "There's no time to be lost."

"Scotland?" Nobody ever actually went to Scotland. Not that she knew.

A great shudder came from him and he pressed a crumpled sheet of paper in her hand as he turned to have a few final words with one of his tenant farmers.

Meg darted hasty eyes over the flawless script and felt Nick move close. "Something's wrong. Isabelle?"

"Yes," Meg whispered, wanting very much to lean against anything firm and steadfast while the foundations of her world slipped out with the tide. She folded the letter with shaking hands, her sister's words escaping at the seams.

"It is an excellent match," Isabelle had written in the end. "When we meet again, I shall be Yours, Lady Ainsley." The signature had been strong, certain, as though Isabelle had practiced it a thousand times.

"If you break your neck, Grandfather, I'll never speak to you again," Meg said in a tight, intense voice. She swallowed back her tears. "Return home to me safely."

A ghost of a smile crossed his face and he swung up on his mount, leaning down. "If they've gone to Scotland, there is a chance I might overtake them, but I'll have to ride like hell, the devil take him," he said, on a furious breath.

"Your friends stand ready to assist you," Nick offered, his formality at odds with how his fingers plowed furrows through his hair.

"Friends," Grandfather spat. "No Ainsley can help us when it's an Ainsley who did it. Seduced her out from under my very roof last night."

"Who? My uncle?" Nick asked, unbelieving.

Meg pressed her hands into her eyes. If reading it had been bad, hearing it spoken aloud was a nightmare. It could not be happening. Isabelle was too precise in her feelings, too careful of them. Even when she stormed, there was a method to it. "She wouldn't—"

"He's old enough to be her father and then some." Grandfather wheeled his mount and raced down the drive, his pace as furious as he was.

As the sound of his words faded away, the summer morning collapsed back into the air made hollow by this news. Meg picked up the distant sound of the sea, the wind that gusted and blew, the four frozen figures standing under the porch of Blythe House.

Meg lifted a hand toward Nick, longing to bridge the distance between them.

"I must find my uncle," he said, stepping back and addressing their companions as though Meg wasn't there.

"I'll accompany you. If you can lend me a horse," Henry said. "Fox, see to Meg."

Meg looked on, numb, as the young men disappeared up the drive.

"Poor Nick. He won't be the next earl, that's for sure," Fox said. "Not now that his uncle has taken a young bride." He looked at Meg and must have seen the burned-out look of desolation on her face. "But it's not bad news for you, Meg. If they marry in a few days, if it's hushed up, if you have the cunning to be in her good graces—"

Meg's mouth opened in confusion. "If?"

"Don't be like that. I know it's a shock, but for a plain gentleman's daughter, Isabelle has made an astonishingly good match. Having a countess for a sister will benefit you."

She blinked at him as though he were speaking a foreign tongue. "But if it takes more than a few days, if it gets out, if I am not so fortunate as to be in her good graces…what then?"

She felt her arm taken and her body turned into the house. Fox's hand brushed hers and a thought blew into her with the strength of a gale.

Ruined.

Chapter One

May 1813

Meg glanced around Aunt Olympia's sparsely populated ballroom and felt laughter bubbling beneath the surface.

"Why are you smiling?" Aunt Olympia asked, managing to scold Meg without moving her lips. "Stop smiling."

Dutifully, Meg straightened her mouth but she couldn't help feeling as if she'd laugh at any moment. Aunt Olympia cast a look heavenward, snapping, "Margaret. You will never marry if you cannot even pretend to be biddable."

Meg choked back a laugh. "I am sorry, Aunt. But we both know this," she sketched an arc with an elegantly gloved hand, encompassing the vases of hothouse flowers, glasses of champagne, and the best hired orchestra in London, "is a waste of Grandfather's money."

Society might find it in the goodness of their collective heart to forgive Isabelle, a beautiful peeress, for running away with an aged earl, but it would not forgive the insufficiently wealthy and well-connected Miss Summers for being her sister. Why should they? Moral depravity, like a streaming head cold, was probably contagious.

It didn't help that Meg had failed to enter Society in a position of grovelling submission, dabbing a handkerchief at the corner of tear-stained eyes as she whispered, "I'm so sorry. I'm so, so sorry," under her breath at every ball.

"It is a perfectly ordinary party," Aunt said, her clipped tones daring Meg to complain.

Meg's smile appeared again. It always did. Aunt Olympia had performed miracles to gather as many people as this, but she was not magic. She could not conjure young ladies anxious to make her acquaintance or honorable young men pressing her for another dance.

"It's lovely, Aunt. But we both know it won't lead to an acceptable offer." Her expression was amused, but if anyone had cared to really look, they might have noticed the sharp edges of her smile. "Grandfather was so puzzled when I didn't return with a clutch of marriage proposals last year."

"Old fool."

Meg's smile disappeared and she lifted her chin. "Hope is not a foolish thing."

Though, as she spoke so certainly, it felt like a lie. Meg's hope that somewhere in London she might find a man who would see her without the disfigurement of her sister's scandal was a tiny, guttering flame.

"I've arranged for Lord Sowell to lead you out for the first dance," said her aunt, running a glance over Meg's elegance—a buttercream silk gown caught under the bust with raspberry pink rosettes. "He's eligible and accepted our invitation, so he must not be put off completely by…for heaven's sake, be agreeable."

"A lord? Isn't that well above my touch?" Meg lifted an amused eyebrow but found herself intrigued as the man approached. Titled. Not bad-looking. Young. Good teeth, too. But there must be something wrong with him or he wouldn't be at a ball like this. Perhaps Aunt had bribed him to come. Meg's eyes narrowed but she could not quell the sudden brightness of optimism.

"Miss Summers?" he asked, taking in the buttercream and raspberries as though he wished he'd brought a spoon. His eyes gleamed as he bent at the waist, extending a gloved hand. She dipped a curtsey while her mind laid out the realistic possibilities. Lord Sowell was either a bore, a pauper, a gambler, a rake, or, most improbable of all, an answer to a maiden's prayer.

"May I have the pleasure of this dance?"

She nodded, gathering her skirt in one hand as he ushered her to the head of a set. "Are you enjoying the Season?" she asked.

"I'm looking forward to Ascot. Have you plans to attend?" he asked, not waiting for her answer but rumbling on. "I've a two-year-old we're training for next year. Sired by Loiterer," he continued, as though that explained his prospects.

"Loiterer?" echoed Meg, in tones of incredulity that seemed to please him.

So it was only her fault that he did not let up on the bloodline of a noble stallion for half an hour. He was a bore. Was there anything so wrong with a bore? Even bores must marry.

As he returned her to a chair, Meg read herself a lecture on the topic of choosy beggars. The satisfaction of half loaves instead of having none at all: the foolishness of wishing for the moon. Pickiness was a luxury she did not have in the matter of husbands, and she determined to redouble her efforts to like Lord Sowell. After all, Grandfather would be so pleased if she found someone. He could stop throwing his fortune at London modistes and flower mongers, finally seeing her settled. And what would she get? She might discover a cure for this nagging loneliness.

Only to find it replaced with nagging boredom. A laugh bubbled from her lips.

It was an unkind thought. Lord Sowell should not be discarded on the strength of a single dance. He must have redeeming qualities if he was willing to consider the idea of allying himself with a girl of little fortune and less reputation.

She sat with him at supper, nibbled on several dishes he had selected for her, and watched as he downed glass after glass of wine. Her resolve to search for his finer aspects drifted when she heard a scrap of conversation from an adjacent table. She leaned back in her chair to catch more of it.

One of Aunt Olympia's guests had a newspaper spread out on the table and read aloud to his companions.

"Despite what people will tell you, there is no such thing as an unmarriageable female. Any gentleman will understand that the problem in firing off a wallflower is primarily economic. Instead of weathering the discomforts of India or joining Wellington's army, a second son may make his fortune by plucking up his courage and taking to wife a girl with a cast eye, a lavender past, or an unfortunate snuff habit. Long experience teaches us all that if the price is right, any girl may marry."

This was greeted with a hearty chorus of male laughter.

"The man's a genius," the reader said, slapping the back of a nearby fellow.

"What man?" This from a merchant's daughter, her wide smile proclaiming her pleasure at being invited to a tonnish party filled with so few females as this one.

"Don't you know?" he asked, pointing to the name under the headline. "This is the celebrated Sir Frederick Magpie, Disinterested Observer of Elegant Ladies and other Alarming Things."

As he went on reading, the arguments began to volley around the table, entered into rather vociferously by the young lady, who asked, quite pointedly, if men thought they were the only ones called upon to pluck up their courage and shelve their tender feelings in the hunt for a mate.

Meg sipped her wine, smiling against the rim of the glass, and wondered what they would all say if she stood and unmasked herself as the author. When she began writing under the name of Sir Frederick Magpie last year, she had no idea the column would stand between her and going stark, staring mad. Her position (not quite in Society but not quite out either) was ridiculous. A joke. Well, Meg enjoyed jokes. She enjoyed making them each week for the exorbitant wage of half a pound per column.

Lord Sowell waved a passing footman closer, urging him to fill his glass. Meg affixed her most agreeable expression on her face, determined to give this man her full attention as his discourse ranged the entire conversational gamut from chestnut horses to dappled horses to bay horses, offering as much texture and richness as the indifferent salmon mousse she pushed around her plate.

"What are your feelings on the subject?" he asked, at last. "Do you prefer a short stirrup or a long?"

"Me?" she asked, surprised he had stopped to breathe. "I never learned to ride properly. I don't like horses."

"What?" he barked, much too loud, as though trying to rattle loose the dissident thought.

"I will have to change your mind for you. Shall I begin to do so as we take some air before the dancing resumes?" he asked, and she stood, taking his arm, allowing herself to be gently escorted through the French doors and down the illuminated path of Aunt Olympia's garden. In her mind she turned over ways to tell her aunt that Lord Sowell would not do.

The air was refreshing after the stuffy warmth of the ballroom and, though the garden was not a large one, the path curved back on itself several times, making for a pleasant walk. But as they came around a dark corner, he stumbled into her, almost knocking her into the high, thorny hedge. She stood firm, righting him at once.

"So strong," he said on a laugh, steadying himself with a grip on her arms.

His wrist grazed the bare skin of her upper arm. His hands fumbled as she was dragged into his thoughts.

Isabelle's sister.

Meg's color rose under the Chinese lanterns, bobbing and swaying as the cool night air brushed around them. Isabelle seemed to be everywhere, infecting each of Meg's tentative interactions like a canker. It was to Lord Sowell's credit, perhaps, that he knew everything but had come anyway.

But his thoughts did not stop there. They splintered under each fingernail and lodged under every flake of skin, pushing their way into her head.

Ripe for ruin.

Meg shuddered, measuring the distance between the house and herself, noting the obstacles that would slow her flight. Dash it. She was much too far from the bright lights for comfort. She forced herself to breathe normally until his gloved hands began to rub up and down her arms in a lazy way. Meg's mouth thinned. "Sir."

He dipped his head and nuzzled her hair, crushing her black, rose-scented curls. "You smell nice too."

"You don't." Meg peeled one of his hands loose. "My aunt will be looking for me."

"You think so?" he asked, capturing her again, seeming to have more hands than the requisite two. His voice dropped and he put his hateful mouth right next to her ear, coating the skin in a moist, flesh-crawling layer of hot breath. "I was under the impression she would like it if I took charge of you. Would you like me to?"

Meg jerked away only to find his grip tightening on her wrist.

"You don't have to act the blushing maiden with me. I know what you are." A chuckle rumbled in his chest. "So play along," he whispered.

Meg twisted. "If you do not unhand me, I will strike you."

He lifted his head and laughed again, the husky sound of it wrapped in the sharp smell of liquor. With a jerk, he shoved her into the spiky bushes and pressed wet lips to her face, searching for her mouth as she twisted in his grasp.

Her traitorous magic pushed his thoughts into her mind, reaping each one as he summed her up with an instinctive cruelty.

You don't marry this kind.

The words screamed through her brain as he squeezed her arms, cutting off the blood and making her hands tingle. He was stronger than she was, but she did not give up as the struggle between them became feral.

She can't ask for better than this.

Meg clamped her mouth shut, succeeding at getting an arm free. She balled her fist, tucking her thumb down as Nick had taught her, and drew back. She caught her elbow against the shrubbery, stifling a grunt as deep scrapes raked along her arm, so she shoved at Sowell and twisted, gaining a precious few inches of space. Then she cocked her fist again, letting it fly and connecting under his jaw, sending a sharp, searing pain through her hand. Dear Lord, why hadn't Nick told her it would hurt so bad?

Lord Sowell yelped, as though her strike was no more painful than the scratch of a kitten, but he let her loose for a moment and she jerked away, alcohol fuddling his response. He made a wild, fumbling grab for her, but Meg spun on her heel, running from him, her slippers digging into the gravel, broadcasting it behind her.

The garden was known to her and she raced through it far quicker than Lord Sowell, who stopped his pursuit at the glow of the lighted windows.

Entering the ballroom with too much purpose for a social occasion, she felt a wave of speculative glances pass from guest to guest. Scandal-brushed Miss Summers out in the garden. Was she really trying to catch a husband? There was ample fodder for the gossip mills. Meg bypassed them all—she had no friends here—and headed straight for the staircase.

Quick feet ran up the treads and, gaining her room, she slammed the door, shooting the bolt home while the beat of her heart roared like a lion in her ears. That would keep them all out. That's all she wished for, in this terrible moment, to be alone. To be safe. To put up barrier after barrier between her and the things that would hurt her.

She rested her forehead on the cool wood panel and pressed the back of her hands to her eyes, counting on fury to burn off the threat of tears. Still, an inarticulate cry peeled from her throat before she could choke it back.

She let it loose for a moment before reining it in. She growled impatiently and straightened, standing there for a few moments like a sailor testing his land legs. Then she moved to pour water from an ewer. Plunging a cloth into the basin, she rinsed her face again and again. Blast this magic. Blast his thoughts.

Meg rubbed until her cheeks were raw, as though she could get rid of his words and the feel of his mouth on her face as fully as she could get rid of the smell of his wine-soaked breath. A hard, desperate thought entered her mind the way a rock might shatter a window. The lock on the door wasn't enough to keep her safe here. She had to get away.

And it wasn't only because of meeting one monster in a garden. Lord Sowell was the final straw. This Season and last, she had found herself popular with cads and rakes, rotters and despoilers of women. At the events Aunt Olympia managed to gain admittance to, they queued up a dozen deep when they found she was sister to the notorious Lady Ainsley. Nor were these the kind of men to do things by partial measures, she thought, slapping the cloth down with a snap. No. Every gouty, pock-marked voluptuary seemed ready to take her half-ruined reputation and finish the job.

She'd had her work cut out for her, keeping things light, keeping them laughing, keeping herself well out of danger when a certain sort of man made advances. And so far, her approach had served her well.

A guttural scraping rattled through her throat. So why hadn't it worked this time? The answer came promptly. She thought she knew what he was, dull and respectable, not dangerous.

A shiver wound through her. She'd fallen into that trap before and not so very long ago, either. Last year one of her oldest friends, Lord Fox, had betrayed her, nearly poisoning her and leaving her tied up on the floor of his townhouse. He had been someone she hadn't thought to mistrust.

The experience had changed her, opening up fissures of vulnerability she had never experienced before, making her far more willing to play Aunt Olympia's games, more willing to entertain the idea of a marriage with a man who might be safe and solid.

Damn.

Meg sat at her dressing table, sliding the slippers from her feet. She looked square into the mirror, taking a long look at her reflection, one of her rosettes dangling by a thread. She yanked it off and threw it on the carpet.

Quickly she undid the fastenings of her dress, letting the raspberries and buttercream pool on the ground. She donned another, more serviceable frock and filled a reticule with a few small necessities. She cinched it shut and sat at her writing desk, dashing off a few lines.

"Dear Aunt Olympia, I am returning to Grandfather. I am also relieving you of the duty of finding me a husband. I find that I cannot be agreeable."

From her aunt's house she hailed a hackney to drop her at the Gloucester Coffee House on Piccadilly, where she bought a seat on a Eastbourne-bound mail coach leaving hours before dawn, a process so seamless that she wondered how long she had known it would come to this.

Oily lamps turned the acrid pooling water of London's streets into copper rivers as the coach got under way, but the light did not penetrate the corner as it slid by. It was then that Meg cried, the clatter of great steel-rimmed wheels rumbling over slick cobblestones muffling her sounds of distress.

Chapter Two

When Meg walked up the long driveway dusk was settling in, and her reticule swung far more jauntily than her own steps. Approaching the front door of Blythe House, she paused to glance for a green glass pebble. Of course it wasn't there. It had not been for six years.

"Grandfather," she shouted, casting her gloves and reticule into a chair. Her voice echoed off the marble tiles of the hall. "Grandfather, I'm back."

Grandfather's head poked out from behind the library door. "Margaret Summers? As I live and breathe. Am I imagining things?"

"Did you miss me?" She grinned, bundling away the numbness and shock of the last hours and making a mammoth effort to don her usual manner: the one he would expect.

He made no answer but simply held his hands out. Her hands were enfolded in his strong, gnarled grip and he leaned down, offering his cheek as a gesture of acquiescence. She went up on her toes, pressing her cheek against his, feeling the whiskers bristle against her face, striving not to burst into tears then and there.

Blessed magic gave her the thought foremost on his mind.

My little Meg.

Home.

It was a bright thread of affection woven around with worry and, though he would ask for an accounting of her flight from London, she basked in the bubbling excitement that told her better than words how he had missed her. A contented sigh escaped her lips.

"I'm sure I've made you dusty." She laughed, brushing a bit of dirt from his midnight blue coat. "You look perfectly gorgeous."

He pulled her along to the library. "Trying to throw me off the scent with flattery? I mean to hear why you've arrived weeks—months—before you should have." He took a seat before the fire where she felt the full weight of his inspection. "I will be imagining all kinds of calamities until you set my mind at ease. Where is your aunt?"

"Still in London." Instead of taking the other chair, Meg carried a stool over and set it at his feet, careful to turn her bruised knuckles away from his view. There was no hesitation in her voice when she peddled half the truth as though it were the whole. "It cannot be a surprise when I tell you we do not get on together."

He grunted. "Few do with that woman. Though I'm her cousin and a good deal older, she makes me feel like she's always slapping my hand away from the jam jar. Was that it?"

She nodded, awash with guilt. "Yes. The mountain of disapproval was affecting my digestion. I had to get away."

"I would have liked to send you to a happier home for your time in London, but we haven't much family. You travelled alone?"

"No. For hours I was squashed up next to a matron with a basket full of jam jars, two naughty children who fought like badgers, a rheumatic clergyman on his way to a wedding, one man who snored the entire way." She laughed, pouring out her tale with so many unnecessary details that he would be lost in the dizzying array.

At the end of it, he squared his mouth and shook his head in gruff warning. "You're not to take such risks again. You don't know what a dangerous world it is for a woman alone."

She bit the tip of her tongue and nodded again, unable to speak.

"Now," he said, "I want to hear all about your Season."

"First, we went to Madame Durand for fittings," Meg began, listing off a dry accounting of frocks and engagements until Grandfather begged for a halt.

"I've heard a lot of rubbish about lace and silver overskirts, young woman, but not one word about who you danced with or who is courting you."

She sent a saucy look and felt like an actress, playing a part. "I like lace and silver overskirts, Grandfather."

His frown chastened her and she sighed. "You won't like what I have to say any better than you like silver overskirts."

"Please tell me it was better than last year. You danced, didn't you?"

"Yes. I danced." Now and again when some decent man had not been warned away from her fast enough. She smiled. "But I like dancing too well to confine myself to one partner as yet."

“I hoped that the next time we met you would bring me some young man, begging for your hand,” he said, touching her fingers where they laced around her knees.

I won’t live forever.

“I’ll take my pick next time, Grandfather.” Shame flooded Meg as she lied, giving him falsity in exchange for the plain honesty her magic could coax from him. But how could she tell a man whose only goal was her happiness and security that he had failed? That he must aim his sights a good deal lower if he hoped to see her wed?

“I have better plans for you next year,” he said.

Her brows raised. “What do you intend?”

For the first time since she returned, Grandfather looked uneasy. Their glances locked, broken only by the sound of the door opening. It would be Jolly. Meg turned with a smile.

Her heart clenched. It wasn’t Jolly at all.

“Well, well. Little Margaret’s all grown up. But what is she doing home?” came a voice, precisely as she had remembered.

Dowager Lady Ainsley. Isabelle.

If Meg had possessed a sillier nature, she might have wondered if this vision was a ghost, but the dark brown hair, caught up in a thick, lustrous knot at the nape of the woman’s neck, though more refined than it had been, was still recognizable. Isabelle’s dress was a widow’s black and it was plain enough that at twenty-three she was even lovelier than she had been at seventeen.

“And she smells like the road, too.” Isabelle smiled indulgently.

Meg stood wishing for the first time that Blythe House had an armory hidden within its snug, tidy walls, a crossbow or a broadsword within reach. The best she could do was place a protective hand on Grandfather’s shoulder and collect herself, standing as straight as a lance at his side.

Grandfather made no sound at all but looked deep into the fire and finally covered Meg’s hand with his own. She saw what he wished her to see. The image was a painting, neither old nor valuable, kept in the back of the hall. The artist had given it a rough beauty that drew the eye to a ragged, half-starved prodigal returning to the open arms of his weeping father. Beneath the joy of reunion was a blunt, plain suffering on the father’s face.

Meg's eyes clouded in confusion and she glanced down. When Grandfather finally raised his head, entreaty softened his expression, holding her gaze until she dragged it away.

"I tried to persuade him to write, Margaret, telling you that I had come. But he insisted on keeping me to himself." Isabelle entered the room as though it was the most natural thing and settled herself on the arm of his chair, perching next to him like a devil at his shoulder.

Grandfather held his palm out and Isabelle set hers against it, briefly dipping her head to rest her cheek next to his. The family ritual was an invitation to use her magic, and Meg, holding his other hand, could feel the old, familiar tug of two magics meeting in one body, the ebb and flow. She pulled away.

Isabelle kissed his forehead. "Mrs Jolly tells me that dinner will be called in a few minutes. I've had her prepare your favorites. Though—" Isabelle bit her lower lip, worrying. "—no one is prepared to receive you, Margaret. Mrs Jolly will have to lay another place setting."

Her words held no admonishment, merely the pleasant tones of a good hostess making the best of a bad job, but Meg bristled. She'd been acting as the lady of the house since she was fifteen years old and Isabelle's manner seemed to brush her to the margins.

"It's a pity your note went astray," Isabelle continued. "The one telling us you were coming. We would have prepared your room."

Meg found her feet. "What a novelty to hear you fretting about the Royal post and the housekeeping, Isabelle. Your interests have broadened so. I didn't write, and unless Jolly has been stricken with a mortal disease, she wouldn't allow so much as a speck of dust to land in my room before driving it off."

The hit must have stung because, with her next words, Isabelle threatened to bring their battle into the open where Grandfather, less aware of the ancient currents swirling between them, could see. "But why have you come?"

"Meg missed me," Grandfather answered before Meg could return the volley. He picked up her hand and pressed it against his cheek with a kiss.

Please, Meg. Welcome her.

It was too much. Perhaps if it had happened another way—a penitent Isabelle, a cautious invitation—but Meg was not in a proper frame of mind. Being shoved into the bushes because a man thought you were an easy mark made her disinclined to wave an airy hand to the consequences of Isabelle's long-ago elopement.

"What a charming thought, Margaret. You have such a loving heart but I would urge caution. The roads are not at all safe when there is no man about," Isabelle murmured, reaching forward to smooth Grandfather's cravat. He turned his head to her and Meg moved toward the fire.

"I did miss you," Meg agreed, dusty and crumpled and wishing to comb her hair and change her dress. Things were so much more easily borne when one was tidy and looking one's best. "I missed picking up your messes and beating you roundly at a game of dominoes."

"She cheats." Grandfather smiled, inviting Isabelle to share in the joke. Isabelle smiled pleasantly.

"Nonsense. I'm too good to cheat." Meg smiled too but her words went to Grandfather and not an inch farther. She had been desperate for home not one hour ago, but now felt a stinging wish to run away again.

"Dominoes?" Isabelle asked. "Why not something that involves a little more strategy? Chess, perhaps. I could give you a good game, Grandfather."

"I'm terrible at chess," Meg answered, leaning back against the cool marble of the mantelpiece, crossing her arms. "I'm not calculating enough. How long will you be visiting, Isabelle?"

How long before Meg could burn everything her sister had touched?

Isabelle laughed, her severe look brightening. "Shall you tell her, Grandfather? Or shall I?"

Grandfather leaned toward Meg, reaching back to hold Isabelle's hands in his.

"Isabelle is home, my girl. Is it not wonderful? She's come home for good and when you go next year to London, Lady Ainsley," he said, stressing her title, "will sponsor you, introducing you to any number of young men."

Meg's mouth drifted open a fraction as she felt the oppressive burden of Grandfather's pleasure. His eyes were looking for some response, some sisterly joy to spill from her lips. But you couldn't spill an empty cup.

"I don't want her patronage and I don't want her here. She has a home of her own," Meg said, casting away the tiny, conversational dagger and resorting to a sledgehammer.

Grandfather sat back. "I am disappointed, Meg. I hoped you would be—"

Isabelle laid a hand on his sleeve. "I warned you she might not see things as we do," she said, giving him a gentle smile. "Will you allow me to explain it to her?"

Grandfather nodded and Isabelle's eyelashes fluttered against her pale cheeks. "When my husband—" There was a catch in her throat and she swallowed thickly before continuing. "When he passed, the solicitor discovered that things had been left quite awkwardly."

Meg's eyes narrowed, her chin cocked to one side.

Grandfather put an arm around Isabelle's narrow shoulders and in response she lifted her chin. "Because I ran away from you all in that terrible fashion…because I eloped," she said, employing no words that would wrap the business up in a pretty package, "I had no dowry to bring him." She waved a hand. "Not that it mattered. Arthur used to say he would take me without a penny and he really did. But, because I abandoned my family, there was no one to act on my behalf, negotiating marriage settlements or insisting that legal documents be drawn up to ensure my future."

Her tale had been liberally salted with self-blame, employing none of the evasions Meg expected Isabelle to use. The words gave her no quarter, made no allowances for youthful folly and romantic illusions. If anyone else had spoken them, Meg would have admitted that they were astonishingly brave, holding the woman to a painful reckoning.

Instead, the words raised the hairs on Meg's neck. This was Isabelle and Isabelle was a liar—a liar and a self-serving cheat. Was six years enough to alter that? Was six hundred?

"You married the wealthiest man in the county. Did he never think to call in the solicitors? Did you?"

"Meg." Grandfather frowned, making Meg feel like a puppy, swatted on the nose with a roll of newspaper.

"No, she's right to ask." Isabelle bore the inquisition with a stoicism Meg wished she could admire. "Living in London is like being a cork, tossed in a river and carried downstream. We were so busy. We thought we would have more time. We thought we would have sons to carry on after him."

Yes. A son would have secured her position. No matter what happened to her husband, Isabelle would have been in control of the Ainsley fortune.

Isabelle gave a wide, pained smile. "I know some people think it's a good thing that I don't have a young child to support. But I wish I had a daughter at least, to have something of him."

For a moment, Meg paused, uncertain. The pantomime was perfect, blurring the lines between what was real and what was not. There was only one way to know for certain if Isabelle was telling the truth. She would have to touch her sister, palm to palm, cheek to cheek. They hadn't done that in more years than Meg could count, and the thought of being inside Isabelle's mind and of letting Isabelle into hers— Meg shuddered.

"Surely the Ainsley estate can support you. You *are* the dowager."

"Meg," Grandfather growled.

Isabelle's eyes flashed but Meg stood her ground, brushing a hand down the rumpled, travel-strained gown, feeling the prickly bush and the hot hands reaching for her, grabbing at her dress, feeling the burning in her lungs as she'd sprinted for the house.

Unlike her sister, Meg had no rich husband and old title to hold those things back when she'd plunged them all into scandal.

Isabelle clasped her hands. "It's better to have it all out, Grandfather, if I'm to really be at home here. The reason I cannot stay in my husband's house is that it belongs to another man now. He is returning from China and there was nowhere else to go."

A door slammed in Meg's mind. She didn't want to think of the new man who would step into old Lord Ainsley's honors. "Nowhere?"

Isabelle laughed. "I'm relieved to see that you're as direct as ever, Margaret. You haven't changed a bit."

"You could certainly have seen for yourself. I've been in Town, this spring and last. Your townhouse was five minutes from Aunt Olympia's home. What stopped you from coming around for tea and cream cakes?"

Grandfather banged the arm of his chair. "Leave off, Margaret. Have some mercy."

Meg felt the stinging rebuke and spun to the fire, the licking flames blurring through her unshed tears. Mercy was beyond her in this moment. There was no room for it alongside the terror and humiliation she'd been running from since the early hours of the morning.

In that silence, Isabelle began to speak. "Arthur had been ill for some time, though he only passed on last winter." Isabelle gave a heavy, careworn sigh that spoke of cool hands resting on his fevered brow, whispered consultations with his doctors, and long nights of sleeplessness.

The lie was there somewhere, though Meg could not see it.

"I should have called upon you but—" Her eyes closed. "You can't know what it is to lose your life's companion," she said, reaching for Grandfather.

As Meg nursed her bitterness, Grandfather dug into his pocket and brought out a cameo, holding it in his palm. He traced the delicate lines of the coral—a face no longer young or beautiful, but precious to her grandfather in a way that no other material thing was.

His wife. Grandmother.

The cameo had softened over time from being held, cherished, and Meg sucked a painful breath of air into her lungs. Grandfather believed Isabelle. He believed this story of the grieving and penniless widow with nowhere else to turn.

Grandfather tucked the cameo away and wiped his eyes. "I think we've had enough of things best left dead and buried," he decreed.

Dead things. Suddenly chill, Meg wrapped her arms around herself, feeling the sting of scratches raised in angry furrows on the back of her arms. Wounds sustained for the sake of those dead things Grandfather was so easily dismissing.

"I'll go tell Jolly to lay another setting at the table," Meg said.

"Don't bother." Isabelle tugged on a bell, every inch the gracious hostess. "It's the housekeeper's duty to attend us."

Again, Meg felt a violent wish to carry a sword. The thought of Isabelle here every day felt like a hand to her throat, slowly squeezing the air from her lungs.

But when Jolly came, standing at stiff attention to receive Isabelle's orders, Meg raced across the room and caught her in a great hug.

"Jolly," she exclaimed, holding tight in case the Jolly she remembered had become slippery—as so many things had turned out to be since she'd crossed the threshold of Blythe House.

"You've brought half of London back with you" Jolly laughed, clutching her cap against her ash blonde hair. She held Meg out and made a careful inspection. "Enough dust into my house to plant a garden." She kissed Meg's cheek nevertheless, taking it as her right, knowing she would be read as their skin made contact.

Cool, minty calm radiated from her touch and Meg saw an image of blinking, yellow-eyed tigers, licking sharp fangs and waving lazy tails. Protective, ferocious.

Meg dropped her forehead to Jolly's and breathed in the familiar scent of home.

"Now, Miss Meg," Jolly said, her dignity slipping a little. "Let's see if we can have you bathed and made presentable before dinner is laid."

Meg sighed, looping her arm though Jolly's. "An actual bath. You don't know how much I've been longing for one."

"No. That won't do at all," Isabelle said, joining them by the door and speaking low. "It's not healthy to keep Grandfather waiting for his meal."

Meg exchanged a look with Jolly but nodded, sending her ahead before addressing her sister. "A few minutes only. He's as healthy as a horse."

"That's what I used to say about my husband before he became ill, and he wasn't so much younger than Grandfather. You cannot be too careful of him." She looked back over her shoulder and dropped her voice still lower. "And consider. You are tired, dirty, and came home in strange circumstances."

Meg faced her squarely. "Are you calling my behavior into question? I'm not the one who took seven weeks to elope."

"Don't be a child." Isabelle sighed, taking care, Meg noticed, that they did not touch. "Do you want to spend the rest of the evening with Grandfather pressing you for answers? It would do neither of you any good. Take your bath, take your meal in bed, and be thankful you don't seem to have brought a scandal down on his head."

"You're worried about scandal now?" Meg laughed.

Isabelle only gave another gusty, forbearing sigh. "I don't want to see him upset anymore."

That was the argument that finally persuaded Meg to do as Isabelle asked. That and the leaden weights that seemed to be hanging from her eyelids. She retreated to her bedroom, safe and quiet, to rest and bathe her wounds.

Though the deep scratches had escaped Grandfather's notice, they did not escape Jolly's.

"What are those?" Jolly asked, as she held a fresh nightgown open for Meg to duck into.

"Nothing," Meg answered, folding her hand over them. But Jolly held her gaze until the truth came spilling from Meg's lips, her words halting.

The actual telling of it was short, but Jolly held Meg for a long time in a fierce embrace, whispering words of love and comfort. Then she drew back, tucking Meg up into bed, sitting on the edge and running gentle hands over her hair, letting Meg feel nothing but the warmth of her affection. Meg could not say how long they stayed like that but, finally, Jolly kissed her brow and doused the light.

When the door clicked behind her, Meg took a long breath, feeling as though the wounds to her heart and spirit had been cleaned and wrapped in fresh linen, the fiery pain of them dulling and leaving her free to think of other things.

Meg sank deep under her covers. *Home.* Home, if only Isabelle had not come.

Meg's thoughts wrinkled as she tried to work it out in the fading light. It didn't seem to make sense. Isabelle wasn't Grandfather's responsibility. It ought to be the duty of the new Lord Ainsley to settle her affairs, see to her widow's jointure, even provide her a dower house.

The new Lord Ainsley.

A ghost of a smile crossed Meg's face. It was such a silly evasion. The new Lord Ainsley who might solve Isabelle's problems was a vague figure, comfortably anonymous. In her head he would be wearing baggy hunting clothes and have a paunch. If she never thought of him by his Christian name, he could remain exactly that.

Nick.

Her smile disappeared and she slipped from her bed to kneel at its side. She rubbed her bare toes along her leg and began her nightly prayer, finishing it off with the usual plea, "…and please, Lord, protect him in China," her brow furrowed, "…or wherever he may be."

Chapter Three

"There," Nick pointed, breathless with the exertion of this final gallop. His bay stallion was lathered with sweat, but the soft breeze blowing in from the ocean cooled them both. Nick surveyed the valley below, matching it against the image he had carried in his mind all these long years. A snug village following the line of land and sea, with tidy cottages strung along gentle hills and tumbling lazily down toward a modest harbor. The ruins of the old Norman castle were a broken ring of walls and turrets rising above the sedate town.

Pevensey. Home.

The stallion danced on impatient hooves, ready for the final sprint down the hill, but Brooks, the man who occupied every position between stable boy and private secretary in Nick's employ, stood in his stirrups. His was a handsome face with a deep sailor's tan and, lifting his hat, he revealed a shock of bright silver hair. After taking a long look he sat again and gave a terse grunt. "This'll do fine."

Nick settled the horse with expert hands and laughed. "You said the same in Canton and you said it again on every ship as you strung up your hammock. I'm beginning to think it's all the same to you."

Nick traced the seams of the countryside, his gaze inspecting every cottage tucked in the folds like a bear turning over rocks. "You'll find it no worse than anywhere else."

"No worse?" Brooks asked, darting him a look as they ambled their mounts down the hillside. "This is your home, sir. You, at least, ought to show some respect."

"Yes, your lordship," Nick said, touching the brim of his hat in mock salute. His smile ebbed away. That word belonged to him now. Lordship.

News of his uncle's death had plucked him, like a ripe tea leaf, from Canton, packing him on a merchant vessel back to England and transforming him from plain Mr Ainsley into a stranger—his lordship, fifth Earl of Ainsley. He certainly looked the part. London tailors had seen to that. His frame civilized by the quiet elegance of a Weston coat and precisely fitted buff breeches. Only the silk of his waistcoat rioted with the gaudy colors favored in Yue embroidery, the single witness that his eyes could no longer accustom themselves to the restrained tones of England.

They entered High Street with its familiar shops, so different than the twisting, fragrant alleyways along the Pearl River, and he dismounted outside Greenley's, ringing the bell as he pushed through the door. The sound of it extinguished the dull hum of chatter, and a knot of young ladies glanced up from the bolts of muslin, several of them straightening with interest. Four or five men clustered around a game of draughts in a corner while Mrs Fletcher, the surgeon's wife, stood at the counter where Mrs Greenley, too intent to pay him any mind, filled her order.

Nick touched the brim of his hat in greeting, setting off a silent echo of warm interest that bobbed and bounced around the room. The shop had seemed to shrink in size in the six years since he was here last, but Mrs Greenley, her hair a little grayer, her frame a touch more wiry, was still measuring walnuts onto a scale.

Mrs Fletcher retreated with her order and when Nick drew near to the counter, Mrs Greenley looked up at him properly and gasped. "Lord Ainsley," she said, casting the scoop into a bin and dropping into a curtsey as she sank up to her neck behind the long counter.

His jaw clenched with the greeting.

Straightening, she folded her hands in front of her serviceable apron. "After your uncle's passing, there was talk that you would be returning," she said, her words heavy with the implication that she, for one, would never gossip. "May I be the first to welcome you home?"

"You are the very first," he said, and her eyes narrowed in triumph. His glance lingered over coils of rope, and squat sacks of barley and vetch.

"I expect you will want to open an account." Mrs Greenley flipped open a heavy ledger to an empty page, laying the credit of Greenley's at his feet. Already she was licking her pencil. "That is, if you plan to stay for any length of time?"

The enquiry was so slight that it hardly deserved to be called a question. Still, he could feel ears straining behind him and knew his answer would be halfway around the village before he stepped out the door. Landless Nick Ainsley, borrowing his prospects from a wealthy relation—prospects covered in so many contingencies that they were worthless—had never invited such interest.

The realization had ceased to be surprising some years ago. Likely the day Isabelle had run off with a title and a fortune, teaching him, to the last farthing, how little someone with no expectations was worth. But it did nothing to improve his mood.

Nick grunted his assent. "Though I haven't been up to the Abbey yet to see what kind of state it is in," he said.

She wrote his name—his full title, even the barony—in a florid script at the top of the page, but his words put a pucker in her brow. "It's not as fine as when his lordship was in residence, but nothing an interested landlord can't put right. I expect it'll be nice, what with Lady Ainsley living with her grandfather again at Blythe House. So easy to settle your business."

"The business is settled, ma'am," he responded, his voice clipped. Then he beckoned Brooks, who had been poking his nose around the shop. "My man will be handling the order, though you must see to the other patrons first," he said, turning to encompass the rest of the shop, noticing that the young men had halted their game to watch him with hard, staring expressions.

Mrs Greenley brushed aside his words, and the other patrons, with the wave of a hand. "Fiddlesticks."

Nick wandered away and her voice faded as he examined the contents of the shop that had taken the better part of every Christmas coin he'd received since the first. He lifted a lid on the jar of loose tea and pushed his nose close, inhaling the aroma. Choking on a cough, he jerked away from the inferior, musty blend with a laugh. Nothing had changed in six years. Certainly not the contents of this jar.

He stepped out into the bright sunshine and looked up the street, seeing the steeple of St. Nicholas's church rising in the distance—the site of every baptism, burial, and wedding in the parish. The sight of it struck sparks against Nick and settled a hard line across his lips.

Brooks followed him and they mounted their horses, wending their way out of town.

"How far is the Abbey?" Brooks asked.

"Another couple of miles east."

"And this?" Brooks nodded at a high brick wall running along the road.

"Blythe House land. It belongs to a Mr Ross." Nick let an uncomplicated memory through, checking it first for burrs and knobs that might splinter his calm. "I used to poach from his streams."

The memory might have been a happy one but as the gates came into view, he found himself reflexively searching the meadow on the other side. A clump of white nigella—ragged lady—grew where the ground was damp, and he remembered his practice of dismounting here and choosing out the best flowers, cutting a choice bunch and tying them off.

He'd been a damned fool.

His fingers slipped into his waistcoat pocket and touched a warm green stone. Impatient with himself, he gripped the reins again before moving on.

Nick frowned all the way to Southdown Abbey.

His mood hardly improved as he came down a drive that was potted and pitted, the lawns shaggy and unkempt. But when he stopped under the arched doors of the ancient structure, he felt a contentment wash over him, sinking into his bones. The old place was as beautiful as ever, the immoveable gray stone growing from the earth like a mountain and the windows glinting in the sun. His uncle had loved this spot, caring for it the way a nursing mother tends a baby, and had taught that love to Nick.

"Your uncle only left a caretaker?" Brooks enquired, banging on the door and casting a squinting look over the massive façade of the house. "They will have found all this a handful."

Nick tried the door to find it locked so he jogged down the steps and around the corner, high-stepping his way through the weeds choking the walled kitchen garden.

"Anyone about?" he called, pushing through the door. The room was dusty and unused, but already Brooks was poking his nose into cupboards, unearthing pots and spoons.

"I'll start a meal if you want to look around."

Nick peered through windows to see Holland covers draping the furniture, filling the once-lively home with shades and ghosts. On the manse's exterior, wind and water, birds and vermin had all made a mark where they could, chewing at wood, swelling and cracking it, tumbling stones on the terrace and blurring the crisp lines in the garden. It spoke of neglect. Why had his uncle left it so completely?

He lingered by the tall conservatory windows, the glass smashed with such abandon that they could only have served as target practice for the local lads. Near a series of sunken storerooms Nick stooped and touched the soft soil marked with fresh tracks.

When he returned to the kitchens, it was to find Brooks standing at the stove, stirring a pot of soup with a thin cloth tied neatly around his waist. "It's not much."

He ladled two bowls of thick fish stew and broke off a hunk of bread for them both.

"It's enough. And you managed to clean," said Nick, tucking into his food. Brooks had swept the debris into a pile, routed the cobwebs, and given the table a hard scrub. A fire crackled in the hearth but the light was beginning to fade and Nick groaned silently. His first night home would be far from comfortable.

"It's a start. Ale?" Brooks asked, offering a common flask. Nick waved it away and Brooks shook his head—exasperated. "The teapot's on the boil. Don't know how you can stomach the stuff that way."

Nick packed his own blend of tea into a plain clay pot, filling it with hot water. It would be milkless. Sugarless. The Chinese way.

"I found tracks right up next to the Abbey."

"What kind?"

Nick nursed his tea and gave a grunt. "Smugglers. You're in Sussex now. A good number of the villagers will have their hand in free trading. There was a cart and several ponies. Recently, too."

"An empty house, too grand for anyone to have any business with. One caretaker. This would be a good place to stash the cargo," Brooks answered, giving a snort. "No one was watching them."

Nick's face hardened as he scraped his chair back. "Someone is now."

He poured hot water into a basin, rolled his sleeves back, and began washing the dirty bowls and cutlery like a man who was used to it. He handed Brooks each dish to dry. "There's damage to the roof."

"A good chance to hire some men," Brooks said. "Put a little money into pockets around the village. And while you're at it, we could do with a few women to help with the housekeeping. It might lighten the grimness some."

Grim. Southdown Abbey had never been that before, and the word stung a response from Nick. "You'd prefer a stinking ship's hold?" he asked.

Brooks raised gentle, rebuking eyebrows. "Not at all, sir. This is perfect. I enjoy living with vermin and bears—" his look was pointed, "—slaving alongside a belted earl like a common charwoman. I could die happy."

Nick laughed. "Any other orders, Brooks? Can I peel your grapes? Air your sheets?"

Brooks stacked the last of the luncheon dishes neatly and turned, flipping his dish rag over his shoulder. "As long as you're so obliging, you could tell me why we stayed at a hotel for a fortnight when you'd a grand London townhouse at your service. You can tell me why you bought horses when the earldom had a stable. You could tell me why you had to run off to an ill-used Abbey."

"The Abbey is the heart of the earldom. If it's not tended, there won't be anything worth having." Nick plucked the cloth away and dried his hands, ignoring the bulk of his servant's inquiry, which was already too impertinent by half. "Too, the conservatory here needs to be in good repair—the glass mended, the furnace operational—before the plants and cuttings I brought can take root."

Brooks leaned against the counter, his expression too shrewd for comfort. To blazes with the man. He should replace him with someone more simple-minded. Someone who wouldn't ask questions. "Now that you've had a go at half-fictions, why don't you try the truth?"

Nick muttered a low curse. "It suits me to be here, Brooks."

That was no answer to give a man who had served him as long as Brooks had, but the real answer made Nick feel weak, vulnerable, like a boy of nineteen betrayed by his sweetheart and guardian.

He wouldn't allow himself to say the reason out loud. Of all of his uncle's properties, this was the only one Isabelle hadn't lived in.

Chapter Four

Blast Lord Sowell and blast the injuries that kept Meg from tearing him to pieces between the pages of a newspaper. Meg dropped the pen, flexing her bruised hand, and set aside the writing desk with her half-finished column. She would allow herself a half hour's rest before resuming her eviscerations. When she was done, Lord Sowell was going to be barred from every decent household in London, reduced to begging for invitations to a cock fight.

She glanced across the room. "What are you doing here, Isabelle?"

Whether by design or accident, the girls had not yet been left alone together. Grandfather kept close, quick to prune back the green shoots of any discord between them. He could not apply himself to it forever and, on the morning of the second day, while the girls joined him in the library, he was called away by a tenant to inspect the fields.

Isabelle raised the faintest questioning brow. Despite the limited colors in her wardrobe she had dressed with care, the deep black of her mourning gown settling against her soft white skin as though she were carved in alabaster.

Meg continued. "Every soul in the village can recite each scandalous detail of your runaway marriage, probably better than yourself. Why would you want to return?"

Isabelle opened Grandfather's correspondence with a long, thin knife, working the blade under wax seals, smoothing each letter open and making a tidy pile on his desk. "I might almost think you didn't want me here, Margaret."

"I don't." Meg's weapon was no thin knife, delicate and finely made.

"A pity. I told you that my husband left me without many funds. It's quite true. Until I marry again, Blythe House is the only home I have."

"For a woman as resourceful as yourself?"

"Oh, Margaret." Isabelle dimpled. "You flatter me."

Meg took a long breath. "Nobody says so to my face, but thanks to our little gift," Meg waved her fingers, "I know there are girls in Pevensey who won't scrub our floors or empty our chamber pots because of the scandal. There are wives who take care to put themselves between me and their husbands, no matter how innocuous the conversation. When I go into town, it's as though I'm a visitor. Isabelle, memories are long in the country and if you are looking for a refuge from London, you will not find it here."

Isabelle tilted her head. "You always were a funny little girl," she said. "The villagers have shown me every kindness. They've been lovely."

Meg's brows narrowed, her memory summoning a chant some of the young lads liked to sing a few bars of as she walked past. "Indifferent? Maybe. Lovely? I doubt it."

"Because they have never treated you in that fashion?"

"Yes. Why would they treat you better?"

Isabelle tapped the flat of her knife against her lips. "Let's see if we can discover why. I am a well-mannered and titled lady with a heart full of charity for our neighbors. Why shouldn't they be kind?" Her knife hand whirled in the air as though vivisecting a wild beast. "I expect the way you are treated has nothing to do with the scandal at all. I invite you to consider that you're simply an unlikable brat."

There it was. The same Isabelle as always. Meg smiled, suddenly on firm ground.

"You're slipping, Bella. That's not even the worst insult I've received this week. I am no longer a little girl to be crying into Jolly's skirts because my sister read my weaknesses and used them to punish me." She lifted her chin and leaned forward, her soft mouth unusually firm. "I don't know why you returned but if you hurt Grandfather—if you break his heart again—I will make you pay for it."

Isabelle's knuckles whitened around the blade and her tone was soft, deadly. "Don't threaten me, Margaret."

"No threat, sister. A vow. I protect what I love."

Their tight silence was broken when a little housemaid entered, bobbing Isabelle the kind of respectful curtsey she never expended on Meg. "Mrs Fletcher is here, my lady," she said before showing in the woman whose bright eyes missed nothing.

Meg straightened. Mrs Fletcher had been one of the few people it had not been a punishment to read, all those years when the storm of scandal was breaking in Pevensey. She had not spoken of Isabelle's elopement but a steady sympathy had thrummed under the surface of her mind, sorrow filling her heart for the motherless child embroiled in such an awkward position.

That had been so long ago.

In the last year, Mrs Fletcher's bright eyes, when turned on Meg, had been pebble-hard, weighing her up, judging her, favoring Meg with the kind of harassed expression one turns on a trampled garden patch and a loosed cow.

Now her lined face was wreathed in smiles. "Lady Ainsley, how fortunate to find you at home. I hope you don't mind that I've come to call."

Isabelle offered her hand and escorted the woman to a seat. "Call me Isabelle. Please. I was hoping you would stop in to tell me more about your son. I vow you didn't tell me the half of it when last you came because Mrs Greenley was so— Oh, I'd better not say."

How strange, thought Meg, watching as Isabelle lapsed into an embarrassed silence, her small hand covering her pursed lips, as though she was too shocked by her own thoughts to finish.

Meg's brow furrowed in confusion until Mrs Fletcher smiled, generously waving away the faux pas as though she had the power, second only to God Himself, to confer forgiveness. There was another something in her smile as well. Delight.

"And you must call me Harriet. Goodness," the woman replied, settling comfortably. "I vow you read my mind. I was so hoping we could continue our conversation from the other day."

Meg thumped her feet to the ground. The blood in her veins, already hot, began to boil. Christian charity, Isabelle had claimed. Politeness and reciprocity. Isabelle prescribed simple homespun ways to find favor with the little community as though Meg had not tried each one of them.

As Meg watched closely, she saw that Isabelle's fingers brushed the woman's hands. She was reading the villagers. An old trick, but effective, to discover what a person wanted in that moment and procure it, twisting one's self into another shape, thereby gaining favor.

Meg had never discovered the knack of being anything but what she was.

"Is Sam enjoying his studies?" Meg asked, taking her seat near the other women.

"You must know he's home," answered Mrs Fletcher, her voice freezing out other questions. As the maid brought ginger biscuits and tea, Mrs Fletcher and Isabelle seemed to enjoy a comfortable coze on the subject of Samuel Fletcher's duties, expectations, and talents, leaving Meg the honor of pouring out and passing around.

They didn't want her, that much was evident, so Meg returned to her writing desk, content to knock Lord Sowell down a peg as the conversation carried to her in bits and bobs.

"I suppose his Lordship has been to see you," said Mrs Fletcher.

His Lordship. The words hung in the air, stirring Meg the way a stick stirs the coals of a fire into sudden brightness. Isabelle's hand froze on the handle of her teacup.

"Did you not find him much changed?" Mrs Fletcher asked. "So handsome."

"He's back?" Meg said, uncaring that her question betrayed the fact that she'd been listening in on a private conversation.

Mrs Fletcher slanted her another one of her hard looks, but Isabelle dropped her eyelashes and answered in a husky voice, "I was sure he would return to Sussex. He loved the Abbey more than anything."

"He came into the village shop looking as fine as fivepence," Mrs Fletcher said as Meg came around to tidy the tea tray, her hands moving as questions swirled in her mind.

How long had Nick been back? Had he left a stone for her? When was the last time she checked? Had she missed it?

"When did you see him, Mrs Fletcher?" she interrupted.

Mrs Fletcher answered in clipped tones. "Day before yesterday."

"Now, Harriet," Isabelle spoke, drawing her around and effectively cutting Meg out of the conversation. "We haven't finished with your boy, Samuel. Such a sad case. I would like to feel my poor efforts might improve his prospects."

Meg retreated to her own thoughts. Nick was home and his return brought with it all the confusion and turmoil of that last day.

The pricking loneliness she thought she'd decided she didn't care about anymore. It was too much for a soft blue frock and a bright afternoon in the library.

"I thank you kindly," said Mrs Fletcher, coming to her feet and pulling Meg from her thoughts.

When she bustled from the room, her fresh handkerchief bulging with ginger biscuits, Isabelle dusted her hands and picked up her knife again. Meg slapped her hand soundly against a low table.

"You read her," Meg hissed, running from thoughts of Nick toward emotions that were clear and uncomplicated. "I saw you do it."

"Of course I read her," Isabelle said, her voice even and ladylike. "The woman put her hand in mine. It could not be avoided. Even you read people like that."

"Do not gammon me, Bella. I *know* what accidental reading looks like. We both know all the tricks of avoiding it. You practiced on that poor woman—"

"Poor woman." Isabelle gave a snort and nodded to the window where the ever-dwindling figure of Mrs Fletcher disappeared down the drive. "How can you defend such a small woman? She brought nothing but ugly, rapacious thoughts to me today. Her greedy little longing for ginger biscuits. Her irritations with the grocer's wife. Her desperate hopes for her hopeless son. And what that 'poor woman' thinks of you is not fit to repeat."

"I already know what she thinks. I know what they all think."

Isabelle clutched a hand to her bosom in dramatic horror. "Don't say you read them, Margaret."

"Not as you did. Not on purpose. I don't touch people like that and I do my best to make sure they don't touch me," Meg insisted.

Isabelle's tone shifted and she blinked in surprise. "What? No one?"

"Jolly. Grandfather, when he allows me." Meg waved a hand.

"No one else?" Isabelle gave a low, throaty laugh. "How utterly stupid. Do you even know what a gift this is?" She lifted her hands and wiggled her fingers. "How else do you expect to bring the people of Pevensey around?"

"I thought you told me it was a matter of maidenly reticence. Charity," was Meg's acid reply.

"I thought you were smart enough to know how the game is really played." Scorn dripped around Isabelle's words as Meg took a strong, steadying breath.

Once, Meg had thought the villagers might be won over in time. If only she was careful and wise and good enough, they would think of her as a beloved, golden child again. How wrong she had been. It had been years since she had entertained such a foolish notion. No matter how correct her behavior was, the best she could hope for was an apparent indifference that masked their feelings. But because of her magic, she would always know how they really felt. Scornful. Suspicious. They wondered when she would be the one dragging her Grandfather through hell.

No. No amount of pleasing them would ever be enough to pay the toll, allowing her escape from this deep, high-walled valley.

So she'd stopped trying. In the last years, she had closed up tighter than a snug seaside cottage in the face of a storm. After London—her mind skittered at the thought—the walls had grown thicker, contracting her world into a tiny circle comprising Grandfather and Jolly, and, lately, Beatrice and former Captain Henry Gracechurch. It was enough. It must be.

If a contradicting voice belied her firm assertion, or if a dark loneliness overtook her from time to time, she could ignore it. She had so far.

"You're wrong to blame me for all of this nonsense," Isabelle said, flicking her fingers to encompass the failed Seasons, the frostiness of a surgeon's wife, the desolation chewing away at the edges of this safe ground Meg had won.

Nonsense, she called it. Meg's eyes dropped to the page she had been working on.

"Every gentleman likes his sport, none more so than horse-mad Lord S. If it's hunting he likes, hedges should be planted to trap a vixen. Sharp thorns to catch and drag on delicate muslins. Dense thickets to allow no retreat."

Her rough lessons from Lord Sowell had been nonsense.

Isabelle continued her attack. "There must be something wrong in you, Margaret. I was able to make a life for myself, mixing in the highest circles of Society, while you've done nothing to cultivate even your tiny scrap of magic. With the smallest exertion, even you could have them eating out of your palm." Isabelle lifted a page of

Grandfather's correspondence, no longer simply sorting them, her eyes darting across the lines. "The truth is that you've no one to blame but yourself."

Meg lashed out. "You are not to do it again in this household. You know Grandfather has forbidden it."

"No one is hurt by it." Isabelle picked up another letter and examined it. "Mrs Fletcher wanted someone to call Mrs Greenley boorish and unrefined. She wanted ginger biscuits and to drone on and on about her worthless son. I gave that to her. She is grateful to me. We were both satisfied. No one was harmed."

"You think it's harmless? Reaching into a person's thoughts and digging—"

"We can't dig, Margaret," Isabelle corrected. "You know as well as I that the best we can do is skim the thoughts of others."

"—digging out," Meg insisted, "what you can use for your own gain? Doing it without permission? It's wrong."

"She will never know."

"But you do." Meg's brows lowered. "And, like you always have, you turn it into a weapon. You despise her."

Isabelle slapped down the paper and raised her voice. "It doesn't hurt her at all," she said, finally roused.

"Then give me your hand, Bella. If it's so harmless, let us read one another." Meg offered her palm, reaching toward her sister, keeping it open, half-terrified with every beat of her shuddering heart. Isabelle stared at it for a long moment and looked away, smoothing her skirts.

"Don't pretend it wouldn't hurt if we read each other," Meg said, her tone deadly. "Out of respect for Grandfather, you will never read anyone else in this house."

"I can and I did, and I will do so again," Isabelle stated, regaining her habitual calm with a tone so even she might have been discussing which flowers to plant in the garden beds. "You're a fool to let any man tell you what you may or may not do with your own power."

"Grandfather is not *any man*. He raised us and loved us and taught one of us good from bad," Meg answered, suddenly embarrassed by the childish simplicity of her words, the way they sounded like a motto to be stitched into a sampler. It was far more complicated than obedience and love for Grandfather keeping her power in check. She didn't use it because it hurt like the devil to do so. It was agony to read the minds of people who thought she was trash.

Isabelle stood and leaned back against the desk, her arms braced behind her. "Grandfather taught us to be pretty, dependent, and sweet. It may satisfy you, little sister, but I'm not afraid of being more than that."

Meg's hand balled into a fist. Thumb tucked down and away. "You'll not read again in this house." The more she said it, the more she sounded like a tiny child taking swipes at a giant.

"Or what? You'll tell Grandfather?" Isabelle said, her eyes wide. "Without even touching you, I can see your weaknesses. If you told Grandfather, it would break his heart, which would easily be enough to break yours."

Meg rubbed her thumb across the discolored skin of her knuckles, prodding at the bruising and tightness, wondering if hitting her sister would hurt as much as hitting Lord Sowell had. Even if it did, it might be worth it. She allowed herself the vision of leveling Isabelle but as her vision got to the good part—the part where Isabelle's nose was bloodied and hopelessly disarranged and making whistling sounds as she breathed—Grandfather poked his head around the door.

"Still here?" he asked, blind to the undercurrents of malice cutting the room to shreds. He smiled, Meg thought, to see them together, keeping company. "I'm going to pop upstairs for a wash but wanted to warn you we'll have company for dinner."

In concert, the sisters, though enemies, worked to dispel the tension.

"Oh?"

Who is it?" Isabelle asked, unfortunately not whistling through her nose.

"Young Nicholas."

Meg faced the window, where Isabelle might not observe any weakness, and felt the blood rush to her cheeks.

Chapter Five

Meg looked down at her frock in a kind of dithering panic. The fabric was creased from the way she sat with her legs curled up as she wrote and thought she saw a blot of ink. She stared at the spot in horror until it rolled off with the brush of a hand, a mere puff of dust. She imagined herself, tearing up the stairs, throwing open her wardrobe and ransacking the contents for something better, meeting Lord Ainsley in a suffocating blaze of sartorial glory.

"There'll be no need to put yourself to any fuss," Grandfather said genially as he flung his hat onto an empty chair. "It's merely a family dinner."

But where Meg wavered in indecision, Isabelle did not.

"How nice," Isabelle said, standing and smoothing her skirts. "Still, I'll pop up to change my frock. I have become rumpled and weary, simply sitting at your desk and opening your letters. I don't know how you manage it each day."

Grandfather gave a low laugh and leaned down for her kiss. "I told you it was no work for women," he said. "You go off and attend to yourself. Meg will keep me company."

So that was that. Meg stood, her stomach shaking like a drunk at a vicar's tea table. *He's back. He's back. He's back.*

Grandfather poured himself a claret and slouched in his large chair before the fire while Meg wandered to the window, leaning this way and that until she gained a poor approximation of her appearance in the reflection. She poked at the knot of hair at the back and licked her fingertips, smoothing down the fly-aways. He would think she'd tumbled into the dining room, fresh from a day of fishing. But what could he expect if he showed up out of the blue?

What would he think of her? The question settled solidly into her midsection, the weight of it chased around by a melee of frenzied stomach puppies.

Grandfather held the glass of claret up to the firelight before tipping it back. "Should I have been more circumspect on account of Isabelle's feelings? Kept my distance from our neighbor?"

Meg opened her mouth, half-ready to tell him that Isabelle hadn't any feelings to speak of.

"She seems much too fragile, still," he continued. "Wandering from room to room like a lovely little ghost, anxious to earn her keep." His glance travelled to the pages on his desk and delivered them a frown. "We were lucky you've always been a sturdy little girl, running with your short legs after the boys. Strong, even if you are so small."

Meg swallowed thickly. He had not seen her in the mail coach, weeping hot tears in the darkness, desperate to be home and safe again. She had felt anything but strong then.

"Between the two of us, we'll look after our Bella again, won't we, Meg? And do a better job of it than we managed before." Again Grandfather frowned. "It could not have been a happy marriage, you agree?"

That statement, at least, had her wholehearted agreement. "They did not have much in common from the outset." Even now, Meg struggled to think of old Lord Ainsley as Isabelle's husband—struggled to think of him anywhere but in the wild Abbey gardens.

Grandfather thumped the arm of his chair. "I can't forgive him."

"Nick?" Meg answered. "Lord Ainsley, I mean."

"His uncle. The man was a blackguard, seducing a young girl from her home and family, pulling her roots out and planting them in foreign soil. How could they have been happy?"

"I—" Meg turned back to the window, recalling every scrap of gossip that had swirled around the fashionable Lady Ainsley in London. The affairs and intrigues. She'd been a glittering figure, running with a high-flying crowd, far removed from the balls that Meg had managed to wrangle an invitation for. The true picture of Isabelle didn't bear the smallest resemblance to Grandfather's imagination. "Bella is stronger than she looks, and I am sure you did right in inviting his lordship. We shall meet him in the village shops and at church, and it is probably best to get the meeting over at once, away from the public eye."

He offered her his hand and she tucked hers within his grip. He turned it over and kissed the back. "That's what I thought."

The big-hearted affection within Grandfather's thoughts was sharpened tonight by an image of old Lord Ainsley waiting at the end of the drive with his carriage on a dark summer night.

He pressed her hand and let it go. "I think young Nicholas thought so too. It certainly wasn't his fault what his uncle did."

His expression was dark and Meg could see the story he told himself, writ plainly on his features. For Isabelle to remain as innocent as a lamb, the fault had to be laid at her dead husband's feet. And he was not around to offer any truths that might tip them over.

Isabelle joined them a short while later, bringing with her the scent of orange blossom. Though she was limited to wearing another black dress, the fabric was attractive and she had tucked tiny white buds into her hair to offset the impression of gloom.

She stopped in the center of the room and rotated in place, brow furrowed in concentration, before taking her place in a chair near Grandfather, scooting it over several inches and arranging her skirts with care. Then she took up a small scrap of needlework, glancing between herself and the doorway several times to gauge the effect. The tableau was complete.

Just in time, too.

"Lord Ainsley," the housemaid announced, moving through the door and holding it for the man following her. When she saw him, Meg's breath caught in her throat and a hand curled around the drapery behind her, gripping the rich cloth.

As he entered the room, the Nick of her memory and imagination began to dissolve, the reliable, calm substance of him breaking apart like clouds scudding toward the horizon.

He was larger now, seeming to fill the doorway with his height and breadth, and he carried with him the aura of a man who spent his days in the sun. His hair rippled back from his forehead, dark as ever but tamed, and her fingers itched to disorder it.

Panic caught her for a moment, and among the many feelings pinging though her heart, she identified an odd, childish sense of loss, already resentful of this stranger who was bowing to Grandfather, flicking a glance at Isabelle.

Meg should say something, join the group near the fire, but her slippers felt glued to the floor as she watched him take Isabelle's raised hand and bow over it, the smooth, confident gesture of a man who knows his worth.

"My lady," he murmured, showing no sign that he felt the awkwardness of their meeting or remembered a day on the front steps when he'd learned of her marriage. He'd looked like a man shot that day. A man whose world had been pulled from his chest. Now he might have been meeting the merest acquaintance.

Isabelle's lashes drifted down across her cheeks like a maiden's veil where a soft blush bloomed, her hand lingering in his a shade too long.

"And Meg," Grandfather prodded. "We can't forget about Meg."

Lord Ainsley straightened and looked full at her, letting Isabelle's hand fall back to her side. His hazel eyes narrowed a fraction and his fingers toyed with the pocket of his waistcoat.

A riot of emotion danced down her veins, but the breath left her as she waited for his mouth to break into a smile, for him to cross his arms and pronounce her an incorrigible hoyden, hardly changed at all. To measure her height against his chest.

"You're back," she breathed.

"Miss Summers." He sent her a solemn half-bow, and a sharp pain went through her at the name. Not Meg. Not even Miss Margaret. But a name her sister had worn until she'd passed it on, spoiled.

It was then that Meg decided she didn't like anything about him anymore. Not his impossibly tailored coat that he wouldn't be able to fish in, or his inane hair, cropped close against his neck, moulding the outline of his profile. She really detested the way he held himself with an air of forbidding confidence, which seemed to hold her, and all of them, at arm's distance.

Meg swallowed her crushing disappointment with an offhand curtsey. "My lord."

"You changed," Grandfather told him as he began ushering the small group into the dining room.

Meg nodded behind his back. Nick had changed. Grandfather saw it too.

"I told you not to," Grandfather continued. "Your clothes were fine."

Nick grunted a laugh, the brief sound of it rolling through Meg's belly, stirring up old memories and new ideas. "I could hardly show up at your door covered in the dust of the fields. It would be terrible manners."

Grandfather seated his granddaughters on either side of him, and Nick at Isabelle's elbow. "That fact did not stop you before, young man. Many was the time you came to my table fresh from some bit of mischief."

A little of the air seemed to go out of the room as the past was acknowledged. Meg's glance flew to Nick, who gave no indication, by fainting fit or howling rage or merest twitch of an eyebrow, that the past meant anything to him.

"Were you riding, Ni—" Isabelle colored. "—my lord? You love horses." Gone was the blazing termagant. Isabelle was Grandfather's "lovely little ghost" again, ladylike in her grief.

"No. He was doing the same as I," Grandfather answered, tucking into his roast chicken. "Inspecting fields, right along the boundary. My father used to say that it's the sign of a good housewife to inspect the linen closets on her second day of marriage. I would add that it's a sign of a good landholder to do the same with his fields."

Isabelle nodded and peeped admiringly up at Nick as Meg's nose twitched in disgust. What was Isabelle playing at? A better settlement from the estate?

"Why can't she do it on the third day of her marriage, Grandfather?" Meg asked with a laugh. "The good housewife inspecting her linen closets. Are the tablecloths going to grow legs and scurry into the fields?"

He pointed his fork at her. "You are a wretch," he declared.

"I *am* a wretch," she agreed, her laugh carrying on though Nick regarded her with such a curious look. She tried to receive it with as much calm as everyone else in the room seemed to have achieved, but with his eyes on her, Meg did not feel calm in the least. She would have a bilious attack if he kept it up.

Isabelle cleared her throat, the small sound drawing the attention of the whole table. "Margaret," she began. "There is something lovely about a woman who rises with the sun and takes stock of her new home, giving her new lord all the loyalty and care she once gave her father. Something beautiful in turning her heart to the work at hand."

Meg lifted a brow and wondered who this precious homily was directed at. Grandfather? Nick? Certainly not Meg. "That's quite a romantic description of crawling through dusty cupboards with a housekeeper looking over your shoulder."

Isabelle shrugged, resting light fingers over Grandfather's hand. "I'm a romantic woman."

"And Meg is not," Grandfather noted, covering Isabelle's hand with his own, once more putting himself between the sisters. Could he feel the tension crackling along the table linens?

"No?" This from Nick. Meg's eyes lifted to meet his cool hazel gaze. Her brow furrowed. How unlike *her* Nick this was. Cool where he had once been warm. Serious when he had been so quick to provoke her, meeting her glance with his own laughing one.

"She has no patience for love," Grandfather teased. "I impoverish myself every year—"

A blush climbed up Meg's neck as she interrupted. "I'm sure our guest doesn't want to hear—"

"Bah," Grandfather did the same, waving a hand. "I've known Lord Ainsley since before he was breeched."

"Well, then," came Meg's saucy reply, praying he would not continue. "I've impoverished you for two years only."

"Yes, but two ruinous years. Each time I hope to find Meg a husband before she takes her place on the shelf." Grandfather laughed and settled back into his chair. He meant it as gentle raillery, but Meg's cheeks burned. Never had he done it in front of witnesses. Never had there been this thread of disappointment she could not ignore. "She's far too picky, that one."

Meg wondered if Nick was looking at her now, and the shame burning her ears turned to irritation.

But she answered as though she were alone with Grandfather, ignoring the undercurrents. "Not picky at all, merely wickedly expensive. You find me a man who will cosset me as you do and I will marry him tomorrow."

He laughed as he was meant to, but Isabelle's look blazed with triumph. Nick continued to regard her with narrowed eyes from across the table.

"You regard yourself as merely selective, Miss Summers?" Nick asked.

"When a woman considers her future, it doesn't pay to be anything else," she replied, feeling his eyes move over her like hands fumbling at an unknown latch. He was curious, trying to understand her.

"Besides," she said, eyes crinkling with laughter, "no one ever tells a man he should turn to the nearest unattached female and hold on for dear life."

For a second his mouth tucked and she thought he was going to laugh with her. Their gazes held until Isabelle broke in, darting a wary look between them. "We were speaking of boundary fences, I think. I want to know how you find Southdown Abbey, my lord. Have you many repairs to make it fit for you?"

Nick dragged his eyes from Meg's and nodded. "Several. The house needs to be protected from the weather, and the gardens are a mess."

"They always were a bit of a mess," Isabelle agreed. "Such a wild, strange thing to lay out on the grounds of a house as grand as the Abbey. Winding paths. Mazes and follies everywhere."

"The hermit's grotto," Meg and Nick said at once. She smiled, her eyes laughing with him, but his retreat was swift and he became a stranger again.

"Well," he said. "The whole of the property has been neglected. I will have my work cut out for me."

"It will keep you in Sussex for some time," Isabelle ventured.

He nodded but his mouth was grim.

"You don't appear pleased about it," Meg observed.

"Margaret," Isabelle scolded.

"We've known him too long to stand on ceremony," Meg said. "Isn't that right, Grandfather?" He nodded, uncertain. "Are you displeased with Sussex?"

"Merely displeased with the state of the Abbey," he assured her. "It looks like no one has stepped into it since my uncle closed the door."

She cocked her head. "No one? Have you inspected the whole of it?"

"Every dusty inch."

"Then you'll have found the tracks leading from the storehouses."

Nick's look sharpened. "How would you be knowing about those?"

Meg brushed the question aside. It would feed his ego, she imagined, to know that she could not stay away from his home. That she had watched it as well as the hired caretaker. Better even. "I'm sure smugglers have been using the Abbey almost from the moment old Lord Ainsley left."

"Then you ought to have informed the magistrate," Nick answered.

"I see no need for that. They're only local lads."

"There is always a need for the law, Miss Summers," he said, his tone inflexible. "I spent six years bound by a rigid system of respect and justice. Trade flourished despite different languages and customs, but it only works when all parties understand and respect the rules of engagement."

"Even if the rules are ridiculous?" she asked. "You cannot walk the length of an English lane to hear someone complaining that the taxes on spirits, lace, and *tea* are absurd." Sir Frederick Magpie had fired off a collection of articles on the subject last winter.

"It is far easier to destroy trust than to build it," he said, his eyes like a frosty autumn morning. "The lies that must be told for smuggling to prosper, the secrets kept, the law ignored…in the long term they can destroy a community."

Meg narrowed her eyes. "Do you know what else can destroy a community, my lord? Transportation. Four of our cottagers were sent off to the penal colonies last year for turning a hand to free trading. Strong young men with a good future on the land. It would be cruel to hand them over to a magistrate and wash my hands when the punishments are so severe."

"The law is clear—" Isabelle began, but Nick spoke over her.

"Four were transported but that's not all of them. The tracks are too fresh. Who else is involved now?"

Meg lifted a shoulder though she knew Sam Fletcher must be involved. Why else would he leave his training? Jim Greenley was in it too, she was sure. "All that lot who loaf around the village all day. Foolish boys who don't care about the risks."

"You take a lively interest in those boys," Isabelle said, sliding her implications through the conversation like her knife under a wax seal.

Nick leaned back in his chair. "I can't blame them for wanting a bit of adventure. I was hungry for that too, once. But if they don't consider the risks, you tell me why I should do it for them."

Meg flinched to hear Nick speaking words so foreign to his tongue that they might as well be Cantonese. "Because they're foolish boys and you are a man," she said, her eyes running over a face that was hard, a mouth bracketed by the cares of manhood. "And it's not adventure they're wanting. It's a shortcut."

His brows raised and he spoke in a tone of surprise. "How can a gentlewoman, cosseted and ringed about in luxury from the moment of her birth, understand the appeal for a man who sees a long, hard road in every direction? I don't blame them for wanting a shortcut, but I do not practice diplomacy with people who abuse my trust. As of today, free-trading is finished on Abbey land."

Meg balled her fist and she saw Nick drop his eyes to her bruised hand. His eyes narrowed as she pulled it under her napkin.

How wrong he was. How little he knew her, she thought, meeting his stormy expression. Daily she fought the temptation of taking the quickest road to where she wanted to go, damn the consequences.

She sat back in her chair, her tone light. "Of course you never ran unchecked in the community from the time you were breeched or engaged in absurd adventures. You certainly wouldn't do something as foolish as…" she tapped a finger to her lip, "… shear a dozen sheep in one night."

Though he had been sipping his wine Nick choked, and the boy he had been came home to her, suddenly laughing with that same light she loved in his golden eyes. "You know we returned the wool the next day."

"I remember that the farmer was sick with worry until he found it in his barn." She chuckled at the memory. "I would think that a man who had that in his ledger wouldn't soon forget that he had benefited from a little mercy and willful blindness."

The light was gone and she was sorry to see it go. Her eyes regarded him seriously now. "Once the magistrate steps in, mercy will have no place. You're Lord Ainsley now, a position endowed with power and trust. Find the men. Speak to them before notifying the authorities."

"But you're not following your own advice, Margaret," Isabelle said, her voice high and puzzled. "You talk of care for the people, but when it comes to the most basic duty of a gentlewoman, a position of great privilege and comfort, you've shirked it. I know for a fact you've not made a regular practice of visiting the poor and sick of our tenants. Why, when I returned, I found that you haven't gone to the cottages in years," she said, amazement in her tone. She looked up at Nick. "She pawns it off on Mrs Jolly." Her glittering eyes swung back to Meg. "It seems that your heart is in the right place, but you stop short when it comes to involving yourself."

Meg's hand shook, remembering the first attempts she'd made as a young, spindly Lady Bountiful, arriving at a cottage with a basket for the newborn only to have the new mother hold herself aloof from Meg's awkward overtures, each touch of their hands telling Meg that she'd heard the gossip. That she thought Meg was far more wild than her sister. That she thought Meg's ruin was only a matter of time.

Maybe she should have tried harder, Meg thought, blotting her lips with her napkin. No. It hurt too much. They would accept her baskets as long as Jolly was the one to deliver them. She needn't thrust herself where she wasn't wanted.

"Isabelle," Grandfather commanded. "Leave her be."

Isabelle dipped her head, the soft jet beads rolling on her neck. "I could teach you how to go on," Isabelle offered, her voice gentle and generous. "The tenants need our consideration."

Meg thought she might choke and she turned from her sister. "If you are determined to push the free traders off your land, my lord, I hope you take care."

Nick's shrewd eyes made her shift, and Meg returned his look, chin high. Worrying about Nick, including him in her prayers each night, was a habit of such vintage that it would not be forsaken in a day or a month.

"I'm sure his lordship is more than capable of seeing to himself," Isabelle said, a slight reprimand in her tone. She turned her face up, recapturing Nick's attention. "I'm sorry the Abbey will need any repairs at all, my lord. I thought my—" she halted before going on, brisk and brave, "—my husband left it in good hands."

"He did not. It looks like he could not afford to keep staff there though my solicitor assures me that was not the case."

Grandfather wiped his lips and settled back in his chair, lacing his fingers over his waistcoat. "I never could understand why your uncle left it in the hands of Miller. Sixty if he is a day. Do you know anything that might shed some light on it, Isabelle?"

Isabelle laid her napkin to the side, the white of it hardly whiter than her skin. If Meg had not, herself, been in a pitched battle with her not an hour ago, she would never believe this was the same woman.

"Concerning my husband's affairs, I would prefer not to discuss them in front of outsiders." Isabelle darted a quick, embarrassed look at her sister. Meg could almost measure the calculation in it. "I wish to respect his privacy."

Grandfather patted her hand. "Very loyal of you, I'm sure. Meg?"

She was to be dismissed.

Meg nodded, setting her napkin down and getting to her feet. The gentlemen rose with her and she saw Nick's glance flicking to her bruised hand once again.

But by the time she was at the door, Meg glanced back to see two masculine heads bent forward in the candlelight to hear Isabelle's low murmuring tones.

What was the game Isabelle was playing at?

Questions nipped at Meg's heels, following her down the stairs to the kitchens, where she found Jolly bustling about like a scullery maid when she ought to have been taking her ease on one of the garden benches that flanked the doorway to the garden, enjoying the cool night air. Surprisingly, Meg found a man there, handsome in a weathered way, bending with his arms resting on his knees, hands loosely clasped between them. He was watching Jolly move about with interested eyes. Meg settled on the opposite bench and plucked a strawberry from a dish. She hulled it, popping it into her mouth.

"Miss Summers," she introduced herself, avoiding the necessity of touch by holding up her berry-stained fingers.

"A pleasure, miss. I'm Brooks from over at the Abbey," he said, tilting his head to point across the fields.

"You came with Nick?" Meg asked, coloring. "Lord Ainsley, I mean. Are you his valet?"

"Valet, surveyor, major domo, butler, secretary, nursemaid, what-have-you," Mr Brooks ticked off, his eyes never straying far from Jolly, who was so careful not to look toward them that it could only have been intentional.

"He brought you from London?"

"He brought me from China." Mr Brooks tore his eyes from Jolly and gave Meg a greater part of his attention. "We've been together a long stretch. Six years."

"So long? Were you on the same ship sailing from England?"

"The very same. And a good thing it was. The lad saved my life." She raised her brow and he went on. "We had a bad captain who would beat his crew as soon as look at them. His lordship kept me from leading a mutiny and hanging for it."

Meg tilted her head appraisingly. "And you never left him. Will you be happy to settle in Pevensey?"

He glanced into the kitchen again and his eyes gleamed. "Aye. I dropped in to meet my neighbors, but there is so much to do."

His slight smile had a knowingness about it that Meg wanted to laugh at. Jolly was receiving a little masculine interest, it would seem. Good for her.

Meg's smile faded.

She regained it, however, and pointed in the direction of the dining room. "Will you do me a favor, Mr Brooks?"

He raised a brow.

"See that he doesn't kill himself getting rid of those smugglers?" she asked, as light as she could manage.

She withstood his scrutiny, more particular this time, until he answered. "I'll do that."

A sharp whistle arced through the sky, sweetly familiar, an arrow piercing her breast.

"And another thing?" she said, their voices muffled in the fading light.

"What's that, miss?" Mr Brooks grinned, collecting his hat. He looked to Jolly, who had paused in her labors, her rigid back turned to him.

"Make him wait the next time he calls you with a whistle." Meg wrinkled her nose. "It's the only way to break him of the habit."

He gave a low chuckle, muffled in the cool spring night.

"Until next time," he said.

Chapter Six

"You'll find them at The Castle Inn," Nick said, looking over his shoulder to make sure he had not lost Brooks in the tumult of market day crowds swelling Pevensey's High Street. "It shouldn't take long. Six or seven strong men should do. We can always hire more if we need them."

"And a housekeeper to manage us all?" Brooks shouted after him.

Nick made an impatient face and hauled Brooks by the elbow into the relative calm of a doorway.

"Not yet. We'll get the rough spots patched and mended a bit before the valuables arrive. Time for a housekeeper then."

"Do you think I could poach Mrs Jolly?" Brooks asked, a narrow, predatory gleam in his smile.

Nick gave a laugh. "You couldn't dislodge her from Blythe House if you tried. Best leave the women of that house well alone, Brooks. They're more trouble than they're worth."

Brooks made a sound of disgust. "You aren't afraid of that dab of a girl I saw last night, are you? That one couldn't have hurt a fly."

"Do you mean Meg? The younger one?" he corrected, pulling Brooks into the stream of people and heading up the street in the direction of the pub. He shouldn't be using the girl's Christian name, even in his own mind, but it was impossible to think of her in any other way. Even now, the name wanted to slip from his mouth as a reluctant grin threatened to advance over his face like rebel troops retaking disputed territory.

His manner, he confessed, had been stilted last night. He had been busy guarding his tongue.

Nick had gone a few paces up the street when he noticed that the going was easier than it should have been. Young men and old stepped out of his path with a tug of their cap as he went. Women walked by him with gentle nods, young ones bursting into a flurry of giggles after he passed. Was this what it meant to be Lord Ainsley? Was this what made his uncle think he had the right to take what he wanted, even from a nephew who had nothing but the hope of a girl? His smile disappeared.

Brooks shrugged. "The Miss Summers who kept me company while I made no headway with Mrs Jolly."

"Headway?" Nick asked his servant, so set in his bachelor ways that he'd developed a crust. "You can't be serious."

Brooks crossed his arms. "As serious as a blow to the head. Lord's truth. I tapped on the kitchen door looking for a cup of tea with the staff, and it wasn't ten minutes before…" He made an exploding noise like a cannonball being blasted from a ship.

The sound of it faded and he gave one terse nod. "I'm serious. That Miss Meg of yours was a nice, comely little thing too," he added generously.

"Not *my* Meg," Nick grunted, his mind fresh with the memory of how she had laughed at him. How he found himself laughing with her, and how they clashed all through dinner. Arguing with her over whether to call the magistrate or not had felt like wrestling a spitting cat into a bag.

His memory served up another moment, before the clashing, when he had been caught off guard by the slim, green-eyed girl standing by the window, her delicate face lit by the setting sun, her curves unimaginably perfect. He had felt like a bale of tea had dropped onto his chest.

While he had been gone, Meg had turned into a beauty.

Nick clamped his lips and shook his head in irritation. The women of Blythe House were trouble. He ought to have learned that lesson well enough to last a lifetime.

"I'll be at Greenley's," he said, parting with Brooks at the inn. A letter from his solicitor was sure to be waiting.

The crowds thinned at this end of town and he found himself following several steps behind a woman, the buttercup ribbon of her dress blowing backward in the wind. As they approached the shop, he heard a knot of little boys, no older than eight or nine, whistling a tune as she passed. Suddenly the small figure swiped a stone from the ground and let it fly across the street in one fluid motion. A yelp followed, as did laughter and the scramble of hasty feet.

Nick's brows lowered. He would know that aim anywhere.

"What are you up to, Miss Summers?"

She dusted her hands, pasting a serene expression on her face, her unconcern contradicted by the bright flakes of red staining her cheeks.

There was a pugilistic set to her chin when she met his look. Meg, who was always in constant motion, moving with the unpredictability of a dancing flame, held his gaze with perfect stillness.

"Good morning, my lord," she finally said. "I have errands."

"Allow me to accompany you," he said, the words surprising him. He had no intention of having more to do with Blythe House than was strictly necessary. Even his acceptance of the dinner invitation had been in the way of getting a chore out of the way. "If only to keep you from throwing rocks at little boys."

She was flushed but cleared her throat. "It hit him in the softest place it could. I wouldn't do any real harm, you know."

Nick felt the breath of a smile lift his cheek. He couldn't help it. It was impossible to be wary of someone as blunt as Meg Summers. "So you meant to aim for the backside. I worried you were slipping," he teased, a little surprised to find himself doing it. This girl would coax another laugh out of him if he gave her the chance.

Her eyes danced and she nodded.

"Why did you do it?" he asked.

Her cheeks pinkened. "That tune they were whistling—"

"Rude, was it? You might have told them so. To whistle at a young lady, they deserved a little more than that rock you hurled."

Her brow lifted with a hint of amusement. "I'll take that into consideration next time." Then Meg bobbed a curtsey and stepped around him so that he had to follow or be dismissed.

He followed. Blast it, why was he following as though one of her ribbons was tied around his wrist? "There doesn't have to be a next time. I'll speak with the fathers if you give me their names. Why do you look at me like that?"

Meg gave a ladylike snort, shaking her head as she turned into Greenley's.

Nick trailed after her in time to hear a low whistle emanate from a young man in the corner. He was a tall, blond Saxon type of boy, about nineteen, and he was rolling a quizzing glass over his fingers, fumbling with the task.

Nick paused at the door, the dusty ring of Greenley's bell echoing behind him. Despite his visit last week, he felt an uncanny sense of unbelonging, of foreignness. Two or three young ladies, their chip straw bonnets and pale spring frocks so similar to Meg's that it might have been a uniform, nodded to her but held themselves ever so slightly aloof. He might have been in Canton again, those first weeks when every word but *haih* and *mh'haih* had been strange and unintelligible.

The lad in the corner straightened. The other fellows in the corner gave him encouraging blows and he cleared his throat as he intercepted the girl.

"Good morning," he said, giving her a bow.

"Good morning, Sam," she said, her steps never pausing even as she stepped around him.

Meg took no note of the atmosphere, but bustled to the counter. "I've come for the post, Mrs Greenley."

"You have one," Mrs Greenley said, scraping none of her cold-butter charm over Meg as she turned to retrieve the letter from the cubbyhole. Her eyes narrowed. "Another long letter from your London gentleman. Eight pence." Meg unrolled one five-pound note.

Mrs Greenley recoiled with the instincts of a jungle explorer spying a venomous snake. "You *must* have something smaller." Her hand rested atop the letter where it lay on the counter and drew it back a fraction. "I don't run a bank. I have—"

"That's a pity," Nick broke in, feeling the locus of interest hum about him like a bird's wing. "I'm expecting a letter from my solicitor, but have nothing smaller than a five-pound note."

It wasn't quite the truth. In fact, it wasn't even cousin to the truth. Nick had an assortment of small coins jangling in his pocket. But something about her manner made him certain Mrs Greenley had been lying. It seemed tied up with the quality of strangeness he was experiencing.

Mrs Greenley's mouth broke into an ingratiating smile. "We can manage to find some way to make change."

"Excellent," he said. "I'll take my place behind Miss Summers while you conclude your business."

"The post, Mrs Greenley," Meg pushed the note across the counter. "And I'll see to his lordship's, as well."

She flicked her green glance up at him, tightening a band around his chest. The girl had been "my lordship"-ing him from the moment he had returned, and he began to feel that if she would only call him Nick, he might feel at home.

Mrs Greenley's eyes widened and she took a lungful of air. "Don't you think that's—"

"Kind," he supplied. "Thank you, Miss Summers. You've saved me another trip into town. And you've saved Mrs Greenley from making so much change."

Mrs Greenley reached for his post and Meg turned to go. He followed her to the street in time to see the lad from the shop standing too close.

"I can borrow a boat," he was saying, fiddling that quizzing glass with clumsy hands. "We could spend the day—"

Nick could feel his hackles rise but before he could speak, a woman's shout carried down the street. "Sam-uel." The voice was sharp and the lad responded to it at once, tipping his hat at Meg and ambling up the road.

As he went, Meg nodded to the woman. The hard-eyed woman responded with a nod so brief it might have been an insult.

"I owe you eight pence," Nick said when Meg turned. Since meeting Meg this morning, it was as though he had returned from China to find that Pevensey, his home, had shifted in some degree, only leaving a blurry image of what it was supposed to be to signal the change. He would understand it.

"It's nothing," she said. "Nothing to fret over."

"I don't like being in anyone's debt," he said, counting the coins and reaching for her gloved hand, pressing them into her palm.

"You had coins all along? What was all that for?" she asked, looking exhausted somehow. "The little game with Mrs Greenley?"

He crossed his arms over his chest. "That's what I wanted to ask. Have you been swiping her walnuts when her back was turned? Why was she so mulish?"

"Mrs Greenley has always been mulish," she offered. "It's you that's changed. You can hardly be surprised that an earl gets better service than a miss."

"Nice try, Miss Summers. Mrs Greenley refused to take your money even before I became involved. If you give me no answer, I'll begin to believe that the entire village has run mad. Little boys whistling a rude tune at a gentleman's granddaughter. Young ladies who throw rocks."

The knot of young women from the shop bobbed from Greenley's like ducks in a row, blushing as they met Nick's eye and giggling on their way.

"Other young ladies utterly indifferent to a girl old enough to be their friend," he continued. "A merchant afraid of money. And then there's the matter of that young man," he said, nodding up the street. "There was something havey-cavey about his offer. And his mother looked as though she wished you to Jericho."

"That's quite a list, my lord," she said, turning away and striding up the street with a speed that surprised him.

He caught up with her. "I didn't imagine it. Something has changed here and I want to understand it. You seem to be right at the heart of it all."

Meg wouldn't stop walking but she couldn't outrun him either.

She seemed to agree because she finally gave him an answer. "The boys were whistling a tune some wit made up for us Summers girls six years ago. Would you like the words? They would make you blush. They make me blush. No one has sung it in ages but it hangs on and hangs on, a sort of Pevensey rite of passage for boys of a certain age. I cannot speak for the girls in the shop. They have never been unkind, their greetings perfectly correct, but we are not intimates. Mrs Greenley enjoys being wretched so I do not take it personally. And Mrs Fletcher? She used to be quite gentle with me, after…after the scandal broke. But now she worries that I will ruin her son," she said.

He halted and she continued on several paces before he was at her shoulder again. As they walked, an image crossed his mind of a fourteen-year-old girl—just past the coltishness of early adolescence—standing in a shallow Sussex chalk stream, skirts hiked above her knees. It was a cool, innocent, English sort of memory and one he pulled out of his mind like a stone from his pocket when the suffocating heat of Canton was ready to melt his bones.

Meg's words cannoned into him, threatening it.

"You couldn't ruin anyone," he said, his voice rough, surprised by the fierceness he felt—the protectiveness—toward that memory from so long ago. His certainty ran up against six years of absence. What did he really know about her, the village, any of it?

Nick had been halfway around the Cape of Good Hope when Isabelle finally married his uncle. Isabelle had the position and money to buy her way out of feeling the consequences of such a ramshackle affair. Nick. Well, Nick was a man, and six thousand miles away. But Meg? If he'd been less self-absorbed, he might have guessed someone so small would fall through a crack that wide.

Meg halted by a horse paddock where the crowds had dispersed, tipping her face up to meet his. He took a deep drag of air. She'd been giving him that defiant look from the time she was six, but she was a woman now and Isabelle's sister. He clamped his hands behind his back.

"Why can't they forget such an old scandal?" he mused.

"Old," she repeated, rubbing the bridge of her nose between two gloved fingers. Her tone was bitter.

"I'm not your enemy, Meg," he said, her name flooding his mind, spilling over the rim and past his lips, well beyond the line he thought he'd set for himself. He sighed. It was impossible to hold this baggage at a distance when he had such a weakness for her company.

The thought was not a welcome one. "Does this happen often?"

"You mean Mrs Fletcher acting as though I'm carrying an exotic disease?" Blustery wind swirled past them, lifting her ribbons, tossing his hair across his forehead. She leaned against the rough fence and plucked one glove from her hand, sliding her tapered fingers from the channels.

"Not often."

"I'm sorry," he said. He reached out to touch her arm and she flinched from him before he could even make contact. The words were pitifully inadequate.

"I don't need your apology, sir. And I don't need your help," she said. His bay stallion wandered near the fence and Meg leaned back, giving the horse a skeptical eye. But, to his surprise, the high-spirited bay dipped his head and began nosing Meg's hand.

"Of course you don't need help. You're doing so well," Nick said, his words light. "Throwing rocks at little boys."

Her tentative hands slipped along the stallion's muzzle. The bay stood perfectly still and Nick's eyes widened. She was handling the beast with a calmness he thought he would never see in her. Meg liked horses about as well as she liked rats.

"The stone was tiny. It couldn't possibly hurt where I threw it," she said.

It took concentration but he tore his glance from her hands. "Someday, one of those boys might take it into his head to throw a rock back at you, Meg. Or Isabelle."

She hopped to the ground. "I can take care of myself," she said. "You may take care of Isabelle."

He turned on her, standing so close that she had to tip her head up to look him square in the face. Her bonnet began to slip and she reached a hand to hold it on as the air seemed to pound in the narrow span dividing them. They'd always been the best of friends. Why did it seem impossible to regain their former footing?

She must have wondered too. "I don't want to fight with you," she said, looking blindly to the horse. Then she tipped a roguish smile at him. "Though I want it strictly understood that I would be sure to win."

"Of course." He chuckled. It was a peace offering and he took it up. "Who's the letter from?" he asked, brushing her reticule with the back of his hand. Though Pevensey was chilly, she must have friends. A London gentleman, he thought, remembering Mrs Greenley's sharp words.

She heaved a breath. "No one you know," she answered, her eyes becoming so evasive that his suspicions were roused, compounding when she slid from the topic with a deft turn. "Did you know that Henry's wife is expecting a child?"

"A child," he exclaimed, as though she had said an elephant or a dragon. "What is she like? Henry's wife." The thought of army-mad Henry Gracechurch settling down in the tame countryside might once have been laughable.

"Brave," Meg answered. He had been expecting her to say she was beautiful, accomplished, clever. Not brave. But Meg had a talent for seeing things. "They are devoted."

He must have betrayed his cynicism in some way because Meg cuffed him on the sleeve.

"My lord, not every man aims to be a desiccated bachelor."

Meg was going to chase him into an early grave with her constant "my lords."

"And how is she brave?"

"She became my friend."

It was simply said and more powerful for all that. She touched gloved fingertips to his wrist, as light as a ladybug walking across a leaf.

"Look."

Nick followed Meg's eyes down the street to where Brooks caught up to Jolly as she exited the draper's shop. From this distance, it was a silent performance: the raised hand, the checked pace, the tip of his hat. Jolly meant to move on but Brooks stopped her with a word. She stood still, awareness sketched along every line of her frame.

"She likes him," Meg whispered.

"How can you tell? Her spine is like a ramrod."

"Don't you see the way she's fidgeting with her purse strings? Jolly never fidgets."

"Perhaps it's nerves. She thinks he's about to maul her," he said, earning a laugh. "He's making it too obvious he likes her. As ready to be a fool as any man ever was."

Meg raised her brows. "That doesn't sound like you."

"Brooks would say it sounds exactly like me. You see the beginnings of a love affair," he said. "I see a man, happy enough in his present condition, risking even that."

Meg gave his horse a final wary pat as she turned from the railing. "You, my lord, are not the same person I used to know."

"Of course I'm not and thank heaven for it."

"Hmmm," Meg murmured, brushing her hands, a gleam of mischief in her eyes. "What a spectacular show it will be, the day you are brought low by love."

He grinned. He could not stop it when she was near. "She would have to be an angel."

"An angel? She sounds like a bore. I wish you joy of her," Meg replied, smiling as she glanced beyond Nick's shoulder. "Good afternoon, Mr Brooks. Have you come to fetch your gargoyle back to the Abbey?"

Brooks touched his cap and grinned. "Unless you have a better use for him."

Meg ran her eyes over Nick and colored, reaching to tuck a few stray hairs into her bonnet. It was a pity she was Isabelle's sister.

Meg looked precisely like an angel now with her flushed cheeks and smooth brow. The way her lower lip curved with fullness.

He coughed.

"There's Isabelle and Grandfather," she said, nodding down the street. "They'll be waiting for me."

Simple words but she squared her shoulders like a knight fitting herself to a suit of armor. Nick could see a deep hollow form at the base of her throat from some sudden rush of emotion.

For the third time that morning he found himself chasing her. "Allow me to escort you."

"I don't need—"

"Don't be such a fractious woman," he said, conscious that he couldn't remember a time when he'd had more fun. "I want to see your family," he answered, stilling her objections.

His gloved hand cupped her elbow and, as they advanced, he noticed how Isabelle's eyes narrowed on him. He had been her willing slave before she cast him aside. Never again.

"Grandfather has exhausted himself, Margaret," Isabelle said, holding her gloves in her fist, hardly acknowledging Nick now that he was here. "While you were off with Lord Ainsley," she said, her lips drawn in a tight line, "I sent for the carriage. It would be best if you came home with us now."

Mr Ross stood with a thin bead of perspiration on his lip, carefully holding himself upright. He leaned hard upon his walking stick, his shoulders as high as his ears, his face drawn and white.

"Too much sun, Grandfather?" Meg asked, pulling the second glove from her hand and stuffing them under her arm. She nodded a silent question to him and he returned a short nod back. Then she touched his cheek. Nick cocked his head to witness the ritual. The family at Blythe House had always had strange ways.

Meg's hand jerked away but she settled it on him again, anxiety lining her face.

"Might I assist you in any way?" Nick asked.

It was Isabelle who answered him, giving him a smile that would have carried him to heaven, once. Now, it only filled him with irritation. "How kind. There is nothing to be done now but I'm sure he would love for you to pay him a visit in the next day or two."

That he could not do. Already there was more contact with this family than he could allow for his peace of mind. He could draw back now. He must.

The carriage drew up and Nick helped Meg up, then Mr Ross. He turned to Isabelle and held his hand out to assist her.

"You will come soon, won't you? Tuesday, perhaps?" she asked, turning soft blue eyes on him. He recalled some shockingly bad poetry scribbled into the margins of his old school books on the subject of blue eyes and made a mental note to dig them out of the attics and add them to the bonfire on Guy Fawkes Night.

He shook his head, taking in a clean lungful of air. He'd returned to Sussex, certain he would be haunted by the ghosts of his past and, though memories met him at every turn, he was surprised to find that one particular ghost could be laid to rest. Isabelle was no temptation. His heart was not moved by her elegance. She had lost her power over him. "Not so very soon, Lady Ainsley. I have estate business, a fancy expression for working in my fields, and I've promised—"

Her hand shifted, grazing his wrist, and a curious languor melted into him—small at first, no more than an opium drop landing on his tongue, but growing every second.

"Oh, but you must. We have so much to talk about."

He struggled to remember his objections, but they seemed so indistinct now in comparison to the excellent reasons he was discovering to come. They had so much to talk about.

The heat of the day rushed in on him, plowing through the veins under his arms, sapping his strength as he handed her up. "Yes," he said, his voice rough. Meg gave him a look full of scorn, but he could not help himself. "Yes."

The carriage started away and he tugged on his cravat, gesturing to Brooks and fighting for a sense of normalcy.

"Araminta," Brooks said, watching the Blythe House party make their way up the hill.

"What?"

"That's her name. She said she expected she would see me in church. So." Brooks spread his palms open as though his case was settled.

"I thought we were avoiding Blythe House women, Brooks. Yet you're chasing after Mrs Jolly."

"That I am," he answered, glancing over Nick, who stood stock-still in the middle of the road, and sending another speculative look toward the carriage. "Which one are you chasing after?"

Chapter Seven

Nick came on Tuesday, cantering his horse down the drive with a look on his face as though he were riding into hell. Meg watched him from the library window, shrinking behind the curtains when he stopped at the porch.

"Who is it?" Grandfather asked her, tucked up like an invalid before the library fire. Meg wandered back to him, even as Isabelle's light laugh and Nick's low answer seemed to carry through the beams of the house, vibrating the floorboards under her slippers.

"Lord Ainsley."

"To see Isabelle."

"I expect so."

Meg dragged her attention to Grandfather, where it ought to be. Three days his energy had been gusting and flagging like petticoats on a wash line. A half-finished game of dominos sat on the small table near his chair. It had been too much for him.

"Don't like the look of me, do you?" he said, lifting his heavy eyelids.

She gave him a grin. "I always like the look of you."

The truth was that she was scared. Meg slid to her knees and reached a hand up to rest against his face, pulling at the threads of his mind, lost and looking for an anchor.

No answering warmth met her touch. No spark of feeling. These were dull, indistinct thoughts. Unreachable. She shook her hand out and tried again, feeling along the barrier between them.

Cold. So cold. She saw a blacksmith's hammer striking sparks as it beat on an anvil. Each chip of glowing fire doused in a thick blanket of snow.

Meg flinched, cradling her fist, hiding it away in the billow of her skirts. "You only want fattening up. Buttered peas, roasted goose, beef steaks…"

"You've better things to do than tend an old man," he said under her litany.

"Oyster patties, prawns, asparagus, orange tarts. That will do for luncheon."

He choked on a laugh and something of his old self returned to his face, but the exertion produced a fat drop of saliva, pooling on his lip, unnoticed. She lifted a handkerchief to wipe it away. Their eyes could hardly meet until he chuckled again. "I'll be as fat as the Regent."

"We cannot hope for such glory." She lifted his hand and kissed the back. "Only a bit of it."

Snow. Choking, blinding snow.

His eyes drifted shut and Meg sat on, listening to the muffled sounds from the drawing room. Finally, less than an hour later, a door opened and shut. She heard the sound of his horse again. Nick hadn't stayed long, but he had come. Was Isabelle so irresistible?

She didn't have the right to have any feelings about that whatsoever. If Nick wanted to make a fool of himself over Isabelle again, it would be an expensive business. He would find himself handing over a dowager house and generous allowance to his uncle's widow. Soon, too, unless she missed her guess.

Meg stifled a heavy sigh, telling herself that it was all good news. The sooner Isabelle could leave Blythe House, the happier Meg would be.

In the meantime, she must get Grandfather well again. She directed a fierce frown at her hand. Reading him, it felt like she had plunged her palm into a bucket of ice. It was so real, so vivid, but no good if it gave her more questions than answers. A string of words such as, "Pity I've got a summer cold. No need to fuss," might have been useful. Instead, she'd skimmed a blasted image needing careful translation, as inscrutable as a Babylonian text.

Jolly came, soft-footed, up the passage and touched Meg on the shoulder, beckoning her into the corridor. "Young Mr Gracechurch has come," she whispered.

"Henry." Meg smiled when she gained the hall, still blanketing her voice in softness though Grandfather was harder and harder to rouse these days. Though Henry had sold out of the army, he stood with the ramrod posture of the soldier he had been. "Grandfather's not receiving. He's under the weather."

"Then he won't miss you at dinner?" he asked, a hopeful lift to his brows. "My wife charged me to bring you to see her and I think she's part witch because I cannot say no to that woman."

Meg grinned at the image of sweet-tempered Beatrice Gracechurch, heavy with child, weaving spells over a cauldron. Meg's smile faded a little. "Grandfather is much too—"

Jolly bustled forward. "Miss Margaret, there's nought that can't be seen to by your sister and me. I'll pop into the kitchens and tell Cook you won't be here for dinner," she said, already out the door.

Meg laughed. The sound of it, even to her ears, was like plaster of Paris raining from the ceiling of a derelict house. If she stayed cooped up, day after day, she would be of no use to Grandfather at all.

"I'll have to change."

"For us?" Henry asked with a shake of his head. "Don't bother."

"All right. But give me a moment to comb my hair and find a hat," she said and raced to her room. When she placed a confection of straw and silk on her head, Isabelle stopped in the doorway of her room.

"Going someplace?"

"Henry's house. He invited me to a family supper." Meg tied the green bow under her chin at a saucy angle. If Meg Summers was nothing else, she was a woman who could not resist a saucy angle.

Isabelle's smile was tight. "In that frock? You look like a crumpled handkerchief."

"The Gracechurches wouldn't care if I turned up neck-deep in mud. They aren't the sort to mind a little simplicity, a little plainness," Meg answered, filling her reticule with her accustomed handkerchief and fishing knife, pulling the strings tight.

Isabelle's laugh was malicious. "Yes, I met Henry's wife at church. Plain as a peahen."

Meg brushed a careless hand down her skirts, flicking at the wrinkles with an ineffectual swipe, and paused as she left the room, her brow knitted in exaggerated confusion. "I wonder why you don't have more friends, Isabelle. Such a puzzle."

She swept from the room feeling she had scored her point but cursed herself for being so stubbornly pious about the virtue of plainness when Henry's gig pulled up to Hawthorne Cottage—the small dwelling Henry occupied on his family property.

"Is that Nick's horse?" she asked. Of course it was. Only a ninny would mistake the big brown creature with a black mane and tail, black fading up the limbs. "Lord Ainsley is here?"

Henry nodded. "Why, yes. I thought I would ask him along."

Meg glowered at his back as he jumped down from the seat. It was no use reminding him that he had assured her it would be a family party and not to fuss over her appearance on their account.

Men were obtuse. They really were.

They entered the pocket-size sitting room together and Beatrice, settled in an armchair as far from the fire as possible and chatting with Nick, levered herself up to welcome Meg.

"You are looking lovely," Meg said, leaning into Beatrice's embrace as Henry poured a drink.

Beatrice shook her head but there was laughter in it, her voice too low to carry. "I know what I look like. It's somehow so much worse being a thousand months pregnant when there is a gorgeous man about the house."

"Henry?"

"Always, darling," she answered promptly. "So much that it doesn't bear mentioning. But I meant that Lord Ainsley of yours."

"Not mine."

"No? We could fix that, you know." Beatrice fanned herself a little. "Henry should have warned me that he was not the disfigured, misanthropic bachelor I was hoping for."

Meg notched her brows and, in answer, Beatrice waved a hand at her figure. "It's so difficult to lift one's self from an armchair elegantly."

Meg laughed, drawing the eyes of the men. "Is your mother coming when you deliver the baby?"

Beatrice sighed. "Yes, though every time she steps through the cottage door she bursts into tears. She's convinced I live in a hovel."

"It is snug," Meg agreed. "But you can always retrench to the Gracechurch home if you had to."

Beatrice shook her head. "I want our privacy for a little while longer. Though, with Mama and Penny here for the birth, there will be precious little of that."

"Penny's coming?" Meg asked in some surprise, remembering Beatrice's irrepressible little sister.

"Oh yes. How we shall keep her from upsetting the whole household with one of her schemes is beyond me. The latest news from home is that she's managed to talk Papa into engaging a fencing master."

"Why not?" Meg's eyes sparkled.

The gentlemen joined them and they sat again, each of them holding their breath until Beatrice had arranged herself just so. Sir Frederick Magpie began to compose a column on the calamities of increasing and childbirth.

"I want to hear all of the stories," Beatrice said as they sat over a dinner far grander than the tiny dining room should have afforded. "I don't think Henry has any older friends."

"None older than Fox and I," Nick answered. "I was sorry to hear of your cousin's death, Henry."

Meg stilled, exchanging a searching glance with Beatrice. Henry slipped his hand over his wife's wrist and rubbed his finger over the fading scars that still ringed it.

Nick gave Meg a puzzled look.

Henry said, papering over the awkward moment. "And Meg trailing after us."

Meg took up the slack. "Pulling me out of scrapes you led me into. Irritating you all with endless questions and requests to re-tie my ribbons."

Henry laughed. "That was Nick's job."

Nick tilted his glass in a salute. "You were a Trojan, Meg."

Meg cocked her brow. "Don't wrap it up in fine linen when I know you think of me like a dreadful little sister."

Nick's gaze sharpened but Henry raised his glass. "True enough. Shall we lift a toast to our little sister?"

At the sound of the crystal clinking together, his knuckles grazed the back of her hand. It was enough to send electric shocks sparking up her veins, bringing a contact both painful and sweet.

One word echoed through her mind before it faded in a fog of disturbed dissatisfaction. *Sister.*

***

Nick drank to the toast, staring at the wine as though it had gone bitter. He was not Meg's brother. The visceral need to repudiate such a thing creeped up on him unaware. She wasn't little either, except in the most literal sense. Her tiny figure would fit comfortably in the curve of his arm, her dark curls brushing his chin. Meg was a grown woman now. He knew it, of course, but the realization seemed to land deep in the pit of his stomach, unsettling him.

The disquiet remained, even after the ladies excused themselves after dinner and left the men to their pipes. Nick watched them go with relief. There had been no ease for him while Meg sat inches from his elbow. Strange, that. In these last days, he felt like a marble rolling across the deck of a sea-tossed ship. But now with her gone, the liveliness of the party went with her.

"What was that bit of awkwardness about Fox?" Nick asked, reaching for the small glass of port Henry handed him. "Why was I not supposed to mention him? Is his death still too raw?"

Henry exhaled sharply. "Raw? No. I wish I had killed him myself," he said, looking down at his hands, opening his mouth and closing it again as though he did not know where to start.

"Beatrice got herself engaged to Fox and had to get out of it," he began. "She didn't want to go to his house alone and begged Meg to accompany her. And you know what Meg is."

"I know what Meg is," Nick murmured.

"She'd never say no to a friend. When they got there to deliver the news, Fox didn't take kindly to coming out on the losing end. He slipped a sleeping draught into their tea and spirited Beatrice away in a coach."

Nick's face hardened as Henry told the story, Nick's lips thinning with each passing moment.

"I found Meg in a heap on the floor of his townhouse, bound like a criminal, almost insensible." Henry gave a short, disbelieving snort. "Even then she was determined to tell what she knew. Beatrice was nowhere to be found, but we patched together some clues and I raced off to Sussex."

Henry went through the facts quickly, which included his chase to find Beatrice, gunshots, ocean swimming, and an escape up a cliff path.

"And Meg?" Nick asked, his throat as tight as his fists.

Nick's chest was tight with emotion, his anger a living thing. "She is recovered?"

Henry raised his brows. "You haven't even asked about my shoulder." He shook his head. "Yes. Meg recovered from the draught in a few hours, I'm told. But somebody talked. Somebody always talks, and never in front of you where you can deny it. It got out that she had possibly been seen going into Fox's townhouse, though there was no mention of Beatrice. She brazened it out, keeping our secrets and giving no indication that she had anything to be ashamed of. The talk died down but we owe her a debt."

Nick set his glass on the table. "Henry," he said, lost for the words that would bring order to his thoughts, and help alleviate the swirl of rage he felt for Meg having to bear up under double scrutiny when she wasn't at fault for either incident. Fox, that bounder, had been a French spy, willing to drug women, and kidnap one to get away.

"We do what we can for Meg in the village," Henry replied, rubbing a hand over his face. "She is accepted where we go, but I am sure that it reverts back to the bad old days as soon as she is on her own. If only it were something you could fight with your fists." He paused, clearly shaken by his memories. "I thank heaven that Meg came home early." He turned to pour out another measure of the tawny port wine. "We need the distraction and the company."

Nick took a glass and raised a brow.

"My wife is not given to nerves, but I've discovered that I am. The strain of waiting—knowing her time could come any moment—is worse than facing a cavalry charge." He rubbed a hand over his face.

Nick chuckled. "Surely not."

"Surely so," Henry countered. "If I thought my sword would be of any use, I wouldn't feel so dashed useless. You laugh now but we shall see how you are when the woman you love is facing it."

"It sounds uncomfortable. I hope I may avoid the affliction."

"Love? You think you're past it?"

"After Isabelle, I don't need it."

Henry leaned back in his chair regarding him with skepticism. "That was calf-love, at best."

Nick shrugged. "Well, no trace of that old madness lingers."

"You'll have to marry sometime."

Nick nodded, looking deeply into his glass. "A lady of good name who understands my need for an heir. And she need not go through the process more than once if it's a boy," he said, half joking.

Henry picked up a fork and leaned forward, pivoting one of the tines against his fingertip, his face pale under the ruddy tan. "Would you believe I don't give a damn about that?" He looked up at Nick, his mouth a thin line and his chin shaking. "I don't care if it's a boy or girl, green or purple as long as Beatrice and the baby come through it." Henry held Nick's searching gaze for a moment before setting the fork down and taking a deep breath. "Anyway, I'll be anxious until it's over. It's easy to think of Meg as nothing but a scapegrace—and she is—but she will be the tonic Beatrice and I need."

Nick reached for his pipe and bag, packing the bowl and lighting the wad. In moments he was drawing smoke, finding himself agreeing with Meg's assessment. Henry and his wife were devoted and, in the face of it, Nick felt unsettled.

A servant came to the window, knocking a finger against the glass, and Henry went to open it. "The mare is near her foaling, sir. Restless and sweating. You said you wanted a look in?"

"Yes," Henry said, making his apologies to Nick, who waved him away.

Alone, Nick wandered into the soft spring night, placing the bit of his pipe between his teeth now and again, pulling in the warm smoke and letting it waft up like a silvery scarf. Then he heard the creaking swing of a window latch and voices drifting like his pipe's smoke on the cool air.

"So much better already, Meg. It's shocking how warm I've become," said Mrs Gracechurch—Beatrice.

"I'm here to do your bidding." Meg.

"Oh good. That means you have to leave off the subject of Isabelle and tell me the truth about London. You may as well tell me now because you are a dreadful liar."

"Excuse me, madam, I am an excellent liar," Meg insisted with a laugh.

Nick let out a quiet chuckle and reached over, setting his pipe on a low wall well away from the window. The smile died on his face as he remembered Henry's words—Meg in a crumpled heap on Fox's floor, insensible with a sleeping draught, determined to save her friend anyway. He sank back into the dark shadows of the ivy, unapologetically listening.

"But tell me why you ran away from London? There are weeks yet in the Season. I know you cannot abide your aunt, but you might yet have found a match."

Silence reigned save for sounds of the country. Birds in the night, the croak of frogs, and the pulsing hum of insects. Nick wished he could dare a peek into the lighted room.

Finally, Meg spoke, her voice teasing. "Fantastical tales are for children, Beatrice, and it isn't my style to go, hat in hand like some beggar, praying for some man to marry me. It is enough, at present, to have Grandfather to care for and your child, who will be horribly spoiled. I hope you know I plan on being an eccentric aunt."

Nick recognized in her voice a certain tense lightness. She wasn't answering Mrs Gracechurch's question.

Beatrice chuckled. "I can't wait for you to undertake a journey to the Bedouin tribes dressed in trousers."

The image of Meg in trousers came to Nick's mind too quickly to be dismissed without leaving an impression of her enticing figure.

"You might be right to leave the stiff-rumped London dandies to look after themselves. If they can't see what a jewel you are, there's no point in bothering. Anyway, there are pickings to be had right under our very nose. That perfectly gorgeous Lord Ainsley, for instance."

Nick held his breath. He could be in the middle of an attack by an army of vicious garden voles and he would not have made a sound.

"He is gorgeous, isn't he?" Meg said. Nick grinned until Meg cut his conceit into ribbons. "But do not even think of matchmaking, Beatrice Gracechurch."

"But why not? I've already imagined what lovely children you will have." Nick could hear the grin in Mrs Gracechurch's voice.

"Because of all the men in England, I could never marry that one."

Nick furrowed his brow.

"Have you noticed that when he looks at me, there's a divot between his brows like I'm a stubborn sum he can't work out." Nick put a hand to his forehead, smoothing the skin. "Then there's the fact that he spent years mooning after Isabelle, which ought to tell you how blind and stupid he is. We are quick to fight."

"Isabelle is not a problem now." Beatrice laughed. "The law won't allow him to marry his uncle's widow. And you like to fight. Tell me you don't."

"Don't like those reasons?" Meg continued, her voice dropping into a throaty, conspiratorial whisper that had Nick leaning toward the window frame. "I have loads more. You should hear how he talks about the local lads, banging on about law and order. Not a speck of mercy at all. After his precious Abbey is restored, I would be surprised if he ever leaves it. And he taught me to spit." Mrs Gracechurch chuckled. "Truly," Meg continued, lifting her voice again, "there's not an ounce of romance in that man. No, Beatrice, you must turn your energies elsewhere. Lord Ainsley and I are not suited to one another."

Nick never allowed himself to be wounded by bare facts. They simply were. Henry called then, and Nick went back inside, swiping his cold pipe as he passed, irritated, for no accountable reason. Meg had suggested he was an ill-tempered bear on more than one occasion. But despite deciding that he definitely wasn't bothered by her words, they vexed him.

The gentlemen joined the ladies then and, as conversation flowed between them, Nick tried hard not to look at Meg at all. Still, he seemed unable to refrain from seeking her out, and he caught himself furrowing his brow on more than one occasion.

"Have you subscribed to a newspaper yet, my lord?" Mrs Gracechurch asked, her expression open and guileless.

"More tea?" Meg interjected, raising the heavy silver pot in his sight line.

Nick ducked and answered his hostess who, too, had to dip her neck to see him. "I haven't. Do you have any recommendations?"

"I think it's time I was getting home," Meg said, setting the pot down with a clatter and getting to her feet.

"*The London Observer* is not so popular as *The Times* but has an excellent weekly column you might enjoy," Mrs Gracechurch went on as though she hadn't heard Meg at all.

"Henry?" Meg called, crossing the room and stumbling over Mrs Gracechurch's feet. That's what it must have been, though it looked more like a kick.

"Of course. I'll hitch up the gig and run you home," Henry replied, setting his cup aside.

Nick's heart sped up and his mouth was half open to object. *No. Let me.* But he had no gig, only a horse he could not, in propriety, take her up on when there were alternatives. Still, as he rode home following the moon, high in the eastern sky, he found himself forming a resolve, that had seemed to come out of nowhere, to order a carriage from London.

Chapter Eight

Meg scratched away at her work—her pen dipping from the inkwell, catching fat blobs of ink on the lip of the glass and returning to the paper again and again, filling the page under the title "The Weaker Sex."

"Any man of sense... Pardon, dear Readers, for my lapse. Any man, being a man, must therefore be sensible—in contrast to the native disorder of feminine minds. Just as male sinews are able to bear greater burdens than the weaker sex, so, too, are their minds."

Meg's lips turned up in a smile so wide she had to bite her lower lip to keep it from breaking across her face. Sir Frederick was in fine form today.

"It is a conundrum worthy of Solomon to discover the purposes of Providence in bestowing the burdens of breeding, confinement, and delivery on a sex so obviously inferior and ill-suited to bear up in the face of them..."

Meg lifted her head as a sharp snore emanated from Grandfather's bed. It was a reassuring sound, deep and healthy, she thought. His rest last night had done him some good and perhaps Isabelle had been right. Meg had been pestering him too much. She bent over her work once more and filled the page with Sir Frederick's guileless certitude.

"If the rigors of childbearing are widely understood, one cannot but conclude that the Fair Sex might be capable of the mental rigors of modern life—the responsibilities attending sufferage, captaining a sailing vessel, or travelling freely among the Bedouins," she wrote, slipping in the ode to Beatrice who was a thoroughgoing knave.

"The mind shrinks from such horrors, but there is a single remedy to such untidiness in the Creator's grand design. My proposal is simple: In order to keep women from the sacred halls of Parliament, men must discover how to bear children."

Meg read it once more, laughing at the conclusion. It was good.

She sanded the paper and folded it, sealing the missive and writing out her publisher's address. Then she made her way to the kitchens. "Jolly, I've got to go into the village to drop this into the post. Will you look in on Grandfather?"

Mist still lingered in the fresh morning air and Meg stepped through the gate of the walled kitchen garden intent on enjoying the great outdoors. The steady clop of hooves brought her up short and she saw Nick riding toward her, leading another mount with Brooks bent over his horse's neck, his arm cradled at a strange angle.

Nick dropped from the saddle in one fluid motion and reached to gather his servant down in his strong, careful arms. His tone was brusque.

"I need some of Jolly's doctoring, Meg."

Meg turned on her heel, racing back to the kitchens, returning with Jolly, who ran with her skirts kilted high above her ankles.

"What have you done to yourself?" Jolly asked, kneeling on the turf where Brooks stretched, her fingers ripping away the sleeve of the man's shirt.

Brooks's breath came in gasps. "The fence."

Nick answered for him. "We were working to repair a paddock fence and a bit of wood whipped around and sliced into his upper arm. There's a piece of it still—"

Not anymore. Jolly had pulled the splinter out and clapped a wad of apron over the gash in one fluid motion as Brooks bellowed loud enough to shake the birds from the trees, English curses intermingling freely with sounds Meg had never heard.

A few paces back, never taking her eyes from the scene, Meg leaned toward Nick, whispering, "Is that Chinese, Lord Ainsley?" Using his formal name was silly—a thin sort of shield to hold between herself and that foolish girl she'd been. Still, she clung to his title.

"Yes." The word was clipped.

"*Puk gaai.*" Her mouth formed around the strange accent as she met his eyes. "What have I just said?"

Nick's jaw clenched. "You've told Brooks he can go fall in the street."

Brooks, white and shaking, stifled a laugh as disapproval lined Nick's mouth. Obviously, he'd given her the most dry, literal translation.

She smiled at Brooks. “I can see that it would be a useful phrase to know.”

“I didn’t mean to say it to you, Araminta,” Brooks gasped, reaching up with his good hand to tuck a few blonde wisps into Jolly’s cap. But Jolly only shook her head as she sponged the wound. Then she clapped an arm across her own stomach, her movements fumbling.

“I’ll thread the needle,” Meg said, settling to her knees.

Jolly looked up at her, mouth tight, hands shaking. Strange. Jolly was never overset.

“Yes,” she said, her eyes sending some entreaty to Meg. Meg nodded when she understood. Jolly couldn’t sew up Brooks. “You’ll have to do the stitching too. Take my apron.”

That sensible article was wadded under Brooks’s arm and Meg nodded briskly, trying to stifle the shiver of fear that went through her. What had she written this morning? That a woman could face her challenges bravely—as bravely as Beatrice was doing, as brave as Jolly. She slipped the gloves from her hands and took command as though she had done this a hundred times instead of the one time she had practiced on the stable dog.

“Jolly, take his other hand. My lord, if you will hold his lower limbs.”

“I’ll not kick you, miss,” Brooks assured, his mouth lined in pain.

She smiled. “Lord Ainsley won’t let you.”

She began to work fifteen small, orderly stitches, drawing the tight skin together and resisting the sloppiness that would have her done with the bloody business in little time by reciting *There is no fear in love* over and over under her breath.

Brooks’s thoughts pinged through her at each stitch.

Hurry now.

Before I disgrace myself.

Then, washing through her mind, Meg saw Jolly’s hand in Brooks’s alongside a feeling she could only describe as deep contentment.

And a whole string of Chinese curses.

“There,” she said as she tied off the thread. Perspiration covered her face and she was sure she looked as pale as Brooks.

"Nicely done, pet," Jolly said, leaning over and kissing her hair as the shaking breath left her lungs. "I'm sure I can dress the wound. Master Nicholas, you will support Miss Margaret as she returns to the house?"

"I was on my way to the village," Meg said, plucking up the letter fluttering on the grass.

"I'll walk with you," Nick said, holding the reins of his horse and holding out an elbow for her. She replaced her gloves and lightly took his arm as though his company was absurd, entirely unnecessary. But her legs felt as though they were India rubber.

For the length of two fields, she could pretend all was well. Then her limbs went cold and her stomach seemed to sway like a top-heavy wagon.

"Meg, why did you keep repeating that bit of scripture *There is no fear in love*?"

She breathed in long, regular cycles before she answered, willing the fresh cool air to brush away this nausea.

"I wanted it to be over so badly that I was afraid I would make three gaping stitches and be done with it. The phrase is part of a sampler Jolly made me do as a girl. Over and over, getting the stitches right. And it served me well, didn't it?"

He threw back his head and laughed, his dark hair lifting from his brow.

But the thought of stitching that long, blood-red gash seemed to kick her in the back of the knees and she went down.

"My lord—" she began before retching on the grass, horrified by the picture she presented: a sick dog, miserably rocking on all fours. Then the nausea redoubled, narrowing her vision, and she could not care that Nick was watching her turn herself inside out.

When the tremors passed, she sat back on her feet and breathed heavily. She passed a shaking hand over her mouth. "My lord—"

He crouched at her side, pulling the bonnet strings and working them loose, lifting it gently from her head.

"Not now, Meg. You need some air." The straw bonnet was tossed in the grass and the letter lay beside it. Nick strode off and she stood, her limbs firm now. She perched herself on a raised root under a spreading tree. He returned a minute later with a wet handkerchief, pressing it into her hands. "I found the spring in the woods. Remember it?" he asked.

"Remember the spring? Of course. While you were having adventures in China, I've been here the whole time."

He ignored her ill humor and collected her bonnet and letter, turning the missive over briefly before dropping them at her feet. Then he sat on the springy grass, one leg drawn up and one stretching before him almost to her skirts. "Was that only reaction?" he asked, tilting his head toward the scene of her humiliation.

"Yes. I'm over it already. Since we lost our surgeon, I've helped Jolly a little. But I've hardly done the stitching before."

She wiped her face, surely daubing it with specks of grass and soil, conscious that he was watching her, conscious that over the last few days he'd visited Isabelle but never asked to see her.

"Shall I tell you something about yourself, Lord Ainsley?" she asked, filling the silence, which had grown awkward.

"Something I don't already know?"

"You accused me of soft-heartedness once, but you're the one who has a soft heart. You were cradling Brooks like a child when you dragged him off his horse."

Nick looked over his shoulder back to the house for a small moment. "He's a servant worthy of his hire. It would be impossible to replace him."

Her eyes met his. "Lies." A slow smile spread across his mouth and the sight of it brought the weakness to the back of her knees again. "He told me that you saved his life on the journey out to Canton."

A dark flush climbed Nick's neck and his eyes skirted hers so that she suspected that his next words really would be lies. Or nearly so.

"He's the one who saved me," Nick declared. "My stomach did not take to sea voyages easily in those days and, in my desperate condition, I promised him a fortune—a fortune I didn't have yet—if he would be my nursemaid. And he was, for a good portion of the voyage."

Meg's eyes narrowed. Nick hadn't suffered a day of seasickness in his life, though heaven knew there had been enough chances for it on the stormy Sussex coast. How uncomfortable he must have made himself on that long-ago voyage, acting the invalid. She wondered when Brooks began to suspect it was all a hum. During that voyage? During subsequent ones? A tiny dimple tucked Meg's cheek.

"He left the ship with you?"

"I couldn't shake him off," Nick replied, still unwilling to admit any softness in his character. "Now he's been with me for years and the man is impossible to set at a distance. He's an anchor in a changing world." Nick looked at her for a long time, the slight wind playing with his hair, tossing it around.

What would he say if he repaid her in her own coin, offering to tell her something about herself? Meg went hot and cold as her secrets poured through her veins. Secrets about her writing. About her powers. About him.

I loved you.

Meg took in his buff breeches and white shirt, stretching over his chest. His hair, still damp from his morning ablutions, curled at the ends. Work in the sun had turned his skin an unfashionable golden brown. That silly little girl she had been was still capable of being very silly indeed. The way she watched him now made it feel like she hadn't changed a jot from the time she was fourteen.

"What need do you have for an anchor? Things don't change in Pevensey." She smiled.

"You have," he said, flicking the dry, rigid stem of a weed away and leaning back on his elbows.

Though the words were softly spoken, they stirred a number of questions within her. Did he think she had changed for the better? For worse? Then there came the suspicion that he was disappointed. She sat as straight as a queen under his steady regard.

Instead of asking him her questions straight out, she retreated into the safe harbor of flippancy. "Did you think I would still be climbing trees in my bare feet? Or that I would be mothering several children by now? Do tell me so that I may remedy it at once," she finished, her words acquiring sharpness as she spoke them.

He pulled another weed and got to his feet, his eyes curiously warm. "That's not at all what I meant. Come, you must be worn out. I will take you home," he said.

"No need," she stood, brushing out her skirts, deaf to what was only good sense. "I have a letter to deliver."

"If you give it to me, I will deliver it to the post."

Exhaustion claimed her and she imagined the indignity of flaking out on the way down the hill. It was that image that decided things and she placed the fat missive in his hand. "It must go out at once."

He nodded and stood, a strange constraint in his manner as he turned the letter over in his hand. "It must be quite important. I'll do my duty."

Chapter Nine

The Abbey was shaking off the decay caused by long neglect. Within weeks, glazing for the conservatory was cut and repaired, in time to receive a precious cargo of cuttings and bulbs Nick had collected in China.

"They'll call you an ogre," Brooks said, coming upon him one evening while Nick carefully nested orchid bulbs into a rock-strewn pot. Warmth emanated from the furnace in the center of the room as he bent over his worktable. "If you don't mix with them, you'll get yourself a reputation. Besides, attending the local assembly is your duty as a landowner. You may live in an abbey, Your Precious, but you're not a monk."

"I'm not suited to parties and dances," Nick said.

Brooks swiped the bulbs from Nick's hand and dropped them carelessly into the dish where, simply to be contrary, they would probably take root and bloom beautifully.

"You can't live in a hothouse forever," Brooks barked, dragging him off to a bath.

So that was that.

Nick wound a high, starched cravat around his neck and slipped into a blue coat, hating the whole business of ribbons and muslins, of rows of gentlemen facing rows of maidens like opposing armies. And when he finally arrived, Nick disappointed everyone by making his way to the end of the long assembly room where the men with gray hair gathered to speak sensibly.

They spoke of the quality of the soil and the chanciness of the weather; wondered aloud about wool prices. Nick, who had been brought up to be his uncle's heir and to know every particular of the estate, entered into the topics with a willingness to listen that earned the approbation of his companions.

Soon he was in close conversation with Mr Thackery, a local solicitor and widower of some means.

"I'm greatly impressed by the innovations coming out of America," Nick said. "If a broken plow can be replaced with ready-made parts—"

Mr Thackery wasn't attending him and Nick followed his gaze to the doorway where Mr Ross stood with a granddaughter on either side.

There were several observations that he made at once. That Mr Ross was well enough to be in society. That Lady Ainsley, black-clad and demure in her widow's weeds, was nevertheless not denying herself the amusements of an assembly. That Meg had somehow become a temptation so great that he ought to have stayed home.

Devil take it.

Isabelle settled into a chair, apparently willing to transgress the boundaries only so far as the door. There was no reason he must speak to her at all tonight, he thought with some relief. Nick watched as Mrs Greenley, the highest stickler, bustled to her side, conferring the verdict that the dashing widow had not passed the bounds of good taste and the lady was soon surrounded by a clutch of matrons.

Mr Ross settled himself a little farther on, sinking into his seat and folding his hands over the head of his cane. He rested his chin atop that and looked like a whirl of skirts might blow him over. He had no business being here.

Then Nick's gaze carried to Meg, like a child who eats his greens first and saves the treat for last. Meg stood with her chin high, back straight, hair—Lord, dark hair curled over the soft crescent of her ear and a few misshapen pearls danced on the end of a simple earring, inviting his eye to explore her delicate-boned neck. No wonder he wanted to pick a fight every time he saw her. It was the only weapon he had.

The longer he looked, the more he saw. There was no welcoming knot of friends to kiss her cheek and spin her around. There was no aunt-like figure to pat a seat and invite confidences. Instead, there was an unspoken border between her and the villagers, as marked as a crescent of water, fragile and rigid, poised high over the rim of a cup. It only took a tiny pinprick to break the tension, erasing the boundary and cause a mess.

The prick was the Fletcher boy bowing before Meg, soliciting a dance. Nick crossed his arms over his chest and felt a grin rise on his face. Meg would send the boy on his way with a bug in his ear.

Though he waited for it, she didn't. Rather, Meg dipped a polite curtsey and followed the whelp into a long set. She certainly didn't look like a woman in need of rescue.

Then Sam Fletcher touched her, twining his hand around hers.

Though Nick might be conflicted about the girl, his body was not. Suddenly, he felt an urgent need to be at her side. Moving with calm decision, his feet took him to Mrs Fletcher. "Ma'am, may I request a dance?"

Her eyes narrowed and she glanced at Mrs Greenley, at Isabelle sitting at her elbow, at the dancers, at any number of wallflowers. "Me?"

"It would be an honor." He nodded a bow.

He led her out, inserting himself next to Meg and the big, blond scapegrace, following the forms of a dance he had learned so long ago that he didn't have to remember the steps.

"Your son is learning a vocation, Mrs Fletcher?" he asked, tearing his attention from Meg's coiled hair and soft neck so that he would not make a scene.

"He began his apprenticeship to a doctor, as his father did, but that…that woman leads him on," accused Mrs Fletcher, as they came together in the figures of the dance.

"I see no sign of that," Nick answered, lending more than half an ear to the other couple. But he could not make out more than the occasional word and none of them made sense. *Woods. Moon. Silk.*

The moment the music died away, Mrs Fletcher darted past him, pulling her son to the wall with the firmness of long practice. Meg lifted her left brow—the one with the arch that gave her a piratical mien—and he followed her, reaching forward to touch her hand hanging at her side with the tips of his fingers. Layers of material parted them.

She halted and looked back over her shoulder, the seed pearls swinging near her velvet cheek. He blamed them for his lack of caution.

"I would warn you to stay clear of that boy, Meg. I'm not convinced his invitations are honorable."

There had been a light of unmistakable pleasure in her face when he'd halted her and, at his words, he watched it extinguish. Now her cheeks flushed and her eyes sparkled as she rounded on him. "I know what he has in mind, but he did me a kindness in asking me to dance. What should I have answered?"

"You might have said you weren't going to dance with him," he said, his voice tightening.

"That's silly. The rules would force me to sit out the rest of the night."

"Then. Sit. Out." He ground each word between his teeth.

She jutted her chin and raised her voice. "I. Don't. Wish. To."

In a moment crackling with tension, Mr Thackery appeared at their side, his hands clasped lightly in front of him. "As neither of you wish to excite public comment…" His voice trailed off meaningfully. "I invite you to find a less-heated topic to discuss in a near-bellow. Miss Summers, may I say how delightful you look tonight? Your grandfather was saying so to me only now."

The frown she was kindling against Nick disappeared and she smiled up at the other gentleman. "I would choose a less heated topic than that, Mr Thackery. Lord Ainsley, no doubt, finds my appearance offensive as well."

"Ah." He looked her over briefly. "We must pity the poor man. I can see how it would disturb him. Shall we discuss the news? There was a wicked column from Sir Frederick Magpie this week. I was delighted to see the topic applied to our little corner of the world."

Nick's temper was cooling—indeed, he was beginning to wonder what had made it so hot in the first place—and he tugged at his lower lip, trying to attend Mr Thackery's point. "What was the title?"

Meg answered in a low voice. "Prudent Economies."

Mr Thackery laughed. "That's right. The man proposed that the only way to end the war with Boney was to increase smuggling, draining France of luxuries. Further, he argued that grammar schools are a ridiculous waste of money and that young scholars must do their duty by smuggling cheap brandy for the upper classes."

Nick grinned. "Yes, if I recall, he went on to suggest that transportation is much too costly. When the poor blighters are nabbed, we might save ourselves the expense of a trial and a ship's passage, dispatching the criminals with a length of rope which might be used and reused endlessly."

"No doubt you would approve of that," Meg said, her tone dry.

The desire to spar with her was irresistible. "I'm not such a penny-pinch, Miss Summers. I would be happy to pay for all the rope they needed. Miles of it."

Her eyes danced and he vowed to stay well away from her next time they met. Next time.

The smile faded from his lips and Mr Thackery filled the silence. "What do you think of Sir Frederick, Miss Summers? Everywhere I go, the country is divided on the question of whether he is a hero or a rogue."

"The man is nothing more than an observer," she answered.

"I'm not convinced he is a man," Nick said. Meg looked up, startled.

"How original." Mr Thackery tilted his head. "What is your reasoning?"

Nick shrugged but his smile was devilish when he glanced at Meg, who was quite pale and still. He couldn't seem to help himself from goading her at every turn. "The way he exasperates me reminds me of a girl I used to know."

She made an aggravated noise at the back of her throat, brushing past him to sit with her grandfather. Somewhere on her way, he lost his smile and was inexplicably overcome with a feeling of longing and hunger.

Mr Thackery knocked Nick in the arm. "She'll be inundated with offers from all the wrong sort in a minute. She would look on a rescuer with a friendly eye."

"Not likely. I have a natural aptitude for upsetting her."

"I wonder why that is," Mr Thackery observed. "You should go ask her. Sit in her pocket all night until she has explained it in painstaking detail."

That was impossible. An emotion he did not dare name scratched at his insides, indifferent to his attempts to be reasonable.

He did the only thing he could do. He turned his back on it and on Meg, going on as though nothing had moved him—definitely not a slim, dark-haired girl in a shimmering dress the color of golden wheat.

"Harewood and Graves were speaking of how to rid a field of standing water," he began.

Mr Thackery made a sound of disgust. "I'm a solicitor, not a farmer, and if young men will waste the advantages of youth and overabundant hair, it's their own fault," he said, leaving Nick to greet Mr Ross and bow over Meg's hand.

He did not take a sedate seat by the pair but pulled Meg from hers.

Nick could not help himself from watching as Mr Thackery led into a dance. Nick backed himself against a wall, bracketed by the two men intent on solving their respective drainage problems, his eyes following her lissome form. Mr Thackery, lighter on his feet than middle age would suggest, said something that made Meg wrinkle her nose in delight. She answered him back, encouraging. Nick scowled.

"What d'you say, Ainsley? Is it another bad year for manure?"

"How old is Mr Thackery? Forties?" he asked, his tone abrupt.

"Oh no, man," Graves said. "He's come through a bad patch last year that turned his hair silver. but he's not more'n thirty-two."

Nick took a breath. "How many children does he have?"

The gentlemen exchanged a look.

"Two? Was it two, Harewood?"

"Mebbe three. Mebbe. The youngest is but a mite. And Mr Thackery is in his prime, you know. He might get another six if he marries again. Yon Summers girl might do for him. None other has tempted him to dance in many a month. He mostly sits out with the wallflowers," he said, pointing a glass to a row of women, which included Henry's sister Esther.

The other man answered. "What of the scandals?"

"What does a seasoned man care for scandals? They'll say he brought her to bridle at last."

The men shared a low laugh, but an unexpected heat blazed through Nick's insides and he pushed his way from the wall, retreating into an alcove. He'd come to this dashed party for the sole reason of meeting his neighbors and he could not even manage to do that properly. What did he want?

He slipped his hand into his pocket and drew out the pebble, holding it loosely in his palm.

He had almost determined to ask her to dance so that at least he could have her to himself for another round of brawling when Isabelle appeared at his side, approaching like a stray cat looking for a meal.

She stretched her neck as she leaned over his hands. “You are fond of that rock, my lord. Is it the same one as before?” She looked up at the end, bringing her face close to his.

Nick slipped the pebble into his pocket again. “A good luck charm.”

She’d noticed it the day he’d gone galloping off to Blythe House on her invitation. Paying a call on Mr Ross, that’s what he told himself. But he hadn’t seen Mr Ross at all, instead spending an awkward hour listening to Isabelle’s reminiscences of their long-ago courtship, sending angry, periodic looks at the clock and turning the little green stone over in his hand. When it came time to take his leave, he found himself promising to come again. He suppressed a shiver as he thought of it.

Isabelle dipped her head. “I hoped we would have an opportunity to speak.”

Nick grunted. He had far too many opportunities to speak to Isabelle. He would come to see her, promising himself it would be the last time, and then find himself succumbing to…to what? Nostalgia for what had passed between them? Honor? As his uncle’s widow, he acknowledged that he had a duty to her. Desire? Sour bile filled his mouth. Whatever reason he kept running back to Blythe House, it was not because he wanted Isabelle.

What about her displeased him? The fact that her conversation was so flat and ladylike? That her temperament was so willing to please him? Even now, she spoke in halting tones, gauging the weight of each word as it dropped from her lips. Nothing like Meg’s hot, fighting words.

“I…I would like you to speak to my grandfather,” she said.

“Any business you have with the Ainsley estate is handled through my solicitor.”

Her face hardened for a fleeting moment—enough to make him wonder how he’d ever been blind to the hurt she was capable of inflicting—but she took a short breath through her nose and softened before his eyes.

"He's been insensible and feverish for a week, my lord. The assembly cannot be good for his health."

"What do you imagine I could say about it?"

"He values your judgment. He must return home and you might help him to see that."

Her cause was that of a dutiful granddaughter, but he had learned to set her word at a distance and observe it sometime before swallowing it whole.

"I'm sure your efforts and those of Meg would serve far better than my persuasions."

Isabelle dipped her head as a flush stole over her cheek. "He will not listen to me and I fear my sister will urge him into greater danger."

"What do you mean?"

Isabelle waved a placating hand. "I cannot blame her for wanting a respite from the discomforts of tending an invalid but…" Her gloved fingers twisted. "Meg was determined to come and…" Isabelle spread her palms wide. "She is rather forceful when there is something she wants."

Nick looked across the ballroom to where Meg was dancing. He could have been the one taking her hand and leading her in a reel, squabbling until they were too out of breath.

Isabelle was still speaking, and he forced his attention back to her.

"She's been flirting outrageously with the Fletcher boy all night and throwing herself at our solicitor," she said.

Though Nick had been fighting some battle within himself these last hours, he had to own that it wasn't true. Meg could captivate every man in the village out of short pants without even trying, but that wasn't her fault.

Isabelle ran a tongue slowly across her lower lip. "I worry that Grandfather will allow his health to be wrecked merely so Margaret can have a bit of fun."

Nick's eyes narrowed as he tried to work out what Isabelle was up to. "Your grandfather is not my business. He must be well enough or he wouldn't be here."

"No? My little sister has him wrapped around her finger, my lord, but I cannot sit idly by while he compromises his health—"

Isabelle's voice choked on the words and her eyes began to fill with tears.

Chapter Ten

The next day, Meg found herself in the woods, following the unmarked path she knew by heart. Though she had not given up fishing when Nick left, she had given up that spot, promising herself that she would not make new memories there until he was home, which would, she had been sure, be a matter of weeks or months. When she realized he wasn't going to come back, she had stayed away from the grief their former location caused.

Meg crouched low and felt for crescent prints pressed into the rich, dark earth. Ponies or mules had been through here, pack animals bearing smuggled cargo somewhere inland where it might be safely stashed. Sam Fletcher and Jim Greenley and the rest of the lads who played at misadventure were running such stupid risks.

And now they were doing it on Blythe House land.

She counted the hoof marks.

They hadn't even the brains to be proper villains. It was Sam who tipped her off to this spot and it had only taken a dance. If she showed an ankle, he might forget himself enough to tell her where the cargo was hidden and where their points of contact were. Not that she would. The information could, she had no doubt, be gleaned with only a little more effort and no corresponding loss of self-respect.

Meg heard a slight jingle and stood still in the slanting light of late afternoon, listening. She picked out wind weaving through the tops of the trees, the skitter of wood mice chasing through the leaves. There it was. The jingle.

She crouched again, lifting her skirts clear of snags and taking long, silent strides toward the river. If Grandfather knew smugglers were operating unchecked across his land, taking advantage of his illness… Meg felt a shudder take hold of her. She would have to stop them.

It felt like a puff of wind would carry Grandfather off and if she could temper it even slightly, she would do it. She prayed he would rally. Hadn't he jumped out of his bed yesterday morning, declaring he wouldn't miss the assembly for the world? He might get better.

Meg's brow lowered to think of it. She'd tried to drag him back to bed but he had shaken her off only to ask a moment later with eyes that were suddenly clear and a voice that sounded like he'd been kicked in the head by a mule, if he might have his cameo back.

"We've turned the house inside out, Grandfather. I'll keep looking," she'd promised.

Meg could hear the jingle more distinctly against the chirp and hum of the woods. A bridle, she was sure. Then her ears pricked up.

"You'll work me into an early grave at this pace, my lord." It was Brooks's voice.

"Untrue." Nick was panting but she strained to hear him over the sound of a good deal of splashing. "Throwing too much money at the problem would hurt their pride. But if we can repair the fences, the tenants can begin the right way."

"We could move faster if you weren't always off to that other house."

Meg crept closer, parting the branches, desperate to hear the answer. She saw Brooks, his hair spiky as he bent low, scrubbing handfuls of water over his head, avoiding the bandage as best as he could. Meg shifted to see more of the clearing and her breath came loud in her ears when she finally spied Nick.

He stepped from the shadows to crouch at the stream, pulling water up his arms. Somehow her gasp did not carry to his ears and she clapped a hand across her mouth to prevent more. Nick's shirt was hooked to a springy branch and he was bare to the waist, braces dangling over his narrow hips.

Her mind spun like a top around that one fixed detail. His skin shone brightly with sweat, his chest sprinkled with dark, curling hair. As he shifted his hands, her eyes widened to see the ink of a long, black figure curving along the inside of his corded forearm.

Shock had her by the hand, tugging at her, telling her to turn and creep back through the woods again. Tattoos belonged to prisoners and sailors, it told her, not titled gentlemen. She shook it off and lifted her chin slightly to watch as a shaft of light played across his muscled back. Another handful of water was scrubbed behind his neck and in his hair.

He paused then, his fingers trailing in the stream. “I can’t seem to help it.”

His words acted as a splash of cold water and Meg stepped back, anxious to get away. A thick, dry twig snapped and the men lifted their heads in unison.

Blast.

Choosing quickly, Meg slid to the bottom of the bank, achieving the feat with a degree of elegance even as Nick spun, knocking himself off balance. He let out a curse and grabbed for his shirt.

“Curse you, Meg, sneaking around like that,” he said, tugging the dry cloth over wet skin. Too soon he was fiddling with his sleeves—pulling them down, doing up the buttons, hiding the tattoo beneath his proper linen. Meg gave a tiny, inaudible sigh as he reconstructed the picture of a civilized gentleman.

Busy hands tucked his shirt into his waistband and Meg turned, apologizing to Brooks. “I would have knocked but…” She shrugged, pleased to realize her voice sounded cool and disinterested.

“No matter, miss,” Brooks answered, laughing. “A country lass isn’t so missish she can’t see a couple of laborers at their work.”

What a delightful fellow Brooks was. Blood pounded through her heart, denying the truth of his words, but she beamed at him.

“I’ve seen nothing to overset me, your lordship,” she lied. Oh how she lied. Nick’s muscles had hardened in the last years, telling her that he must have done far more than work in a stuffy export office all day. “I’ll let you get back to work,” she answered with admirable self-possession, her calmness at odds with Nick who, even now, was stooping to douse a neckerchief in water and wipe his face.

She spun in her boots, preparing to mount the bank again, determined to be graceful and dignified. Instead, she stepped into a tiny hole, rolling her foot. Pain knifed through her ankle and she plopped down in a billow of skirts.

“Ruin your grand exit?” Nick said, his voice hateful and amused. But he stood over her, offering a hand.

She looked up at him, unshed tears pooling in her eyes. She opened her mouth to tell him which circle of hell he might take up residence in, but her lip shook and she bit it.

"Are you really hurt?" he asked, his voice softened, and he knelt beside her.

"It will pass." She cleared her throat, willing the tears to retreat. She knew what she looked like, sitting in the dirt with her nose stuck up in the air—half Mayfair grand dame, half offended pig. "I only want a few minutes. You've no need to stay and laugh at me, either of you," she said, including Brooks, who stood several paces away.

"Tosh," Brooks answered.

Nick was already plucking the hem of her skirt. She slapped his hand away. "What are you about, Lord Ainsley?"

He grinned. "I do love it when you're officious with me, Meg Summers, but I need your obedience now. Show me your foot."

"It's nothing."

"Then it won't take long for me to agree with you. Think how superior you will feel, knowing you're right and I'm wrong," he said with a wink.

She gave him a look that she hoped would have him bursting into flames, but she gathered her skirts and stuck the foot out, almost managing it without allowing her breath to hitch and a tiny whimper to escape. At last the whole boot could be seen but not even a fraction of stocking.

"Are you going to take off the boot?" she asked through gritted teeth.

"No," he answered, cupping the heel with gentle hands. "Wiggle your toes."

She did. He grunted.

"Point them."

She did. He grunted.

"Rotate your ankle."

She did. She gasped and pushed him onto his backside, pulling the foot away from the source of pain and taking a few hard breaths.

"How bad is it? I do not need a broken foot at this time, sir," she said, her dignity injured at least as badly as her ankle.

"You don't?" he asked, balancing on his knees again. "Why?"

She could swear he was biting back a grin.

"Grandfather needs a good deal of tending."

His eyes explored hers more intently than they had the foot. "Wasn't he well last night?"

"Looks are deceiving. He is very ill indeed."

“Then why did he come to the assembly?”

“I cannot account for that. It was madness, and so I told him.”

“You could have stopped him.”

“A girl of eight stone? If it turned into a wrestling match, I didn’t like my chances.”

Strangely, he did smile then and her insides grew soft, pliable. She shook her head in disgust, flinching away from the meaning of her response. Even on the very best day, Meg, with her burdensome reputation, would struggle to win any man. Nick Ainsley was not simply any man. He was the bearer of an ancient title, a respected landholder. His position was a pillar of the community. Moreover, he couldn’t stay away from Isabelle.

His words returned to her. *I can’t seem to help it.*

Meg had caught glimpses of them last night, how they spoke low and intensely. It was insanity to let this…this attraction take root when the links binding him to Isabelle seemed to re-forge each day.

No. She didn’t know what to do with this man, but she could not keep him even if he made her mouth dry, her heart beat wildly, and her fingers itch to pull back his shirtsleeves and explore the mark on his forearm.

These feelings were complicated, but pain was simple. She had to keep herself from feeling more of it.

“Is my foot broken?”

Chapter Eleven

Nick frowned. "You have a sprain, unless Jolly says otherwise. But I'm fairly sure you'll be up and getting yourself into scrapes within the week."

"Excellent," Meg said, the pain subsiding as long as she didn't move. "I'll be sure to take it easy on my walk home." She reached her hands up and Nick laughed.

"You're not going anywhere unless I take you. Brooks," he called, "can I trust you to entertain Miss Summers until I find that dashed horse?"

"Horse?" Meg squeaked. "No, my lord—"

"Pleasure, sir." Brooks settled himself next to Meg, stretching his legs out. "Miss Summers has a rare ear for Chinese curses."

Nick strode off, leaving Meg's laughter chasing after him. This was how to handle it. Keep it light. Keep her laughing. Keep her fighting. He would be safe enough from this attraction if he could stay away from her emerald eyes, and the temptation to draw so close to her that he might feel her breath on his skin.

The high-spirited horse was not yet obedient, and it took a quarter of an hour to chase him down.

"I thought you'd gotten lost," Meg said, when he returned to the clearing. She had a hopeful expression he hated to squash. "I could manage to walk if Brooks here lent me his arm."

"Let's not put off the inevitable, Meg," he said, looking up and measuring the length of the shadows.

She muttered something insulting but, with Brooks's help, managed to stand. "You will not make yourself a stranger to Blythe House, Brooks?" she said, gripping Brooks's forearms with her gloved hands in order to keep her balance.

Brooks touched his forelock like she was the lady of the house and he one of her dashed under gardeners.

"Come on," Nick said, running a finger under the girth.

"There has to be a better way than riding pillion," she said, an uncertainty in her voice that served her right. He had offered to teach her to ride dozens of times.

"Not unless you've become an expert horsewoman in the last six years."

She raised a pointed little chin. "And if I have?"

"Then I will hand you the reins to this huge bay and would jog along after you. There is every possibility that he might break your neck and I would be rid of your meddlesome ways."

Even then she hesitated. Poor Meg. He shouldn't have to goad her to behave with sense. Walking a mile on that ankle would lame her for a month.

Finally, she let go of Brooks and reached for him, chin raised defiantly. "Well, I haven't," she snapped.

Nick squared himself in front of her and Meg lifted her hands to his shoulders as she had done countless times before—so many that he didn't think it through. Reflexively he reached for her waist, completely feminine under his hands, and realized his mistake at once. A child would be hoisted in this manner, or a wife.

He lifted her up and she sat as though on a side saddle, bending one knee forward, letting let one hang straight, attempting to tug her skirts into order. When he swung himself up behind her, his arm circled her waist and Meg gripped his sleeve with both of her hands.

"You don't need to—"

"I don't want you to fall off, Meg," he answered, his voice rough. Then, to Brooks, "I won't be long."

Already he regretted his decision to come down to Sussex without a cart or trap, something with a bench that would have set her from him a little. Her nearness was like a tiny sliver of wood stuck in the pad of his finger. Painful. Impossible to ignore. "I want to explore around the east marshland before sunset."

"Do you?" Brooks watched him with laughing eyes. "No rush."

Nick frowned at the man, clicking his tongue and prodding his mount along at a slow pace, rocking with the gentle movement of the horse. Meg banged into him several times, holding herself so ramrod straight that she would be aching by the time they reached their destination.

"How is it possible that your seat has gotten worse? Soften your limbs, Meg. You're going to crack my jaw if you don't lean back and let this beast do the work."

He congratulated himself on his tone until her narrow shoulders settled against his chest and his nose filled with the particular scent she wore. He inhaled. Lemons and rose petals. Astringency and sweetness.

"This beast?" she asked. "Hasn't it a name?"

"It's a task I've not gotten to. Have you any suggestions?"

"*Puk gaai*," she declared.

He choked back a laugh. "Not at all the thing." Young ladies did not tell people to go to hell. Still, a slow, unwilling grin spread across his mouth all while she kept her face tantalizingly averted. His view consisted of a few ribbons of her bonnet and the curve of her cheek. Not nearly enough.

"Why are you going to the east marshlands?" she asked, shaking him from his idiotic mooning. "Don't you remember how badly they stink?"

"I remember." He grinned again at a memory of how he'd tried to ferry her down one of the channels in a shallow-bottomed boat. Of tipping her out of the craft and having to walk the long way back to Blythe House, the rankness of rotten eggs billowing from her. She had not smelled lovely then. His smile widened. Meg had looked as filthy as a goblin and her people had bathed her outside. Several times.

"Was it so bad?" he asked.

"Grandfather almost made me cut my hair off. They wouldn't even use my dress for rags." She gave him a blunt jab between the ribs with her elbow. "What are you looking for in the marshes?"

"Smugglers seem to have stayed clear of the Abbey since I returned. But I mean to find out if they're using my land. Do you know if they might be?"

Nick felt her ribs lift as she exhaled a large breath. "I'm not in anyone's confidence, my lord," she said.

He bumped her shoulder.

Her answer was grudging. "I know that when these lads get some money in their pocket, they spend it on little luxuries that are hard to hide—laces and ribbons for their sweethearts, new boots…" She nudged his midsection again. "What makes you think they want anything to do with the east marshes?"

His face was grim. "There've been signs of activity down on the beaches, but I think they're stowing cargo somewhere. I figured—"

"Where better than a boggy marsh that stinks like a carcass?" she said, leaping ahead of him like a nimble-limbed doe. "I hadn't thought of it. Clever."

"It's possible I'm wrong."

"I don't think you are," she said, and the feeling her warm approval gave him made him want more of it. "Did you notice the signs of their passage in the woods?"

He stilled. "Is that why you were there?"

"Yes. I'll keep my ears open down in the village."

"You'll do nothing of the sort, Margaret Summers," he growled, fueled with a scorching protectiveness that seemed to come from nowhere. His arm cinched her close. "It's far too dangerous."

"Of course, my lord," she answered, and he could almost hear her teeth grinding together. "Will you let me loose? I'm going to suffocate."

Nick almost dropped her in his haste to untangle himself. He'd all but pulled her onto his lap.

Where was the comfort of their old, easy friendship? As they rode together, he found it elusive. Perhaps it would return one day when she was safely married and he had settled himself, tending the orchids and chrysanthemums in his conservatory. Avoiding his wife.

He imagined Meg already wed to some gentleman. It wasn't difficult to do. Meg would make someone an excellent wife—likely to spend her afternoon bowling cricket balls to the nursery party instead of managing the household, unfortunately. But she would teach her daughters the knack she had mastered of being tart-tongued and winsome. Lemon and rose petals.

Nick shifted, causing *Puk Gaai* to dance. He smiled at the name. "We'll call him Puck. It's a respectable compromise."

Despite her reputation, Meg would be snapped up by the first young man who realized that the key to her heart would be promising to clean all the fish she could catch. The sooner it happened, the better for his peace of mind. The unfolding plan was perfect. The only unaccountable hitch was the way his heart ached at the thought.

The sun was low in the sky as they approached Blythe House and he swung out of the saddle. "Don't try to get down, Meg," he said, trying to sound irritated and out of patience with her. "You'll only hurt yourself."

"How do you expect me—"

He dismounted and plucked her from the horse, lifting her into his arms. Her face was in profile, the russet light settling on her firm chin and lotus-soft skin.

As he carried her into the house, he tried not to enjoy it at all. But he admitted that he did. He also knew that each contact with Isabelle was dangerous. That she would find a way to drag him back to her side like some desperate whale, harpooned and hunted. These dark thoughts gave his face a sharp, forbidding aspect.

He had no business being attracted to Isabelle's sister. This had to be the end of coming to Blythe House.

Chapter Twelve

In the week following the assembly, Grandfather had been like a man possessed—up at all hours writing letters, posting them off to every business and legal connection he had, burning candles down to the wick. While Meg's foot mended, Isabelle acted as his secretary, copying out his correspondence and being his scribe, arranging for him to meet with his solicitor, Mr Thackery. She even offered to carry Meg's post and seemed content to go on little errands for Jolly in the village shop.

Meg hated to admit it but, despite being a perfect wretch to Meg, Isabelle was proving her worth. It was taking a toll, however. Her sister was looking more ragged around the edges than usual, less like a sleek, well-fed housecat. Tired lines radiated from her eyes.

One morning as Meg sat before the library fire with a stack of old periodicals at her side, Mr Thackery was announced. Isabelle glanced up from her writing table, setting her pen down with a sharp click.

"Your grandfather asked me to tell you it's finished," he said, setting his hand over a sheaf of papers. "He's gone up to rest."

"Mr Thackery." Meg smiled. "I didn't know you had come about business. I was sure Grandfather was routing you in a game of chess."

He gave no answering smile. "Not this time."

He declined to stay when Isabelle offered refreshments and, as he went, Isabelle raised her hand to her high-necked gown, pressing the ruffled collar at her throat. She whirled and Meg thought she detected a gleam of something triumphant in her eyes.

Meg stood, favoring her wrapped ankle, and made her way to the desk. Her injury still troubled her but improved each day.

"What is all this about, Isabelle? He's not well."

"I don't know why you say that, Margaret," Isabelle answered, standing at Grandfather's desk and sorting letters into tidy stacks.

Her head was bent over the work and she did not pause or raise her shadowed eyes. "It's perfectly normal to emerge from a period of poor health, feeling anxious to complete some business one has put off too long."

"What business is so important that he cannot put it off?" Meg asked.

Meg could see the rim of Isabelle's smile under her bent head. "I feel sure that if he wished you to know, he would have told you."

Meg slapped a hand on the desk and raised her voice. "This isn't a game to me, Bella. You must make him stop."

"Make?" Isabelle did look up, then. "I'm not making him do anything. Haven't you seen how demanding he has been? How there is never enough time to accomplish all he wishes to?"

Isabelle was not speaking falsely. Since Meg had returned home, Grandfather had become exacting and troublesome. And though Isabelle had not goaded Grandfather to these excesses, neither was she protesting them. Meg's eyes narrowed and then she exhaled a long breath.

"If you cannot make him stop, then I will."

Again, Isabelle's fingers went to her throat. "I wish you luck with that, little sister."

***

In the end, Meg never had the chance to make Grandfather do anything. He did not return from the drawing room that day but retired to his bed, where he had been ever since. After a week of sleepless nights, Meg could not deny that Grandfather was dying.

Sometimes she would listen as his breathing became shallow and labored, staring at the firelight dancing on the ceiling. Now, she sat next to him on the bed with her feet curled up under her nightdress as Mrs Jolly watched over them from the doorway.

Meg's hand rested on his heart, beating through the thin lawn of his nightclothes, beating out of his chest, and she sang in a gentle, thready whisper, "Oranges and lemons, say the bells of St. Clement's. Pancakes and fritters, say the bells of St. Peter's…" He joined her for scraps of it, when he surfaced from the heavy drag of unconsciousness.

In the middle of one of the repetitions, he clutched her bare arm, pulling her into his mind. The heavy blanket of snow that had shrouded his mind these long weeks was finally gone, burned away by the image of cracking hot dragon's breath. The monster was iridescent greens and blues with diamond-bright claws that clicked as it paced the confines of his thoughts. Its fire was livid orange, shimmering with heat.

Meg forced herself to leave her arm in Grandfather's grasp though some part of her feared it would take her too, consuming her in the merciless blaze.

"Not real. Not real," she whispered to herself. This was death, at least Grandfather's vision of it.

"Help me," he gasped. "Use your magic."

Meg nodded. Anything. Anything. She concentrated, watching for some thought to surface, the way she would watch for fish leaping in a brook. There must be something inside him that wasn't death or pain or fear. "I can see a—"

"No." He cut her off, pulling at the bedclothes, grinding his hand against his heart. His breath came faster now. "Get rid of it. Push it away."

Blind panic was clouding his mind and she struggled to see through it. "Push? I draw your thoughts. I read them."

You can push them too. She heard the words in her head as his mind was suddenly lucid.

The exertion was killing him. He gritted his teeth and the words shifted from her mind. Now he was showing her the most complete image she had ever seen. It wasn't the raggedy end of a thought or smudged likeness, but Grandmother sitting at a child's bedside. The child's eyes were wide with fright and the older woman pushed her hand over and over the little one's forehead, smoothing back her hair until the fright was no more.

This.

Grandfather's breath came in short, hard gasps and his pulse beat like a hammer in his neck. Death would take him like this if she didn't do something. But replace his thoughts? How?

"Please," he said, his voice breaking. It was her undoing as, childlike, he called for her. "Help me go."

Compassion moved Meg to take a deep breath and pass a hand across Grandfather's forehead. "There, there," she crooned and knew it was no more effective than a pat on the hand. She tried again, focused on her thoughts—thoughts of ease and comfort. Again, nothing and she felt tears sting her eyes and course down her cheeks. He had given her so much in his life and was asking so little. Still, she was failing him.

In her helplessness, she turned to the only magic she had and felt her fingertips pulling a shallow net through the thoughts running in his mind.

"Grandmother," she whispered. "Will you think about Grandmother? Think of when you first met."

Meg tucked her small hand into his larger one, his knuckles knobby and sharp. Frail as he was, it still looked like it had the power to protect her.

"Think of what she was wearing. Pink. I see it. Keep thinking. That's it," she said, guiding him with her words. Love hummed along their connection, pulling up the floorboards of his mind, delving deeper than she ever had before. It was suffocating, banding her heart and chest, clenching her veins. She wanted to turn back. *No.* Love for Grandfather tugged her onward, leading her to the dark fathoms, giving her the courage to reach for them. Her eyes drifted closed and, in a single, distilled moment, she saw everything.

It was too much, at first. His fright echoed back at her, dragging her into it, making her feel that his fear was her own, that it was her body on the precipice of death. But bit by bit, the dragon fell apart, shedding one dish-like scale at a time, and in the shards bloomed a garden. A garden at sunset with the air humming with insects—too beautiful to be real. Meg closed her eyes and felt the rising excitement of new love as though it were her own.

"Is that her, Grandfather?" she asked of the image in her head. But she already knew it was. The girl wore an old-fashioned pink dress, caught at the elbows by rows of generous ruffles. More ruffles banded her neck and above them was a laughing, heart-shaped face.

"Aye," he sighed. "Maria."

It was and it wasn't. Meg's vision was more than a re-creation of an event. Her memory was Grandfather's, layered over with emotion and remembrance. Light didn't *seem* to shine from his Maria, in Grandfather's mind, it actually did. And she felt her own heart give way as his had done that day.

"It was the first time I ever saw her," he said, his agitation dissipating slowly, like a fine mist blowing slowly out to sea. "She cheated, you know. She touched my hand and knew exactly how I felt."

Meg stayed like that for hours, asking him questions when the dragon threatened to return, tugging out threads of the things he saw and prodding him to remember more, absorbing the gentle succession of memories as they picked themselves from the review, feeling the lump of emotion form in her own throat as her idea of who Grandfather was and had been grew and stretched.

She saw his strong hands rest on the backs of two little orphaned girls, guiding them down the long, narrow aisle of the medieval church in the village. Those same hands as they fastened the clasp of their mother's ruby pendant around Isabelle's neck. His worry for her that was more than worry. Wild, heart-splitting loss. Loneliness.

And then love. Love carrying him on through the night, stretching his hand into eternity, believing it would be grasped on the other side. When the brilliance of dawn reached over the horizon, Meg sang, "I'm sure I don't know, says the great bell at Bow…"

She halted, touching his face and—nothing. He was gone.

***

When the day of the funeral came, Meg stood straight and serene in a frock of strawberry pink. The shade Grandmother had worn when she met Grandfather. How she longed to have stayed in bed, screwing her eyes shut tight against the dawn, instead of burying the old man.

She blinked her eyes against the dazzling sun as the harness jangled with the strain of sudden motion and she began to walk, following the coach bearing Grandfather's coffin, to the village church.

She supposed she should have grown accustomed to thinking herself an orphan, but she never had. Grandfather filled in all the spaces—mother, father, nurse—so that now she felt the sudden loss like wading into the shallows and stepping off a ledge into deep water. Meg bit the inside of her lip, nearly drawing blood.

Don't cry. He wouldn't want you to cry.

She focused on how the rocks crunched under her slippers. How the black paint on the coach was worn on the back where the coffin would be lifted down.

Then a figure fell into step beside her.

"You didn't wish to wear black?" Henry Gracechurch asked, a smile in his eyes.

Meg exhaled, surprised to find herself disappointed. He was a dear to come and this walk would surely be easier with a companion, but in the moment between hearing the crunch of his boots on the gravel drive and hearing him speak, she had felt a wild hope that it would be Nick.

A foolish hope. He had stayed away from Blythe House after delivering her home that day she'd sprained her ankle, and she doubted if he had news of Grandfather's final decline until he was already gone. Of course, his response to Grandfather's passing had been perfectly correct. A generous haunch of venison and a cask of brandy had been sent from Southdown Abbey to ease the funeral preparations, along with long a note of condolence that Isabelle had taken it upon herself to respond to. He had done the correct things—generously—but there had been nothing of him in them.

"Grandfather said black reminded him of my mama's passing," Meg replied, tugging the cuff of her sleeve over the tight kid gloves, making sure every scrap of skin was covered. Her feelings were too raw to risk reading someone else's.

"You look lovely," Henry said, offering her an arm and giving no hint that he thought any delicate woman would be expected to weep at home, leaving the public mourning to the men. Judging from their set, troubled faces, the men of the village who lined the way, caps doffed, believed she was upsetting some delicate order. But where else should she be? Grandfather was going to his final resting place. The least she could do was walk awhile with him.

The glossy black Friesians pulling the carriage nodded their heads, shaking the plumes of ostrich feathers mounted on their tack.

"I hope your sister is faring well."

Meg felt a searing pain. Isabelle had kept well away from Grandfather's sick room during the last days. She organized hanging the mourning baize and wrote a long letter to Aunt Olympia. She dabbed at wet eyes when Mrs Greenley or any of the local gentry stopped at the house but was, in all material respects, fully in command of herself.

The funeral service was simple. Mourners filled the church in Pevensey and, as Meg felt their eyes pressing into the back of her chip straw bonnet, likely wondered why a woman had come.

She clutched her handkerchief and waited for the tears to fall. She had as much right to be here as the tenant farmers, or Grandfather's grocer, or the knot of younger men whose sullen expressions seemed to ask if Grandfather's death would mean that the coast along Blythe House would be more favorable to free-trading.

It was easier to think about the disapproval. Easier to cast her thoughts toward the back of the church instead of forward to the chancel steps where the casket rested, making real her nightmare.

"Come along," Henry said when the last of the mourners had filed out, hardly able to look at her but dipping a respectful nod in Henry's direction. "Mrs Jolly will have a meal ready."

She shook her head. "I'm not going yet. I'm sure I scandalized the vicar with my request but I've asked to be at the graveside."

Henry hid his shock quickly, but she saw the slight check of his hand. Convention and faith said it was no task for women. But who would stand there if she didn't?

"Grandfather was—" With effort, she kept herself from unleashing a flood of tears onto Henry's navy blue coat and simply finished, "I have to see him home."

He nodded. In the end, it was Henry who stood beside her at the graveside as the vicar said the words. When it was finished, she threw a pitiful handful of dirt onto his coffin. A meager effort to close up the wound that felt gaping and raw.

Henry lent an arm as they picked their way across the churchyard. They halted outside the wall, underneath a huge black alder tree, and Meg took a lungful of air. It was over, and the emotion of it, floating like some enormous gray thundercloud waiting until she could shut the door and be alone, pulsed with fullness.

Oh Lord. When would he go?

"With Mr Thackery away with his family, when will they read the will?" Henry asked, his face stern. He hardly resembled the open-faced young man she had spent hours fishing the river with.

"Two months, at least," Meg answered but Henry scowled.

"I dislike this habit England has of settling property so far from a female. I can't imagine a stranger taking up residence at Blythe House."

Meg smiled, the first all day. Her publisher had been understanding while she trafficked in the grim business of death, but soon, Sir Frederick would take pen to paper again. He would have many thoughts on the subject of primogeniture. "You've no need to worry about my prospects. I'm sure Grandfather provided for Isabelle and me."

Henry grunted. And then, "You saw Nick?" he asked. His name took Meg by surprise and she had to tamp down a sudden longing for him that seemed to materialize from the back of her mind, where he often kept her company.

She raised shadowed eyes to Henry. "He came?" she asked, shutting the gate behind each word, not willing to let any more out than was strictly necessary unless she unleashed a flood.

"He would not miss such an occasion. You really didn't see him?"

Meg scraped a piece of mustard-yellow lichen out of a rocky crevice in the wall, digging her soft gloves in the rough stone. She shook her head.

Henry continued. "He was behind us. I thought he would be at your side at the funeral."

"Why should he? He has paid his respects as he ought. Grandfather was only a neighbor."

Henry's look was dark. "Yes. But you aren't. I expected—"

"You can hardly expect him to think of me—of all of us at Blythe House—fondly," she declared. But the truth was that she did expect it, to have him come to her now, absorbing a flood of tears and standing her on her feet again as he had when she was a child.

Meg's eyes swept the horizon, the slim ribbon of sea caught between heaven and earth, and the chapel bells began to ring.

Where can he be? Say the bells of Pevensey.

Chapter Thirteen

Nick was like a bear in a cage—a miserable bear, pacing the confines his pen. He hadn't seen anyone. Meg, a voice in his head corrected. It's Meg you haven't seen. It had been three weeks since the funeral when he had stood in the nave of the church and watched the girl, gallant and unflinching, walk up the aisle on Henry's arm.

He had allowed himself to walk along with the rest of the men as they left, giving a nod to Henry, whose eyes had widened as he turned.

Half of him justified the action. Meg had all the support she could wish for in Henry and his wife. Jolly. Isabelle, even, would better share Meg's grief than Nick could. And, heaven knew, Nick needed the distance from Blythe House.

This last month he had not known himself, and it was terrifying to feel inexplicably drawn to Isabelle when he wanted nothing to do with her, no more master of his actions than a dog on a lead. His ties to Meg should be cut while they were yet weak.

He frowned at the tray of seedlings, plowing a hand through his hair, and turned, casting himself into a battered armchair. The Abbey was beginning to look like a home and the conservatory was showing signs of promise. He should be happy. Staying away from Blythe House meant that he finally felt like himself.

He rested his forearms on his knees and looked down at his boots. The problem with that was that he didn't much like the man he was.

A soft rap on the conservatory door brought him around. "Come," he called.

Brooks leaned into the room, holding a bundle of books Nick had ordered from Town. "Araminta wants to tell Miss Summers about the baskets," he said.

"No. It's nothing." He took the volumes and selecting one, setting it in a plain basket so that it looked like an afterthought instead of the considered choice of a man who wished to please a particular woman. “She doesn’t need to know.”

Meg didn’t need to know about the books, spices, or ingredients for her favorite dishes carried to Blythe House in a series of anonymous baskets. She didn’t need to know about anything else that might coax a happy thought from her making its way from Southdown Abbey to Blythe House in the last weeks.

“When the orchid starts blooming in her bedroom window, she’s going to wonder who sent it.”

“Mrs Jolly can say that someone must have mislaid the card. It happens during such a time.” Nick turned back to the windows overlooking the garden. Much of it was in bloom now, sweet fragrances and rioting color on the other side of the glass. “She’s not to know.”

“Yes, sir,” Brooks muttered, pulling the handle.

Before it had quite closed, Nick spoke, arresting him. “How is she?”

Brooks gave him a hard stare. “Grieving.”

When he had gone, Nick found no comfort in his thoughts, wandering the estate until unconscious feet carried him to the edge of the woods. Verdant green. Rustling with life. He always thought of Meg here.

There were no ghosts of Isabelle—she hadn’t liked anything the least bit wild—only the memory of a slip of a girl racing through the trees, laughing as she ran.

Nick bent back the boughs of a tree blocking his way as he followed the familiar path to the river. His steps quickened as he neared the clearing until a voice, attractive and sweet, carried to his ears. “Hold still while I bash your brains in.”

Nick pushed his way to the edge of the rise overlooking the riverbank. “Meg? Is that you?”

She did not look up from her task. Indeed, her figure froze and a long moment stretched out. Then she took a sharp breath and, with the other hand, brought a rock down on the fish, ending the catch in a quick, unfussy way.

“Lord Ainsley,” she said. Then Meg turned shadowed, moss green eyes on him and he felt a sudden, half-expected tug on his heart.

"I hate it when you call me that," he said, breaking off incautious thoughts and jogging down the bank.

"Nice to see you, too," she said.

Nick nodded at her hands. "Do you still hate cleaning fish?"

Her answer was to dig her pocketknife from her pocket. "I'm always prepared to do so. It's interesting what you can get used to if you have no other choice."

He held his hand out and she hesitated. Finally she tossed him the fish and then the knife.

He bent the blade open and began to clean her catch as she washed her hands, finding, as he did so, that her pull had not diminished.

"I didn't get a chance to speak with you at the funeral," he said, closing his eyes a moment at how weaselly it sounded. "I was sorry to hear about your grandfather." Nick tucked the fish in her basket where he counted two others and smiled briefly. "He was a fine old man."

"Thank you." A jagged hurt look conquered the tidy, blank nursery expression on her face. She spun away, holding her arms across her stomach. He hated to see it but was glad too. This was a real emotion. She continued on, her voice confused and broken. "Why didn't you come?"

They both understood what she meant. *Why didn't you come to me?* But he had no answer that would give either of them satisfaction. The sounds of the river rippling by filled the silence.

At last she turned, straightening her shoulders and drawing herself up to her ridiculous height—just to his collarbone. "Your reasons are your own," she said, careful again. Remote. But then her lip began to shake—as it had when she was a young girl—and she bit down on it.

"Meg." He reached for her, past the polite wall she had erected, and pulled her into his arms, instinctively, automatically, as he had so many times before.

A storm of weeping broke from her, shaking her frame. "Meg," he repeated, suddenly lost. For long years his life had been one of commerce—silver on one hand, tea on the other—bartering, trading, dealing. But there was no coin to exchange for her tears. No bargain to strike that would erase these battered feelings.

Whatever else he had done to assuage his guilt or comfort her was nothing next to the plainness of his presence: the willingness to witness her mourning and grieve with her. Whatever the complexity of his feelings, she was his friend and he had failed her. So he whispered her name over and over as she held onto his neckcloth.

His voice was broken. "Forgive me."

At last, the fearsomeness of her tears subsided, slowly ebbing like the tide, to be replaced by deep shuddering breaths and then her gentle breathing. They stood for a long moment, as though each were hesitant to break the contact.

"Why didn't you come?" she asked again, as she lifted her head.

"Meg, I should have." Could he explain? "Your sister—"

At that she whirled away from him, pushing tears from her cheeks with the flat of her hands. He felt bereft of her, felt how she fitted there in his arms.

"She's managing it all," she said, not looking at him now, retreating a little into that dignified young lady who kept her distance from him. She swallowed and Nick could see the effort to maintain her composure. "I haven't had a thing to do but think."

Alone. Lord, he ought to be shot.

"I stayed away because—" How could he say it? It sounded stupid and he hadn't even said it out loud. *The way my will slips around your sister frightens me.* He shrugged.

"I missed you. I like having a good fight now and then." She offered a wobbly smile.

He could not yet match her mood. "I'm so sorry, Meg."

She nodded though her smile twisted with pain before she had command of it. "And I'm sorry to have cried all over you. Things are not so bleak as your neckcloth indicates." She reached her hands to smooth it and it was as much as he could do not to pull her into his arms again.

He spoke before he thought. "Will you meet me sometimes? Not at Blythe House," he added. "Here?"

"For some fishing?" she asked, her brows came together. But he'd intrigued her, he could see.

"Like old times."

"Will you send Brooks to tell Jolly to tell me?" She laughed at the absurdity.

Lord, he loved her laugh. His heart was beating so hard he thought it might escape his chest. He dug into his waistcoat and brought out a green pebble that moved each day from pocket to pocket.

Her eyes widened in surprise and recognition.

"I said, like old times."

Chapter Fourteen

Isabelle lifted a morsel of flaky trout with the prongs of her fork, giving it a skeptical look. "Fish again, Margaret? You'll empty the stream at this rate."

Usually, Isabelle didn't bother speaking to Meg at mealtimes, or in-between times for that matter, so Meg felt bound to reply.

"It gives me something to do." That was the truth, anyway. Over the last weeks, Meg followed her familiar habit of rising with the sun and looking for the sign that Nick had a couple of hours to waste with his old friend.

The sharpness of Grandfather's death sometimes hit her like a wave slipping up the beach, reaching for her, threatening to pull her back, but those mornings spent with Nick, Meg could feel the wave cresting more softly—coming and going still, yet ebbing out in a natural tide. Nick made no demands that she pretend to be happy when she wasn't and it eased some hard, painful block in her that she could step into the pattern that was already set, finding the pebble, filling a bag, standing on the bank and casting her line. No complications.

"Mourning is tedious," Isabelle said, casting her napkin down. "Seeing no one. Going nowhere."

Meg slipped a bit of fish into her mouth, feeling the layers separate on her tongue. These weeks had been anything but tedious.

One day she had raced to the riverbank, casting her satchel on the dirt. "A boy. No name yet. Henry looks like he's taken a cannon to the head."

Nick had been adjusting his line and grinned over his shoulder. "Were you there?"

She nodded. "I must look a fright. Jolly woke me around two or three saying that Beatrice was asking for me."

"Because of your vast store of experience?" he teased, casting his line.

"No, idiot. She wanted a friend. Only her sister and mother attended her, not a midwife to be seen, and you won't believe it but when I was allowed to see her, Beatrice was tucked up in bed holding the wee babe, and her mother was *sitting on her limbs*."

Meg pulled a shocked face and he mirrored it.

"Some strange Dorset custom, no doubt," he said, which set her to make up more outlandish ones, earning a grunt or a grin from him.

Meg smiled now, remembering it.

"I hate mourning. I hate this hideous black, though you have managed to upset the natural order and escape it," Isabelle said, a sting in her voice. She tapped her fingers on the table and cast her eyes over Meg's cream gown with daffodil ribbons. "I'm sure some of our neighbors are shocked by your mode of dress."

"Who?"

"Lord Ainsley is, I'm sure. He likes order. Speaking of which, has Jolly told you any news from over at the Abbey?"

So, that was her reason for this unaccustomed friendliness. Nick.

Meg's answer was sedate. "I see the same as you. Mended fences and plowed fields."

"Some of the women from the village have said he's hired more workers—he took on Mrs Miller as the housekeeper and hired maids, even."

Meg smiled. Nick had told her about how, now that the crops were sown, he could begin to address the more neglected parts of the Abbey, finding room for his treasures.

He'd been stretched out on a blanket, smoking his pipe. "The south-facing roof has fallen into disrepair, but if I can get men from the village to patch it before the weather turns, an incalculable amount of damage can be prevented. I don't dare take some of the pottery from the packing straw until I know there won't be plaster raining down on our heads."

She'd given him advice. "Get Mrs Miller, if she will come to you. The woman's half-demon but honest."

Nick had turned, resting his chin on stacked fists, the grass tickling his nose. "It's Jolly I want, or someone like her."

How had she resisted him? But she had, and smiled while she had done it. "There is no one like her and she wouldn't leave her wee chick for any sum of money."

"Wee chick? She used to call you her little magpie," he said, eyes narrowing.

It had shocked her to know he remembered the name and she turned the topic quickly.

Now, Isabelle set her glass down with a snap. "I expected all our neighbors to pay their respects but we've heard precious little from the Abbey. I've an urge to give Lord Ainsley a piece of my mind."

Meg's stomach tightened but she struggled to identify her fear. Fear for Nick, encountering an Isabelle who had repeatedly managed to bring him into her orbit? Or fear for what it would mean for her if Nick and Isabelle met again?

"Better to meet him at church," Meg offered, wanting to put off the day of reckoning for as long as she could.

Not that Meg blamed Isabelle for her frustration, being hemmed in by convention, looking forward to sedate teas with sycophantic acquaintances, the weekly outing to church. Meg felt none of it. She had her writing. She had the river. For now, she had Nick. It was enough.

The next day, Henry invited her to dine, and Meg had returned to him wearing a sky-blue gown and a sapphire blue ribbon threaded bandeau-style through her hair.

"Isabelle didn't kick up much of a fuss when you said you were coming," he said, handing her into the gig.

"You managed to suggest I'd end the night with little Charles being sick all down my back."

They arrived at Hawthorne Cottage as the wind freshened from the sea and Meg spied two other carriages. She turned to Henry with a furrow in her brows. "You've other guests?"

"It's only my sister, Esther. Mr Thackery has returned as well."

"Delightful." Meg collected her wrap and prepared to alight.

"Meg, it's Nick too." He waved an exculpatory hand. "Now, I know you must be furious at him. You'll let me know if I need to beat him over the head some, won't you?"

"Why ever for?"

"I know for a fact he hasn't visited Blythe House in more than two months. Isabelle tried to wring me for information while I waited for you to change. But he's my oldest friend, Meg. I had to make him Charlie's godfather."

Meg cocked her head as he gathered her down from the carriage like she was a sack of parsnips. "It's to be a surprise for you too, so, for pity's sake, look shocked when Beatrice asks you."

Delight washed over her features and it returned a few minutes later when Beatrice made her own petition.

"Godmother?" Meg said, looking up from Master Charles, who was dribbling down her front. "Of course."

Beatrice grinned "We're to do the christening in the autumn when my parents return with Penny."

Then, hearing the voices raised downstairs, she tucked her arm through Meg's and leaned close, leading her off to dinner. "We'll keep him out of your way, Meg. Henry and I discussed it beforehand. I plonked the largest bouquet of flowers you've ever seen, right in the middle of the table so that you wouldn't even have to see Lord Ainsley tonight."

Then she moved on to arrange her guests before Meg could correct her. She was seated at Henry's right hand at one end of the table and Nick was at Beatrice's side on the other end. The arrangement of blooms blocked her view of him—a pity because he was such a beautiful creature in evening clothes. He occasionally sat up tall, peering over the odd assortment of tea roses, corncockles, and spears of lavender to wink at her.

There was amusement in his face, but occasionally something warmer that made her cheeks tingle and her eyes skitter away from meeting his.

The group retired together at the end of the meal, to sit comfortably in the parlor, the conversation roving like a nomad from topic to topic.

"You look exhausted, Henry," his sister said, her tone teasing. Meg noticed that pain tightened the skin around her mouth but, since Esther had tucked away her cane, the only other sign of her weak limb was a series of surreptitious stretches Meg observed as they sat close together. "You've lost the fresh, well-rested look of a bachelor at last."

Henry rubbed a hand over his face. "I would like to return the compliment sometime. We must turn ourselves to the occupation of finding you a husband."

"Stronger minds than yours have tried, little brother," Esther said, sipping her tea, her expression as serene as a goddess. "At twenty-eight I'm a little long in the tooth to be a blushing bride. Anyway, being an aunt is a lovely occupation. So restful."

It set everyone in the room laughing except Mr Thackery, who seemed intent on opening a book, flipping through the pages, and shutting it again with an irritated snap. He tossed it aside. "You've been saying you were too old since you were twenty-five, at least, Miss Gracechurch."

Meg saw it, a slight wobble in Esther's smile, even if she answered breezily enough, "So I have."

"I ought to be going," Mr Thackery answered, feeling for his pocket watch. "Rose has a nightmare about midnight each night and I hate to miss her running to my bed." His smile was rueful.

Beatrice yawned, stifling it behind her hand.

"It's getting late, Henry," Meg said. "I think it's time for me to say good night, as well. I'm ready to go home when you are ready to take me."

"No need for Henry to take you," Nick said, his long limbs stretched out before him. He looked half asleep. "I brought a gig and I'm practically running past your door."

There was no reason to decline. No reason to feel some feathering of excitement brushing through her veins. Hadn't she spent hours with him this month, alone and unchaperoned? But even as rationality marshalled its arguments, sensibility had its own say. A wide riverbank in the bright sun was a different prospect than a bench seat in the moonlight.

Beatrice's eyes widened in mortification and she mouthed, "Sorry," behind her hand as they moved to the door. Meg shrugged away her apologies. It couldn't be helped. Anyway, she could keep Nick laughing the whole way home with tales of Gracechurch meddling.

She stood still as Mr Thackery helped her with her wrap. In the process, their skin grazed, no more than his hand brushing an arm.

"I can drop Miss Gracechurch home over the hill, if she likes," the solicitor said as tight coils of longing dragged around Meg's heart, plunging her fathoms deep into the ocean of his thoughts as they had done when she read Grandfather.

Esther. Mr Thackery loved Esther and had done for a long time.

Meg's eyes widened in wonder as she looked at him. Not her idea of a romantic figure. His hair was silver, tufting boyishly forward. His face inspired trust rather than passion. His waistcoats were plain. But she staggered under the weight of his longing.

Felt his desperate craving unearth her own for Nick until it was roaring in her ears.

Chapter Fifteen

Meg was jerked from her reverie by Nick and it was all she could do to prevent herself from walking into his arms right then and there.

"Come along, Miss Summers," he said, his tone brusque. As he strode through the door, Meg caught a look of narrow irritation cross Beatrice's face.

Meg climbed up to the bench and scooted away from him so thoroughly that she was in great danger of falling onto the ground. He flicked the reins, jerking the light carriage into motion and bowling past torches lining the drive. Once they were on the main road, they would have only the moon to lead them home.

An ideal time for lovers, she thought. If they had been that, he would walk the horses as slowly as possible and she would lean her head on his shoulder, an hour stolen from a proper courtship.

As it was, Meg could hardly speak. She sat perfectly still on the narrow seat and counted the lighted windows set in the snug cottages along their way, straining to hold her concentration steady while the inexorable thought of how thoroughly reasonable it would be to press her lips against Nick's battered at her mind.

Meg sucked in a lungful of air and tried to sort it out, distracting herself with the particulars of her diagnosis. This new power of hers, reaped on the night of Grandfather's passing, came with a cost. Lord, why was there always a cost? She might be able to discover the deepest facets of a human soul, but she could not emerge from the experience untouched. It was akin to exploring the attics, she thought, searching for a crushing workaday metaphor. One might find innumerable treasures, but one would return with a head full of cobwebs and a spider or two. Mr Thackery loved Esther, and Meg had gotten the cobwebs of it all over her own hair.

That's not quite true, Meg. It wasn't Mr Thackery's desire that licked along her veins now, gripping her in a storm of wanting. It was her own. The reading had simply taken the lid off the pot, as it were.

"What did you think of the baby?" Nick's voice was low, rumbling from his chest, pushing her ever nearer a precipice from which her control would slip.

Her voice hardly carried in the soft darkness as she gripped her seat. Even to her own ears she sounded strained. "Adorable."

"The weather is certainly fine."

Again, she felt him trying to rouse some response, but her hands shook with the effort to calm her reaction to his nearness. "Yes. Very fine," she said, followed by a deep, quavering breath.

"Are you quite well? You're not nauseous, are you?" he asked.

"Quite well. I'm merely enjoying the fresh air." They must get home before she made a fool of herself and climbed into his lap. "Can we go any faster?"

"Of course." Almost imperceptibly she felt him check their pace. "Mr Thackery would benefit from having a wife," he stated, his voice clipped.

"I suppose."

"Do you think of him as a young man?"

Irritation flicked along Meg's veins, threading sharply through the pleasant heaviness of longing. Why was he speaking of nothings when she wished to be kissed? "He's not old."

Nick released what she thought was an exasperated breath and gave the horse another flick, picking up the pace.

The gig entered the gates of Blythe House, and moon shadows slid over them as they traveled under the spreading oak trees. Pools of lantern light cast a warm glow on the porch, where he helped her alight.

Her hand perched atop his and her stomach clenched.

"Meg—" he started and the pressure which had been building up all this time—not merely tonight but every day for the last six years—rushed through her, burning away reason and sense. She turned her face up to him, half-veiled in shadow and, swiftly, before she could argue herself from it, she rose on her slippered tiptoes, tugged against his lapels, and pressed her lips to his.

She felt his start of surprise and the scrape of stubble on his chin, the way he fit against her. Then she gave a soft sigh as the pent-up emotions found some relief. Dimly she understood that she might regret this action at some later date. But not now.

As she began to draw away, Nick brought his hands to her narrow back, folding her to him.

Had he wanted this too? Meg hardly had a corner of her mind to spare for such thoughts as his warm lips moved over hers. She struggled to focus, able to anchor herself only to how much *she* wanted this. She had done so, almost from the moment Nick had come home. It had been there all the time, so interwoven with their friendship that the two things could not be untangled.

This would change things.

She pushed the thought away, wishing reason to the devil, blind and deaf to anything that wasn't the spicy aroma of his skin or the ragged sound of him drawing a breath. Then a voice broke them apart.

"Margaret," came a fierce exclamation. "What on earth are you doing?"

***

She moved from him and Nick staggered at the sudden loss of Meg in his arms. He turned toward her, ready to face the consequences, running toward them, when he saw her raise her hand against her mouth. Her eyes were wide.

"Wanton girl." Isabelle's voice shook. "I'm ashamed of you. My lord, you have my humblest apologies."

Nick blinked in the sudden light of the open door, his heart hammering in his chest, broken wide with wanting. "It was nothing," he said, chest heaving still.

He looked back but Meg was on the move, slipping between them, rushing into the house before he could call her back.

Isabelle stepped into the doorway, blocking his path. "Please forgive her, my lord," Isabelle pleaded. "She is young, impetuous. She will come to her senses, I am sure. Can I beg you to forget this incident?"

Forget? No. Not in a hundred years. If he lived to be an old man, this would be the last memory he would surrender. He glanced over Isabelle's shoulder, surprised to find not so much as a fluttering tapestry heralding Meg's passage.

"You may be assured, my lord, that we will not make any demands upon you. You were the injured party." Isabelle's voice recalled him to the porch. "But I must ask a delicate question. How did she come to be in your company tonight?"

He shook his head, doing little to clear it. "We were dining at the Gracechurches' and I offered her a lift home in my carriage."

"To have repaid your generous nature like that." Isabelle bowed her head into her hands. "Managing her on my own has been difficult." She gave a large breath, swelling her expanse of bosom. "Since we've brought you out of your way, may I invite you in for a drink?"

He glanced to the top of the stairs, his heart banded in his chest. He thought he and Meg had been building a foundation these past weeks, falling into a comfort with one another that would survive outside the peculiarities of time and place. Had that sweet kiss shattered the fragile trust they had forged?

"No?" Isabelle said, reaching her hand to his, a slim finger slipping beyond the rim of his glove, one pad of her finger touching the veins that lay close to the skin at his wrist. "Grandfather's solicitor is reading the will tomorrow. You'll come the next day, though."

He didn't want to. He wouldn't.

He heard himself say, "Yes."

Chapter Sixteen

When Meg had a moment to think of it (a moment that comprised every minute between last night and this morning), a wave of hot mortification mottled her cheeks. She came down for breakfast, cowardice carrying her feet past the door, and well past the pebble Nick might have left for her. Panic seemed to grip her at the thought that it was there, almost as much as it did if it wasn't.

Now, the library clock ticked away as Meg waited on Mr Thackery. She might have spent her time wondering why it was that Grandfather's heir, young Mr Ross, had not made an appearance. Or what Grandfather's will would have to say about the prodigal granddaughter.

Instead, her wayward mind was intent on replaying her recklessness of the night before. What had possessed her to kiss a man who had shown no particular interest in kissing her first? She knew why, but no matter how dispassionately she tried to explain it away, her mind unspooled the memory, her lids a little heavy as she dwelled on the feeling of his large hands spanning the width of her back with little effort.

"That's hardly appropriate, Margaret," Isabelle snapped while striding into the room.

Meg blinked her eyes wide, folding away the horrible, wonderful recollection of Nick Ainsley bending his head low, surprised to feel a tiny flicker of hope lit in her breast.

Isabelle pointed to Meg's primrose hair ribbons, as sunny as the weather. Isabelle wore her widow's weeds with small black earrings swinging against a soft white neck—a sketch of modest womanliness, fragile with grief. An illusion.

Meg ran light fingers over the woven fabric of Grandfather's chair—fabric he had rested against only months ago. Isabelle would be gone soon. She must be. No sense in beginning a war.

Isabelle did not feel the same.

"Mrs Greenley thinks you're a little whore," she began. Against the brightness of the window, she might have been a cool statue. "That's the word that sticks in her mind every time I read her. *Whore.* Mrs Fletcher is more charitable but wonders if Sam has had you yet. Has he?"

"Good morning, Isabelle," Meg said, her color high. "Did you have a tiring night riding your broomstick terrorizing the village?"

Isabelle ignored her jibe. "You think, after throwing yourself at him, that you know what Nicholas feels? You think you read him last night? You're wrong. Desire is the only thing you can read when you're in a man's arms. They are simple creatures and that emotion means nothing to them."

Meg hadn't even been sure she had read that. Poor Jacob Thackery, his longing for Esther had run roughshod over her emotions, and the echoes of it might well have muted anything she hoped to read from Nick. When his lips were on hers, there had been desire between them. But was any of it his?

Isabelle gripped her seat and her voice took on a rough tone. "Do you think he's going to want a strumpet as his countess?" she asked, tearing the spool of memory from Meg's hands, dashing it onto the flagstones and grinding it under her booted foot.

Meg lifted her chin. "When I was a child, I would weep into my pillow and wonder why you could never like me—why you never even pretended to. But I know now."

Isabelle let out a short gust of breath. "Don't be absurd, Margaret. I don't think of you at all."

Meg gave her head a slight shake. "I see you, Bella. I'm the only one who can. Even when you take such pains not to touch me, I know what you are, and I always have. How you must hate that."

The air between them bristled, dense with old arguments and old battles.

Isabelle recovered first. When she smiled, the skin around her eyes was as smooth as a grey seal. "It's easy to forget you're not a child, Margaret. You behave as one so often."

Meg's mouth opened to tell her what she could do with her memory when Mr Thackery was announced.

"Now then," he said, settling himself behind Grandfather's desk and making careful a pile of his papers. "As you know, Mr Ross was full of energy in his final months to dispatch his affairs exactly as he wished. He stressed that over and over to me as we met." His eyes darted to Meg and skipped away so quickly that she tensed.

"The reading of it is simple enough," Mr Thackery continued, his fingers beating on the desk like a baker pressing a fork into the top of a pie.

Finally, he placed spectacles on the bridge of his nose, took up a piece of paper, and began to read. Meg's mind wandered back to Nick as he related the preliminaries until her attention was suddenly captured. "—having gained the permission of my presumed heir, one Mr Malcolm Ross of Coille na Cyarlin, Penicuik, Scotland, to break the entail—"

Meg sat up, her eyes wide. "He broke the entail? That's…that's impossible."

The spectacles came off. "Your grandfather spent a considerable amount of wealth to buy young Mr Ross out, settling a sum of money on him. Forty thousand pounds and the thing was done. The circumstances are unusual, I grant you. But perfectly legal."

"Forty thousand?" Meg gasped. Without an infusion of capital, such a sum would ruin them.

He adjusted spectacles on his nose and read on. "The estate, including Blythe House in its totalities, the rents owing to it, animals, monies, and all other chattel therein shall be settled on my granddaughter Lady Isabelle Ainsley, nee Summers."

The air seemed sucked from the room, leaching from Meg's heart and limbs and lips.

"Am I to understand," Meg said, her voice a whisper, "am I to understand—" She looked to Isabelle, who sat with her soft hands folded neatly on her lap.

"What does he say about me?" Meg asked. Mr Thackery shuffled his papers and Meg held her breath. There had been such encompassing words in Isabelle's bequest. *All. Totalities.*

"Margaret Summers, spinster, having had the benefit of Blythe House these last years and not seeing fit to establish herself creditably during the Seasons she has been offered, must benefit from the charity of her sister."

What had Grandfather done? No safe annuity. No sum to tide her over until— Her mind fumbled. Until what? Meg held a hand over her mouth, clamping back the shock as she repeated the words in her mind. *Not seeing fit to establish herself.* There was no mercy in them—no understanding of her position in Society, of how, in the eyes of some, she had absorbed Isabelle's ruin like it had been her own. This was worse than the gutting pain of grief. It was the turn of the knife.

"There's another small provision, Miss Summers," said Mr Thackery, his look as gentle as it must be when he comforted his small child from her nightmare. "He wrote it out and handed it to me at the assembly before I left for Town. So he hasn't forgotten you, you know."

"What is it?" Isabelle asked, her voice sharp.

"She is to receive her grandmother's trunk."

"A trunk? Oh. That's quite all right." Isabelle subsided in her chair.

"Is she my guardian now, too?" Meg asked, unable to even look at Isabelle though she was not the one who had dealt this blow. *Oh Grandfather. Why?*

"Until your birthday." Mr Thackery rifled through the papers. "In a month, I think."

"As it should be," Isabelle said, triumphant. Meg could hear it.

"What does it mean?" Meg meant the shocking will but Mr Thackery explained the guardianship.

"Your sister will provide for you," he said kindly. "She will decide where you live and, in the event that you wish to be married, your sister will have the right to withhold consent or give it. You understand?"

Meg mutely nodded. Why would Isabelle want her? There was no love lost between the sisters. Perhaps she simply wanted to keep a close eye on her oldest enemy.

When the thing was settled at last, and Mr Thackery had taken his leave, Meg went straight to the point. "How did you get Grandfather to do it?

"I don't know what you mean, Margaret," Isabelle said, sweeping her skirts out of the way as she sat behind Grandfather's desk.

"He wouldn't have left the estate to a woman. We both knew that."

Isabelle's face was serene. "He had some old-fashioned ideas of what a woman was fit for, certainly, but he repented of those feelings when I returned home, seeing that I was capable of taking up so much of his business affairs."

Meg's brows caved in. "Is that what all that help was for? You hoped to win Blythe House?" Her mouth twisted in disgust. "But you didn't get everything your way."

"Didn't I, Margaret? I'll have one of the footmen bring Grandmother's old trunk from the attic and leave it in your room. I'm sure it's filled with treasures."

Chapter Seventeen

Nick held the pew door for Brooks, stepping in after him.

The village church had once been grand when Pevensey Bay had been a busy seaport but, as its fortunes had dwindled, the chancel had been walled off from the nave, converting the main space into a preaching box. Lovely things were hidden by an uncompromising brick wall, which cut the church in two. The delicate lancet windows above the high altar could no longer be seen, nor could the cradle roof above the chancel—built sound by shipbuilders. No more than a rough stable now, whose architectural wonders were appreciated by the sheep and goats that grazed the churchyard.

Six hundred years this parish church had been here, and it hardly seemed to take note of Nick's absence, folding him back into the flock as though he had wandered away for a night and been lost on the downs.

As he looked about him, his neighbors dipped their chins in greeting and he felt a faint echo of cynicism. Months of living here had not been enough to accustom himself to the way he had become a favor to be dispensed, a wealthy neighbor to be cultivated or a title to be wed. Comfortable as an old coat, it'd kept him together body and soul from the time his wealthy uncle ran away with his bride. But these months with Meg made him see that this cynicism would create chasms between himself and his neighbors that he could not hope to bridge.

Nick thumbed through his prayer book, tattered from his travels, and felt a rustle of interest animate the congregation. He lifted his head, looking to the top of the nave where light spilled through the dim church like a fire. A figure in black made her way up the aisle, her pace decorous and measured like a nun at her prayers. Isabelle. Each Sunday she made such an entrance, a veil over her face, appearing to pay no heed to her audience.

Mrs Greenley whispered to Mrs Fletcher from the pew behind him. "What a proper lady ought to be."

Nick only saw something studied in the extreme smoothness of her walk that bristled the hairs on the back of his neck.

"Agatha, look." Mrs Fletcher gasped. "She's finally done it. Her ladyship got that girl into some proper mourning clothes."

Nick's gaze slid from Isabelle with her downcast eyes, farther up the aisle, to encounter Meg. Head to toe in black. Her thick raven hair was drawn into a demure knot exposing the nape of her neck. Tiny black curls escaped from her bun and a plain black chip straw bonnet tilted unremarkably on her head, secured by a miserly ribbon tied at a rakish angle under her chin. Her dress, too, was extremely simple. Made of coarse cotton, it fell straight to her toes without the diversion of a ruffle or a gather anywhere. She ought to have looked like a crow. Most women did when they wore mourning.

Meg did not.

Instead, the deep color picked out in greater relief the graceful line of her neck, the delicate scoop above each collarbone, the brilliant green of her eyes. She began to move, and his breath caught in his chest as though he had run a mile. The rough fabric hitched and clung to her petite curves. He gripped the edge of the pew.

Nick could not peel his eyes away as Meg wiggled past her sister, finally settling into her seat with no concern for the way she had winded him. He inhaled sharply and crossed his arms over his chest, facing forward and sending a scowl at the surprised reverend.

"Well, now," Brooks murmured, a twinkle in his eye.

"How do you ruin a black dress?" Mrs Fletcher muttered. "That dress is a sack and she doesn't even have the decency to look bad."

Mrs Greenley hissed, "The sooner her sister brings her to bridle, the better for all of us."

Nick set his mouth into a thin line. The villagers wanted to see Meg tamed. They wanted the tokens of penance when there had been no evidence of sin. They wanted to see her grief worn on her back as though any amount of murky crepe fabric might hope to communicate the sorrow he had felt that first day at the river. Little wonder Meg had taken to throwing rocks.

Nick lent half an ear to the familiar words of the service, repeating the patterns he'd followed from the time he was a young boy. But, while his mouth was singing "Lo! He Comes With Clouds Descending," his mind continued to turn.

An emotion, buried so deep that it radiated like an underground earthquake, rumbled through his chest, powerful but hardly felt. The faintest reverberation of it, the only part he allowed himself to acknowledge, was the consciousness of how little he wanted Meg Summers to be docile and broken.

He darted a look backward across the aisle to find Meg's eyes trained on the performance of the rites and admonished himself that he should do the same. But when he turned forward again, the vision filling his mind was of Meg, tugging at his lapels, pulling his head low enough to reach. Of kissing her and wishing that surprise and reason had not wasted so much of his chance.

By the time the congregation rose to repeat the words of the Apostle's Creed, Nick understood himself. He'd been willing for some time to admit a grudging attraction to the girl. When he had named the emotion, it had even given him a sense of satisfaction to know he was the kind of man who would tell himself uncomfortable truths in order to subdue his unruly emotions. Yes, he had a weakness for Meg, but when he had recognized the danger that weakness posed for his peace of mind, he knew he might take steps to prevent himself from further entanglement.

What a dashed fool he'd been.

It was time for a true confession, not the half-measure of honesty he had meted out. The willingness to admit an attraction had been a shield: a brick wall hiding away more intense, vivid emotions. Ones there would be no walling up again.

He loved Meg.

As soon as the words formed in his mind, they set off a rock fall, oversetting assumptions and plans, changing the landscape in one massive slide. He loved Meg.

What a strange courtship it would be, he thought, a wry half-smile playing on his lips. It was too late to begin the correct way: bringing her posies and paying her compliments. Mourning was no time for lovers, even if she had kissed him.

The thought made him grin, inadvertently upsetting Reverend Moss in his rituals again. He drew a more solemn expression and turned it over in his mind. Meg had kissed him, though heaven only knew why, and before he could discover the reason, she'd dashed away like a stunned rabbit. The pebble he laid down the next morning was ignored.

As she was ignoring him now.

He turned his head over his shoulder only to encounter Isabelle's wide, innocent eyes. Rumors were flying around the village that old Mr Ross had left the whole of his estate to her.

And where did that leave Meg? In need. Would it be enough to convince her to consider his proposal? He hated to think of it in those once comfortable terms—a transaction, or commercial exchange. Still, any advantage might tip the balance in his favor and he would not discard it. In that moment he recognized a ruthlessness in himself, out of place in a church.

When, at last, the service concluded, Nick surged to his feet but she was too fast for him. He turned to find that she was already halfway up the crowded aisle. It was Isabelle who met him at the end of her pew, her hand fluttering to her breast as though he were a snake or lizard, startling her in her path. He felt the sharp sting of alarm travel his own veins.

No. He must conquer it if he hoped to make Meg his wife. This was her sister. They were being observed by the better part of Pevensey parish and so he offered her an arm.

"An excellent sermon, was it not, my lord?" Isabelle asked, stepping into the sunshine and turning to him as she unveiled her face in one graceful movement. He had imagined something like that once, when she might come to him as a bride, making her vows in front of God and man.

Now it left him cold.

"I don't know if the gossips have let it out yet, but my grandfather's will made me Margaret's guardian. I hoped to discuss it with you," she said. "Tomorrow or the next day."

"I can have nothing to do with that," he said, wondering if tomorrow's pebble would be ignored too.

"No? I think your wisdom and experience could be enormously helpful," Isabelle said, inching her glove from her hand. "She has been properly chastened after her actions the other night. The girl admitted that she was curious, foolish child. Wanted to know if kissing an earl were any different than kissing a… Well, you of all people should remember what a curious child she was. You needn't distress yourself by meeting with her. We could—"

Nick cut in. “Meg ought to be there,” he said, looking away, tracking Meg with his eyes. She was sharing some joke with Jolly.

Suddenly, Nick felt the light touch of Isabelle’s cold fingers on his cheek and heaviness charged through his bones, shaking him, pushing him out of his own mind. Tomorrow. He must meet with Isabelle tomorrow. He fought against it, his neck straining against the sharp folds of the cravat, sweat picking out on his brow. Damn and blast, he was tired. So tired. And what did he want? He couldn’t remember. Not this.

A pain wriggled underneath his ribs, pooling around his heart, as smudgy black spots dotted his vision.

“Tomorrow?” he breathed.

“Yes,” she said, “I insist.”

Chapter Eighteen

Meg laughed as she sent an arcing look across the churchyard so it wouldn't be so obvious that she was looking for Nick. She found him easily enough, staring thunderstruck into Isabelle's face. Isabelle's hand reached to his jaw in an intimate gesture, sure to add grist to the village gossip mill. His eyes were confounded, exploring.

He loves Isabelle still. Meg released a breath she didn't know she was holding.

"Is that what has you so upset, little Meg?" Jolly asked, following her gaze.

Meg gave a reflexive smile and shook her head. "Upset? Why should I be upset?" she asked, unable to take her eyes from Nick standing passively near Isabelle as she mauled him in the churchyard. "My grandfather disinherited me, my sister is my guardian, I hate wearing black and, worst of all," she said, tearing her glove from her hand and holding up her finger. "I've developed a blister."

Jolly gave a low laugh. "I'm the one who should have the blister. I worked all night to give you something fit to wear from that pile of rags your sister left you."

"God bless you, Jolly," she answered, profoundly grateful. Meg had returned from collecting the post yesterday to find every stitch of her clothing burning in a garden bonfire as though they were a heap of autumn leaves. Isabelle had been watching nearby and urging a shame-faced gardener to poke them with a stick.

Meg could still hear her scream of genuine outrage that even an unmolested length of fabric, a pretty patterned muslin, dear at ten shillings a yard, was not spared. It lay across the fire, shot through with gaping black holes. Isabelle had turned with a look of pleasant satisfaction and told Meg that she was dispensing with (here she gave a slight cough) "all other chattel therein." Meg, of course, was welcome to three of her castoffs. Heaven only knew how Meg stopped herself from ripping Isabelle's hair out by the roots.

Jolly had wrought miracles, plying her needle for hours to turn the long, gaping frocks into tidy, workmanlike dresses, suitable for any depressing occasion. Or would have been if she had been able to resist the temptation to cut them rather dashingly.

Meg, stepping into and out of the dresses as they were fitted, had earned her blister accomplishing another task. The fury of Isabelle's high-handedness, added to the crushing weight of Grandfather's will, had set off a storm of inspiration. Though it had taken a colossal effort, Meg had found rich veins of humor in the situation, amassing page after page of polished work. Mr Morgan would likely be publishing her broadsides for months to come.

"As plain as these frocks are, you look far too well in them," Jolly said. "His lordship couldn't take his eyes from you."

A hot flush bloomed across Meg's neck, though her voice was even. "Yes. I can see the man is mesmerized," she said, sketching a hand toward Nick whose whole being was riveted on Isabelle.

They watched as Nick handed Isabelle up into the carriage, leaving Meg and Jolly to make their way together on foot. As they turned to do so, a voice stopped them.

"Mrs Jolly," Brooks called, his cloth hat stuffed under his arm, pewter hair tossed in the breeze. "Are you walking home?"

Meg wondered how long he had been there, waiting for an opportunity to speak.

She looked to Jolly for an answer, but she stood as still as one of the headstones dotting the ground. Jolly had allowed herself to walk out in the garden with him. She had allowed him occasionally to call her by her Christian name. But there seemed an unspoken impasse.

Meg had a hint of deviltry in her smile. "Yes. It's such a lovely day, Mr Brooks. Araminta—" Jolly's eyes flew open at that but Meg persevered. "Araminta and I fancied a walk."

"It is a lovely day," Mr Brooks agreed, not taking the easy opportunity Meg had offered. He was waiting for Jolly to decide her fate.

Finally Jolly spoke through dry lips. "You are welcome to join us."

Brooks tugged his cap onto his head and threaded her arm through his without another word. Jolly looked at Meg in some alarm, then curled her hand in the crook of his elbow where it was covered at once with his own.

"I'll follow in a few minutes," Meg said, her voice placid and careless even as she gave Jolly a wink that Mr Brooks couldn't see. "Go on without me."

Meg watched them go through the gate, going up on her toes to see the last of them as delight beamed from her face.

"Are you going to let them go off without a chaperone?" came a voice that sent her thumping to solid ground. Nick.

"Can he be trusted?" she asked, not turning yet.

"As much as any man with the woman he wants." Meg's cheeks flamed but he did not pause. "Brooks can be depended upon to be a gentleman, but that's why you might want to put a stop to it," he said. He stood closer than she liked but, as she worked her lungs in and out, she wondered how much farther away he would have to be in order for her to breathe properly. One step? No. Two? No. Fifty?

He raised his arm to point over her shoulder and she felt his closeness. He gestured to the winding trail their servants had taken. "I know you said it wasn't possible, but I wager that Southdown Abbey will be poaching your housekeeper before long."

She looked at the woods. Anything to keep her from looking at him. She felt herself every minute fighting the wish to tug his head down and reach up as high as she could go. Shame burned in the stew alongside wanting. He wanted Isabelle. Meg was insane to want him for herself.

"Perhaps I will gain a butler," she countered. "I don't put it past you to cheat to win her," she said, moving briskly and plucking a dandelion from the base of the stone wall, already pulling it to pieces as she turned to face him.

It didn't matter. He closed the distance again and this time she had a stone wall at her back. A strategic misstep.

"I've nothing to cheat with. See for yourself," he said, spreading his arms wide.

Meg saw the muscled arms and broad chest.

She sucked in a breath. "I…I…"

She looked away, feeling stupid. Had she ever stopped loving him? No. Her heart still slammed away like a puppy's tail whenever he was about, eager for any crumb of affection. She sent a measure of self-disgust inward, irritated to see that it didn't matter. She would continue on, quick to want to want him, and brave enough to weave foolish dreams.

"Lord Ainsley," Mrs Fletcher said, coming upon them as their attention focused so narrowly. Her eyes glinted at Meg, who would have scrambled over the wall if she thought it would have given her any peace from Nick's large frame.

"It's so naughty of Miss Summers to take you all for herself when so many are anxious to continue our acquaintance."

Mrs Fletcher nudged Meg with her elbow but the tiny action made Meg flinch away, slapping a hand over her arm where Mrs Fletcher had touched her. An inferno of emotion poured through her at the contact and she lifted her fingers, half expecting to see skin that blistered and shone from the heat of a raging fire.

Meg rushed away, ignoring Nick's hasty call, hardly gaining the cover of the trees before she collapsed on the path, her breath coming in hard, shaking gasps. The images gleaned from Mrs Fletcher—as conventional and placid a matron as had ever sprung from good English stock—ran like a boiling river within her veins.

In the flash of an instant, Meg had seen it all. The little headstones in the churchyard for each of Mrs Fletcher's babies, the larger one for her husband who had died last winter. Only Samuel, grown as tall as a man now, was left and, through Mrs Fletcher's eyes, Meg felt her throat swell with pride and fierce protectiveness over that boy, the only one who had survived to be tall enough to throw an arm over her shoulder, kiss the top of her head.

"When will you return?" she asked.

Sam's voice echoed in Meg's mind. "Sometime."

Lord, now this dreadful business would take him too.

Meg clapped her hands over her ears and curled her body inward as the phrase repeated in a dark whisper, hissing through her skull. *Dreadful business. Dreadful business.*

Beneath the clamor, Meg's own thoughts were buried under a mountain of sights and sounds. The sinking moon. The tar-black sea. Then she felt the astonishing wild cry of ordinary Mrs Fletcher pierce through her.

Help.

Meg sobbed out feelings of helplessness and loss, too spent to wonder how a woman she saw through the uncompromising lens of judgment should have her own sorrows and fears. It was enough to know that she did.

She stumbled home, the punishing echo of Mrs Fletcher's thoughts still clanging through her body when she mounted the front steps of Blythe House on shaky legs. Her reflection in the hall mirror showed her dark circles under her eyes, dark curls pasted against her damp brow.

She slumped into a chair, head resting in the crook of her arm where it bent against the hall table. She closed her eyes breathing in and out, losing herself to the dragging tide of fatigue.

By and by, she felt a hand jostle her from the doze and before her eyes even opened, she saw another vision. It was a forest of rickety branches bearing furry green knobs that would soon burst into blossom. The forest floor was covered in a mat of fallen leaves as the essence sunk into the rich, black soil. The air was fresh and uncertain, a forest on the verge of the ebullient joy of spring.

She blinked her eyes open.

"Jolly." Meg straightened, rubbing her arm. The residue of fear and exhaustion left her in a staggering rush, blown away by Jolly's freshness. "You're back."

"Yes," Jolly replied, unwrapping her neat blue shawl, her briskness at odds with that quiet, expectant hope in her expression. "We thought you would catch up but when you didn't come—"

"Mr Brooks pulled you into a clinch?"

A blush travelled up Jolly's neck to where the wheat-blond hair mixed with threads of gray, but her look was severe. "Miss Margaret."

Meg raised her palms in surrender but did not wholly retreat. Again there was a wicked gleam in her eye. "When will you marry?"

"Whatever do you mean?" Jolly laid her shawl over her arm and trained her eyes on the baize door at the back of the hall, her face in profile to Meg. "He escorted me home, I thanked him for the service, church is next week."

Meg stood, surprised to feel no slackness in her limbs left over from Mrs Fletcher, and surprised that Jolly's emotions should be so fine and strong. "But I'm sure he wants to…and you—"

"I've still a household to tend to, and a stubborn girl to manage."

A pang shot through Meg as she followed Jolly into the kitchens where preparations for supper were well in hand.

"You worry too much," Meg said as Jolly pulled an apron around her waist. "I can look after myself."

"As well as a newly shorn lamb," Jolly teased.

Meg had her worries and now she made herself say them aloud. "I don't know what the future holds, Jolly. I have precious little money and can't go on living with Isabelle. You shouldn't tie yourself down at Blythe House for my sake."

Jolly opened a cupboard, the heavy sarcasm in her voice muffled as she searched. "Yes, Miss Margaret. You are the only thing keeping a forty-three-year-old widow with respectable employment from pulling up her roots in order to join a ship's crew as cook and swabby."

Meg laughed at the image. "But I'm keeping you from the Abbey."

Jolly gave an exasperated huff and thrust a bowl into Meg's hands.

"What?" Meg asked. "Next time your sweetheart walks with you into a wood—"

"Shhhh," Jolly hissed, looking over her shoulder at the well-oiled staff of the Blythe House kitchens. "You get busy shelling those peas and give your imagination over to finding a man of your own to worry about."

It wasn't a request but a command. The waiting forest would have to wait a little longer for spring to come. Meg plopped onto a chair at the long table and dumped the peas onto the rough table. Taking up one, she cracked a pod open, running her thumb under the plump peas and feeling the satisfaction of depositing them with a rumble into the bowl.

Jolly returned with a plate of carrots, peeling away the skins in long, rolling coils. They worked in silence for a while with their own thoughts, but Meg's dwelled too long on Nick Ainsley's wide, outstretched arms.

See for yourself.

She shivered and cast about for another occupation. "What have you heard about Sam Fletcher lately?"

"Not him," Jolly said, waving her knife in the air. "Find another man. That boy hasn't got the brains of—"

"A pea?" Meg asked, holding one aloft and then popped it into her mouth. "Never fear. He is safe from me."

Jolly grunted. "He began his apprenticeship under a surgeon in Brighton last..." she wrinkled her brow in concentration, "...March or May it was. But it didn't last."

"Why not?"

"He's got nothing better to do than keep company with Jim Greenley and the other members of the Pevensey Intellectual Society."

Meg snorted a laugh and moved her hands in the rhythmic motion of popping the shell, dumping the peas, and grabbing another. "And what do you think about that?"

Jolly's hand stilled on the knife and leaned forward. "I think that young Sam's associates don't give a rap that Pevensey has no proper surgeon and that our only prayer of one is whistling his future down the wind. The whole topic of smuggling makes me furious. If your grandfather had been in better health, been less distracted—"

Memories of Grandfather crowded in on Meg. Would the pain of the disinheritance ever dull? She had begun to feel like a pot thrown down a well, clanging and clattering as she fell, never hitting bottom. Just when she thought she had taken it in, the betrayal, the cruel words of the will, she hoped some remembrance of Grandfather's loving nature would jar the smooth descent. It was as though she had not only lost him, but her memories of him, too.

"Miss Margaret, are you well?" Meg looked up to encounter Jolly's searching look.

She nodded. "Quite well."

But Jolly's look sharpened and she sent her up to her bedroom via the narrow, winding servants' stairs, and as she climbed, she spread her hands, grazing the close walls as she went.

She had gotten into the habit, these last years, of thinking of her dearest loved ones—Grandfather, Jolly, Beatrice, Henry—and no one else. But a strange sense of being too alone, too isolated, had drawn over her since Grandfather's passing.

Involving herself in the daily cares of the village would hurt. She knew that well enough. Years of spoken taunts and unspoken coldness had transformed the warm-hearted girl she had been into a pugilist—ready to strike to avoid a blow. But in one afternoon, poor Mrs Fletcher had reminded her that she was a woman with the heavy burden of cares and worries that had nothing to do with Meg. And Meg had been too afraid to see them.

She stopped on a tight bend in the stairs.

I have good reasons for being frightened.

She was the injured party, the innocent victim of her sister. Meg deserved none of the unkindness the villagers turned on her. Was it any wonder she hunched protectively over her heart?

But as she unfurled the long list of reasons, she could see no end to it. Her world would continue to shrink as she grew old: the resentments hardening to form a high wall, keeping others out, while it kept her in.

Her good reasons to draw away from others were becoming a prison.

Meg had opened Grandmother's trunk yesterday, glancing through the assortment of items in a storm of confusion and grief, finally closing the lid to all that. The gift Grandfather had given her at parting was far more complicated than a trunk of old clothes and keepsakes.

In his last hours on earth he had shown her a deeper way of reading. She had a chance now to really see others—Mrs Fletcher and Mr Thackery thus far—in all their complexity. This new power would not make saints of them, but it had wrested from her the comfort that she'd believed they were demons.

I don't want to came a childish thought.

But isn't that what she wished for? That Grandfather would have really seen and understood what it was she had been up against in London. That Society would know her past and be gentle with it. Those were treasures she longed for and had been denied.

A shaking breath loosed from her chest. Now it was in her power to offer this gift to others.

She sat on the stairs with a bump and balled her fist. It wasn't fair.

You're not a child.

What would it cost her to understand her neighbors? Pain? Yes, she would pay that price. Heartbreak? That too. Her righteous judgments?

Those most of all.

She wandered to her bedroom and sat at her vanity table, far too bewildered for rest, until Isabelle entered the room, a satchel swinging from her fingers. "Margaret, you and I have several matters to discuss."

Meg dragged a breath through her lungs, thankful for Jolly's touch. Without it, she would be staggering on her feet. "What is it?" she asked, picking up a comb and turning to the mirror. She wasted no time on pleasantries.

Isabelle tossed the sack on the table, looked over Meg's shoulder into the mirror, and ran hands over her hips, smoothing the line of her gown. Finally she said with a level, even voice, "I've discovered some disturbing things over the last few months but didn't like to do anything about it until all was settled."

"Things?" repeated Meg, glancing at the sack, which had landed with the rustle of a bag of leaves.

"This and that," Isabelle answered, tucking wayward strands of hair more securely into the sleek bun. "Papers, money…a good deal of correspondence. Why, Margaret, I never knew you had literary aspirations."

A thick bubble of horror began to surface in Meg's mind and she set the comb down, turning. "You went pawing through my things like a…like a…?"

"Guardian, sister. Guardian. It's my duty to see that you're behaving yourself under my roof. Gently bred young ladies do not write newspaper columns."

"It's good, then, that I am not a gently bred young lady."

"No. No you're not," she said, flicking Meg's disheveled appearance a scathing look. "I took the liberty of writing to Mr Morgan, telling him that any business arrangements you had formed were without the consent of your legal guardian and must be at an end."

"I'll write him back. He—"

"He is bound to refuse the services of a minor. Anyway, where would you get the money for the post?" Isabelle asked, as though the problem posed an impossible riddle.

"I have money of my own," Meg said, suddenly wishing to ransack her drawers for the small box that held her rather generous wages.

"I think you'll find you do not. Further, the servants will be instructed not to dip into their savings. In short, to keep themselves separate from our affairs or risk dismissal."

"You filthy thief," Meg growled, shooting to her feet.

"Thief? Oh I think not. If you think about it," Isabelle went on, "the only thing you're legally entitled to in this house is Grandmother's trunk. And, of course, you're welcome to this," she said, plucking up the corner of the sack and tipping the contents onto the table. Out rained a thousand pieces of paper, some of them scraps so small that no words could be deciphered from them.

Meg recognized them at once. The letters from Mr Morgan. The columns she'd poured her pain and questions into. Her livelihood. Lost.

Meg's heart seemed to stop at the realization and she drew a shaking breath between her teeth. "What could you hope to gain?"

"Cooperation." Isabelle smiled. "I want your cooperation."

"For what?"

"Only one thing. Simple, really." Isabelle leaned close. "I'm going to become Lord Ainsley's wife."

Meg's stomach recoiled at the sudden image of Nick drawing Isabelle into an embrace, of him slipping a ring down her finger.

"Seems a bit repetitive. Haven't you already done that once?" Meg asked, sheer force of will smoothing her tones.

"And I'll do it again."

"It's illegal on this sceptered isle. Are you planning to lead a revolution?"

"We can marry quietly in Denmark when my mourning period is finished." She spoke with such certainty and determination that Meg could imagine that the thing was an accomplished fact. It would take a good deal of money and position to sail through, but such a step wasn't unheard of. "And then I intend to return to my place in Society."

Meg's eyes closed briefly. Isabelle hadn't been after a belated marriage settlement. Not when she might win an earl. "So that's it."

"No, that is not it." Isabelle's voice lifted. "I'm marrying him because he loves me. I've read it over and over again this summer."

A muscle in Meg's jaw jumped. "I didn't think you were the kind of woman to accept a proposal based on that emotion. I'll have to congratulate you both."

"No."

Meg's brow lifted a shade.

Isabelle's control frayed. "I've read the words in his mind a thousand times but I cannot allow him to speak them until after I put off my blacks," she said.

"You seem to have worked it all out, but what does your marriage," Meg said, almost choking on the word, "have to do with all this?" Her hand, clenched around a sheaf of ripped paper, dropped them in a fluttering pile. "Surely leaving me to pursue an independence would be beneficial for us all."

"You have a knack for being in the way, Margaret. I trust that that disgusting display on the porch the other night will not be repeated as long as you remember who is in control here."

Meg's blazing eyes stared at her sister's ordered countenance.

"Remember who holds the whip hand, Margaret, and I may even allow you to get your little job back someday."

The sisters measured glances for a hard moment.

Then, with a twirl of her skirts, Isabelle was gone.

Chapter Nineteen

A list lay at Meg's elbow as she bent over the writing desk in her bedroom. The rough sheet of paper contained the titles and summaries of the lost columns, as best she could remember. Working late into the night, she had managed to reconstruct three:

Take An Entail By the Tail: A Gentleman's Guide to the Problems of Primogeniture, *Cheap Women: How Females Make Ends Meet When They Haven't Got a Six-pence to Scratch With*, and *Beware the Bluestockings: The Dangers of Proposing Matrimony to a Woman who Reads.*

Meg stopped and stretched, dark shadows under her eyes. But she smiled over her growing pile of papers. Maybe Isabelle would think she was sulking.

Or maybe Isabelle wasn't thinking of her at all.

Nick had come almost an hour ago and their murmured voices from the drawing room had slowed her progress, seeming to drift unintelligibly around the closed bedroom door, under the crack, through the keyhole. It would drive Meg wild if she didn't get some fresh air.

She sanded the half-finished page and added it to the stack, rolling them into a slim tube. Then she walked to a decorative vase and slid them inside. If Isabelle found them, Meg would begin again. And again. And again.

Meg grabbed a straw bonnet, so intent on getting out of doors that she remembered her forgotten gloves when she was halfway down the stairs. Too late. She stepped into the hall as Isabelle and Nick entered, and Meg noted that Isabelle's little hand was swallowed up in his brown one. Why wouldn't it be when the thoughts she was reading were bound to be so pleasant? The couple stopped at the door, both figures in stark silhouette.

"I don't know how I shall manage," Isabelle murmured, her voice catching a little. She cast her eyes wide beyond the porch, her words seeming to include the complications of the hen house and pigsty, barns and tenants.

Nick inched closer. “You shall manage,” he said.

Meg’s fingers shook as she placed the bonnet on her curls, tying off the ribbon. She thought Isabelle flicked her a look.

“You’ll help me sometimes?” Isabelle said, swinging his hand lightly between them. Meg’s path was effectively blocked and she held her breath, watching Nick’s throat work against the brown skin of his neck.

“Sometimes.” The word was ragged and forced from his lips.

“Excuse me,” Meg said.

Isabelle’s head didn’t even turn in acknowledgment. “You could come tomorrow and help me sort out the particulars of the will. Without my late husband to guide me, I’m terribly confused.”

Helpless Isabelle. If God was going to strike her dead for all these lies, he was taking his time.

Nick was going to say no, that nothing would induce him to return to her orbit. Meg could read it in the hard set of his lips and the way his body leaned from her sister.

Then, as she had done in the churchyard, Isabelle touched his face, resting her palm along the hard line of his jaw in an intimate, familiar way. It was a lover’s touch and Meg felt the pain of it land hard in her chest.

“Please.”

He had been skittish, as high-strung as Puck, but Meg watched a change come over him. Ragged breathing smoothed, shoulders dropped, lungs filled with air. He was tranquil.

“Anything.”

Suddenly his eyes fastened on Meg’s and there was something glazed-over and feverish in his look.

Isabelle spoke in a slow, methodical way. “Thank heavens you’re here to help me with this mess.”

“Yes, there’s nothing worse than becoming the greatest heiress in the county,” Meg said, brushing past the pair, intent on getting away as soon as may be. “What might exceed that misfortune, I cannot imagine.”

As she passed him, Nick snatched Meg’s wrist in a shaking, clammy grip that crushed the bones.

Meg braced herself to feel the crippling rush of emotion that her new powers conferred.

Ice-cold river.

Her eyes widened as they met his and, in the space of a heartbeat, she saw that his dazed expression held no flicker of will.

Cold water tipping in a basin.

At first, Meg thought they were both reading him. She could always feel when Isabelle was touching Grandfather, how their magic would mix and tug within a shared vessel. But it wasn't quite like that. Instead, Meg felt like she was on the banks of a stream, over-full and swelling, pushing her back. There was definitely magic coming from Isabelle and it wasn't as benign as reading.

She jerked loose from Nick and ran, sprinting down the drive, her mind a whirl of questions. She stopped at the gates, leaning against a pillar and holding her hand on her stomach until he came, minutes later, riding Puck.

When he saw her, he swung down, switching the reins from one hand to the other behind his back. She would have backed up but there was nowhere to go.

He held her gaze for several heartbeats. "You're upset," he said, his eyes no longer blank and unfocused.

"Why do you keep coming to Blythe House?" she asked, looking into his face. "I thought you had an Abbey to manage and property to restore. I thought you were going to catch some smugglers."

"You don't like seeing me?" he asked, closing the space between them a fraction.

"It's not that. It's…my lord, you can't marry Isabelle," she blurted, making a grimace. Meg Summers was no good at subtleties. Blast. Blast. Blast.

"Who said I was going to marry Isabelle?" Light danced in his eyes. "Does it matter to you?"

Meg dropped her eyes, warm all over. "I don't care who you marry," she insisted. Maybe God was ignoring all the lies coming from this corner of Sussex this summer. "But a friend would warn you away from Isabelle."

Nick smiled. "Warn me? Is there danger?"

She walked along the boundary wall, weaving in and out of a low stand of trees. "Isabelle is a danger to you."

"Well, then ease your mind," he said, following close. "I have no intention of marrying your sister."

Meg let out a sigh of frustration and turned, thumping a fist against his chest. "It doesn't matter what your intentions are."

"No? Do you want to know what I intend?"

She stared up into his face, skimming over planes and angles so familiar that she could see them when her eyes were closed. Why wouldn't he listen? Didn't he understand that force and power were not merely things a man wielded though muscle and might? Though she was a woman, Isabelle's power ought to frighten him.

If he knew of it.

Meg bit her lower lip, tugging at it with her teeth. She looked up at him, confused by the intensity of his expression. There would be no going back after this. No easy embraces. No friendly intimacy.

Likely, he would never let her touch him again.

But it meant his safety. She held her palm open, training her eyes on it, and plunged ahead.

"Isabelle has a way to make you do what she wishes. She has magic," she began.

Nick gave her a slow smile—he smiled so often now. "Isabelle has no magic for me."

"She does," Meg said, looking up suddenly. "I have magic too."

"That I believe."

"You don't. Not really. But I'll show you, if you want." He cocked his head, curious.

Her ability to read was certain. What made her cautious was the ability to read too much. Since Grandfather's death, the ability seemed out of her control, but she commanded her mind now to touch only the outer rim of his thoughts. Perhaps she could close her eyes and imagine herself touching Mr Thackery or Henry.

"Think of something… Think of what you had for breakfast."

His tethered his horse and nodded, every line of his frame telling her that he was humoring her.

Meg looked all over him. His face was the easiest to access, but if her control slipped, it would be because she was touching him there. She tugged down the edge of his glove, exposing the wrist and base of his hand, the dark hair slanting across the skin.

"What are you…?" he began then shut up as soon as her slim fingers banded the spot.

She closed her eyes and tried to ignore the smell of his dark cologne. "Toast and butter and marmalade. The light shines through the marmalade like a jewel. You think Mrs Miller is a better cook than she is a housekeeper. You want Jolly for that. You're determined to have her. And fish. Brooks caught fish. It was fresh and well prepared. But you prefer to catch your own fish. You haven't been out in days. And you're tired of eating alone."

With a gasp, Meg jerked her hand back as soon as the snaking impression of Nick's shock began to supplant the banalities of breakfast.

"What did you do?" he asked, pulling off his glove and examining his hand, turning it over in the dappled light. Despite his attempt to speak lightly, she knew she had shaken him.

"I haven't injured you. You needn't look for marks." Meg put a hand to her temple. "I read the thoughts of people I touch. Many of the women in my family have the ability to read, including Isabelle."

Nick looked down, his expression still wary but shifting. "You've been reading my thoughts your whole life?"

Her glance skipped away from his. They were supposed to be speaking of Isabelle. "No. If you think over it now, you'll realize that I don't touch you very often. Not since I was a little girl. Not without gloves. It's not a nice thing to do."

"It's not nice to be inside my head?" he asked, his brows lifting.

She smiled. "I mean it's not sporting."

"I see. And Isabelle. You think she's…reading my mind?"

"Yes, but there's something more she's doing. You grabbed my hand when I passed you at the doorway and I could feel her magic. But it was strange. I ought to have heard or seen your thoughts but there wasn't any of *you* there."

Nick crossed his arms over his chest and leaned against a tree trunk. "All I could think was to catch hold of you," he said, shaking his head.

"It was the right thing. Then you promised to help her with the will."

"I didn't mean to do that. It—" Bewilderment lined his brow. "It came out of my mouth."

Meg stalked a few paces away.

"What haven't you told me?" he pressed.

"I'm not sure. I think she's pushing you," she said, at the same time she questioned her presumption. At his look she supplied a definition. "I think it's like brushing aside your will and replacing it with her own."

He bent back his wrist, holding it toward her again. "You'd do better to show me what you mean."

"I don't know how she's doing it," she yelped, coming no closer. "I certainly can't do it myself."

"But you have magic," he said, repeating her own simple words.

"There's no school for these things. The first I ever heard of this kind of magic was when Grandfather was dying. He wanted me to push him at the end, to make him less afraid."

"Was it Isabelle who did it?"

Meg shook her head. "The magic works by touching and she wouldn't come near the room," she said, looking away, avoiding the sympathy she was sure to see in his face. "I can't think what else it would be. Did you remember promising her anything?"

Nick's mouth was grim. "I promised to come back tomorrow and spend some time going over estate business with her."

Meg nodded. "Did you wish to?"

His voice was careful, picking over this new information like a jeweler at his worktable. "I had other plans. I could not account for my offer. You have to undo it," he said, thrusting his wrist at her.

"I told you, I can't push people," she said, raising her voice.

"Have you even tried?"

"Grandfather—"

"You were grief-stricken. One could hardly imagine that you had the capacity to discover some new—" He fumbled for the words. "Some new ability you'd never practiced."

But she had. She had discovered a deep well of unwanted empathy that cried out for use. What would happen when she touched Nick with a heart open enough to see all of him? The prospect terrified her.

"You can try it on me," he said, beckoning her further into the small stand of trees coiling along the boundary wall. The air was cool here, away from the glare of the sun. "We've nothing to lose."

She followed him, well and truly hidden from the house. They'd climbed these trees from the time she could first remember.

"You trust me?" she asked. She wouldn't blame him if he ran as far from anyone related to Isabelle as he could get.

He tossed a grin over his shoulder and sank to his knees on the soft grass. "What should I think of? What she wants me to do?"

"That might be best," she answered, kneeling opposite him, not yet taking the hand he held for her. "Give me a minute," she said, looking away.

She knew what her magic wanted to do. It wanted to dive inside him, reaping his thoughts like they were a field of barley in high summer. Her magic wanted to know him, and she had to muster every ounce of will she had to keep herself from doing that. Only the surface, she told herself.

"I'm ready," she said, reaching for his wrist again, bracing herself against the seam opening between them as though her magic would nose through and go bounding up his arm. She bit her lips as she let tiny threads of information through. Only a little. Only a little. A drop at a time.

Within seconds she knew it was working.

His mind was laid out like the Abbey garden, wild and beautiful, and she seemed to know that brushing her hand along bristle-topped lavender and soft, bouncing tea roses would glean his memories. She shook, keeping her feet to the winding paths only to find herself blocked by a massive, smooth, black monolith.

Tomorrow I will come again.

The thought was planted right in the middle of his mind, the solid weight of it strange against the soft play of flowers, blowing in the sea breeze.

Meg closed her eyes and seemed to see her own hand pressing against the block, leaning into it with all her might. *Go. Move. Be gone.*

She put her back into it, straining with all the might of her tiny frame. Nothing seemed to work.

Within the vision, Meg lifted her head, surveying the garden, finding similar blocks of varying sizes hovering insubstantially above the cunning twists of the gravel path. She approached one and reached for it, pressing her palm against the implacable surface.

Ask Isabelle to dance.

She felt another.

Tell Isabelle about the rock.

Meg approached the largest of them, transparent and high.

Ask Isabelle to marry you.

Meg's heart lurched, even as she beat her fists against the walls of the intruding thought.

Dreamlike, the garden rushed past her in a dizzying array of colors and she found her hands pressed against the aged stones of the Abbey. Solid. Immovable. She put an ear to the smooth warm stones and felt love. Unrequited love. Love he wanted but could not have.

Meg jerked her hands and felt herself tumble backwards on the grass, staring up into the canopy of trees above.

"Are you all right, Meg?" Nick asked, leaning forward on his knuckles, an arm on either side of her waist. "Did it work?"

"Put your gloves back on," she said, scrambling out from under him. He loved Isabelle. Still. Even knowing her terrible power, and what dangers she presented.

"It didn't work. I've no ability that matches that." She curled her knees under her chin, clasping her arms around her limbs as he crouched near. She had controlled herself—mostly—and the thought should have given her happiness. When she was prepared, she didn't have to feel the suffocation of empathy.

"Isabelle has tried to push you lots of times," she said, glancing up at him. "There's evidence of it all around the garden."

"Garden?" His eyes creased with silent laughter.

"Your mind is laid out like the gardens at the Abbey. I don't get to decide how I read people, and you are quite attached to your home, my lord." And to Isabelle. She stripped her hat from her head and fanned it across her face.

Then Nick grew earnest. "Why is she bothering with me?"

Meg closed her eyes. She could not bear to read Nick's expression. "She wants you to marry her."

He waved a hand. "That's illegal."

"Not if you leave the country to do it. The thought was there, half-formed in your mind already." Meg struggled to her feet. If Nick loved Isabelle, maybe he wouldn't care. "She's got the idea into your head and if she manages to fix it there, you won't be able to stop it."

"Of course I will."

Meg shook her head, exasperated. "Are you coming back tomorrow?"

"Yes," Nick replied. He gripped his hat and slapped it against his thighs. "I didn't mean to say that."

"But you couldn't help yourself. You'll be here tomorrow. If you take care to keep your skin well covered and make any excuse not to touch her, you have a chance to get on your horse, ride off home, build a castle's worth of fortifications between yourself and Isabelle. Leave England. Go back to China. Please. I beg you, as your friend—"

It made her sick to say it and she began to walk briskly back to the drive until his next words halted her.

"What of you? Are you not in any danger?"

Meg took a short breath and turned. "Isabelle won't touch me. I'm not as powerful as she is but she doesn't dare open herself up in that way. Go away, Nick, and don't come back until you're safely wed."

Nick gave her an intense look. "That would please you?"

"Yes," she answered, capturing the inside of her lip between her teeth. "It would please me." The pain of saying it felt like a bandage, clotted with blood, ripped away from the skin.

"There's a solution in front of us," he called after her retreating form.

"What's that, your lordship?"

"Stop lordshipping me, Meg," he commanded, "and come back here so I can ask you to marry me."

Chapter Twenty

Meg stopped as abruptly as if he had shot an arrow between her shoulder blades. She turned, wariness in her eyes, arms folded across her midsection. All in all, she seemed less like a girl who was about to receive an honorable proposal from a peer of the realm, and more like a cross and ill-done-by child.

"It's the solution to our problems," he said reasonably, fighting to keep his mind far from the tantalizing memory of Meg inching back his glove and taking hold of his wrist. He would think of it later.

"I have no problems," she stated.

"No? Everyone has heard about that shocking will, Meg." He held up his fingers and began ticking them off. "You've no money. No home but with your sister. And you don't trust her. Marriage would solve all of these problems."

Her eyelids flickered with some unreadable emotion. "You're so interested in my problems that you can't see yours," she said. Up went her fingers, counting off her own litany. "You've discovered magic and you can't tell me that it doesn't scare you. You're being pursued by a woman you…who left you for your uncle. And now you've foolishly proposed marriage to a friend, simply because you can't be bothered to protect yourself. My lord, you are in a great deal of trouble."

"Friend?" he challenged. "And I think you've called me foolish and lazy. Right now I want to wring your neck."

Meg was getting it all wrong. He accepted the fantastical idea that she could read him, but it was as though she were peering through ancient glass, warped and sagging at the bottom, distorting her view. She couldn't even imagine that he might love her.

"See?" She laughed. "Marriage between us would cause a good deal of trouble."

Nick grunted. His heart had fastened onto this opinionated, wrong-headed girl who seemed determined not to take him. He tried another approach.

"I know I can't marry Isabelle," he said, hoping to wipe that idea from her mind. "It would be foolish to do so if she has the power to push my will aside."

Meg nodded. "There ought to be trust when two people marry, at least."

Nick saw an open path and took it. "We have that, you and I. You trust me. What better foundation could there be?"

Meg's lip caught in a row of her even teeth and then she swallowed hard.

"Are you still trying to propose?" She shook her head with a tiny smile, as though she thought him addled. "Despite what it looks like at the moment, I know I will come around right. The guardianship will end. I don't need saving."

"We all need a little saving from time to time."

Meg heaved a full breath. "Then let me save you from my sister and from yourself, my lord. Run away from us Summers women because heaven knows, you can do better."

He couldn't do better than her. Not in a thousand years of looking. But she really believed what she was saying, in no frame of mind to listen to the whispered vows that pressed against his skin from the inside, desperate for an outlet.

"The Ainsleys may live in an abbey but we haven't been saints. For all our sins, the title has been a durable one and can certainly stand a bit of gossip. Think what it would be like swanning into Greenley's as a new-minted countess, dripping with jewels—"

"Merely for sending the post?" She laughed.

"—and making everyone grovel," he went on, coaxing. "I can assure you that I have the means to support a family."

Though this elicited another laugh, she soon sobered, regarding him with a tilt to her chin. "You think I would marry you for money? Or petty revenge? Or a title?"

He didn't. Since his return from Canton, he'd been so wary of people, so suspicious, but never with Meg. She knew his moods. She knew his passions. She knew the jokes he would tell even before they left his mouth. Meg saw him as he was. Little wonder his heart was hers.

"You're too much my friend—"

"We'll do the thing right," he said, painting a picture, feeling his lungs banded with the effort to persuade her. "Acres of orange blossoms, your grandmother's veil, a frightfully expensive wedding breakfast, and a church full of people."

Her smile faded and he knew, even before she spoke, what her answer would be. He tried to forestall it. "You did kiss me," he reminded her of the indiscretion as only a bounder would. "I know you cannot find me entirely detestable."

A hot blush washed over her features. "Don't remind me of that. I cannot explain that action and I'm horribly ashamed. I am sorry that it caused you embarrassment."

"Meg." Her name was a scold on his lips. How could she think he'd been embarrassed?

"But it's one more reason not to marry me. I throw myself at helpless men." She smiled, but this time it was he who felt grave.

She was demolishing his arguments, setting him away from her with a decisiveness he feared would calcify into an impenetrable shield. And what if he told her he loved her? What if he swore that his only hope of happiness lay in her hands?

Nick's eyes narrowed on her. Meg had magic and she might trust the evidence of that far more than anything he might say. She said she could read the truth in him, but he had not been thinking of her when she'd feathered soft fingers around his wrist. There was so much more of him to read.

He was a gambler down to his last coin. His voice came thickly from his throat. "Let me show you how good we would be."

Meg's eyes narrowed in confusion but he stepped close, and they widened. When he slid his arms around her slim waist and dipped his head, they fluttered closed. She lifted her chin though her face took on a look of firm concentration.

"Don't be such a martyr," he teased, and her nose crinkled as her mouth turned up into a smile. A bare second later he claimed it.

He meant to take his time, to be the one in control, to think about how much he loved her.

But the moment his mouth settled on her soft lips, he couldn't think at all. Her touch ignited him like fireworks during festival time as heat and pressure snaked through his veins, shooting off bursts of light against eyelids tightly closed. Though she held herself stiffly, her palm uncurled on his chest, pushing aside the heaviness of his coat to press against the thin material over his heart and doing nothing to subdue its furious beating.

He gathered her closer, his fingers tracing the curve of her cheek before plunging into her hair, burrowing into its softness. She would know now that he loved her.

How could she help but know?

Meg made a sound, the faintest sigh, exploding through him, forcing him to brace his hand on a tree limb above her head while she kissed him senseless. Finally, as he held her within the close shelter of his arm, he lifted his mouth from hers, his breath coming in shaking waves.

Her eyes opened, the deep green of them like jade, the breath breaking from her throat. She was affected, too.

"See, Meg. It's not so bad," he began, an odd mixture of power and weakness coursing through his veins. "We could—"

Her eyes lost the hazy, unfocused look and she stepped away, turning to retrieve her hat. Each of her movements was brisk and precise. Time seemed to stop and rotate around them in an orbit for the space of several heartbeats.

He had no pride left. "Meg Summers, I beg you to be my wife."

Her chin lifted. She smiled. Lord, why had he ever loved her smiles? He hated this one. "No, thank you."

He'd failed. She had not seen his love or had not cared. There were no more cards to play.

"No, thank you? Why?"

Meg started to walk away, putting distance between them, turning with a little skip. Her hand came up to shade her eyes. "You only want to know my reasons so that you can dismiss them out of hand, but my mind is made up."

As she got farther away, her voice lifted to bridge the distance. "You are not in such great danger that you must escape in so drastic a manner. I know the magic must frighten you but do as I suggested. Watch after yourself tomorrow, don't let her touch you and leave my sister as soon as you can. Someday you will find a girl who is more than mere protection and when you've married her at last, come home. You'll thank me for this."

Helpless frustration made him want to hit something.

"Never, Meg."

Chapter Twenty-one

Meg walked to the village the next morning, desperate for anything to keep her mind off Nick. It wasn't working.

Even a long night spent muttering up at the ceiling had not been enough to sort out how she had been able to withstand the engulfing temptation to read every bit of Nick as he kissed her. As soon as she saw that he was going to do so, a panicked sense of urgency lit into her and she'd locked his thoughts out more securely than the King's crown was locked away in the Tower.

The longer the kiss went on, the fewer thoughts she held in her head at all. Her mind dwelled on the memory until she blinked it away.

Meg Summers, I beg you to be my wife. Lord. How had she summoned the strength to resist his roughly spoken appeal?

The sound of it echoed in her ears even now, telling her to run up the coast toward the Abbey and repent of her foolishness. Nick was certainly willing to marry her and there were benefits that would accrue to both sides of the arrangement—he would get protection from Isabelle, and she would have a home and position that would insulate her from the insults of Society. Add to that was the simple fact that he'd been quite persuasive.

The memory of how persuasive he had been set off a shiver that she quenched only by listing off her reasons for denying him. The man didn't seem to understand that marriage between them would bring him more closely into Isabelle's dangerous orbit. Even if she could not marry him, Isabelle was a force to be reckoned with and one would be foolish to underestimate her. Finally, Meg could not marry a man who looked upon her as a friend and little sister.

Another shiver went through her at the thought of the loneliness such an arrangement would bring.

She swung through the door of Greenley's, her face warm with confusion. It would be far better to turn her mind to something much less troublesome. Something like international smuggling.

Her interest in it had been limited to keeping it off Blythe House land, but now her thoughts focused on Mrs Fletcher, making it a personal concern. Despite the wall that divided them now, the woman had once shown Meg kindness. In the days after the elopement, when news of Isabelle's flight had gotten out, but no news of Isabelle's marriage had come, Mrs Fletcher had not hesitated to touch the girlish face, running a hand over her braids, offering wordless sympathy. Now she was the one who needed help and Meg was in a position to offer it.

"I've purchases to make, ma'am," Meg said to Mrs Greenley, flicking her eyes to the knot of young men loafing by the barrels. She made sure to flash a tiny smile at Sam. "Mrs Jolly sent me to pick up her order for the housekeeping."

She slid her list across the counter and Mrs Greenley began to stack the items in Meg's basket, flitting around the store like a crazed hummingbird. Jim Greenley barely lifted an eye, much less a finger to help her.

"That is all?" she asked, as Meg hoisted the basket into her arms. It was heavy-laden but would not be difficult to manage. Still, Meg gave an elegant stagger and Sam took the bait, striding over, no mother to stop him this time.

"Allow me," he said, taking hold of the basket. She surrendered it at once and he looked down in surprise. Meg's usual response to his offers was to tell him where, and in what manner, he might put them.

"How kind, Mr Fletcher," she said, a smile wreathing her face. "If you'll follow me."

And he did.

He followed her through the village and up the lane toward Blythe House and she set about her task of gathering information. "I thought that you planned on beginning an apprenticeship with a surgeon?" she asked.

He shrugged and the basket shrugged with him. "Don't know. Not much money in it."

"No? Your father saved Henry Gracechurch last year, I remember. Dug a ball out of his shoulder in the middle of the night. That's what I heard."

Sam's chest seemed to swell a little, shifting the bottles in the basket and setting off a rattle. "He saved lots of people. Most of them come banging the door after nightfall and he'd set to, doing his work whether they could pay or not. He let me help some."

Sam was as big as a man, but his face was still a boy's and it reflected his feelings now. "He died doing it, leaving me to care for my ma. He took cold after a storm and the sick never left his lungs."

If she touched him now, she would read his grief.

"Your father was a brave man, Mr Fletcher. He chose a hard path but the whole community looked up to him."

They approached the Blythe House steps and Meg turned. "Thank you, Mr Fletcher. It was kind of you to accompany me."

Sam shook off the melancholy that had gripped him in the last minutes and set the basket at her feet. His handling of it wasn't gentle and she heard the blistering crash of breaking glass.

"You've broken it," Meg cried, going to her knees and gathering the shards of glass from a small bottle of brandy.

He crouched at her side, fumbling to scoop a handful of glass and deposit it under a lilac bush. "I'm so sorry. Miss Summers," he said, his thick neck banded in a too-elaborate cravat. His face was near. "I've been meaning to speak to you for some time."

Meg glanced at him and bit her lip in consternation until she remembered the desperation of his mother. *Help.* She kept her voice light and easy. "Forgive me if I sounded upset. Brandy is so hard to come by."

"Not so hard if you know where to get it. I can get you a bigger bottle within a fortnight."

"Oh?" she said, putting the basket to rights.

"When there's no moon to give us away, that's when the boats come, right up next to the little cliff by your stretch of coast. Surgeons aren't the only men on call in the middle of the night," he said, stopping there like it was some riddle she had to work out.

"But he saved lives and you run brandy," she said, pleased to see that Sam flushed and looked away, shamefaced. "Don't you see how dangerous it is? You could be hauled before a magistrate, sent to the penal colonies. Sam, think what that would do to your mother. I can help you, if you're in trouble. Promise you won't forget?"

Some latent, learned chivalry must have spurred him to put his own hand out and, as he helped her rise to her feet, she braced herself, reading the lingering echos of grief and the brash arrogance of a little boy who hadn't learned that a thing can be out of reach. He meant to kiss her and was sure, what with all he'd heard of her, that she'd be willing.

Meg stepped back.

"I would have to pay you," she said, "for the brandy."

"No need for that." He smiled. Sam tugged her against him, awkwardly tipping her against an arm that was more solid than she expected. His eyes closed as she began to calculate the precise pain her blow should inflict as a price for his presumption.

"I don't wish—" she began as he began to lower his head.

She began to raise her arm when she heard a crack.

Samuel Fletcher cannoned into a column and slithered down its length.

***

Nick didn't think. He approached the door to see Meg wrapped in Samuel Fletcher's arms and the compulsion moved too fast for sense. He crossed the porch, not drawing breath until he'd bashed his fist into the young idiot's nose.

It was a pity Samuel hadn't been knocked out, but blood, crimson and copious, dripped onto his cravat and the lad put a probing hand to his face. "You broke my nose," came the muffled and outraged cry.

Nick was sorely tempted to haul him up and hit him again, breaking his jaw.

"If I ever catch you pestering Miss Summers again," he began, his imagination conjuring rewarding, bloodthirsty punishments.

"Pestering?" The boy's voice was an offended squeak. "Pestering?"

He scrambled to his feet, one hand cupping his face while the other pointed an accusing finger. "We were having a bit of a flirtation. She wanted me to walk out with her. If it's anyone's fault—"

His words choked off as Nick shoved him against the column and lifted him by the neck, his boots dangling. Meg would never invite this puppy's kisses. Never. Nick balled his hand into a fist and drew back.

"Let him go," Meg demanded and, when he didn't obey, she jumped and hung all her weight onto his cocked fist. "Let him go."

Nick jerked his hand loose of her and dropped the young man into a crumpled heap.

"Go."

Samuel clambered away, leaving Nick and Meg on the porch. His own breathing was all he could hear for some time and he did not trust himself to speak. Meg packed her basket, replacing the items that had scattered across the steps by Samuel's hasty leave-taking.

"You were quite effective, my lord. I hope the boy is not too damaged," she said, with a light, shaking laugh.

He growled low in his throat. "Did you really invite the company of that imbecile?" The question was harsh—far harsher than he intended. "Did you want to be made love to by a young fool?"

Her hand arrested and her brows lifted. "Sam Fletcher's almost my own age and it's none of your business what I intended."

His eyes widened. She was not denying it. "Do you have any clue about the danger you were courting?"

"Why don't you tell me," she said, and if he'd been less outraged, he might have noted the deadly calm in her voice.

"Young Fletcher doesn't see you as a respectable female. Not quite. He might have tried to have his way with you."

She laughed at him. Laughed. "What you saw was clumsy optimism, not malevolence."

Nick's stomach dropped. "And if his intent had shifted?" His voice softened as the pressure in his veins began to abate. She dropped her head and her long black eyelashes fanned across her cheeks. What a blasted monster he was, tearing a strip off her to relieve his own feelings. "Perhaps you didn't realize—" he began, and her chin shot up, fire in her eyes.

"Why does a man always think women are incapable of understanding danger? As though we are pudding-brained creatures saved from constant disaster by an army of minders and keepers. Perhaps when *you* wander into a bear pit, relying on the good nature and civilized manners of the bears not to tear you limb from limb, you may comprehend what it is to be a woman. Ladies are, each of us, constantly aware of our dangers."

She had a point, but he did not pause to examine it. "I'll believe you are capable of watching over yourself when you exhibit any genius for it. The evidence—"

"Evidence?" she shouted. "It was only a kiss and I was handling him."

His voice rose to a roar. "That's what it looked like. Another five minutes and you could have been on your back. Less time if you wanted it."

He felt the blow before he saw it coming. The flat of her hand cracked across his face in an inferno of rage.

***

Seeds of mortification began to bloom on her cheeks as she spun from him. Anything to keep him from seeing the hurt she knew must be in her eyes.

"Meg," he began as she picked up her basket. "I only wanted—"

"No more advice, please," she said, swallowing thickly against a tide of hurt. "I've had quite enough. And I'm not going to apologize for that blow. You deserved it."

His hand slipped to his throbbing cheek. "I didn't mean to suggest—"

"If you are any kind of gentleman," she said, packing her words with doubt and scorn, knowing it would prick him. Lord, anything to hide the sorrow. "You will leave off. I will not ask him to carry my basket again."

"Why did you? Fletcher said…" He trailed away.

It felt too late to tuck her arm into his and speak to him confidingly. She would rather go to Mr Thackery or even her sister with the news that there would be a shipment within the next fortnight. Or no one at all.

So she lied.

"I wanted to kiss him."

A muscle jumped in his cheek but he stood like a granite statue of a perfect gentleman. "Will you not accept my apologies?"

"I would thank you if you let me alone."

Her gaze met his and then Isabelle stepped into the doorway, a tight smile on her lips. “Nick, you’re early. But I’m pleased you’ve come. We have quite a lot to discuss. Margaret, I’ll see the basket gets to the kitchens. You look in need of a rest.”

Meg could not return to her room fast enough.

***

“What are we going to do with her, your lordship?” Isabelle asked, settling into a chair and pouring out the tea. “You see what a wild thing I have on my hands. I saw her walking up the drive with the Fletcher cub. She’s been encouraging him for weeks.”

“Indeed,” he said, carefully taking the cup with a gloved hand, arranging his fingers as far from Isabelle as possible.

What would Isabelle read if she reached into his mind now? Frustration. Desire. Love. None of it for her.

Afternoon sun spilled through the window and he watched the patterns of light and shade chasing one another across the rug as he remembered each painful moment on the porch. Not his fist making contact with a nose, or even of her palm striking his face. That pain was already fading. No, the pain was from jealousy, the unjust words hurled at Meg. His mouth twisted as he let out a silent sigh. What a hole he had dug for himself. He had been in the wrong. Entirely.

Damn. He ought to have his ears boxed.

“May I refill your cup?” Isabelle asked, reaching forward.

“No,” he said, settling the saucer and cup down. He stood, striding to the mantel. “I am all ears, ready to hear what it is you brought me to your home for.”

“The problem with Margaret,” Isabelle began, reaching for a newspaper at her side, “is far bigger than I knew. It’s not merely her outlandish apparel and her total want of propriety in the village. Lately, I’ve come to discover that she’s been penning a series of columns for a newspaper. Being paid. Corresponding with a man.”

Nick straightened, his mind leafing through sheaves of remembrances, which seemed to bear out Isabelle’s…accusation. He found that he’d half-guessed already.

“She’s Sir Frederick Magpie, isn’t she?” Nick reached for the paper and Isabelle stood, stumbling forward as he stepped clear of her flailing arms. She caught herself on the mantelpiece, gasping.

"Pardon me, Lady Ainsley," he said, taking the paper from her hands, relief settling into his stomach. Meg had a publisher. This would explain fat letters to Mr Augustus Morgan, and it would also explain her secrecy. Thank heavens he hadn't taxed her on the subject. He would have looked more like an ass than he already was.

He moved to the light of the window and spread it open on a column titled *The British Way of Grieving*.

"Women do not feel true sorrow," it began. He choked on a laugh. Lord, he loved this girl. "Funeral and burial rites are meant to be witnessed by stout-hearted men of unparallelled bravery instead of women who cry over the least little thing…"

"She's going to ruin our family name, mocking the traditions of the country, my lord," Isabelle exclaimed, sidling up behind him. He turned on his heel, thrusting the paper into her hands.

Meg had put herself beyond the reach of his apologies, but he could have sense enough to perfectly obey her warnings about Isabelle now. "She's a credit to you."

"A credit? Nicholas—"

"Lord Ainsley, madam. Your sister is a credit to your family name. Sir Frederick Magpie is famous for his wit." He lowered his brows. "He is known as someone who sees things no one else does, shining a light on notions that are no less silly because they have been cherished for so long. If Pevensey had any sense, they'd put up a monument in Meg's honor on the village green."

Isabelle advanced. "You were arguing with her, out there on the porch. I could hear your muffled roars. Yet you defend her now."

"What of it?" he countered. He always fought with Meg, aware on some level that most of their skirmishes presaged warmth between them that could not, at present, find any other outlet.

"Nothing," Isabelle said, her smile cold. "There's nothing to be said. Shall I see you out?" she asked, drawing near him once more.

"No," he exclaimed. "I'll see myself out." He saw her eyes take on a hard, determined expression and said, allaying her desperation, "May I come again tomorrow? We have much more to discuss."

Her raised hand slipped to her side.

"Promise?"

"Of course," he lied. He should ride away, as Meg said. Run and keep on running from Isabelle. She would throw herself into his arms next time and he would be helpless to resist her. "I'll see myself out," he said, gathering his things, pretending a muddle he did not feel in order to escape bowing over her hand.

Once the front door closed behind him, he took a deep, clean breath. Lord, Meg was right about all of it. He turned and cast a look toward her windows, wishing they'd really had it out, fought and yelled until the root of the matter had been uncovered, the canker drained.

Nick pulled his glove from his hand and pushed searching fingers into the seam of his waistcoat pocket. The green pebble caught the noonday sun. He raised it to his lips, kissing the uneven surface, sealing his action with a vow and a prayer. Then he set it behind the column and turned toward the stables, heedless of the shadow in the library window.

Chapter Twenty-two

"What are you doing, grubbing like a peasant?" Isabelle asked.

Meg hitched her black skirts out of the way and stood, her slippers crunching the fine grains of sand on the porch steps as she turned. He had not left a pebble. All signs indicated that Nick had done what she urged him to do on the day he had proposed. He had escaped and she should be happy about it.

"Nothing," she answered. "I thought I saw a coin."

Isabelle murmured, sweeping through the door. Despite the heat of the day, a shawl was drawn over her shoulders and her face wore a pinched, exhausted look. "Ask Jolly to attend me in the drawing room. We have menus to settle."

"Is anyone coming to dinner? Lord Ainsley?" Meg asked.

"Nicholas? No. He has a life of his own. I can't expect him to dance attendance on me each day."

Meg narrowed her eyes as she swung through the baize door. It had been three days since Nick had come, and Isabelle's unconcern reeked like a pile of manure in the hot sun.

"Jolly," she said, entering the kitchens and coming upon that lady packing a small crate. "Have you heard anything from the Abbey?"

"I sent a kitchen maid over this morning when Mr Brooks didn't—" she clamped up, setting a covered pie on top of a layer of straw. "Well, I expected him and he didn't come. I was told Mr Brooks can't get away for even a minute."

"Why not?"

"His lordship. He took ill and they all thought it would get better but it's only gotten worse."

"How bad?" Meg's mouth was dry. There was no rationale to explain away this hard, brittle fear that took hold of her now.

"Bad enough. I'm sending sick room provisions."

"Are you going yourself? Who's taking them?" Meg's questions shattered from her fumbling grasp. She had to see Nick. Had to assure herself that all was well.

"One of the gardeners is going to drive up a cart."

"He'll take me, too."

When Meg arrived at the Abbey, there was no polite staff to welcome her with refreshments or turn her away on account of a slight illness in the household. Her feet took her up the stairs without being stopped, and it wasn't until she approached the private bedrooms that she met the least resistance.

It came in the form of Mrs Miller, planting herself in front of the door handles and lifting the bunch of household keys, attached to her bodice on a thin chain and conferring no lesser authority than an archbishop's staff and mitre.

The first request had been gently made but Mrs Miller would not budge. "His lordship is in no state to receive—"

"I don't care about his state," Meg said through gritted teeth. She pointed at the panelled door. "That gentleman and I are engaged to be married."

It took no more than a moment for Mrs Miller to perform the necessary mental calculations. One lord of the Abbey, plus one affianced bride. The sum totted up to one new mistress. Mrs Miller stepped away from the door, performing a low curtsey as Meg turned the handle.

Racing through a small sitting room and into the bedroom beyond, she let fear carried her feet quickly into the strange territory of a man's private chambers. She had no time to appreciate the rich materials and ancient furniture. What greeted her was Nick, bathed in sweat, his back arched off the bed, limbs and sinews stiff with agony. Low, feral groans tore from his throat. He looked like a man on the edge of death.

At her gasp, Brooks looked up from a basin of water, as limp as the rag he wrung out.

"Miss, you shouldn't be—"

Meg cast her gloves and bonnet into a chair. "I didn't know. I didn't know he was sick," she said, voice trembling. "Please. Brooks, please don't toss me out. I can be of some help."

He took a breath, glancing about the room and the wreckage of three days of illness, and finally beckoned her closer.

"I don't know that anyone could help. Nothing I try seems to do the slightest good and I've seen typhoid, scurvy, grippe, cholera, malaria…" he said, sinking into onto the window seat with an arm on his knee and running a hand roughly across his face. He pointed to the bed. "This hasn't let up for three days. Shaking and thrashing. Hardly a rest. He'll kill himself if—"

Meg made a cry she could not suppress, an animal in pain.

"Pardon," he breathed.

Meg sat next to Brooks and let a wave of sorrow dash against her, swirling around her feet and threatening to swamp her. Six years Nick had been gone and the only prayer she'd had was that he return safe—sometime before it was too late. She would not lose him now.

"What needs to be done?" she asked, sniffing and wiping her cheeks with the back of her hands.

He threw his hands out in confusion. "I've been doing what seems best at the moment. Talking to him. Cooling him."

Meg took in the scene. Nick had kicked off his linens and wore a simple open-necked nightshirt, the end of which was screwed in a tangle around his knees. He breathed like a man hanging off the edge of a cliff, straining for every lungful of air. There was no use pretending she was an experienced nurse, but she wanted him well more than anyone in the world. That had to count for something.

"I can't do any harm, Brooks, and you'll be no good to anybody if you don't get some rest. Let me stay with him while you do."

Brooks took a long look at the figure on the bed. "He's been a difficult man, no lie," he said, his voice breaking. "Hard, angry. Not so you could see." He put a fist against his chest, his face twisted with grief. "But way down, mistrustful like a dog that's been kicked too many times. But fair for all that. Plain dealing. I didn't know he could smile until these last months."

"I know, Brooks," she whispered. "We'll get him back to us."

She sent him on his way with the ghost of a smile, and when he had departed, Meg inched closer to the bed, reaching out to Nick, who shivered at her touch. The muscles of his shoulder tightened under her hand.

Snow.

Meg snatched her hand away, cradling like it had been singed. No. No. Not again. She reached for him once more.

Chilled to the bones. It's cold. So cold.

Meg leaned over him. "My lord," she whispered, so close to his ear that she could feel the heat of him—the fever—warm her skin. "My lord, wake up." Her words tumbled out, half sob, half command. "Wake up. If you die on me, I'll tell everyone how you really broke your arm. Wake up."

She laid a hand on his chest, the hair of it prickly under her hand where it escaped the open neck of his nightshirt. She dropped her head, unable to keep the tears from coming. Shaking sobs broke from her and her back bent like a rod. "Nick—"

"Yes." His voice was gravelly and weak, and his grip weaker still where he held her hand, trapped against his heart. The hand was damp with sweat but she would not have moved it for a fortune. "You never call me Nick anymore."

She lifted her head, wiping away the tears with a shaking laugh. He was gray with exhaustion and great breaths worked his lungs, but he was awake, and even more of a wonder, his body no longer strained against the bed linen.

"I should get Brooks," she said, tugging at her hand only to find that his grip was strong enough to keep her. No. It was she who was not strong enough to break it.

"Not yet," he said. "Water."

Only then did he release her. She turned, lightning quick to fill the cup. When she returned, his face again twisted in pain, his mouth drawn tight in agony. With great effort, he lifted himself onto one elbow and she moved to brace him up.

"I'm sorry, Meg," he breathed, as she held the cup to his lips. "About Sam."

"Shhhh," she said, leaning her head against his for a moment. "Not now."

He fell back to his pillows, exhausted. "Stay?"

She looked for a chair or stool where she might adopt the position she had imagined for herself, sitting near enough to lay a cool hand on a fevered brow from time to time. Reading to him if he was bored.

"No," he insisted, and tugged on her hand. "Stay with me."

Despite the impropriety, she could not deny him. Meg clambered onto the bed to sit, straight-backed, nested in the bed sheets like a princess in a palanquin, leaving her hand in his.

Snow. It was different now, if only by degree. The snow she imagined was beyond a window. Without, sleet pinged against the glass. Within, a fire crackled in the hearth.

Meg wrinkled her brow at this vision, frustrated as never before that her power was not often as straightforward as an unmistakable message carved into stone. But this was better than the blinding storm of snow she felt before. It felt better—less fraught and menacing. Over time, Nick's breathing became steady and even as he dropped off into a healing sleep, and she turned the meaning of the snow over and over in her mind.

It could not be a coincidence that so much of her grandfather's last days were filled with that same suffocating snow as well. The feel of it on Nick's skin threatened to pull her back into the freshness of grief and more.

Could it have something to do with Isabelle? With pushing?

Meg stared at her hand holding Nick's until her vision blurred, remembering the sensation of rushing water when Nick had reached for her that day at Blythe House. How cold the water had been: how similar the feeling of Nick fighting, growing weak.

So similar. But Isabelle wasn't touching Nick now. That alone should absolve her sister of any blame. Meg turned the pieces of the puzzle around in her mind, looking for the proper fit. If she wasn't touching him, how was Isabelle pushing him?

Shadows lengthened in the room, stretching thinly up the walls and vanishing in the fading light. Meg's muscles cramped in her legs, her back tightened. She stretched as unobtrusively as she could but still her limbs tingled with fatigue.

Brooks poked his head around the corner of the door, appearing better for having a meal and a wash. But his face was still drawn in sharp lines as he looked down at his master, dozing peacefully now, and caught Meg's eyes.

"Why kind of witchcraft have you wrought?"

She smiled, feeling the weight of her eyelids, and shook her head slightly. "I was lucky enough to come when his fever broke."

He answered with a low grunt. "Lucky."

She felt his eyes on her, taking in the rumpled dress and stockinged feet.

"We'd best get you back home, miss, before there's talk."

Meg gave a low chuckle. "There is bound to be talk. I told Mrs Miller that I'm Nick's fiancée. The woman must be spreading it around the village now, unless I miss my mark." Meg sighed. "Never fear, Brooks. It will simply be one more story to tell in the scandalous history of Margaret Summers. She was within a hair's breadth of respectability by marrying an earl, but nothing came of it."

She shook her dark mood away preparing to hand off her patient to more experienced hands than her own.

"You could have him, you know." Brooks laid speculative eyes on her. "He's an honorable man." Meg gave him a long look and he sighed. "And you're an honorable woman. Ah, well. It was a fancy I had along with Araminta."

Meg smiled. "He's sleeping well but he doesn't seem to want to be left. So make sure you—" Meg began to withdraw her hand from Nick's but the moment contact was broken, he went rigid, pulling her down so that she lost her balance and tumbled into the depression at his side. The snow had returned with a suddenness that shocked her, but one word pierced the storm.

Stay.

This was no simple handclasp. Nick's arm fastened around her, cradling her against him from neck to knee. Meg looked over Nick's shoulder and widened her eyes at Brooks. What now? He widened his own back. The impropriety of it made her cheeks burn.

"He needs his sleep," Brooks said, already backing out of the room.

"Brooks, don't you dare," she hissed in laughing outrage, all command lost as Nick's arm tightened. "What should I do?"

"Get some sleep, my lady?" he suggested, calling her "my lady" in such a pointed fashion that she could not mistake his meaning. He bowed, not even trying to hide his smile, and left.

She glared at his back, but the irritation seemed to leave her as soon as she heard the click of the door closing. She wished the discomfort of her stays would disappear, but she would not wish herself anywhere else but right where she was.

She turned in Nick's arms and he shifted, dropping a hand against the linens. Light from a distant candle gently caressed them and she traced a finger over his forearm, the muscles firm even in sleep. She followed the sinuous black lines of a fearsome dragon, the tail trailing off over the sensitive skin in the bend of his elbow. Gently, she drew an arc across the hollow.

Nick's arm tightened, stealing away this interesting image, and Meg felt her eyelids slide shut. She would rest them for a moment—only for a moment. She would rouse soon. But, instead of climbing the ladder to wakefulness, she sank into heavy fatigue, welcoming sleep when it came.

Dawn lightened the curtains, too feeble to spill light across the bed but nosing at the window. Meg blinked her eyes, making out the soft blue color of the furnishings in the dimness, the ornamentation that had been added, generation by generation, over the top of what had once been an austere abbey, filled with praying monks.

She yawned, stretching her hand out in a fist that returned to scrub away the sleep in her eyes. It was soft here. Comfortable. Warm.

"You snore."

Meg turned her head to regard Nick, alert and watchful. His chin was scratchy with three days of whiskers and he propped himself up, holding her hand in his and rubbing the back of it along his rough jawline.

She wrinkled her nose at him, afraid that if she didn't, she would press a kiss there. Nick was a trial of handsomeness in evening clothes, but devastating to her resolves even now. "I don't."

"You do." He flopped onto his back and the action sent her rolling toward him, fitting them together like an egg nestled in a cup. "It's adorable."

Her stomach rumbled.

"How long has it been?" he said, his laughing voice a little dry.

"Since you got sick? Three days," she answered, feeling her lips move against his neck and the way their breathing began to synchronize. With great concentration she kept his thoughts at bay.

"No. Since you came."

"Hours? Twelve maybe? Fourteen." His embrace tightened.

"How did you get past Mrs Miller?"

She smiled. Thank heaven he was pestering her with questions, distracting her from the feeling of rightness and belonging that would not shift from her heart. She raised her face and lifted her brow in a wicked arch. "I lied."

"My Meg, lied?" he said, kissing that same brow, sending a spiral of longing into her stomach. "That's not your way. You prefer to tell the truth and shame the devil."

"Don't be mad, my lord," she demanded, a little breathless, snuggling her head down in the crook where his neck met his hard shoulder.

He gave her hand a light pinch. "Nick."

"Nick, then," she amended. "I told her I was your fiancée."

Meg stilled, waiting for a response. Nick stilled, heaven knew why. The blasted birds outside in the trees kept up their noisome singing, marking time in wild crescendos that seemed to catch the breath from her throat.

"You didn't lie," he said, in a voice that could only be described as careful. "I asked you to marry me. Though," he found his smile, she could hear it in his voice, "I thought when you finally accepted me, I might be the first to know."

Stay. The thought had repeated all night like the beat of his heart.

"There wasn't anything else that would budge her. She watched your door like a trained assassin. Nick. I am sorry."

"I don't know what you're apologizing for. Barging into a sickroom? Spending the night? Saving my life?"

"I didn't—"

"You've ruined me," he interrupted, and it turned into a yawn. She shook her head. They both knew who would bear the cost from this night's work. His yawn finished. "Whether you want to or not, you'll have to marry me now." His eyes closed, dry lips lifting into a roguish smile.

She stared at the light, filtering through the gauzy curtains. If the light were water, the whole room would be in danger of flooding. What was she running from? "If you still want."

He was silent for so long that she wondered if he had fallen asleep, but as she began to lift her head he tugged at her braid, tugging the berry-red ribbon loose, settling her on his shoulder.

"I want."

Chapter Twenty-three

She woke again to find they had been covered in a thin blanket. Brooks had brought it, she hoped, though that thought was mortifying enough. Gradually, reality intruded and she could not find the words to be truly delicate. Nick shifted, giving the matter a sense of urgency that trespassed the boundaries of ladylike reticence.

"I am desperate to relieve myself, Nick. If you don't let me go, I'll never be able to look you in the eye again."

He laughed, loud and strong, the sound of it rumbling his chest and filling the room, but he lifted his arm from her waist. "I don't want a wife who can't look me in the eye. Go."

Wife. He meant to hold her to it. Her thoughts could hardly even allow herself to think the words plainly. It was far easier to pretend that she had no hand in this and that he was forcing her. But the words she'd spoken to Mrs Miller had been so ready on Meg's lips. She wanted this.

Meg blushed but sat up, tugging her frock into some order, only to feel her hair pulled. She looked over her shoulder to see him yanking the crumpled, trailing ribbon from the tail of her braid.

"Ow."

"I'll take this as a ransom so you come back."

She scooted off the bed, her glance taking in every bit of him, looking for signs he might revert to that tortured creature she found last night, but his gaze was steady and her eyes slid away from his.

She forced a laugh. "After this adventure, I can promise that I'll never come back to your private rooms. Not for a king's ransom."

When he didn't answer, she chanced a look at him to find that, even flat on his back, he was still commanding.

"When we are wed, this will be as much my room as it is yours," he said, his blazing eyes reminding her that the future would arrive sometime, instead of floating distantly out of reach forever.

She felt herself blush, but she managed to respond. “Married people don’t share rooms,” she said. “Unless they’re poor.”

“Then I’ll follow the fashion of the poor. I don’t intend to be separated from my wife.”

His look set Meg’s heart pounding, but she lifted an unconcerned shoulder, quitting the room before her blushes betrayed her.

When she returned, she caught sight of herself in the mirror and grimaced at her reflection. “I look dreadful. Why didn’t you say something?” Jolly was going to murder her on the laundress’s behalf. Her dress was creased from neck to hem and her tidy braid had become a frizzy halo.

“I’ve a comb on the dresser and a robe over the chair,” he said. “I lay all my worldly goods at your feet.” Nick laced his hands behind his head and stared at the ceiling as though their circumstances didn’t matter much. His eyes shuttered like he might fall asleep again.

Meg touched the robe, feeling the silkiness slip through her fingers. It was a loose banyan shape, embroidered in the exuberant colors found on his waistcoats, and she put a tentative arm through the sleeve, half wearing it, liking the capacious fit and the smell of Nick that clung both to the article and to herself.

When she looked to the bed, she found Nick regarding her with a watchful eye. She hurriedly slipped out of it, settling it back on the arm of the chair with a pat, and went to find his comb.

It was on a high dresser. Higher still was a small mirror and, even by tilting it, she had to stand on her tiptoes to see her likeness.

“You don’t want a wife, Nicholas Ainsley. There is no room for me here.”

“I’ll allow you to bring in a single footstool,” came his high-handed reply, but the teasing caused a piercing pain in her breast. Meg might live here. She might share Nick’s bed and home. Would she belong?

“What did it feel like?” she asked him, slipping her fingers through the coils of her braid and sliding the plaited strands free. “Before I came last night.”

When he didn’t answer, she looked at his reflection in the mirror and caught an intent expression on his face that made her twist her neck around.

But it was gone or imagined when she faced him because he answered blandly enough. "Like there wasn't room enough in my head for me to think. Like I was hacking away at a thicket or being buried alive under a snowfall."

Meg turned back to the mirror, plucking up the tortoiseshell comb, and continued her ministrations, all the while chewing her lip. She lifted her hair in a bunch and worked the ends free of tangles in short, brisk strokes.

"What is it?" he asked.

"Did you feel like there was something you had to do?"

His eyes narrowed. "No. It was more like I couldn't get inside my head to think at all. What are you thinking?"

"Brooks said it was nothing like any sickness he's ever seen. I'm trying to figure out if it had something to do with pushing."

Nick sat up, throwing his bare feet over the edge of the bed, and she tried to ignore how the sight of it made her feel. He was far easier to deal with as an invalid.

He slipped into the banyan robe and sank into the chair. The riot of color ought to have made him look womanish or old-fashioned, like something stepped out of the last century when men wore heels and patches. But the contrast between the delicate embroidery and his brown skin, taut against the cords of his neck, pleased her.

"How could it? Isabelle wasn't touching me."

Meg let out another length of hair and began to untangle a new section. "That's what's puzzling me. Perhaps it operates in another way—" She gave a vicious yank, snarling a knot of hair. If only he would stop watching her. "But perhaps I'm wrong."

"Perhaps." Nick stood, placing himself behind Meg and taking the comb from her fingers. Then he began smoothing her dark curls, working the ends loose and running his strong hands through her hair. She stood like a block of statuary under the stonemason's chisel, cold and still, certain the beat of her heart would give her away.

"'Perhaps' is a dangerous word, Meg," he said, plaiting her hair with inexpert fingers.

"My ribbon?" she demanded when he had done. She held her hand out.

He grinned, patting his pocket. "It's mine now. Your ransom, remember? I'll give you one of mine to pledge our troth." He reached past her to pull open a drawer and she wondered if he had any idea he was stealing the breath from her lungs.

He found a length of thin cord and retreated a few inches to tie it in a bow. He was brushing the tail end of her hair against his lips as he thought. "I'm worried about that 'perhaps.' You saw me last night. I was half mad. If it was pushing, how much longer could I have withstood it?"

That question haunted Meg.

"And if she has a way to push me when I'm out of her sight, then what broke the—" he shook his head, searching, "—spell?"

She made a moue of distaste at the word. "I don't know that either. This is foreign territory."

He looked up, capturing her gaze in the mirror. "It's your power, Meg. Why don't you know anything about it?"

"Grandfather didn't like it. He said it was unsporting—" she began.

"That wouldn't have stopped you."

"Why do you say so? I owed him so much. He raised us."

"Meg, holding you back from something you really wanted used to be as easy as holding back the sunlight. Are you telling me you never read Henry or Fox? Or me?"

Meg lifted her chin. "Conceited man. You think you're so interesting. There wasn't enough in your heads to fill one side of a pound note."

"So you did read me." He grinned.

"Only once. It's not at all pleasant most of the time so I don't make a habit of it. You can read things that feel like a slap across the mouth."

His face changed and he got there before she could head him off with something amusing. His eyes rested on her with an expression of tenderness. "Oh, Meg. All this time? You've been reading the village—"

She colored as she interrupted him. "Anyway, I never learned about pushing."

He acquiesced to the change of topic. "Your sister did."

Another shrug. "You know Isabelle."

"No," he answered, dropping her braid though he did not move away. "I'm not sure I did. You tell me."

"I was curious. You'll remember how I would trail after you boys until you taught me all you knew. But Isabelle—" Meg shook her head. "She wanted things. We had no guidance, no mentor. Only Grandfather telling us to stop doing what he had caught us doing that he thought inappropriate. She never saw the point of that."

"And you did?"

"People aren't tools to be used." She took a breath and moved from the closeness of him. "And that's enough of the inquisition. I wish I had more answers for you, but I don't. We shall simply have to take care until it's time for us to wed."

"It's time now."

Meg plucked at the sleeve of her black gown. "Not quite—"

He folded his arms across his chest, implacable. "We won't be waiting until you're out of mourning, Meg. I'm meeting the vicar today. Little more than two weeks for the banns to be read three times and we'll have the thing done the day after your birthday. Isabelle won't be your guardian any longer and we won't need her permission."

"Marry while I'm in mourning?" she asked, a thread of joy rising in her that she could not help. "You're determined to set the tongues wagging."

He grinned. "Needs must when the devil drives."

Meg's lightness faded. These were all the soft words she could expect.

It was Brooks who carted her home, stopping well away from the house and watching as she ran, soft-footed across the garden, coming up to the house near the kitchens. She tapped on Jolly's window and it was thankfully swung back with little delay.

"How is he?" Jolly asked as she poked her head out. She looked Meg's gown over with a frown.

"I left him well enough. The fits stopped and the fever has broken. There's more—" Meg looked over her shoulder. "Get me to my room and I'll tell you all."

Jolly whisked her through the kitchens, not taking time to send the cook away or busy the little kitchen maid in some other corner of the house. They shot furtive glances at her, eyes slipping from her face as though it were coated in axle grease. Meg's cheeks flamed.

"I was sneaking so I wouldn't be seen," she hissed to Jolly's back as they climbed the servant's staircase.

"You're too late for secrecy. Mrs Miller was over here at first light to tell the tale to every footman and maid around the place. She said…she said you were alone with him all night in his bedchamber and then tried to brazen it out with some nonsense about an engagement."

Meg's eyes drifted shut in mortification. "Does Isabelle know?"

"You mean it's true?" Jolly whirled on the small stairs, her mouth dropping open.

Encountering that look returned her to the child of nine, caught out in some transgression Jolly would get to the bottom of. "I couldn't leave him. He had one foot in the grave."

"Where was his other foot?"

"He was near death," Meg explained, flattening the truth, simplifying it, skating over the fact that, like Juliet, she'd wished dawn had never come. "What would you have had me do?"

Jolly turned to resume her ascent. "You had trouble enough in the village with things as they were. This certainly won't mend it." She stiffened her spine. "The engagement. Is that true, too?"

Meg's voice was small and tired. "It is now."

Jolly must have stopped because Meg walked right into her embrace and she held back her tears with a dam as thin as tissue paper as Jolly wrapped motherly arms about her. She wanted to cry for Nick, losing faith in the woman he'd once loved. And cry that Isabelle had caught them both in a trap that would bind them together. She wanted to cry, too, for loving him and being happy that this was so. Meg clung to Jolly, her joy and sorrow buffeting like a high wind between the close walls of the stairwell. She could not halt a few from spilling over.

"There now," Jolly said. She wiped Meg's tears with her apron and cupped her face, tilting it up until their eyes met. When they touched, Meg saw a pool of still water, peaceful, endless. Here was Jolly's love for her.

"If you agreed to it, no doubt it's for the best."

Meg could read that it was a lie, but a gentle one. Meg loved her for saying it.

"There's more. Isabelle is practicing a new kind of magic. She's pushing his own thoughts away and replacing them with her own."

Jolly hustled her up the stairs, down the hallway, and into her room. "So that's it," she said, sending the bolt home. She seemed to accept that there was a new power at Blythe House as easily as she accepted that Isabelle would not use it for good. "What's to be done about it?"

Meg was stepping out of her gown and pretended not to hear. She handed it off to a waiting Jolly and donned a robe. Plain material. Frills. No yards of extra fabric. She cinched it tightly about her waist and sat at her vanity, with her brushes and combs and ribbons in easy reach. But she wasn't at home anymore.

"Nick and I will be married in a few weeks," she said, slipping Nick's tie from her hair and coiling it around her finger.

Jolly gasped but she only said, "So soon?"

"If Isabelle can somehow push him, even when she's not touching him…"

"He'd have to wed her, yes. But I don't see why you should give up your happiness for his…comfort."

"Not his comfort, Jolly. His life. Nick was too exhausted to work it out, but during the long night I did. I was so confused as to why Grandfather cut me out of the will. I came around to thinking Isabelle might have something to do with it but didn't know how. She never touched him in the end."

"Aye," Jolly said, "I remember."

"He felt like snow for weeks before he went, and when I went to him last night, Nick felt that way too. You should have seen him, shaking and straining like his heart would break open. The strain of it was killing him and I think—" She halted on the precipice, her feet tingling to consider the height. And then she leapt. "I think that Isabelle's pushing might have killed Grandfather. And if it did, it's possible she killed her husband, too."

Jolly plopped to the bed, her eyes wide. "How?"

"I don't know."

"What does Lord Ainsley think about this?"

"I don't think he would have let me leave his room if he understood what Isabelle was capable of."

"And he'd be right to keep you from danger." Jolly sprung up, clutching at Meg's elbow with fingers closing like a steel trap. "Get up. We have to go. We have to leave this house this instant."

Habitual obedience to that voice made Meg rise to her feet but she ripped her arm away when they stumbled into Grandmother's trunk.

"No," she said on an intense whisper. "I don't know what her powers are. I don't know her limitations. I don't even know if she did it on purpose. But if she could get to Nick while he was miles away in his bed, he'll not be safe from her ever. That's why I agreed to marry him. I have to know how she does it, Jolly. And when I know, I'm going to stop it."

Chapter Twenty-four

Even in the blaze of August, the church was shadowed and cool. Meg shifted on her seat, never taking her eyes from the back of Nick's neckcloth. He'd inclined his head when he came down the aisle, seating himself on the other side, and she'd exhaled a breath of relief.

They had exchanged no words since she left his rooms yesterday morning. She'd said, tying the ribbons of her hat, "You will call for me, Brooks, if he has a relapse?"

"Yes, my lady," he'd said, and she did not trust herself to give him a proper response to that bit of impertinence tacked on to the end.

So she'd looked back at Nick, which was the wrong thing to do with his hair all over the place, and reached to comb her fingers through the tangle.

Stay.

"You'll be in good hands," she said, pulling her own back.

"But not in yours."

She chose the safest interpretation of that. "You said you can manage now on your own."

His answer was grudging. "True. The pushing is still there, I can feel it, but it's like a distant drum. It's silenced when we touch," he said, tracing a knuckle over her jaw. "Why do you think that is?"

Stay.

"You'll have to explain that to me."

Shaken, Meg stepped away from the warmth of his tall form. "Only when I discover the reason myself," she had said, following Brooks to the waiting cart.

After the Offertory, Reverend Moss lifted his voice, saying, "I publish the Banns of marriage between The Earl Ainsley—" An excited gasp echoed through the church. "—of Pevensey parish and Miss Summers—" This time it was a cry and a babble of voices. "—

of Pevensey parish. If any of you know cause or just impediment why these two persons should not be joined together in Holy matrimony, ye are to declare it. This is the first time of asking."

He delivered this in a tone of bland unconcern, but Nick turned, sending a faint smile across the aisle to Meg as the dull hiss of poorly suppressed gossip spread across the nave like liquid glass.

"What is this?" Isabelle asked, her form rigid, her lips hardly moving. "What have you done to him?"

Meg lifted her chin, content to maintain her posture of queenly silence as the service continued heedless of the bomb the vicar let off in the village…until she felt a jab between her shoulder blades and a note dropped into her lap.

Her head swiveled and her nearest neighbor jerked her head toward the Gracechurch pew, several rows and an aisle between them.

Beatrice stared back, seeming to point with her eyeballs and tight-pinched mouth.

Meg unfolded the note, penciled on what looked like the ripped flyleaf of a prayer book and read the terse word. "Answers."

Meg folded the note, biting hard into her cheek to keep the tears back as the voices swelled and eddied behind her. Isabelle sat by her, a malevolent presence hardly exorcised by the hymn singing. As the service ended, a young voice broke the silence. "Why do you say he *has* to marry her, Mama?"

Then Isabelle was blasting up the aisle while Nick met Meg at the end of her pew and offered his arm as though it were a commonplace event. The congregation didn't seem to know what to do. Meg knew what was due him in the way of congratulations, and marked every difference with pain. A ripple of curtseys brushed before them, uneager, curious, halting.

Once outside, no ring of ladies rushed to her side to ask her to tell them how it had all come about. But there were well wishes, nevertheless. Mr Thackery, holding the hands of two young girls, approached and said he'd seen it a mile off. The older Mrs Gracechurch offered her felicitations with as much interest as she ever spared those who were not her children. Esther leaned on her cane and bent to kiss Meg's cheek, her manner nothing less than delighted though there was a thread of wishing in her touch and an image of the Pevensey solicitor.

Henry approached with Beatrice, slapping his hat against Nick's arm. "I can't believe you've been nursing a hidden passion for our Meg," he exclaimed. "Nick, you dark horse, how long has it been?"

"Weeks," Meg said, choosing the time period that would excite the least curiosity.

"Ages," Nick answered. She pinched his hand but Nick's eyes twinkled. "From the time I taught her to fish, really. With Meg as my wife, I will never starve."

Meg shot him a withering look and then Beatrice tugged at Meg's arm. "Excuse us, my lord. I must offer my congratulations more privately," she said, leading Meg off to a quiet spot in the corner of the churchyard. They did not speak at once but leaned against the stone wall.

"More people are coming to him now," Meg said, looking back to the knot of villagers surrounding her fiancé. "Now that I'm not at his side, reminding people that it's me he's marrying."

"That sounds bitter."

"I don't mean it to be. I worried that my reputation would become his."

"You speak as though it's contagious."

"Isn't it?" Meg had reason to believe it was. Only, how far could Isabelle's ruin travel? To Nick? To their children? "If the only difference between him having a place of influence and importance in the community and not having one is that I stay in the background, then that's what I'll do."

"Background?" Beatrice's eyes crinkled and she laughed. "You?"

Meg grinned. Being circumspect was not her strong suit, but she could try.

The merry light faded from Beatrice's eyes and she gave a large sigh. "Don't turn the topic when I demand answers. Why are you doing this? You told me you cannot stand the man. That he's opinionated, arrogant, and reclusive. If you need a place to live instead of Blythe House, you should come to us."

"At the cottage?" Meg asked, raising a skeptical brow. "Three rooms upstairs and a little warren of rooms downstairs. It's a wonder you have space for Charlie."

"I could make my parents hire you as Penny's companion. The mischief-maker needs one, heaven knows. It's not too late."

Meg glanced back at Nick. “It’s far too late.”

“If this is about his illness, let us put it to rest at once. He didn’t ruin you in the sickroom. Mrs Miller will vouch for how sickly he was, and no one seriously thinks he was capable of a dalliance, no matter what the gossips say. There is no reason for this.”

“He asked me to marry him, Beatrice. I said yes.”

“Why does he want to marry you, Meg? To salvage your reputation? To somehow get back at Isabelle?”

“Stop there, Beatrice Gracechurch, before you go too far,” Meg said, her posture straightening.

Beatrice’s eyes were sad, but her tone was gentle. “A year ago you begged me not to make the mistake of marrying Lord Fox when he could not make me happy. What sort of friend would I be if I didn’t do the same?”

Meg turned. “You were in love with Henry, Beatrice. Marrying another man would have been monstrous.”

“And what will you do, Meg, when you find someone to love and you’re already tied up to some irascible beast?” Beatrice said.

“Beast?” Meg laughed.

Beatrice made an irritated noise. “He is not a beast. But please, please, *please* tell me he loves you.”

Meg bit her lip. “He does, after a fashion.”

“I hear how Henry and Lord Ainsley speak of you. It’s affectionate. You’re a little sister to them. But does he love you as a woman?”

The question stung. Meg shook her head.

“Then make me understand this.”

Meg crossed her arms, her eyes blinking against the sunlight as she scanned the churchyard. “There,” she pointed, lifting her finger toward a flowering bush growing under one of the narrow lancet windows. “That’s where Nick buried a stillborn kitten. I was seven—no more than that—and I’d come crying to him because it was dead. I didn’t think to go to anyone else. Not Henry, though he has a soft heart, and certainly not Fox, who would have laughed in my face. Nick crouched low, dried my eyes, and promised he’d give it a funeral service. And then I told him it had to be in the churchyard because you couldn’t go to heaven if you were buried anywhere else. He didn’t utter a word of protest but snuck in with a spade and," Meg smiled to remember it, "conducted the funeral service with all the solemnity of a priest."

"Meg." Beatrice's voice was gentle now, pitying.

"He's fiercely loyal and caring. And when he kisses me, I want to explode. Beatrice, I could never love anyone but Nick Ainsley." She wiped the back of her hand across both cheeks. "That's why I'm marrying him."

The relief of saying the words out loud broke inside Meg like a sunrise.

"But when you spoke of him—"

"You wouldn't believe how angry I was that he left for China and didn't take me with him." She choked back a cry and laughed, bracing her forearms on the stone wall. "It hurt so badly to lose him last time and I couldn't—" She sucked in a breath. "I was supposed to miss my sister and I didn't. I missed Nick." She patted her face to make certain it dried. "Anyway, he really is opinionated, arrogant, reclusive…" She spun her hand with a laugh, continuing the list.

Beatrice touched her arm and said, her voice meant to carry a little. "Meg is listing your virtues, my lord. I am almost convinced you deserve her."

Meg straightened and spun to see Nick closing the distance with long, sure strides. "I'm not such a fool as to believe I do."

The answer seemed to please her and, aside from the obscuring fog of reserve Beatrice always seemed to carry within her, Meg read tenderness and hope as Henry led her away.

Meg hoped too. Despite all that had been before, Meg would be Nick's wife. Surely they could build on that.

Nick turned back from Beatrice and Henry, clasping Meg's hands in both of his. "We've one more hurdle to cross."

She looked up in confusion.

"Your sister," he explained. "We have to face her."

They made the short trip to Blythe House together, travelling on the same bench seat that seemed too narrow not so long ago. She would have to accustom herself to the size of it, and of travelling at Nick's side when, irrespective of her magic, each touch seemed to throw sparks into dry kindling.

Halting before the front door, Meg looked up. "Are you certain we can't elope? We could board a ship to Scotland and be married in three days," she proposed, laughing. But the smile faded from her gaze as she met his blazing eyes. He came around to lift her down and she tipped her face to follow his.

"I am sorry, Nick. I'm too used to turning everything into a joke. I didn't mean to stir up old ghosts with talk of elopement. Forgive me?"

"It's nothing," he answered, swiftly dropping his hands from her waist, breaking her light grip on his forearms. When he turned to the house, his mouth was strained.

Isabelle was waiting for them in the drawing room.

"I heard a rumor," she began, pouring out a cup of tea, "on my way out of church. Mrs Greenley said how singular it was that you were allowed to nurse Lord Ainsley through his sickness, even with a standing engagement. Would you care to explain why I had no knowledge of this, Margaret? And why you would countenance such behavior, my lord?"

"I was deathly sick, half out of my mind, Isabelle," Nick answered, dropping the formality of her title. "In no position to wave off a willing nurse."

"You're not some penniless cottager, Nicholas," she shouted, her anger almost stirring the curtains. She dropped her voice. "You've money to hire an army of servants if you wish and you certainly don't have to offer marriage to the girl." Her head swung around. "You have certainly *not* been ruined, Margaret."

"I haven't?" Meg replied, amusement lacing her words. "Having people stumble over themselves to inform me that I'm not ruined is quite a new sensation." She pulled at the strings of her bonnet and pulled it off, settling into a chair. "Is that what comes of becoming a countess, Isabelle?"

"I find that remark in vulgar taste, Margaret."

"I find bellowing like a fishwife when you don't get your way to be in vulgar taste."

Nick stood behind Meg and laid a hand on her shoulder, looking square at Isabelle. "You seem to think that I proposed because I had done Meg some injury. That this is a matter of honor."

"Isn't it?"

Meg was engaged to Nick, secure in the fact that their claim on one another had been proclaimed in public for all to hear. But the sound of that question, and the sight of Isabelle, magnificent in her rage, sent a rivulet of apprehension coiling down Meg's spine. Isabelle was not beaten yet.

"It's simple, really. I asked Meg to become my wife because I love her."

Meg's heart was in her throat and she swallowed hard, turning hot and cold. How it must have cost Nick to say those words to Isabelle.

"Simple?" repeated Isabelle, her voice sweet like poison. "This is not simple. Simple things don't require secrecy. Simple things don't set off a firestorm of speculation and gossip." Isabelle rose, smoothing dark skirts against slim hips. She neared and Nick stepped back. A faint smile played on her lips and her brow lifted. "It's unlike you, Nicholas, to fail in your manners. You didn't even ask for my blessing. See how my little sister has guided you already? She'll have you believing her fairy stories soon. But then you've always had such stirring faith in the people you love."

Nick's mouth set and Meg inched closer, not touching him but standing close. "Thank you for your kind wishes, Isabelle. You've taken the news so well."

Isabelle didn't waste her smiles on Meg. She left the room then and Meg could swear that the swish of her skirts flicking against the doorjamb echoed the undulating scratch of a viper wending its way.

Meg glanced up at Nick, a question in her eyes. "I'm fine," he reassured her, sucking in a deep breath. "Only the pushing was louder." He wrapped his arms around her waist, drawing her into an embrace. No skin touched but the cords of his frame seemed to loosen. "It's better now."

Chapter Twenty-five

"What are you writing?" asked Nick, throwing away a stalk of grass. He lay down by Meg's feet so that the billow of his sleeve touched her skirts and settled his battered straw hat over his face.

Since he could not see her looking at him, she paused her pencil and took him in. Over the past week, he had lost the tight, spare look of ill health, returning to the kind of potent wholeness that kept her continually on guard. Now, they were in the bottom of the kitchen garden, hidden by a row of berry bushes where Isabelle might not spy.

"Meg?" he prompted, his voice muffled by the hat.

"Thanks to your help in reestablishing my professional connections, I plan to send my publisher a column about being engaged. Sir Frederick Magpie is expressing thoughts about the process."

Nick gave a rumble of laughter. "Have him write that banns take much too long."

"Oh no. He would take the line that the time should be doubled, trebled, even." She laughed. "We could be married by common license to speed up the process, if you wish," she reminded him. "If you think I'm worth the expense of a few shillings."

He slapped a blind hand out, whacking her slipper. "I don't want to look like we're in any rush. As though I *had* to marry you."

She had her mouth open to ask him why. Isabelle had made no fresh attacks in the last several days, but she was a menace nonetheless. Was Nick unsure?

"Anyway, I'm quite busy right now."

"Oh?"

"Yes. I've been rooting out smugglers. I found a few casks buried near the swamps and dashed them to pieces. I left the shattered remains in a conspicuous place. We'll hope that sends a message that there is no safe passage on Abbey lands."

She nudged him with her foot. "That'll only push them to Blythe House land, Nick, or farther up the coast."

"I've set a watch for you too."

"I worry for the families of those men." She sighed, thinking of poor Mrs Fletcher.

"What would you have me do? My tenants bring me reports of trampled crops and stolen sheep. Free traders pass within yards of respectable homes and some have been threatened to hold their tongues. This isn't only about local lads having a bit of a lark anymore. There are whispers that larger sums of money from London are backing professional gangs."

"Whispers? Tell me you haven't been talking to the magistrate."

"Who else? Meg, it cannot go on like this. Not every trader is some blokey John Bull. There are enormous sums of money attached to this enterprise, and when that is the case, my people will be in danger."

"Nick, he'll call in the revenue officers."

"You're worried about those boys," he said with a faint question.

"We grew up together."

"The magistrate tells me that officers can't possibly come for several weeks. I have no wish to catch anyone in the act," he said, winding a piece of red ribbon around his fingers. "There will be time enough to warn them, and if they are wise, they will listen."

"Wise." Meg snorted. This was the time to tell him about Sam, but the thought of what he would do with the information worried her. He'd shown no mercy toward Sam at all.

Her eyes narrowed. "That's my ribbon, Nick. You've yet to return it."

The fingers stopped and he folded it over, tucking it into his waistcoat pocket. "We pledged a troth. I will return it when you come back to the Abbey."

His words sank in her chest and set her heart to beating. When would that be?

"I hope you plan to continue writing after we are married," he said. "We could use the money."

She laughed and threw a clump of grass at him.

"I had Brooks bring me every copy of the *The London Observer* he could find," he said. "Twenty-three articles. Have I read them all?"

Meg flushed. Aside from Beatrice and her sister, no one else knew she was Sir Frederick. No one else would read them knowing what lay beyond the silly facade. "More or less. My publisher doesn't require them weekly. He isn't a demon."

"What is he, then?" Nick's voice was as lazy and low as a fat bumblebee circling a bud.

Her brow lifted and a wicked light came into her eyes. "A handsome young devil who kissed me soundly the first time I walked into his office."

Nick jerked the hat off his face, a perfect scowl of irritation on his features, and Meg chortled with laughter. "I'm joking. I wrote a letter to the editor as Sir Frederick Magpie and he traced it back to Aunt Olympia's house, asking if I ever got mad at other things, not only ladies being hidden out of sight at Parliament like inmates of a seraglio."

Nick's grin was lazy. "I liked that one. Sir Frederick claimed it would be more efficient to dispense pierced fans for women to hold in front of their faces at all times." And then, "You were working out your frustrations?"

Meg nodded. "I wanted to scream so often. But it was so much more bearable when I could give Sir Frederick his head."

Nick rolled over, hitching himself onto one elbow. "You weren't merely frustrated." His bright hazel eyes bored into hers. "I read the one about the bushes, Meg."

Meg's insides settled hard into the base of her abdomen and her breathing caught and dragged like her skin and hair on those sharp hedges in Aunt Olympia's garden. She looked anywhere but at him.

"The one you titled *A True Sport*." He plucked another stalk of grass.

Meg gathered up her writing materials and shook out her shawl. "It's time I got back to Jolly. Isabelle has been finding fault with every little thing these days." What idea did Nick have of ruin? The same as everyone else. That a woman was used up and broken the moment a whiff of scandal clung to her skirts. The moment she was pressed into an unforgiving hedge… It wasn't the definition Meg had. Thankfully, Isabelle's adventure had taught her to look more deeply at the word. But why should Nick?

He put a hand on her boot, not restraining her in any way but stilling her, his face as stern as it had been when he first returned home.

"I've been meaning to say something," he began, his eyes shifting away from her, only to be dragged back like a truant. Her spirit dimmed. He was going to ask her how far Lord Sowell got, and if she got away at all.

"That day on the porch, when I punched Sam in the nose—"

Meg's cheeks flushed. "We both said a lot of things, Nick."

He held up a hand. "True. But what I said was unconscionable, thinking I knew better." He swallowed. "I'm sorry, Meg."

Meg's jaw felt as though it had fused shut.

His eyes trained on hers. "Forgive me?"

"Yes."

"Don't you want to ring a peal over my head?" Nick asked.

"I remember slapping you across the face," she answered. "And I still think you deserved it."

Nick nodded, rolling to his back, the colors of his waistcoat contending with the flowers in the garden.

"Why do you wear such eye-melting waistcoats?" she asked, keen to relieve her curiosity on one point even if there were so many things they could not say to one another. "They are not at all fashionable."

"Are they not?" he asked, lifting a lazy eyelid. She pushed him with her toe until he would answer her seriously. "I do know they are not quite the thing, but I hope I have the good sense to recognize what I want when I see it without regard to what anyone else may say."

He tipped his head back to glance at her. "Good?"

She nodded.

"Good. Now it's my turn to get an answer out of you." She shifted slightly as he continued. "Why don't you like horses?"

"I like Puck."

"You tolerate Puck far better than any other horse. Well?"

Meg shifted on her seat. "It's going to sound silly."

"Only silly?" He reached above his shoulder and tugged her slipper off, running a tickling finger up the arch of her stockinged foot.

"Peace," she gasped, pulling her foot to the safety of her petticoats. "Peace. I'll tell you. When I touch them, I can read horse thoughts."

"Can you really?" he said, sitting up. "You can read what Puck is thinking?"

"Puck and every hack I ever tried to ride. It's not the same as reading people—it's far more blurry and diffuse—but they do not respect my authority. It's insulting."

"Puck doesn't respect you?" He grinned and she threw another clump of grass at him.

"If you can't even believe me, we'll make a miserable match."

"No we won't," came his soft, certain reply. Then he stood, brushing out his trousers. "If you're worried about Isabelle plaguing Jolly, send her to the Abbey. She'll come to us eventually, I'm sure. Brooks is walking around like a man smelling of April and May."

Meg laughed as she gained her feet. "She would not leave me now. Time enough when we wed. You need to get back to your scything, my lord. Only a lazy man takes time during a harvest for a nap."

"There's always time for a little light wooing, Meg," he said, giving her a wink as he stepped past her. She watched him stride away far longer than she ought to.

"Hot out there?" Jolly asked when Meg returned to the kitchen. She put a hand up to her flushed cheeks. Nick's light wooing had her flushing, and her heart pounded away in her breast. What was she to do when Nick went to the trouble of conducting a little heavy wooing?

What was her position to be at all? She had intended on being his savior. And friend. And she would nurse her love for him like a little bird in a cage, feeding it morsels of stale, day-old bread and wondering when it would finally die so that she could reclaim her sanity. But being Nick's wife promised to be better than that.

She could sense the first shoots of hope springing from the ground. He would be loyal to her—the false declaration of his love for her in front of Isabelle had proved that. And there was a thread of pleasure in one another's company that seemed promising.

A warm flush dusted her skin as she thought about what it was like to be with him. Not all friendliness and comfort. Hadn't she hoped, even a little as she baited him, that he would tumble her back into the grass and kiss her soundly? Hadn't there been something in his eyes that promised he might? The thought sent hope winging from her hands no matter how she tried to restrain it.

"Jolly," Meg called. "You've been married."

"Yes, I was," she answered, shaping dough into large round loaves to feed the laborers during harvest. "And I wasn't. It wasn't much of a marriage. Is it time we have a discussion on what you might expect?"

The way she picked her words, deliberately vague, had Meg's cheeks growing warmer and she found herself shaking her head before the words were out. "No, Jolly. It is not. But…but I did have a question."

"What's that?"

"How long before things settle down?" Meg pinched off a knot of dough and formed it into a tiny ball. "How long before you didn't…you weren't…" Meg pressed the dough into a flat disk. "How long before you were good friends?"

Jolly smiled but answered in perfect innocence. "You should always be good friends, Miss Margaret."

"No, I mean," Meg began, her voice low and desperate. "How long before you can go back to being a sensible woman without—" Her hands fluttered around her stomach.

Jolly laughed. "How can I answer? My Tom preferred curling up in his bottle of brandy, and I was too busy wishing he was some other kind of man."

Meg did not wish Nick were anything other than exactly what he was.

"There are other ways of going about it," Jolly continued.

Meg cocked her head. "Does that mean Mr Brooks will be rewarded with your fair hand at last?"

Jolly laughed. "Perhaps. I hardly know my own mind."

"I can help you there," Meg offered.

Jolly held her palm out with bits of dough clinging to the skin. "What can you tell me?"

Meg ran two thumbs along the creases in Jolly's hand, feeling the calluses of hard use. She was a housekeeper now, but not too high and mighty to help the cook and maids at their work.

"I see an apple tree, so laden with fruit that the boughs sweep the ground. The tending is over. The harvest is about to begin. Acres of apples will be dropped in baskets and carried in overflowing aprons."

Jolly gave her a curious look but said nothing.

Meg halted there, allowing herself to go no farther into Jolly's mind. Standing on the edge was enough to see how terribly she wanted Brooks and the ordering of the Abbey and Meg to go along with it. How close it was.

She felt herself become saturated with Jolly's love and hope, and felt the light pouring from every fiber of her being. This was the time to try her hand at pushing. She gripped Jolly's palm.

Hand Meg a cup.

It was a small request. Meg did not want to disorder anything by asking Jolly for more.

Jolly made no move.

Hand Meg a cup.

Meg gathered all the warmth of their bond, all the love that intermingled them and…

"I best be getting back to work," Jolly said, patting a soft knuckle to Meg's cheek. She went back to the dough, and Meg scooped up her own papers, making her way up the stairs with a furrowed brow. It wasn't an overabundance of will that would allow her to push or else Grandfather would have had his wish and been spared the fear of death. And it wasn't love. She loved Jolly as much as she loved anyone. So what was it?

She plopped the papers on her desk and put her feet up on the top of Grandmother's trunk, chewing on the end of her pencil.

Chapter Twenty-six

Mrs Fletcher was the first domino to fall. When the banns were read the second time, she approached Meg and Nick after the service with a tight little bob and an invitation to take tea with her.

"Samuel has spoken so highly of you, Miss Summers," she added, earning Nick's hard frown.

"Next week, perhaps," Meg replied.

"I told you the village would come around," Nick said, giving her hand a light squeeze.

Meg, privy to Mrs Fletcher's private thoughts, snorted. The woman was desperate for help and would ruthlessly seek it in any quarter, no matter what.

"She has not quite come around." Meg re-tied the bow under her chin. "She hardly looked at me as she said it."

"But you'll go?" he asked, handing her up into his carriage. "Perhaps you'll see young Mr Fletcher."

He gave her a searching look, but she made no answer and they rode in silence as Meg turned over the gleanings from Mrs Fletcher's mind. His mother feared Sam would be caught free-trading. He was going out tonight, Mrs Fletcher was sure of it. Anxiety swept through her at the thought. But the earl and his lady would be powerful allies in the event her son was swept up in a raid.

"Are you quite sure I can't interest you in a Sunday drive?" Nick asked, slowing near the gates of Blythe House. His smile tucked and there was a comically lecherous gleam in his eyes. "The road goes on and on. We could—"

"No." Meg cut him off with a sharp exclamation, extinguishing his merry look.

She wished to coax it back, but it was all she could do this week to meet him as a friend in the garden when he came in from the fields, hair damp from the quick wetting. Shirt dry. Even imagining the process whereby that was achieved made her want to wave her fan.

She plied it now, giving his stern profile a glance. Men were strange creatures. How could he wish for a dalliance when his feelings for Isabelle had not died? The mere thought of being touched by any other man made her skin crawl. The thought of any woman but her touching him made her unusually murderous.

He pulled up before the door of Blythe House, aiming a hard, watchful eye at the windows. "I don't like to send you away from me like this."

"Nonsense," she reassured him, tucking away her fan. "It's my home."

His mouth thinned into a line she thought might signify disappointment, but his only answer was to trace the back of his gloved hand softly along her jaw. "Be safe, Meg."

She alighted from the carriage before he could make a move to hand her down and she waved him away, turning to walk into the house. He didn't understand that she was far safer than he was. Isabelle had passed the point of shouting, and though they occupied the same space, it never seemed to be at the same time.

A good thing it was, too. Meg could not count on her talents as an actress to carry her through eating and conversing with a woman she suspected of carving her inheritance from Grandfather's life. Shortening it. Snuffing it out.

In the meantime, the problem of Mrs Fletcher could occupy her. Hardly pausing to deposit her hat and prayer book on her bed, Meg made her way to the attic, finding one of Grandfather's trunks and bracing herself against the memories as she opened the lid. She quickly drew out a linen shirt and trousers, holding them up to her chest, checking the fit. She kicked out both feet, noting several inches of striped trousers pooling on the ground, and bundled them up, fishing in the trunk until she discovered a pair of braces. She had resolved to wear her oldest pair of slippers when she found a smallish pair of shoes, silver buckled and dull black, which might do. Then, she crept down the attic stairs with her treasure, making her list. Hat. Scarf. These would enable her to complete her ensemble.

After sawing off seven inches of material, she laid the clothes on the bed and waited in her room while the sun set and a weak moon rose, casting faint shadows on the lawn. She waited still longer as the glow from the kitchen candles dimmed. All was silent.

Meg drew off her dress and petticoat, electing to keep her chemise, stays, and stockings. Picking up the shirt, she billowed it in her hands for a moment, sorting out the armholes, but sank onto the bed, pressing the fabric to her nose. The scent of sweet-smelling tobacco that had always clung to Grandfather's clothes clung to this shirt and she inhaled it.

"You'll come along with me, then?" she asked the thin air. "I'll feel better if you do."

She dropped it over her head and began doing up the buttons at the neck. The trousers were next and if they didn't make her look like a pirate, she didn't know what would. One leg hung longer than the other and the braces outlined her bosom more than she liked, but they would keep the trousers from sliding off.

A low knot of dark hair was covered with a scarf and a plain straw hat, "borrowed" from the garden shed and drooping low over one eye. She stuck her tongue out at her reflection. Meg Summers made a very ugly boy.

There was little light to guide her way and she picked over the ground by memory

more than sight and prayed now that she was out here that she would not be a nuisance. Her aims were clear: watch for officers. Collect information about the smuggling operation. Approach Sam later. She would not be in any danger if she were cunning and cautious.

Nearing the village, she fumbled over a gnarly tree root in time to see Samuel Fletcher creep from his house. She caught herself, but her hands were scraped. Stifling a cry, she pressed them under her arms to stem the blood flowing from, hopefully, tiny abrasions. The dashed trousers were supposed to protect her from these things.

She followed his dark form for more than a mile east along the coast road in the direction of the Abbey.

"Are you worth it?" she whispered at his back as she watched him slant toward the ocean. Deep shadows hid her now as she scurried along behind a hedgerow and reminded herself why she was here. Sam was precious to his mother and those emotions had roused Meg's own tender heart. It would be far easier to ignore the dark pit of fear and anxiety in Mrs Fletcher's breast—to feed her own animosity and judgment—but Meg could not.

Sam disappeared down a pony track, which led down to a thumbnail beach, and Meg chewed a knuckle as she decided what to do. There would be nowhere to hide once she started onto the track. And once she gained the beach, there would be nowhere to run. As much as she wished to help Mrs Fletcher, she did not wish to risk her life.

"Have some sense, Meg," she whispered, echoing what she was sure would be Nick's admonition. So she rolled under a bush and waited, listening to the distant sigh of waves washing up the rocky beach, and the scuttle of night creatures in the grass. She was yawning into her fist when they came up again.

"How long are we going to keep doing this?"

"Scared, Sam?" The voice belonged to Jim Greenley.

She picked out the gentle snuffling and clomping of small ponies coming up the track.

"Of transportation I am." Meg slowed her breathing and counted the horses that came up the track. *Two. Three.* "You're not?"

"The money's good."

"No good if we're caught."

Four. Five.

"We won't be if you keep your mouth shut."

Six. How many more could there be?

"We're right under his Lordship's nose and we're running out of places to hide the cargo, Jim. Our network was never meant to handle anything this big. We'll get picked up or run afoul of one of the professional gangs and then we'd be in for a fight."

"Get one thing clear, Sam. We *are* a professional gang."

"Who? You and me and those men already rowing away?"

"Our tidy operation came to the attention of an investor this summer. We picked up a patron. In the next week or two, we've plans to expand."

"What?" Sam exclaimed. "When were you going to share that information?"

"When I could trust you to keep your gob shut," Jim spat. "Spouting off every time you get a pint in you. If you keep your head down, the patron says there's a way around his lordship discovering us. We'll recruit more hands and—"

"More?" Despite his great size, Sam's voice sounded lost. "I was meant to be a surgeon, Jim. My father planned for me to heal people, not drag them into danger. Lord, why did I let you talk me into this?"

Seven. Eight.

Jim ignored him. "You'll cut on the far side of Abbey land before entering the woods. I'll go along the west track and meet you at the cottage," Jim said. "Let's hope you won't pick up another flattened nose when you skirt near Blythe House."

The silence that followed was so long that Meg swore she could hear Sam's face redden in the darkness.

"What?" Jim laughed, bawdy. "A gentleman never tells?"

"Leave off, Jim. I've nothing to be proud of there."

In the end four ponies went one way, four more went the other. Meg followed Sam. She could get him alone, talk to him—

Meg shivered. No. Not in the dark all alone. Sam might be as she had said—a clumsy boy with more enthusiasm than sense—but he wasn't Nick. She would follow closely and see what good she could do. Crouching low, she cut inland, racing across an open meadow when her too-large boot hit an obstacle and she went flying.

"Oof," was her only exclamation and she squeaked when a low, familiar voice gave a harsh whisper.

"What in the name of heaven?"

Nick.

Weak moonlight filtered through scudding clouds, but he was no more than a dark shadow looming above her.

She scrambled like a mouse from a cat but, after a short fight, he grabbed out and caught her thin arms, pressing her back into the tall grass. A booted leg trapped her own. "You're one of those runners?" he asked, his shape eclipsing the sky.

Blast. Meg clamped her lips shut and prayed no betraying sound would escape her. She tried to wriggle her arms free, but his hands were like twin vises and the movement seemed to spark off some anger.

"You don't know what you're involved in," he said, his voice an intense growl. "You're just a boy but you don't have to be stupid. Come around the Abbey tomorrow and I'll set you to work at a fair wage. But go home, lad. This game could get you killed."

Tears of confusion pooled in the corners of her eyes. Where was the Nick who had sworn to fight for his land? Where was the man who had been implacable, threatening to send the magistrate after them? Now he offered work and warnings.

Still, he waited in the dark to catch these men. Perhaps his mercy extended to her because he thought her a mere lad.

His hands eased and she saw her escape, but along came the gentle clopping of ponies. He pushed his weight into hers and settled a large hand over her mouth.

Hush.

The thought was too simple to hold her attention and it was soon claimed by his scent—the sweet smell of ripe hay, and the lemon of his soap. And that hand, too rough and calloused for a gentleman, earned in working the land with his tenants, pressed against her lips. His length, heavy and warm, pinned her down while a shrinking sliver of her mind preached against the sins of becoming an overwrought, excitable female.

Then she felt him tense and one word, wrapped around with violent intent entered her mind.

Fletcher.

He would spring away in a moment, and she bit at his finger shouting, “Sam, run.”

A rustle of movement followed and then, suddenly, the sound of ponies was swallowed up in the woods. Nick rolled from her and said in a rough, furious voice, “He’s safe from me. Go home, Meg.”

***

Nick sat back in the grass, his arms resting atop his bent knees and the bowl of heaven turning above. He breathed heavily and had no thought of the runners keeping him from his warm bed. He pressed the palm of his right hand to his mouth where it had lain against Meg’s seeking any of the warmth she had left behind.

She hadn’t said a word but her breath had hitched and he seemed to recognize that catch, nosing for clues and finding them in the smell of her hair and the delicate lines of her jaw under his hand. This couldn’t be anyone but Meg. His Meg.

And then she shouted for Sam.

That had prevented him from hauling her up onto her feet and then on to the Abbey, discovering what in the blazes she was thinking to be scampering over the countryside in the middle of the night when no body or soul meant any good.

He thought he'd been winning her over, approaching her as gently as a spooked cat. The engagement was a dashed inconvenience, casting a pall over his attempts to woo her. But there was friendship between them even if her response to his invitations was in turns amused and skittish.

He thought he'd managed, sometimes, to pierce that armor she wore at all times. But he hadn't done it at all. It wasn't for him that she'd left her bed, donned a ridiculous costume, and went skulking through the grass. It was for Samuel Fletcher.

The thought was hard and sharp in his chest, hollowing it out like a spade turning over fresh earth.

Nick swiped the grass, found his coat and before long he was striding off toward Blythe House, trafficking all but forgotten. He would see her safely home whether she wished it or not.

Chapter Twenty-seven

Meg pushed through the door of Greenley's shop and Sam Fletcher lifted his head, his tired eyes widening. He almost disappeared in the dim corners of the shop, but she called out, as brazen as anything, "Sam," so that there was nothing for him but to come back.

"Miss Summers," he said, joining her on the street. He flicked the brim of his hat though his eyes darted left and right, possibly looking for Nick Ainsley to blast him in the nose again. She turned and led him up the street, in sight of half the village, tucking her arm in his as though they had agreed on an afternoon stroll.

"I need to apologize," he began, trailing off in the face of her green eyes. "For…for…"

"Your advances," she finished baldly.

"Yes. I thought you wanted—"

"I didn't want," she said, nodding placidly to a passerby.

He reddened like an apple as her gaze blazed at him.

He swallowed hard, the shame of it crisping every surface of skin. "I deserved this," he said, indicating his face, no longer black and blue, but faintly green, and possessed of a slight jog in the once straight ridge.

"It is no shame to look like a rogue as long as one behaves like a gentleman."

"I hope to earn the name."

"Excellent," she said, snapping open a parasol. "Now then, we have other matters to discuss."

"We have?"

"You were almost caught last night."

"I…I…"

"How long have we known one another, Sam? Thirteen years? You were in short pants when I came to live with my grandfather." She did not scruple to use her sister's name. "I don't think I need to tell you that if you are found crossing Blythe House land, Lady

Ainsley will bring the full weight of the law down on your head. She protects what is hers. You were trailed by a young woman last night, Sam. How much easier would it be for a trained officer to follow you?"

"I—"

"Lord Ainsley would not scruple to clap the lot of you in irons," she said, far less certain of that than she once was.

They came to the end of town where the shops and cottages strung out in a ragged line, and Meg peeked around her parasol at the sound of a passing horse, her eyes met and held by Nick.

A shiver went through her. He had known it was her in the grass last night, but he hadn't bellowed at her, then marched her off home to bellow at her some more. But his hazel eyes held an unaccustomed chill as he nodded his greeting and her cheeks flamed.

Lord, she hoped Mrs Fletcher proved to be worth it.

Sam, elbows perched against a gate, saw nothing of this. "There's nothing I can do. I'm caught tight." He ground his palms together as though in agony. "I didn't mean to get in so deep, but I was furious when my father died—out in the middle of a storm helping some fool who didn't deserve it. After, I couldn't take anything to do with the surgery."

"Could you now?"

"I think so," he began, uncertainty lining his brow. "But now that I'm in this business, I can't see a way out."

"Why not?" she asked, her mind halfway down the village street, trotting after Puck and shouting excuses at Nick's back.

"The—the other man—" he began, and it was all she could do not to cast her eyes heavenward. Bless his heart for trying to protect his confederate, but Jim Greenley was as obvious as the goods for sale in his mother's shop. "—is in it up to his neck. I can't leave him on his own."

Meg touched the sleeve of his coat and looked up into his eyes. "You must persuade him. Truly, Mr Fletcher," she said, "merest chance kept you from being brought before a magistrate this morning. I repeat my promise to give you any aid you stand in need of."

"Why?" he asked. "No one here has ever treated you nice at all."

She lifted a careless shoulder. "Everyone knows I'm an adventuress."

***

Nick rode out that morning with no destination in mind, his only purpose to outrun the wish to break the Fletcher boy's nose again. He found himself admitted into the small parlor at Hawthorne Cottage, a room too cramped and small to fit him properly.

Mrs Gracechurch found him there, crushing his hat.

"Do not let me keep you from being comfortable," he said, loath to sit as she stood, swaying with her burden.

She shook her head and laughed. "He knows when I sit. The more comfortable I am, the more strenuously he objects. The nursery maid will collect him soon."

The door opened then and they both expected the maid, but it was Henry, bringing in the sunshine. He did not waste his greeting on Nick but went to his wife, curving an arm about her waist and planting a kiss on her temple. "Sleeping?"

"Finally," she breathed, sharing a look with him that made Nick glance away.

The nursery maid did come then, and the fragile bundle was passed from arms to arms like a charge of gunpowder as the tea things were brought in.

Plain English blends, he noted, taking his without sugar.

"What brings you?" Henry asked, stretching his arm along the back of the sofa behind his wife.

"Meg—Miss Summers," he said, and watched as Mrs Gracechurch's hand stilled.

"What's the little baggage done now?" Henry enquired, his smile not taking Nick's grave manner seriously.

It was this that made the truth burst from Nick's mouth, incautious of his audience. "The little baggage is running a smuggling gang."

"Smuggling?" Henry's brows arched. "Come, Nick. You can't possibly—"

"Surely not," Mrs Gracechurch exclaimed, snapping her teacup down.

Blast. If he had any hope of reforming her, this good matron was exactly the sort Meg must impress with her respectability. And here he was, blackening her character with outrageous accusations he himself did not quite believe.

"I—I—" he stumbled.

"She is more than capable of it, of course," Mrs Gracechurch said, surprising him with her firm acceptance. He turned a look on Henry. *See?*

Mrs Gracechurch continued. "But Meg doesn't court danger without reason. Now, if you told me she was helping a friend, then I would believe you. Meg would put herself through any trouble for those she cares for. She does not seem to calculate costs in the same way as others do," she said, her voice soft but firm.

Are you sure?" Henry asked, and Nick's thoughts shifted to the memory of Meg—certainly Meg—stretched on the grass beneath him in the darkness of a summer night.

"Yes," he said, hearing the roughness in his voice. He cleared his throat. "I found her acting as lookout for Sam Fletcher last night. I don't need to tell you the risks."

Henry nodded. "The taxes are so high and the custom houses so corrupt that the smugglers are almost heroes in the village. And the money is good if you are clever enough to elude the revenue men."

"It's not as simple as that," his wife said. "In Parliament there is talk of gold being smuggled across the Channel to support the French government. They're cracking down now, and the risks… Meg could be exposing herself to imprisonment, transportation…"

"Exactly, ma'am."

"Beatrice. Please."

"And you must call me Nick." They nodded in accord.

"Now then, there must be some simple explanation for why she is involved with smuggling."

"Money?" Lord, Nick hoped it was money. "She has precious little after her Grandfather died. And she wants to leave her sister's home."

"We offered her a place after we found out about the will, but Hawthorne Cottage has little room and your mama," she said, turning her head to give Henry a glance, "doesn't say it, but I think she worries about Esther's chances if Meg came to stay."

"Esther's chances. Esther says she is quite happy to remain as she is, my love," he said, kissing her brow. Nick laughed to see Beatrice's disbelieving expression.

"At my next dinner party, I'm going to accidentally lock her and Jacob Thackery in a broom closet until they sort themselves out."

Henry choked on a laugh. “In any event, Meg refused to consider removing to our home.”

“Could Meg be doing this for a man?” Nick asked, his face grim.

“She’s a newly engaged woman.” Beatrice’s eyes widened with a kind of suspect innocence. “You are uncertain of her regard?”

Henry chuckled. “Meg doesn’t leave anyone uncertain about her feelings. I’m sure she loves Nick very much…”

Nick felt a spreading glow of comfort in the words only to have it ooze out in the next moment.

“…after a fashion. But we can’t blame her if she’s restless.”

“We can’t?” Beatrice said, snatching the words from Nick’s mouth.

“No.” Henry’s eyes danced and Nick could swear there was something knowing and wicked in his look. “He only offered her a place at the Abbey out of an overabundance of friendly concern. What woman would be excited over the prospect of that? Don’t you agree, Nick?”

Nick had never wanted to pummel Henry so roundly.

Beatrice sat back, right into the crook of Henry’s arm, and tapped the bowl of her teacup in contemplation. He noticed the number of white scars wrapping her wrists, the marks telling a mute story of her ordeal last year. This woman wouldn’t shrink from a challenge.

“We could find her employment,” she said. “What about Godmama?”

“Does Lady Sherbourne need a companion?” Henry asked, yawning hugely. “Meg is not exactly restful.”

Beatrice nudged him and Henry, laughing, sent Nick a look that meant, “Do you see how I suffer?” followed by a wink to his wife.

“She’s a lovely, high-spirited woman,” she insisted. “I’ll dash off a letter to Lady Sherbourne, who will offer Meg some employment so that she may leave her sister’s house and get out of the engagement.”

“What? No.” This was not what Nick wished.

“Isn’t that the solution?” Beatrice asked.

Henry was half asleep, his face almost buried in his wife’s hair, but Beatrice looked at Nick sharply, and he wondered at himself—at that sudden need to conceal his thoughts.

She went on, “The engagement has clouded things, has it not?” and he felt exposed, as though she saw it all.

“Perhaps,” he conceded. Like a fool he had taken a shortcut, grasping Meg’s offer to help him with Isabelle with both hands. It had seemed simple then, to rush her off to be married when circumstances had presented him with the opportunity. She would be glad of it later, he told himself. She would learn to love him.

But now, instead of the reckless hope that had fired him at the first, he could not stave off a growing sense of guilt. Meg had only agreed to the engagement because of his weakness around Isabelle, and instead of finding other ways to escape her grasp, he had seized on the option that abused Meg’s soft heart.

Henry was gently snoring now and Beatrice said, her voice low, “You should ask her what she wants, my lord. The answer might surprise you.”

“Breaking the engagement will leave her worse off than she was before. Cast off from an earl,” he said, not yet willing to yield.

“Ask her.”

Chapter Twenty-eight

Nick meant to do exactly that. He worked all the next morning, cutting hay with his tenants under the blazing sun as his mind composed and discarded the words he would use as though they were tall stalks of wheat and his love for Meg a razor-sharp blade.

At midday, while the men lay in the shade of the spreading oaks to eat and smoke, he knew he could not put it off any longer and crossed the stubby fields, stopping by the stream to wash the dirt and sweat away. Then through the formal gardens and into the kitchen gardens, where he hardly dared hope she would be waiting.

She was. Meg was arrayed in the shade of the berry canes with a tidy kit of fishing lures spread open on her lap. Her scissors were nearby as were bits of fluff and feathers she was fashioning into a new fly. Bees were industrially weaving through the late summer lavender bloom. A curl of hair kept blowing against her cheek, brushed back with a hasty hand.

"Meg." His mouth was open to form the words that might set her from him forever. He would offer her a way out and could not believe she wouldn't take it.

She looked up, shading her eyes with her hand against the sun, hiding all but her full lower lip.

He dropped to his knees.

"There you are," Isabelle exclaimed, and Nick had to prevent himself from scrambling backward from her.

Isabelle glanced around. "How cunning of you to hide yourselves away here. Jolly kept telling me you were in the garden and I must have travelled the gravel walk for miles before it dawned on me that you two were not the sort to seek out romantic vistas. It's refreshing to find a couple so at home with one another that they don't mind being in sight of the compost heap."

"What did you wish to say, Isabelle?" Meg asked, winding a thread around a bit of woolen fluff with insulting precision. She never even looked at her sister.

"Only this. I have been unfair to you both. Your engagement was a surprise, I admit it, and I have behaved like a spoiled child."

Nick cocked his head, not in a sense of wonder, but in wariness. Isabelle had taught him that she was at her most dangerous when she employed honesty.

"The village must be abuzz in speculation and I have only added to it by failing to add my approbation of the match."

"You have approbation to give?" Meg asked, setting the fly on her black skirts.

"Certainly. My only sister marrying my…my…"

"Nephew?" Nick supplied, unable to resist the jibe.

"Nearest neighbor," Isabelle finished. "What would please me more?"

Nick and Meg shared a laughing look that seemed to catch them both off guard. Hasty glances slid away and he felt an empty jolt in his belly.

"So," Isabelle said, beginning afresh. "In that spirit, I would like to throw a party for you. An engagement party."

"Is that necessary? We thought to do the whole thing quietly," Meg said.

"If I've learned one thing as Lady Ainsley, it's that you can see anything through if you don't skulk around. So it's to be on Friday of this week."

"On my birthday?" Meg asked.

"Any later and you'll be wed. Your final banns will be read on Sunday. Speaking of which, I've heard nothing about the date."

"We've not settled on anything yet," Nick said while looking at Meg, gauging her reaction.

Meg offered, "There will be no moon on Friday. It would be terrible to ask our neighbors to travel on such a night."

"It's the only night I could possibly do," Isabelle replied, swirling away in a storm of petticoats.

Meg picked up the work again, turning the hook this way and that in the manner of a sailor with his cutlass. He tugged on a trailing line, pulling the fly to her lap.

"We have to talk."

Meg did not meet his eyes. "Yes, I know. I'm suspicious of Isabelle too. I don't know what she's planning."

"Not about that, Meg. I—" he began, knowing that his next words would secure his future happiness or no. "There are other ways to keep me safe. We don't *have* to marry."

She flinched. "I'm wedding you to keep you safe. Now you don't think she's dangerous?" she asked, her voice rising. Meg scrambled to her feet and he followed.

"That's not what I said. It was an agreement that made sense at one time, but you'll be able to earn an independence soon and—"

"I never agreed to marry you because I was looking to be saved, and I certainly never told you we had to marry. That was your idea. I supplied you with choices and you took the most idiotic one," she snapped.

He felt a mounting fury. "You're the one who told everyone we were engaged."

Meg sucked her lip in and folded away her work. "We wouldn't be in this mess if you could stay away from my sister."

The guilt of it cascaded through him and he reached for her hand. At the point of contact he felt himself jerked into a will-breaking stampede, sucking him under and burying him beneath whatever it was Meg Summers wanted.

Shut up, Nick Ainsley.

So he did.

All the words he wanted to say dammed in his throat, crashing like a jam of wagons and curricles on a busy London thoroughfare. A shaking sweat took over him, far more intense and sudden than the toil of the morning had caused. His heart strained in its cavity, jumping out of time.

Meg turned, her mouth open, eyes wide with shock. Her breath came heavily from her lungs and she looked down at her hands. When she looked up again, her eyes were wide, frightened.

"I pushed you? Haven't I?"

He touched the pads of his fingers to his mouth, helpless to answer her. Not even wishing to. He reached for her hand and laid it over his mouth with a little nod.

"You feel like snow," she cried. "I don't know what to do."

What had she been doing when he touched her? Fighting him.

He scowled, his angry expression cutting in and out until she understood.

"How am I supposed to get mad at you again?"

He tilted his head toward the house where Isabelle had gone.

Meg nodded, closing her eyes.

It didn't come at once, but after a minute or two it arose like a bubble surfacing in a muddy swamp. One moment he could not speak, and the next he gasped, "I knew you could do it."

She slumped against him, her feet collapsing under her. Meg's breath was labored and tears choked her throat. "I don't like it. I don't like it." And then, "Put me down."

He'd been holding her up.

"My brave, brave girl. I knew you could do it."

***

Shadows danced against the walls when Meg woke. She remembered dimly that Nick had scooped her up, collecting Jolly as he went inside and up to her room.

"She needs to rest," he'd said, and so she did, tucked under a light blanket. As she'd dropped off, she felt a light kiss to her brow and a shadow of fear.

It might have been funny, the memory of Nick's face scrunching into an ogre's fierce scowl until she understood what he asked of her. Get angry. Use that anger. The anger will fuel the pushing. She thought he was right. Love had not done it. A desperate need had not done it either. Maybe anger would do the trick.

So she'd gotten mad at Isabelle again, stoking a flame of fury that Isabelle was once more meddling in her life, once more grasping Meg's things and tearing them to pieces. But no answering flame licked through her fingers, burning away the freezing snow of Nick's inertia.

What if nothing could help him?

That's when the fear had come. And she remembered shouting at Nick, hot words that sounded like anger, but tasted like fear.

The act of summoning up that emotion, sticking and staining every surface it touched, sapped her strength as it boiled over and became more concentrated than grief. Fear for Nick shaking and straining under Isabelle's power. Fear she wouldn't be able to save him. Fear he didn't really want her to.

Fear had fueled the pushing.

In the end, she had saved him, but at what cost? She was more afraid than ever that he wished for Isabelle. She was more hopeless. There were no answers save the single realization that Meg never wanted to feel that way again.

Meg struggled to sit up, drawing her knees up and resting her chin on them. If only Grandmother had been the one to teach her. Her gaze passed over Grandmother's trunk. Such a small remembrance, this inheritance, but when Grandfather hardly had a thought to call his own, he had managed to leave this single, surprising item to Meg. Why? It had seemed the mercurial whim of a sick old man, but now that she knew what he must have been fighting in those last weeks, her eyes narrowed. Padding over to the thing, she unstrapped the top and flung it open, conscious in some innermost part that she was searching for answers.

She lifted out a packet of letters wrapped in a blue ribbon, garments stiff and brittle with age. The wedding veil Nick wished her to be married in.

One by one the items were unearthed, her search far more particular this time, until she got to the bottom of the box where she found a slim volume titled "The Days of Miss Maria Felicity Bagshaw, June 1763" in a girlish hand. Meg smiled to imagine the young woman at twelve penning those words. Meg walked back to bed and settled against the pillows. The words fell on her like a cart tipping over.

"It is a great privilege to be magic, linked in a chain that goes back from daughter to mother as far as any in our family can remember, and governed by principles taught to us in our earliest days." Meg bolted upright, scanning the fly-spotted and water-warped page with eyes that darted in every direction. Governed by principles? Meg had not been: she had been governed by her Grandfather.

Finally, she forced herself to slow down, taking it in. "Within this diary I will set down the attempts to develop my character so as to deserve the power I have. Having a scientific mind, I feel it incumbent to set out the rules and limitations of my gift."

The author of it was a haphazard correspondent, referencing long-deceased ancestors, picking up her narrative with apologies, only to drop again the following day. Leaving gaps between entries lasting weeks, sometimes months. But when she did write, it was always for a purpose.

Here, laid out in black and white, Meg discovered things she had only groped toward herself: that there were degrees of reading someone's thoughts. A shallow skimming that took only the most immediate thoughts of the subject and deeper readings that might include avenues never guessed at.

That there were consequences to the reader, some more grave than others. That one might read things one didn't wish to. That one would feel a kind of emotional jolt, similar to the discharge of a gun that would rebound onto the reader if the subject were sufficiently overcome.

And then there was this:

Have discovered a curious thing today. I was riding out with Mr Ross, allowing him to hold my hand now and again, and he let the horses have their head. It ought to have been exhilarating but I was quite terrified and grabbed his wrist while wearing my little lace glove. I did not shout, "Stop" but he did so at once.

Though it is not a practice Mother knew anything about, I have discovered that it is possible to push thoughts into a head, as it is possible to glean them. I shrink from the danger of having such power. How easily I might be twisted by having such a hold on another mind. But it opens up the possibility that each of my powers has an opposite.

There was a long gap. Then:

My husband says that motherhood agrees with me, but I cannot believe him. I am more fearful, more anxious that some calamity will befall my little one. The baby is four now and no others have followed. I fear my womb is closed. I fear to lose the one I have. I push her often, now. Take care on the path. Don't go near the river. Don't run. I have discovered that I can do it when I'm not touching her as long as I'm holding a favorite toy or blanket. Pushing doesn't exhaust me anymore. I find that worrisome.

That was the last entry signed in an elegant hand: *Mrs Maria Ross.*

Meg closed the book, resting her palm on the cover, opening the sluice gates of her mind to Grandmother's revelations. She could easily imagine the girl Grandfather had shown her in his memories: lovely, rosy with promise, possessing the same endowment Meg and Isabelle shared.

She had died shortly after Meg was born and, touching the pages now, she felt the loss keenly. How much they, Isabelle and herself, might have learned from Grandmother even though it had seemed to go terribly wrong.

Meg flipped open the pages to the last and read again. *I fear to lose the one I have. I push her often, now.* Grandmother had used fear to push her daughter, digging into that dark emotion for security and safety, peace and reassurance. Had she hated the sensation as Meg had hated it today?

Small wonder she lost control, finding it to be a bottomless mine, producing more of the fear she hated, the promised rewards always tantalizingly out of reach.

Meg drew up her legs, resting her chin on her knees once more. "Did you mean me to find this? Is this what you wanted me to know?" she murmured. The inheritance of Grandmother's trunk had seemed such a strange, small bequest in Grandfather's will, hardly worth bothering over. But it had surprised Isabelle all the same. "Were you watching over me, even when your mind was bound?"

Though she had known that Isabelle had pushed Grandfather in some way, she allowed the full import of what that meant to break over her. It wasn't a nice little story she could tell herself to let the pain of Grandfather's final actions dull. It had really happened.

Meg bent around the pain of his loss, almost feeling the weight of his heavy hand on the crown of her bowed head, and felt it dissipate. Tears came and with them cleansing. He hadn't meant it. Not the harsh words of the will. Not cutting her out. Not abandoning Meg to her sister's devices, fighting Isabelle to the last.

The joy of his return shook through her, pushing an ebullience through her veins as renewing as a spring wind. Grandfather loved her. That hadn't changed. And he'd managed to give her Grandmother's legacy, even while he'd been crushed under Isabelle's power.

After a good howl, Meg reached for a handkerchief. "How?" she asked, speaking to Grandfather though he was gone. "How did she push you when you weren't even touching? How did she push Nick?"

Meg returned to the text, poring over it and coming, again, to the image of young Mrs Ross in the garden with her child, out of reach as her daughter ran toward some danger. She saw the toy in her hand. She pushed.

Some favorite toy.

"What was your favorite toy, Grandfather?"

The answer came at once and Meg slipped off the bed, eschewing her slippers. Opening the door, she listened for sounds of dinner being served. The glow of candlelight pressed from under the dining room door, and the clink of dishes and glass created a reassuring picture of Isabelle at her meal.

Meg turned toward the end of the hall where Isabelle's room was and tapped on the door. No answering murmur met her, and she poked her head around the gap.

Where would she put it?

Quick fingers pawed through a jewelry box on the top of her dressing table (a too-obvious choice) and every drawer in the room. She lifted the mattress back to no avail. Meg had almost given up her search when she found a small, plain box in the back of Isabelle's wardrobe, too small for a hat.

When she shook it, it rattled. The lid was stuck tight but when Meg pried it back, it popped open, knocking Meg onto her backside and spilling the contents onto her skirts.

There it was—the small cameo Grandfather had not dared part from until it became inexplicably lost. This sentimental keepsake, cherished for decades, had been the instrument Isabelle had used to drive her will into the heart of their grandfather.

Sick rage coated Meg's mouth and she gripped it tightly, moving to scoop the remaining items back in the box. Her eyes automatically sorted them: A battered chess piece, an ornate thimble, a button, an enameled snuffbox, a locket containing a curl of pale yellow hair: things of monetary value alongside things of no value at all. Her hand arrested, hovering over a plain, green glass pebble. She plucked it up, her thumb running over the crescent shape, and she saw Nick's body arching against his bedclothes, tense and straining.

This is how the witch had done it.

A murmur of voices drifted up the hall and Meg hastily tipped a handful of items into her bodice and snapped the lid closed, shoving the box deep into the wardrobe. Moving quickly through the hall, she had her hand on the door of her bedroom when Isabelle stepped from the stairs. Meg's heartbeat would give her away, she was sure.

"You missed dinner," Isabelle said, with that particular mix of superiority and amusement that made Meg want to slap the faint smile from her mouth. "Were you indisposed? Don't you think it's rather worrisome for a future countess to be sick? How will Nicholas get an heir off you?"

Meg ignored the crudeness, though her smile didn't reach her eyes. "It's generous of you to throw a party for us, Bella, when I know you don't want to." The falsity wanted to fuse her jaws together.

"This is my home and you will be my neighbor. I have no intention of being ostracized in the community."

Saving face. Using other people to further her own ends. It was of a piece with Isabelle's way of living.

Isabelle continued. "Do you wish to know the details of the dinner?"

Meg pressed a hand to her bodice, feeling the items shift in her short stays, and sucked down a deal of air. She let out a loud, sustained belch that made Isabelle's nose wrinkle.

"No," Meg gasped, pressing a fist to her mouth. Like a skipping rock, she let out another smaller belch and she made a note to thank Henry for teaching her how. "I should lie down again."

Chapter Twenty-nine

Meg dressed with care, though her choices were limited to funereal black, midnight black, or crow black. Jolly brushed her hair until it shone and dressed it in thick coils ornamented with some unknown scarlet flowers, sent from Nick for his bride-to-be.

Cultivated blooms, Meg thought, fingering the scalloped petals that grew in orderly precision near the center and sprang in wild disarray at the edge. They were so unlike the hand-gathered posies he'd offered to her sister so long ago. Those had been simple and personal. What did these mean?

She could not ask him. Aside from the flowers, it seemed he had forgotten about her entirely. No coming around the kitchen door. No teasing to watch her blush rise. No wet hair to show that he'd cleaned himself up for her, however hastily. Her involvement with the smuggling must have been his last straw.

When they last met, he had been fumbling for a way to end their engagement, and then she'd pushed him. Maybe that had been the breaking point. He might be frightened of her now.

But she screwed a jet earbob to the lobe of her ear, anyway, and saw it dance in the candlelight, giving off a faint shine despite the deep color.

"That'll be him," Jolly said, listening for the bustle downstairs. "And about time, too."

"He's perfectly punctual," Meg replied, assaying a look in the long mirror, though she admitted to herself that he had cut it awfully close. Not a lover eager for her company.

Jolly looked over her shoulder at Meg reflected in the glass. "I wish you didn't have to be in black." Jolly smiled. "But I suppose he couldn't wait for you."

Meg turned her lips up at that, but she gathered her fan and squared her shoulders. It was time to meet her fiancé.

Nick tilted his head back, removing his hat and handing it off to a maid as he watched her descend the staircase. She picked out the details she would remember when he left her. His curly hair that needed a clipping, the intricate stock he'd likely allowed Brooks free rein on, another one of those waistcoats he liked so well.

There are other ways to keep me safe. We don't have to marry.

The next time he brought it up, she would have herself well in hand. She would let him go.

There were good arguments for keeping him. The laws of propriety demanded that he wed her after the banns had been called, and after being unchaperoned all that time at the Abbey. When they parted, it would be she who bore the brunt of it, new fissures of gossip opening up wherever she went.

And she loved him.

"You look well," he said, clearing his throat. "I knew chrysanthemums would look well—" He bit off his words and glanced into the drawing room where Isabelle, attired in a glorious half-mourning gown of lavender silk moved about fluffing the cushions into particular positions.

"We must speak," he said, stepping into the shadows of the hall where they would not be seen.

Meg willed her feet to follow him, feeling the wobbling *blancmange* of her engagement slipping on its dish, threatening to splatter on the ground.

He dug into the shallow pocket of his waistcoat, pulling free her red ribbon, carefully wound into a coil. He held it flat on his gloved palm.

She stared mutely at it.

"I've no right to hold this ransom," he said, looking into her eyes with a message that sent her wishing for a deciphering key. "It's yours now, to do what you will."

What she wanted was to fold his fingers over the ribbon, closing them tight in a fist that nothing would break. She wanted to tell him she would collect it on their wedding day. She wanted to scream the house down.

"Thank you," she said, holding her palm out as he dropped it in her hand. He gave her a hard look as she tucked it into the sleeve of her gown.

How confused he would be if she threw it right back in his face. So she made her voice pleasant and polite. "Have you felt more pushing?"

He shook his head, his mouth a grim line. Did he resent the reminder that Isabelle was not merely a lovely hostess tonight, but a danger to him?

"No. At least, I feel it distantly from time to time, but nothing like before. Perhaps I've become immune."

It didn't work like that. "My lord—"

"Nick," he snapped, striding away and greeting Isabelle, who turned to him with a coo of pleasure. Meg trailed after him, observing the correct little exchange between neighbors. He was gloved. She was gloved. Their stone was no longer in Isabelle's possession. There was nothing more to be done.

Guests began to arrive then, trailing in to greet the couple. Isabelle met them first, passing them along to her little sister, most of whom directed sour glances at Meg, hardly concealing their disdain.

Mrs Fletcher was no longer the polite matron, intent on winning Meg's confidence with an invitation to tea. As Meg slid a finger along her skin, she felt a driving sleet. Meg's eyes widened. What a poisonous, petty thing for Isabelle to do, pushing her guests to reject Meg even more than they were already inclined to do. It wasn't snow, however. Perhaps there were too many guests for Isabelle to push effectively. Perhaps she lacked the personal items that would make her pushing more durable.

Still, Meg longed for one friendly face. "Where are the Gracechurches?"

"Did they not come?" Isabelle asked, her eyes widening. "Oh I do hope the invitation wasn't lost in the post."

"What do you hope to gain from such a small-minded trick, Bella?" Meg whispered, smiling at the guests though her jaw was clenched.

"You might be surprised by my answer, Margaret." She wandered away then, mixing with the guests and leaving Meg on her own. Nick should have been the one to stand at her side, but it was Mr Thackery who came to her at last.

"Where is Miss Gracechurch?" he asked, a little brusque. "I hoped she—they—would be here."

No doubt Isabelle had pushed him too, but Meg had had her fill of being the subject of irritation. "So you can continue your glacial wooing?" she snapped. "She was not on my sister's guest list, but if you want to see her, Mr Thackery, you know where to find her."

He plucked a glass of wine from a passing tray and thrust it into her hands. "You resent my speed? She has not given me the slightest encouragement. A woman wants to be a man's first love. She doesn't want him to come with memories and sorrows and a house full of children. She says she's happy as she is."

Perhaps it was the impending dissolution of her own engagement that made Meg speak. "I'm going to be a worm, Jacob Thackery, and tell you that Esther holds you in her heart. That she has far too much pride to show it. That she's likely to deny it for the first month. What you do with that information is your own business. I do not have patience today for stupidities and unspoken sentiments."

Mr Thackery looked into his glass for a moment, letting out a long-held breath. "I'll speak to her tomorrow."

"Then at least one happy thing can come from this party. If only I could please the rest of the guests," she said, gesturing around the room.

"They're upset about the harvest," he said, taking a drink. "The hay has yet to be taken in and the chance of losing the last quarter to frost or hail or some dashed inexplicable blight has every man here on edge. You can't blame them."

"I don't blame them at all," Meg said, sipping the liquid in her glass, hardly warmed by it. "It's a terrible time for a party. There's no moon to light your way home."

"Bad for parties, perfect for free-trading." He smiled.

At his words, Meg blanched. With all of Isabelle's machinations, Meg had not given it a thought. Of course there would be free traders afoot on such a night as this. Her finger flicked over Mr Thackery's wrist as deftly as a cutpurse. There was the faintest echo of Isabelle's pushing alongside a steady uneasiness. Meg let herself skim his thoughts a degree more deeply. A banging at his door in the dead of night: revenue officers. A country solicitor asked to mount a hopeless defense in front of an implacable magistrate.

Mr Thackery set down his glass of wine. "Let's talk of happier things. When is the wedding to be?"

Meg opened her mouth as she felt Nick's solid presence behind her.

"Not yet," he answered, smoothly as though he'd taken some thought. What had once been a matter of urgency had become something he was putting off. The wrinkled ribbon peeked from her sleeve and she tucked it in again. "As you said, there is the harvest to be gotten in."

Mr Thackery aimcd a look of irritation at Nick and wandered away, muttering the word glacial under his breath.

Meg tilted up an amused smile up at Nick. For a brief moment, they shared a smile that broke her heart. "I'm worried about Sam and the others," she said. Nick's smile faded. "I think the magistrate has called in officers."

"Did Thackery say so?"

Meg held up her finger. "Sam won't stay away if his friend is down there."

"How do you know he's not there on his own account? If he knows the risks and pursues them anyway, he's a reckless child."

She was already shaking her head at him, the chrysanthemums tickling the rim of her ear. "He's not like that at all. He's loyal. He wants to do the right thing."

"Do you care so much?" he asked, and she lifted her chin in surprise at the roughness in his tone.

"I do," she said, willing him to understand. She'd spent years on the receiving end of judgment, praying for a little mercy. Mrs Fetcher needed some now. How could she withhold it?

A muscle jumped in Nick's jaw and Meg turned from him as Jolly rang the bell for dinner. Nick moved to escort Isabelle, and Meg entered the room on Mr Thackery's arm to see the glittering china lined up in military rows, nary a fork or a glass out of step.

Isabelle, looking every inch the dowager Lady Ainsley, occupied the head of the table while Nick sat at the foot. Meg, who ought to have occupied a position of honor, was lumped in the middle with Mr Thackery, happy to be assured a degree of politeness from her dinner partner, at least.

Quiet conversation bubbled along the length of the table as the night wore on. She lifted her wine glass as Mr Thackery began what promised to be an amusing story about his girls naming the family cat when she heard the sound of shattering glass and a muffled curse.

"There they are," she murmured, setting her glass down.

"Who?" Mr Thackery asked.

"The Pevensey Intellectual Society," she answered, shoving back her chair and standing as two figures stumbled into the room, blinking in the sudden glare of candlelight. She might have guessed they couldn't manage discretion. Their clothes were torn and Sam was holding up a sagging Jim. Several women uttered sharp cries as Meg waved them down and strode around the table to meet the men.

"Sam said we could come to you if there was trouble," Jim said, his shock of ginger hair dark matted to his head with sweat.

Her guests, half standing, looked to Meg.

"What kind of trouble?" she asked.

"Officers, a couple of them mounted, but most of them on foot."

"How far behind you?"

"Five minutes?" Jim shrugged. He held his side and gasped for breath.

Meg gave a low curse.

A gentleman in the party was less restrained. "You imbeciles broke a window. They're sure to tear the house apart looking for you if they find that."

"What are you doing here?" Mrs Fletcher, her voice rising in agitation. Her hands wrung together. "You'll be shipped away. Or worse—"

"There's no time for hysterics, ma'am. We must act." Meg scanned the faces of the assembled guests, tense, frozen in shock. "I'm going to hide them. Anyone who wishes to leave now may do so."

To her surprise, no one stirred. "Nick?"

He was already at her side, so close that she could lean into his solid chest. "Where will you put them? Blythe House is sadly lacking priest holes," he said, the glint in his eye reminding her of how many adventures they'd managed together.

"Here. In plain sight. Will you add those two chairs to the table?" she said, pointing to the wall, then turned, addressing the guests. "If you will scoot your place settings six inches toward either end of the table to make room in the middle. Yes. That's it. Isabelle, get Jolly and tell her to bring two place settings while I see to their clothes."

"This is wholly illegal," Isabelle said, pressing a hand to her breast. She stood, pushing away her chair. "Turn them out at once."

Meg swung on her sister. “Over my dead body.”

“You won’t like it much, ma’am, if we’re caught,” Jim spoke through gritted teeth. “In it up to your neck with hands no cleaner than ours. It would go bad for you if we talked.”

A shocked silence rippled from the center of the room.

“How dare you speak to me.” Isabelle’s eyes glittered, the picture of outrage. She shot a fiery glance at Meg. “I won’t be any part of this.”

“Then leave,” Meg challenged. “And for your sake, pray these boys don’t get caught.”

Casting her napkin on the table, Isabelle turned in a flurry of lavender magnificence, knocking into a surprised Jolly.

“What was—” Jolly began as Isabelle’s form retreated.

“Mrs Fletcher,” Meg said, pulling the boys after her, “please see to the table. Get Mrs Jolly to even out the party. I’ll find some evening clothes for these gentlemen.”

“There was a ruckus down on the beach,” Sam said, following her quick feet as she made her way to the attics. “We were hauling in the catch when we heard them barreling down the cliff path at us, lanterns swinging away and guns drawn. Our boat crew pulled hard for the open sea but the officers had them fast with ropes and hooks. It was chaos. Men jumped for it, kicking for France as hard as they might.”

“And you?” Meg breathed, winding up the narrow stairs.

“We don’t know anything about France, but knowing the land like we do, we managed to climb up a narrower path farther on—”

“Not the one that goes straight up,” she exclaimed.

“That one. Jim fell a piece. I checked him. No ribs broken. Just winded.”

“And frightened,” she said, pawing through Grandfather’s trunks and holding up the relics of his wardrobe against the broad shoulder points of these overgrown boys, tearing at the spotted neckcloths and tossing them lengths of linen. “Tie them simply,” she said, prodding them down the stairs again. “Your shirts and trousers will have to do. Try not to stand up and, if you must, stand behind someone.”

They nodded, squeezing themselves into the coats as they arrived in the dining room. What a mess it would look, if there was a close inspection, with coats far too short in the arms for her liking, but there was nothing more to be done. The table was set out for the extra guests and she stuffed them into their seats as Nick dished food onto their plates.

"Push it around," he commanded, moving to the other side of the table with a dish of buttered beans and scraping off a generous portion. This was the man who had cursed their business and called for their arrests. What had happened to him?

Meg shook her head. "Take my place, Jolly, and I'll sit in Isabelle's seat." She ran her eyes over the housekeeper. Mrs Fletcher had lent her cut-glass broach to dress up Jolly's plain frock, and another woman must have handed down a shawl. Already Meg could hear shouts and footsteps on the gravel outside.

"What else? What else?" Her voice rising in panic as she surveyed the scene.

Jim's and Sam's faces were streaked with mud and sweat. Meg snatched up a napkin and looked around.

It was Nick who read her mind. "In the vase," he called, taking his seat. So she plucked up the blooms and shoved the napkin in the vase, soaking up the water with the cloth before plonking them down again.

"Face," she said, taking the cloth to Jim's upturned brow. Then she whipped around to get Sam, taking a hard scouring hand to his cheeks.

I'm frightened.

She looked into his eyes and set a comforting palm against his cheek, looking into his eyes with a soft smile. She glanced away to encounter Nick's sharp expression when an urgent banging sounded against the door. Meg whipped into her seat.

Jolly directed a housemaid to answer. "Go slowly, little miss."

She returned, giving an excellent performance of befuddlement. "Revenue officers from Eastbourne, ma'am. They say there's been a disturbance."

Meg lifted her voice so that it would carry into the hall. "How exciting. Show them in."

A middle-aged man in a red coat entered, his hat secured at his side. "Major Norris, ma'am." He bowed. "My sincere apologies for interrupting your party. It's a nasty business that calls us out on such a night."

"Oh?"

He stepped forward, nodding to the guests, slipping his glance up and down the table. Meg held her breath as his eyes skipped past Jim and then Sam. "We broke up a band of smugglers tonight, down on your beach."

The ladies of the party gave satisfying gasps of horror. "Have you caught them?"

"Not at all. These were men well versed in villainy," he growled, warming to his topic. "They know how to evade capture. Most grabbed an oar and swam for it, no doubt to be picked up by larger vessels off the coast."

Meg stood, reaching a hand toward Nick. He joined her and placed an arm around her waist. "Most?"

"You've hit on the nub of it. At least two were on the cliffs when we raided the boats. They made inland, straight here."

Meg turned frightened, childlike eyes to Nick. "But they would know to avoid the lights of the house, surely?"

"I hope so, my love," Nick answered, looking so like a man bent on soothing his sweetheart that she almost believed it.

Major Norris responded. "I'm afraid we can't be certain of that. A broken window was discovered outside the library. We think the rogues are in the house. Did you not hear the glass shatter?"

"They're always dropping things in the kitchen," Meg said, her voice a mix of horror and awe. "You say they've broken in?"

Again, the ladies responded with frightened gasps. Sam and Jim sat still—too still, if she had a criticism to make.

"You haven't heard anything as you dined?" the major asked, tilting his head to include the company who duly shook their heads. "Then I request permission to search the house."

Nick cast a glance down at Meg and answered for them both. "If it's the only way to be assured that my fiancée is safe."

"My sister, Lady Ainsley, wasn't feeling well and took to her bed some time ago," Meg interrupted, touching Major Norris on the wrist.

Suspicion flared like a fire in his veins, given sudden fuel.

Meg amended her words to allay his fears. "Perhaps I may accompany you up to that room?"

He nodded and they made their way, the stomp of military boots sounding throughout the house.

"Isabelle?" she called, hoping her sister would be on the bed or otherwise appear indisposed. "Are you well? I have an officer who needs to search the room for smugglers."

After a few moments, the door swung back and Isabelle's face was indeed white. In fact, she looked haggard. "Smugglers? In Pevensey?" She opened the door wider.

Major Norris bowed and walked past her. "Pevensey, Norman's Bay, Eastbourne… In hundreds of tiny inlets up and down the coast." He checked the most obvious places, behind curtains, under the bed, but he also tapped the walls and floors for hollows. Meg's stomach clenched like a vinegar-soaked towel, squeezing sourness through her veins. If she had attempted to hide the boys, they would have certainly been discovered.

"What's that smell?" Isabelle asked, lifting her nose.

Major Norris answered from deep inside the wardrobe. "That'll be the boats. We set them ablaze."

"With all the cargo?" Isabelle looked genuinely shocked. "I thought you were after the traders."

Meg's eyes narrowed on her sister. This agitation was real. It felt real.

"Smugglers, ma'am. We prefer to call them smugglers. We burn the boats because we never pick up the patrons—"

"I don't understand," Isabelle said.

"Prosperous men who hope to get rich, or rich men plotting to stay that way, avoiding the risk and reaping the rewards," he said, rising to his feet. "Cowards. But this night will wreck his fleet and cut into his ventures quite tidily. He'll wake to find his little empire gone."

Isabelle blinked, sinking on the bed.

"That will be all, my lady. Apologies for discommoding you and best wishes for your good health."

They returned to the hall. Meg stood near and he began to take reports from his men as they returned from the search. Nothing in the kitchens, nothing in the library, and nothing in the other bedrooms: with each report, his frown deepened.

"May I offer you a glass of wine, sir?" Meg asked, fear feathering her skin like a spider walking down her arm. She could harness it, pushing the officer out the door in a moment. She held her breath instead, waiting for an opportunity to get them away, ready to seize upon it.

"Not at all professional, ma'am," he answered, peering into the gloom of the hall, staring hard at a carved chest by the stairs. He strode to it, lifting the cover, and slammed it shut it again. "They must be here."

She couched her words in innocent speculation. "Isn't it likely that such a pair would lay traps and diversions for you if they are as professional as you say?"

She touched his wrist and read his skepticism. *Silly chit of a girl.*

"Nick?" Meg called and he came. She asked with her voice pitched higher than usual, "Do you think it's possible the broken glass is a false trail? The major is considering it." She squeezed his arm but didn't need to. He was already following her lead.

"Clever of you to think of it, sir. I'm surprised I didn't see it, myself."

The major rubbed his jaw. "You are not trained for such things, my lord. The smugglers wanted me to find the glass."

Things moved quickly then. Major Norris gave a high, piercing whistle, rallying his officers, and they bolted into the night, bent on searching every shed and cottage in Pevensey if it would gain them their men.

Nick closed the front door, leaning against it while Meg's heart beat hard under her ribs. He made no move as noises faded down the drive, only watched her with his bright, golden eyes. The silence stretched and stretched, tied like a rope between them, taut. They only needed to bridge the distance. He bumped away from the door and she tensed, warmth rising over her neck and chin.

"Miss Summers," Mrs Fletcher said, jerking Meg's attention from him. She stood in the door of the dining room, unable to keep her seat. Tears brightened her eyes and a hand pressed against her side as though it had been she, not Sam, running for his life.

"He's safe," Meg answered, suddenly weary. "You've no—"

Mrs Fletcher wasn't listening. She threw her arms around Meg, swallowing her in a fierce embrace and choking off all attempts at talk. Guests streamed from the dining room into the hall, pushing closer, edging Nick farther away. Meg swam through a wave of impressions as they touched her: a smothering blanket of gratitude, delight—sheer delight—to be in the middle of such an adventure, the enervating fatigue that follows exertion.

"Mrs Jolly was a treasure, an absolute treasure…" she heard someone say.

"I thought I would die when I saw those flowers tumbling out of the vase…"

"Quick thinking, Miss Summers," said a peppery and irritable squire. "Sign of a superior mind…"

Meg could not take any of it in, but she felt each touch, so warm with approbation that she finally did cry, bursting into tears so soundly that Mrs Fletcher took charge, shooing everyone off to the dining room, and leading Meg to the sofa, calling a housemaid to bring a restorative cup of tea.

Chapter Thirty

When wraps and cloaks were collected, the hour was late, and the carriages began the long caravan back to the village. Jolly closed the door with a dazed expression.

"I never thought I would see the day," she said. "Not in all my life."

"Nor I," Meg said, stretching her arms in a long reach. "Did Lord Ainsley come down to the kitchens for a little peace?"

"No. But if he didn't say good night, he must be about somewhere."

Suddenly Meg wanted it finished. Though returning her crumpled ribbon had seemed to signify an end, Meg found she needed it in plain English. He must know she wouldn't hold him to an engagement he wanted no part of.

The thought of it, *in plain English*, twisted her stomach still further.

It didn't have to be a tragedy. In this brief respite, before the village remembered all her sins, she might even get away with being cast off from an earl with far less damage than might otherwise be the case. Yes, Meg squared her shoulders for the second time tonight. They must end it at once. She walked down the halls and peeked into empty rooms. It would be like him to take himself out of the center of the party, wishing to find some quiet corner to rest.

Meg would walk into a sitting room and his length would be sprawled along a sofa and he would wake and she'd say, "I agree, there must be a better way to keep you safe than by marrying. Let's find one." And the thing would be done. He would go his way and she would cry her eyes out for a month.

Lord, let it only be a month.

Downstairs, Meg quickly ran out of places to look and she strode into the garden with a rising sense of unease. Perhaps Nick was having a pipe.

"Lord Ainsley," she called, switching it to Nick as her search extended to the wooly lawn near the coast where only hours ago gun-wielding free traders had been seen. Her skin prickled. It wasn't safe out here.

"Still not found him?" Jolly asked as she came back through the kitchens, red-cheeked and anxious. She always did have a wretchedly good imagination. It was too easy to imagine that Nick had been hit over the head with the butt of a pistol, bleeding out behind a hedge.

"No," she answered, forcing her tone to be easy. Staff had done all the washing by now, tidying up for the morning. Everything was in its place. But not Nick.

"I'll look upstairs. He could be sleeping."

"That would be strange," Jolly said, and the words repeated in Meg's head as she climbed the stairs, her heart beginning to charge wildly in her breast. She checked each of the bedrooms before facing down the door at the end of the hall, a manic flock of birds swooping in her chest, not knowing what she dreaded more: Finding him with Isabelle? Or not finding him at all?

She neared, unable to hear anything but her ragged breathing in the small, dark hall. She scratched on the door. No answer. "Isabelle?" she called. No answer.

Meg swung the door back, hoping to face her sister's mulishness at having her privacy invaded, only to find a flat, rumpled coverlet and the small, wooden box upended and dashed against the fireplace mantel. The lavender gown was draped over a chair and the wardrobe hung open, the door at a drunken angle as though it had been ripped from its hinges. A hasty inspection told her that things were missing—Isabelle's set of combs, valise, a few frocks—thrusting Meg back to that day so many years ago when she had made another, similar inventory.

Isabelle was gone. Nick was gone.

Bile rose in Meg's throat and she swallowed it back.

"Where are you?" Meg whispered under her breath as she raced to the stables. "Nick?" she called, heedless of who heard her now. "Nick?"

Blythe House kept a small stable, but Isabelle's mount and a small cart were gone. A high whinny pierced the night air, jerking her from the dead end this answer was.

Puck. She could see his dark head nodding over the stall door, and she grabbed a lantern, racing to his box, so certain she would find Nick bending over a hoof or reaching for his saddle.

She lifted the lantern to a hook only to find the stall empty.

"Where are you, Nick?" Could they have eloped? Had Nick gone with Isabelle voluntarily? He'd not felt a moment of serious pushing since his illness. He even thought himself immune. Had he gone with Isabelle because he wished to go?

Meg crossed her arms over her stomach and rested her head against a railing. She pushed away, wiping impatient hands over her eyes, and saw the berry-red ribbon half-pulled from her sleeve. Nick had hardly been without it these last weeks, winding it around his fingers, teasing her with it. Her eyes narrowed on the slim scrap of silk as a thought fluttered out of reach. If she was perfectly still, it would come to her. Grandmother, she thought, and the story of holding a favorite toy and pushing her daughter. Of wondering if each of her powers had an opposite.

If Isabelle could push from a distance, might Meg be able to read Nick from a distance? Nothing in Grandmother's record indicated so, but even as she thought the words she wound the ribbon around her fingers feeling the warmth of his fingers each time they'd touched her skin.

Cold. Jagged shards of ice blowing back from a snow field. Breathing in air so cold it made her chest ache.

Meg's breath caught on a whimper of pain. He was being pushed. Nick wasn't master of himself, but heavens, she needed more than this.

Give me more.

Meg screwed her eyes shut and when she blinked them open, her eyelids were heavy with exhaustion. She wasn't in the stable anymore, leaning against a box, pleading for knowledge. She was stumbling along a spray-slick wharf, light spilling from dockside taverns.

Stop, she cried, *stop, let me see where I—*

Her hand was tugged forward and her sluggish gaze focused on it. Isabelle. Isabelle stopped next to a small merchant vessel, the name picked out in white on the hull. *HDMS Færøe.*

A Danish ship.

Meg blinked again, focusing her eyes on Puck, on the sweet smell of fresh hay and his gentle, huffing breaths.

"Can you get me there?" she asked the horse. Puck sniffed her rolled hand, shaking his long mane in the dim light. "You'll have to."

In her haste and fright, she did not get him saddled. While she managed the bridle easily enough, Puck danced away each time she raised the saddle over her head, and she finally cast it down at her feet with an exhausted cry. Climbing the rails of the stall, she got eye to eye with the beast and slid a palm around the curve of his jaw. "Be good to me."

Horse thoughts were muffled and indistinct, impossibly superior and reticent. But Meg stayed completely still until Puck closed his eyes. Affirmation nosed through the thick barrier between human and animal.

Then Meg kilted her skirts and scrambled onto his back, pressing her heels into his flanks and achieving a trot that was much faster than her own feet would carry her. How she wished she had let Nick teach her to ride now.

The trip was quick, rattling the teeth in her head, threatening to jar her from her perch. Finally, she slid off his back in the harbor paddock.

"Thank you," she whispered, her knees jellied and shaking.

She skulked along the narrow street, clenching her ribbon again. The ice was gone but in its place she felt straining and fighting. She quickened her steps to the side of the *Færøe,* picking her way among nets and crates near the entry.

Thank heavens she was still shrouded in black. Her lithe shadow moved up the gangplank, her leather-shod feet landing soundlessly on the main deck. Isabelle's voice travelled from the quarterdeck where she struggled to communicate with the captain.

"We must go at once," came her commanding tones.

"I can do nothing, ma'am." The reply in heavily accented English. "The tide is against us. A half hour at least."

"Move from the wharf now…"

Meg turned away from their voices along a narrow walkway, littered with ropes, and found Nick, tied up on the forecastle deck, his wrists and feet bound with complicated knots to the bowsprit. A woman's lacy handkerchief had been stuffed into his mouth and a filthy neckcloth anchored it in place. Even his eyes were covered.

She moved to his back and leaned forward, her mouth close to his ear. "Is that you, Nick Ainsley?" she said, a low laugh edging her voice.

He cocked his head and went absolutely still.

***

He gasped when she'd loosened the gag, his voice a hoarse whisper. "I can't get these off," he said, shifting his hands. "I've been working on them for half an hour and they're still as tight as ever."

She grinned, holding up a blade. Her fishing knife.

"Even at a dinner party, Meg?" he asked as she began sawing through the thick hemp, strands snapping back on her hand as they pinged open.

"Sir Frederick is going to have a lot to say about the contents of a lady's pockets," she whispered, the amused sound of it washing through him like a torrent, cleaning away the rancid aftertaste of Isabelle's pushing. Her warm breath tickled his ear, and it was as much as he could do to remind himself of their peril: that it was no time to take her in his arms.

She handed him the knife and he went to work at the knots binding his feet, one eye on the aft and another on the ropes. When he broke free, a prickling pain rushed into his fingers. Moving slowly, he dragged himself behind a load of cargo with Meg, flexing his wrists and ankles.

"How did she get you?"

"She touched my hand," he answered. "I was in the hall watching you with Mrs Fletcher and she came up next to me and grabbed a hold of my mind." A shudder overtook him.

***

Meg could see how he hated it—anything to do with this power. As he shook with revulsion, she shifted. "Are you recovered? We have to go quietly."

But Isabelle cried out, the high sharpness piercing the night. Nick jerked to his feet. "It's too late for that," he said, gripping the knife in his hand. A rough seaman charged, short blade at the ready. Nick shoved Meg at his back and crouched, his feet braced apart.

"Can you swim?" he asked, grappling with the man even as he asked her. Their muscles strained, but Nick had the advantage, shoving the man onto his back.

Meg found a rough coil of rope, aiming it at the man's feet, and threw, tangling him up. "You're the one who taught me. I might drown if I jump in with all my skirts," she said, reaching for some new weapon. Her hand closed on a hammer.

Sailors poured onto the deck only to halt in confusion.

"Get them," Isabelle shouted, but her words carried no weight. Either they spoke no English or hesitated to obey a mad Englishwoman. Meg and Nick exchanged a look. Perhaps they could simply walk down the gangplank and into safety. They began to edge down the walkway when Isabelle ran into the group, touching the men, pushing them, sending them on the attack with grim efficiency.

"Nick, we'll never—" Meg said, taking a step back.

"Where's my girl?" Nick baited her, choking up on his knife and urging her to do the same with her hammer. Then his expression became businesslike, his sentences choppy. "If I go down, you keep swinging. Jump if there's nothing else."

She nodded as he kicked his first attacker square in the chest, knocking him into two more. Caught by a low railing, the two slipped over the side. Meg picked up a bucket and bashed the first in the jaw before he could close the distance.

Still dazed, she shoved him off the port side, throwing a cask into the water after him. "Grab on," she shouted to the man, turning when she heard Nick utter a howl of rage.

Nick had plucked an attacker right over her and held him by his throat.

"You can't kill them," Meg grunted, throwing her hammer in the face of another man, hearing the sickly, lettuce-tearing crunch of his nose. Her stomach lurched, but as he lunged for her, she shifted her weight, his momentum taking him over the railing.

"They don't know what they're doing," she shouted. "If you get them over the side, they're swimming off."

Nick nodded, shaking his captive until the man's knife dropped from his hand, and sent him sailing over the hull, pulling another man over his back in a strange twisting movement Meg had never seen before. Her eyes widened at the ease with which Nick handled himself. Clearly, this was not his first brush with combat.

But, though the narrow deck had been working in their favor, now men were crawling over the bales and casks to reach them.

"Four of them," she counted.

"Is that all?" he asked, breathing hard.

She gasped a laugh and retrieved the hammer, sending it flying once more. Her aim was slightly off and it didn't stop the man as he leapt the final distance, landing a glancing blow to her temple with his fist. She fell hard against the deck, kicking and biting where she could.

He twisted her arm behind her and she choked off a scream. Abandoning his attackers, Nick fought to her side. Hands grabbed at him but not before he tore the man off her and threw him so far into the bay that the ripples hardly reached the boat.

As she struggled to her feet Nick dispatched two more. The last sailor, taller than the others, slashed at Nick, bringing his dagger down in a deadly arc. Meg threw her arm up and felt the sting of it curve over her skin, slitting her forearm as neatly as running a knife up the belly of a fish. Nick reached for her but the sailor caught Nick under his chin, dragging his neck back. Against the expanse of skin, so thin she thought she might see his heartbeat thrumming in his veins, he rested the point of his bright blade.

In a moment, the tumult of combat was over.

"Bring him here," Isabelle said, her voice carrying across the deck, in no hurry to prevent harm. A thin bead of blood slid from the point, marking a slow trail down his neck. Meg looked to where her own knife lay, wondering how fast she would have to move, how good her aim would have to be while her own wound spilled blood over her fingertips.

Perhaps she could push him. She lifted a hand and summoned her fear, but the sailor grunted and pressed the knife deeper into the wound. Meg's eyes steeled and she walked before them, making their way to Isabelle.

"I have so many questions," Isabelle said, as they arrived on the quarter deck, the sailor dragging Nick to the far side where Meg could not hope to reach him. Under her pelisse, Isabelle was attired in the simple white of a much younger woman. "How did you know we are eloping?"

"We're eloping?" Nick interrupted, his words forced through his teeth as the sailor dragged his hair back. "What a lot of fuss, Isabelle. You only had to ask."

Isabelle's smile was slight and she moved to secure Nick's hands behind his back in a hasty knot. She touched the sailor on the arm and his efforts to hold Nick redoubled.

"I had hoped to avoid this, Nicholas," Isabelle said, moving away, "but you were stubborn."

"What was I supposed to do, Isabelle? Marrying my uncle's widow is illegal. My hands were tied." He raised his bound wrists, a lock of hair falling over his forehead. "Well, figuratively."

She flicked him a sour look before pinning Meg down with narrow, cat-like eyes. "It's obvious that you were flattered by my little sister being so much in love with you."

Meg felt the blood leave her cheeks, but she never stopped looking for an opening, running scenario after scenario through her head. What could she do to get Nick safe away?

"Isn't that right, Margaret?"

"Let him go," Meg demanded. "You have what you want."

"What is it that I want?" Isabelle asked, her head tilted, curious.

"Everything from Grandfather's will. Blythe House. Money."

"Money? You think there's money left after Grandfather paid off his heir? Some stranger who would have taken it by virtue of being born a man?" she spat. "There's no money. Not enough to matter. Not enough to get me out of this backwater."

"Did you kill him for it? And your husband too?"

Isabelle collected herself. "I didn't do anything to them," she insisted, and Meg felt the chill of her set, tea-drinking smile as she spoke about death. "If they'd bent to my wishes, we would have all sailed on together quite nicely."

"But they didn't. So you pushed them."

Isabelle raised an eyebrow. "Bravo, Margaret. What with all your bending to Grandfather's wishes, I was beginning to wonder if you would ever discover your real power."

"Yes," Meg answered, determined to keep Isabelle's focus on her, no matter what. Nick would seize any opening, no matter how small, if she gave him one. "You forced old Lord Ainsley to run away with you, didn't you? It struck me as so strange at the time, but you were the most beautiful girl I had ever seen. Why wouldn't a man lose his head in your presence? And then, when he died, there was nothing suspicious about that either. But when Grandfather—" Meg choked back the knot of tears in her throat. "You went too far, there. He became another person in those last weeks. Cruel. Dismissive."

"He was always cruel and dismissive," Isabelle hissed. "Put away your powers, girls. Walk a narrow line. Be as pretty and sweet as a dish of *comfits*. Don't be powerful. Take what men are willing to give you. Ignore what you want. Grandfather forced us into tiny, gilded cages."

"Don't talk to me of force, Isabelle," Meg raged. "I was there when it killed him."

Isabelle's command faltered. "It doesn't hurt anyone if they'd do what I want."

"Grandfather was fighting it. He died trying to keep Blythe House from you. How can you say it isn't even really what you wanted?" Meg asked, her voice breaking in a ragged edge. The gash in her arm continued to bleed, blood leaking through the fingers she'd clapped over it. "What could possibly be enough for you?"

The ship moved with the tide and shipboards, butting up against one another, refused to give way, signaling their struggle in long, creaking groans.

"Look at yourself, Isabelle. You're trying to force Nick into marriage. For what? A title? Wealth? A position in Society? You have so much already."

"So much," she spat. "Six years of pushing. Six years of fighting for what was mine. And now I've got nothing. Not even those pitiful boats smoking on the beach."

The soft noise of a rope slipping to the deck stopped her mouth, and Meg turned to watch Nick drop his chin to his shoulder, trapping the sailor's knife. He raised his arm and threw himself to the side, twisting his assailant's limb before turning in a fluid motion and applying a hard knee to the man's groin. There was a distressed moan as Nick tossed him overboard.

Then he rushed at Isabelle.

“Don’t—” Meg shouted, cut off as quickly as Nick’s charge. Isabelle, pale and feminine, grasped him by the arm, holding him easily. In a heartbeat, Nick dropped to his knees, shaking.

Meg went on all fours, looking up into his face. “Resist it,” she said. His eyes narrowed on her, but he could not even nod.

“Having power means wielding it, Margaret. It is our proper sphere to dominate weak creatures.”

“Creatures?” Meg ground out, fury clouding her vision. “You think that carrying Nick off to Denmark will end any better than your last attempt? You’re going to kill him.” Meg sprang to her feet and lunged. For the first time in more than a decade, the Summers sisters touched.

An icy blast of thought engulfed Meg’s arm, dragging at her will, clawing up her shoulder.

Do as I wish.

Leave us.

Leave Nick.

Meg’s brow beaded with sweat as fear marshalled at her back like thousands of soldiers, crouched and ready: all her fear for Nick, all her worry about Grandfather, old fears. Fear and hopelessness piled high in the pit of Meg’s stomach until she looked Isabelle in the eyes, her expression cold, remote.

Isabelle had loved her once. What happened?

Such a small question, but as she wondered, fear dissolved like sugar crystals under a hot stream of tea and in its place came curiosity, understanding, compassion. She sent them skimming along the surface of Isabelle’s thoughts.

Triumph.

Disdain.

Meg held her breath, afraid but welling with grace too. Then she dove down until she was looking through Isabelle’s eyes, watching handsome young Nick Ainsley bring her refreshments at the village *fête*. She felt the pleasure of wearing a pink bow in her hair, of reading him and making a game out of being what he wanted, of winning his devotion, of weighing his worth.

If only he was going to be the earl.

Time slipped through her hands and Meg caught it like a ribbon. She was at Blythe House now, leaning toward the mirror and seeing Isabelle’s reflection, her face blemished with faint pockmarks. *I’m hideous.* Mrs Jolly came to bring her to dinner, touching her hand. "You must come down, Miss Summers."

I won't.

And so she doesn't. She'd discovered how to push instead.

Meg's blinked, surprised to find herself still on the rocking deck of a Danish ship, her arm turning to ice. A pounding in her brain grew louder and louder. She could not resist it much longer.

Meg jerked into Isabelle's head again, crossing her arms as she sits watching dancers at a ball. She looks at her gloved hands. The pushing frightens her but she can't stop. It is so much easier to get what she wants. Dresses, parties, a Season of her own.

But Aunt Olympia is difficult to push. She doesn't like touching. Childlike, Isabelle tries to hex her, gathering an assortment of items and stealing her words from Shakespeare's witches. She knows it won't work. But touching Aunt Olympia's garnet ring and wishing she would stop her mouth works very well, indeed.

She watches the dancers swinging and twirling and boils in anger. She isn't anybody who matters. All they see is a little country nobody with a tiny dowry.

If only...

Isabelle is in the library now. Grandfather is showing her off to his friend while they play a game of chess. The old earl doesn't like her. She feels that from the indifferent brush of his hand. He doesn't like young ladies, but she can make him like her.

Meg felt the cool sea air wrapping around her and her arm began to burn with cold, as though the flesh and sinews were peeling off in long strips. She would be on her knees in another moment. Scenes from Isabelle's life whirled past, faster and faster.

Isabelle at the altar alongside an erratic and shaking groom, and the priest asks her in a low, searching voice if she is being forced to marry. She turns a look up at old Lord Ainsley, offering him her youth and her beauty.

Why won't he take it?

Meg rocked back from the fury breaking like an ocean storm in her breast and redoubled her grip on Isabelle's wrist, fused to her sister's mind.

Isabelle is weak with pushing every moment, simply to keep him at her side. Her husband never gives her a rest. He never gives her a child either. A son.

I only want a son.

The constant pushing dries up her womb and now he's dying, curled up in the corner and frightened of her.

Grief.

Meg felt her sister's emotion devour her, fermenting in every sinew, levering open her own heart and finding the grief she held for Grandfather, the pain of loss.

Isabelle's grief was not like that. But it was honest, nonetheless. She grieved, not for a husband she had never loved or even known, but for herself. Counting out the years of toil and weighing it against all she had gained. No home to call her own. No child to secure her future. No wealth amassed. No friends.

I see their eyes when I'm not pushing them to like me.

Isabelle strides through the door of a shop and hears the ring of a bell. Shrewd eyes make calculations about her worth. A ripping, rending animal instinct takes Isabelle now. It's so easy to change their minds, to make them respect her, to watch them dance. It only costs a button or a thimble, a book. Come closer.

Let me touch you.

People move farther away, out of reach. She opens a solicitor's letter. Nick is coming home.

Meg felt herself grow warm and breathless in Isabelle's remembrance of what it was like to be adored for being one's self. Or almost one's self.

He loved me once.

He will love me again.

No need to push him.

Meg howled as the ice burned, concentrating in her elbow, grappling up her bones. She wanted to stop. She wanted to leave Nick to Isabelle. Let them sail away. Let them leave. It wouldn't hurt her at all.

A spasm rattled through Meg's frame and she looked up, as though from under a fathom of water at the fear that might save her, pulling her out of Isabelle's grip and making her master over her sister. The path whispered dark promises that she might forget every pain, every ill. It would give her peace. She would be at peace.

Reach for it.

Meg trembled, never more desperate in her life to end the pain. She wanted to stop feeling so much pain.

Her eyes fastened on Nick and she turned, diving harder for Isabelle's center though the agony in her ears and arms was narrowing her vision into tiny glittering pinpricks.

Isabelle is in Blythe House now, trying not to push, trying to win Grandfather over on her own. It is far easier than she imagined. Touching, almost. He wants her back.

She can start again.

And then her little sister returns. Margaret. She's exquisitely beautiful. Isabelle knew she would be. Isabelle resists the urge to touch her hair as she used to. So long ago in another life.

Then Margaret begins taking Grandfather's attention. Reminds Isabelle of how she wronged the little sister. She pushes away from it. There's no room for that in her plans.

She watches for Nick, waits for him to remember how he loved her. Margaret ruins everything. She's in the way. She's always in the way.

I have to push him.

Nick. Meg would do anything to keep him safe. She reached for Nick with her free hand, feeling his grasping hand seize hers like a lifeline. *There is no fear in love...*

At that, a warm melting heat moved down her arms, passing through her fingers. The warmth dropped like a marble into a pool of water, falling, falling into the center of Isabelle's power.

There it rested until it heated and heated, melting the ice. It didn't stop. Meg looked at Isabelle, saw her eyes widen, saw the fear swim in her pupils until a radiating wave of light and heat blasted through Isabelle, cauterizing old wounds. Finishing it.

All of it.

Light seemed to go out of Isabelle altogether, spilling into the night sky. Meg fell backward, stumbling against the wheel, and Nick fell away.

"You've taken it," Isabelle howled.

"I didn't do anything," Meg murmured, doubled over in grief and weariness, the words smashing through her. Sleep wanted to claim her. Tears and sleep. Thin clouds streamed past a night sky filled with stars. White spray blew from the water, setting the boat rocking. Nick began to rise, propping himself up on his hands.

"What did you do?" Isabelle shouted, flinging herself on Meg and beating her arms. Meg fought her off until Nick, rising to his feet, wrestled her from behind. “Give me my magic back,” she snarled.

Meg dropped to her knees and gave a tiny shake of her head, blood coursing down her arm in a slow rivulet. “I could not be so cruel, Isabelle.” The words came in a sob. “You can be free of it now. I saw how trapped you were, you are. I saw you—” she gasped, dark, blurry dots spotting her vision.

“You see nothing,” Isabelle spat, falling to her knees. Weariness was catching up with her too.

Nick dragged the rope from the deck and bound Isabelle to the railing, his movements deft and secure. Then he rushed to collect Meg as she sagged to the deck, holding her to him, smearing blood across the glorious waistcoat. “Nick—”

“Shh,” he said, bending over her, looking at her with eyes that shone. “We have to see to your arm, sweetheart.”

She frowned, not wanting easy endearments.

“Is it bad?” she asked, wishing to wail like a baby. All of Isabelle’s demons roiled in her still. If it would leave her along with the blood, she would as soon bleed a while more.

“Hardly a scratch,” he said, but faintly, through the maelstrom, she read his terror.

“Take me to Sam,” she breathed, hanging onto consciousness by the thinnest thread. “Promise me.”

“Yes, my love.”

“Don’t call me that,” she grouched, just as the sweetness of oblivion rose up to meet her.

***

Nick advanced up the wharf with Meg in his arms, within sight of every drunkard and wastrel in Pevensey. He had no cloak to protect her privacy or draw across her face, and the light from the taverns gave him no place to hide. Her reputation, already on the floorboards, slipped between the cracks and tumbled even lower. God forgive him when she woke up.

Cutting inland to High Street, he worked his way east until he stopped at a cottage with a bow-fronted window. He raised a fist to the door and did not stop beating until it swung open.

"You," Samuel Fletcher said, pressing back against the door and closing it quickly behind him. "I thought you were the revenue officers."

"No, Meg is hurt and I need a surgeon."

Sam bent over his bundle. "Mrs Jolly is far more skilled at this sort—"

"We weren't at Blythe House," Nick cut him off.

"I'm not—"

"You'll do your best for her."

Samuel Fletcher nodded, leading Nick down a narrow hall into his father's surgery. Nick had expected the surfaces to be dusty and ill kept but, as he lit the candles around the room, he saw it was gleaming.

He set her carefully on the table and Samuel leaned over his shoulder, rolling back the sleeves of his nightshirt. "How did this happen?"

Nick relived the horror of watching a knife swing over his head, striking Meg when he should have been the one to take the blow. He could only grunt, "Knife. Can you fix it?"

Samuel brushed him aside and picked up Meg's arm, lifting away the neckcloth that had served as a makeshift bandage. Blood was everywhere and Sam clapped the cloth down again. "Hold this there," he commanded, turning to thread a needle near the candlelight. "Why is she still out? She hasn't lost as much blood as that. See?" He pointed and Nick looked to a thin, crusty seam peeking from the bottom of the cloth. "It's clotting already."

"She's exhausted," he said, at a loss for words to describe the otherworldly battle Meg had fought and won. *My brave girl.*

Sam nodded. "Best to do it while she's out."

His stitches were uneven, those of an apprentice still, but, inch by inch, the wound began to close. He was managing the last when Meg's head rolled to the side, jerking her into wakefulness.

"There you are," Sam said, smiling at her. He knotted the bandage around her arm and put a hand to her brow as Nick looked on, outside the pool of light illuminating those two, so near in age. Meg seemed to see something in Sam that no one else had guessed at.

"I knew you could do it," she whispered, her voice coming out in a croak, before slipping beneath the waves of unconsciousness once more. Sam turned to tidy his basins and tools and Nick felt more certain than ever that he had been a monster to corner Meg into an engagement she didn't want.

It seemed obvious she wanted this unutterably stupid young man who, nevertheless, had the good sense to recognize what a treasure she was. With Meg at his side, Nick conceded that there was a narrow possibility he might become worthwhile.

She'd changed Nick, hadn't she? Wedging her tiny frame against him, prying him from the mistrust and bitterness he'd clung to, leaving him defenseless when she wound her way around his heart. There was no telling what she might do for a boy who was merely untried and foolish.

He drew close, slipping his hand into hers. He had to let her go. If what she told Isabelle was the truth, that the woman had a hand in his uncle's death and her grandfather's too, Meg had only agreed to marry him because she thought he might die at Isabelle's hand. Not, as he had hoped, because she was beginning to love him and was too cussed to admit it.

An angry man—a selfish man—would keep her for himself, but she had stripped him of even these shields.

He glanced to her hand in his and saw a raggedy red ribbon tucked in her sleeve. How was he ever going to let her go? Nick pulled on the ribbon, twining it around his fingers.

Samuel hung his apron on a hook by the door and unrolled his sleeves. "There's room upstairs for her to sleep and I'll take her back to Blythe House in the morning. You look all in," he said, buttoning his cuffs. He was no longer the wastrel son of Mrs Fletcher but the promising surgeon he was meant to be. And making Nick feel fifty, at least. "Go on home."

"No," Nick said, his good intentions dashing against a hard, implacable grief. He would give her up, he promised, but not today. "I'm her fiancé. She returns to the Abbey with me."

And so she had.

That state of affairs lasted no more than a day. While Meg snored gently in his bed, Nick carried on an argument with sweet Beatrice Gracechurch, who had become as immovable as a mountain.

"She will want to be among friends at a time like this," Beatrice whispered.

"I *am* her friend," he replied. Pansy-coloured bruises ran along his jaw and his hair jumbled on his head. He looked like he'd slept in a chair all night, which he had.

"We both know it's a good deal more complicated than that," Beatrice answered, seeming to spare no pity for him and his poor heart that beat in time with Meg's. She turned from the window looking out across the downs bright in the September sun and sat at his side. "Nick, if you've any hope of sorting this mess out, she can't be here, recovering from an injury with a rubbish engagement hanging over the both of you."

"You'll not take her back to Blythe House," he declared, scowling. Isabelle was there, waiting for his decision about the magistrate. Lord, letting her suffer for her crimes was what he wanted. But there was Meg to consider. Yes, and those two foolish boys as well. Any action taken against Lady Ainsley would have far-reaching repercussions.

"You can't frighten me with your black looks, Nick," Beatrice said, pity in her eyes. "I know this is killing you."

Then why was she taking Meg from him? Nick ran fingers through his rumpled hair and made one final request.

"Don't let her near her sister."

"You haven't heard? The magistrate hasn't been able to find any local connection to those boats on the beach and Isabelle packed off to London." Damn. If he had been in his right mind, he would have set a watch. Now he would have to chase her down.

Beatrice touched his hand. "In any case, Meg will come to us at the cottage. You may find her there."

And so Jolly and Beatrice had bathed and dressed her, walking on either side of her as she left his home, leaning heavily on their arms. The steps were folded up, the door was shut, the coachman flicked his whip and Meg left, casting no look backward as she was driven from the grounds.

He stood at the bottom of the Abbey steps, rain pelting his face as the carriage curved out of sight. Repairs began in the spring assured him that the Abbey was watertight, and well situated to stand the winter storms ahead. It was in fine shape.

He was not.

Chapter Thirty-one

Meg swung through the door at Greenley's and the little bell bounced on its spring. Patrons of the village shop paused to glance at her, as they always did.

It had been a fortnight since Isabelle's disappearance and Meg was well-bundled in a warm pink pelisse against a sudden cold snap that had settled on the downs, bringing frosty mornings and thoughts of autumn.

Esther Gracechurch approached, her steps making a waltzing rhythm with her cane. "It's you I have to thank," she said, "but my brother told me to keep myself out of the way and leave you be. So I'll say it now. Because of something you said, Jacob Thackery asked me to marry him and I—"

"Henry told me." Meg smiled, though it was an effort these days. However, her pleasure was genuine. "I saw how much Mr Thackery wanted to ask you. I hoped he would do so."

Esther grinned at the memory. "The madman appeared at my parents' door one morning to beg for my hand. The entire household was still in their nightclothes and he was shouting up the stairwell, 'It's high time, woman! It's high time!'"

Meg choked. "Just like a man to forget the best part. Of course you said yes?"

"Heavens no. I thought he was bosky. But he kept asking. Three days of it. And then in the middle of a family dinner we somehow got ourselves locked in a pantry." Esther coloured becomingly. "We emerged most definitely engaged."

Meg laughed, the first real laugh she had let loose in two weeks and it was as though she was shaking off her sister's shadow.

She had spent far too much time wrestling with Isabelle's demons. In moments when her mind stilled, she turned over what it all meant, wondering where Isabelle was, wondering if being stripped of her powers had rendered her impotent.

Meg traced her fingers along the raised scab underneath her sleeve, feeling an odd compulsion to prod the tender spots.

Discovering Isabelle's treachery had given her back the memory of her grandfather—the tenderness and care he'd offered at every turn. It ought to be enough. But Isabelle had also stirred old memories and frustrations of Grandfather wrapping Meg in wool cloth after Isabelle's elopement, of how she hid her writing, instinctively knowing that it would upset him.

Reaching into her enemy's heart had given her eyes to see complexity, intricacy, and colors as vibrant and varied as the stained glass of the village church, but bleeding into one another rather than demarcated into patterns of good and bad, wise and foolish, loved and hated.

"Will you still be with Henry at Michaelmas?" Esther asked. "You're probably impatient for your own nuptials."

"Of course," she answered, knowing that there would never be any. If Nick wanted her, he had known where to find her. And, beyond a few short notes, he hadn't.

Whenever Meg touched Henry or Beatrice, the contact was enough to tell her how they loved her, how they worried over her, and faintly, woven through with a streak of shame, how they wondered when she might be well enough to leave. She ought to beg Aunt Olympia for a home and have done with it.

Tomorrow, she decided, for today's letter was another bit of nonsense for *The London Observer*.

No, not nonsense, she thought, clutching the precious missive. It dishonored her work to call it so. Her pen gave her a voice. It kept her from clinging to Isabelle's kind of magic to fill the voids.

Little Rose Thackery tucked her hand into Esther's and looked up with entreaty. Esther smiled down at her, then said to Meg, "If you need a respite from Henry's Lilliputian cottage, do drop in and see me."

Then she was gone with another ring of the bell and Meg turned to the counter to face Mrs Greenley, as sour as ever.

"Merely something for the post, Mrs Greenley," Meg said, digging into her reticule for a coin, "and a packet of pins."

"I don't serve your kind of woman."

The silence that descended over the shop could have been no less pronounced in a graveyard.

Shock had clamped Meg's mouth shut. "Pardon me?" The outraged words came from Mrs Fletcher.

"Don't pretend you don't know, Mrs Fletcher. This girl was seen in a drunken state being paraded along the taverns by the wharf. There's a name for that kind of woman and it—"

A roar tore from Mrs Fletcher's throat and she snatched a long-handled broom, banging it hard against the counter. "If you don't shut your mouth, Agatha, I'm going to stuff it for you," she shouted, spitting like an angry goose in the center of Greenley's.

"But she's—"

Mrs Fletcher took a wide swing and whacked walnuts from the crate, spilling them across the floor with a dull rumble. "The tea crocks go next, Agatha. Make your mind up that you never saw such a thing yourself, and that you will never repeat such a scandalous bit of gossip or, so help me, I might lose my grip."

The proprietress was pale with shock, her back lance-straight, but she complied with Mrs Fletcher's demand. "I never saw such a thing."

"You have an awfully nice window." Mrs Fletcher waved the broomstick handle menacingly at the mullioned glass. "It would be a pity if it shattered into a thousand tiny pieces."

Mrs Greenley nodded shortly and slid a packet of pins across the counter to Meg, who dropped a coin along with her post and scooped them up. "I would never repeat any such story or allow it to be repeated in my hearing."

"Excellent," Mrs Fletcher said, setting the broom aside and dusting her hands. Her voice rose above the babble of the other patrons. "I remember that night well. Miss Summers's brave actions saved Sam's life…and the lives of other boys in this town. She's the reason Pevensey will have a trained surgeon in a few years."

Her words set off another flowering of talk and Meg took Mrs Fletcher by the sleeve as she left the shop. "Is he really going to be trained?" she asked, standing in the road.

The woman nodded, her mouth wobbling now that she no longer wielded the broom like a Scottish highlander with a broadsword and a blood feud. "He left last week for Brighton. If he squanders this chance, I swear that I will take a broomstick to his head. I don't think he will this time."

Meg smiled. Then her eyes clouded. "About that night I arrived at your doorstep so unceremoniously, Mrs Fletcher. Do you want to know the reason I was on the wharf in such a condition?"

"No." That's all she said. *No*.

Then Mrs Fletcher leaned forward, her bright eyes intense. "You've given my son a fresh start," she said. "And I—" She bit her lip.

Meg nodded, understanding at last. Mrs Fletcher was offering Meg the same in return. Like Sam, she would not dare squander it.

But, when finally Mrs Fletcher composed herself, she said, "I hope you'll give me a second chance, too."

Meg opened her mouth, but no words arrived in tidy, well-mannered regiments to leap from her tongue. She had supposed that Mrs Fletcher would, over the last fortnight, be busily sweeping her gratitude away like an unsightly mess of ale and sawdust, no more to mar the smooth, clean surface of her skepticism and judgment.

"After causing such a scene," Meg smiled, "I think I must."

"I wish it meant that the tittle-tattle would stop, Miss Summers, but Pevensey is too small for that. Still, most of the talk from the gossips this winter will be about how they were in the actual room when Mrs Fletcher lost her mind."

Mrs Fletcher reached out a hand, and Meg made herself stand perfectly still as she received the touch. With some difficulty, she resisted the impulse to flinch away. Mrs Fletcher's thoughts tumbled from her mind like a walnut, a whirl of plain gratitude and motherly concern, interlarded with the wicked pleasure of giving Mrs Greenley her just desserts.

It wasn't anything earth shattering but, nevertheless, Meg felt the circle around her widen to encompass the woman, felt the pleasure of opening her heart, felt herself take a brick from the wall that divided her from others.

She wanted more of that. Whatever else her future brought, she wanted more trust, more grace, more people. It wouldn't be easy. It was sure to bring upsets and disappointments, but it would be interesting, and far more rewarding, than her previous way. Meg smiled and began to walk with Mrs Fletcher up the road.

"And now," Mrs Fletcher continued, "that the earl has returned from London, you'll be wed. I assure you that there is nothing more dampening to loose talk than a happily married couple."

Nick was home? Meg blushed as she cast her eyes up the coast. She had learned from one of Nick's notes that the magistrates were not to be called in on Isabelle's case. There was too much risk for Jim and Sam, she supposed. For all her acquaintance with scandal, Meg could not regret that it would be handled discreetly.

"And now that Lord Ainsley owns Blythe House, your sister won't be stirring things up. I'm sure he doesn't need the property but that's love for you. It's an awfully expensive wedding present, what with you already owning an abbey next door."

"Nick owns Blythe House?" Meg's feet rooted into the compact soil. Her face must have been as blank as her mind because Mrs Fletcher pinched her lips together.

"It was meant as a surprise, wasn't it? I've let the cat out of the bag."

Meg turned her face east, toward the watery sun. It would be a long walk. A cold one too. She'd better get started.

Meg bobbed a curtsey to Mrs Fletcher. "Excuse me, ma'am. I have to pay a call on my fiancé."

***

Meg walked three miles over a rutted road toward the spires of Southdown Abbey, her nose growing colder by the minute.

Why had Nick bought Blythe House?

Answers presented themselves, but she was unable to give them any weight. That he seized a sensible investment opportunity seemed quite as likely as the idea that he was using the house to channel cash into Isabelle's coffers.

He had not even hinted at the possibility.

Jolly had come to visit her at the cottage as often as time permitted but, more and more, Meg felt her loyalty divided by the pleasure of managing domestic catastrophes at the Abbey with Brooks and seeing to her former charge. She brought baskets filled with bright apples, homemade tarts, and always some flowers rooted in a cast-off pot. She spoke not a word about Nick, only tucking his miserly notes in among the other things.

Brooks opened the door to her, a smile crossing his handsome features. "Finally. Come away out of that cold. We need some proper sorting out and you're the girl to do it."

Was she? Meg felt as though she had far more questions than answers. But she followed along after Brooks as he led her to the conservatory.

"He's likely to eat you, miss," he whispered. "Been like a dragon since that Mrs Gracechurch stole his horde away."

"His horde?"

"You, miss. It's a metaphor."

Meg laughed but, not given to fretfulness, tightened her gloves, pulling on the edge of the cuffs. "You wouldn't come in with me, would you?"

"Not for all the gold in Christendom, miss." He smiled, turning on his heel and leaving her to stare at the dark wood of the conservatory door.

Then she remembered her manners and tapped a knuckle against the door, not lasting through the sickening silence that ensued before leaning her head around it.

The sight that greeted her made her eyes widen in wonder. When had he done all this? Trailing vines and verdant shrubs filled half of the large, warm room. Bright color sprouted in beds and pots: vibrant yellows, waxy reds, feathering purples. Nick's strong back bent over a potting table, working in the fading mid-afternoon light, a watery sun penetrating the windows.

"I'm not finished," Nick said, not lifting his head. His bare hands bore an orangey clump of delicate flowers from an ornate blue and white pot into a small terracotta one with a chip along the rim.

Meg dug into her reticule and closed her hand around the green glass pebble.

She could have clasped it anytime this last month to know what Nick was thinking but how could she? Isabelle had caused so much trouble trespassing in his mind that she only wished to leave him be. Now, crossing the room with silent footsteps, she slipped past his elbow and slid the stone across the table.

Stillness settled across the planes of his shoulders and she held her breath. Then Nick set his hand over the rock, closing it in a dirt-grimed fist.

"Have you come to invite me fishing?" he asked, straightening to his full height, turning and looking down at her. Her heart rose in her throat to see the shadows around his eyes, the stern lines bracketing his mouth. Her hand lifted, wishing to smooth the grooves. She dropped it to her side.

"I've come to see an old friend." She glanced at the rock in his hand.

He towered over her for a moment before slipping the stone into his waistcoat pocket. The room contained a mismatched collection of furniture nearby, more comfortable than fashionable, and he walked to a table to pour out a small measure of Madeira, sending her a questioning look, which she answered with a shake of her head.

"Why have you come?" he asked, downing the liquid in a single swallow.

Meg bit her tongue before hot words tumbled from her lips. *Why haven't you come?* "I received a strange bit of news this morning from Mrs Fletcher." Watching Nick closely, she could swear she saw him flinch at the woman's name. "That you bought Blythe House from my sister."

Nick's brows lowered as he gazed at the door. "Brooks," he growled. "He's got a tongue hinged in the middle, the meddling old spinster."

"If it's not too much trouble," Meg began, "I'd like to know why."

"I couldn't stand the thought of Isabelle next door." He held himself tense, as though she were a wild animal who might turn on him at any minute.

"She has no power over you anymore. I stole it away."

His mouth lifted on one side. "Yes you did. But it wouldn't matter if you'd shrunk her to the size of a mouse and carried her around in a cage: she'd still be dangerous. I didn't want her in the neighborhood."

"So instead, you gave her money," Meg said, her eyes trained on his face.

"I would give her a fortune to see her gone from Blythe House, but that's not what she got from me. I didn't have to with the threat of legal action hanging over her head. In the end, we struck a bargain. I would purchase the property for a third of its worth, doled out as a modest living. And she agreed to make her permanent home north of Hadrian's Wall. The moment that she crosses it, she surrenders all income."

"You sent her to Scotland? Made her leave the country?"

"Yes," he answered. "And I hope she freezes her toes off."

His tone—dismissive, scathing—told her better than his words that Isabelle's happiness was no more part of his reckoning. The thought of it made her heart beat harder and she gripped the table.

"What will you do with it now?" she asked, half-afraid he wished to burn her home to the ground, laying waste to the rubble.

He stared into the empty glass hanging from his dirt-rimmed fingers, rolling imaginary liquid around the bowl. "I thought you might take it."

The beat of her heart shifted into her stomach, and each beat meant something different. Love. Sorrow. Hope.

Why was he being so off-hand, as though the expenditure of more than ten thousand pounds was a manner of little importance? "Your notions of propriety are disarranged, my lord."

"Nick," his name ground between his teeth and he snapped the glass on the table.

"Someone has to think of your character, *my lord*," she retorted, baiting him, knowing they must cut through this thicket of niceties at any cost. She raised her voice. "You can't go around giving a house to an unmarried lady."

"Then what will you take from me?" he roared, shaking the rafters, the ferocity of it lingering long after the last echo.

His chest heaved and he let out a breath, raising his hand to her in contrition.

"Nothing," Meg whispered. "I want nothing."

He turned away from her, bracing his arms across his chest and staring through the tall glass windows that lent the room a delicate, sacred atmosphere more fitting to a house of worship than a garden. Lord, how they both loved their armor.

"There is one thing you'll have to take from me. Something within my power to give you."

She waited, every word he spoke another uneven step on a rutted road.

"The banns have been read, but I will not hold you to them. You are free."

The blade sliding into her arm had hurt her less and she dropped her eyes to his waistcoat, blinking away the film of sudden tears.

"I—" she began, halting at a curious sight. Curling out of his pocket was a bright red ribbon, the color of ripe berries. Her ribbon.

When had she last had it? The last night she saw him. He'd returned it and she'd shoved it into a sleeve. But there it was, tucked into his pocket as though it had been there all along.

She stared at the door. Brooks might be meddlesome, but he was an excellent valet. That ribbon would have been removed each day. But there it was.

She caught her breath and turned to the worktable. Her tongue ran along dry lips. "I thank you for casting me off. It's bound to be a nine-days' wonder. Perhaps I'll go away for a little while."

"Where?" he asked, his voice sounding as rough as a boat scraping along a rocky beach.

"Aunt Olympia might not toss me from her doorstep. And then again, Beatrice offered to write to her godmother asking if she needed a companion. As Blythe House is not my home anymore," she said, trying to sound as unemotional and direct as possible when her stomach was lurching as wildly as she did atop Puck's back. "There are places I might live quietly for a time," she said, running the tips of her fingers along the scratched grain of the tabletop.

And then there was the house, purchased merely to pass it over to her, as though it were less important than her crumpled bit of ribbon. Oh Lord. How had she not seen it? Hope began to blaze within her. The pebble. The ribbon.

"You? Quiet?" he said, working himself into a fine fury. "You'll make a dreadful companion for someone who wants peace. And I don't like to think of you crammed into a corner with a bit of sewing while some old lady orders you about until—"

"You paint such a picture, my lord," she went on, conscious that the heaviness she'd carried these past weeks was lifting like a lacy veil. Now the ground felt firm under her feet and a heady optimism sang through her blood.

"Very well," she said, unable to stifle a coquettish drift of her eyelashes. Was he noticing? Oh yes he was. "Because all my other choices are so terribly bleak, I agree to marry you, instead."

There was some satisfaction that she'd managed the same casual tone he'd used when offering her the ancestral home.

His face settled into the hard lines she loved.

"No, Meg. No. I refuse."

She lifted her brow. The one he'd kissed that night. "Refuse? But, Lord Ainsley, the banns have been read, I spent the night in your rooms—"

"I was half dead."

"Only half." She smiled as she remembered Jolly's words. "Anyway, you can't refuse."

"But I do." His brows lowered.

The man really was a beast, securing himself behind high walls and thick defenses. Meg conjured a scowl. "Then I'll sue you for breach of promise, drag your family name through the swamp, and make you wish your ancestors had never been born."

He blinked heavily as he took a deep breath. When they opened again, his eyes were tender, full of sorrow. Didn't he know she'd caught him yet?

"You wouldn't dare," he said. "Your heart is too soft. Meg, you can't stand me—"

"That hasn't been true for days."

"It is true. You think I'm an uncaring, reclusive cad. And I am a cad, Meg. I backed you into this engagement by throwing myself on your mercy," he said, leaning back against the table at her side.

"And I am willful, belligerent, and ruined," she answered.

He made an aggravated face. "Not ruined a speck, Meg."

Her heart glowed at that, but she sailed right on, giving a tiny shrug, tugging him along like a trout on a hook. "I expect there will be a period of adjustment for both of us, but I am prepared to make concessions."

"Why?" he snapped, his patience at an end. "Why change your mind?"

"A coronet and the emeralds?" she offered. With a nimble leap, Meg boosted herself up to the surface of the potting table, sitting still, her hands curling over the edge, inches from where Nick leaned, both of them facing the same direction.

"Utter rubbish."

"The Ainsley emeralds? Everyone says they're lovely even if they haven't been out from under lock and key in thirty years."

"You turned down a house, Meg. You're not likely to get soft-eyed over some paltry gems. Give me a better reason." His muscled arm bumped hers coaxingly.

The brief contact almost wrecked her control, but she breathed hard, feeling the constriction only grow as he turned to step in front of her. Her eyelids drifted down. "The Abbey is so much larger than Blythe House. You once laid all your worldly goods at my feet and I cannot resist them. In return…" She reached toward him, giving the faintest tug at his waistcoat, slipping her ribbon from his pocket. "I'll let you keep this."

The ribbon lay on her palm in a spool. His breath stopped and she lifted her eyes only to find his gaze seemed tethered to her gloved hand.

She must be brave now. Their heads were bent together, examining the ribbon as though it was an exotic insect. In a low voice, "It took me a long time—too long—to work out why Isabelle couldn't push you after your sickness. I wondered if it was because she lost focus or that I had somehow managed to push you after all. I didn't understand it until I saw you had this," she said, winding the ribbon onto a finger.

Nick opened his mouth, closed it again.

"She couldn't push you because you had a talisman that you must have carried at all times."

His mouth tucked as he thought. "Did you infuse it with some of your magic?"

"No." She smiled. Heavens, she was almost laughing. "You did. In order to push you from far away, Isabelle needed something you treasured. Do you know what she took?" Meg pulled the green stone across the table, the sound of it scraping along the finish. "In order for you to be protected from her pushing, you needed a talisman that mattered equally as much."

Meg set the ribbon alongside the pebble.

She looked up and found that his eyes were on her face. "I am a horrible brat, Nick, to tease you about marriage. I pledge to let you be forevermore if you answer one question with perfect honesty."

He looked like a man in front of his own gallows. "I will."

She would not use her magic on him. He must tell her on his own. "Why does this scrap of ribbon matter to you? Why does the rock?"

Nick put the lightest finger on the trailing ribbon. His eyes lifted to hers and he simply stood there for a long moment, his large shoulders and great height no longer armor against her insistence. "I love you. Is that what you wanted to hear?" His voice ragged.

Yes, that was what she wanted to hear. From the day she'd stood, knee-deep in a stream, wondering how her best friend had become something dearer. Her stays felt constricting as she took a great breath and blinked. But the man sounded profoundly put out at the thought of loving her. Perhaps he still needed to be persuaded on some material points.

"Then why won't you marry me?"

His hazel eyes softened. "I'm not the same man I was when I came home, Meg, looking after his own interests, caring only for his own comforts. You saw to that. You and Sir Frederick, and that damned soft heart of yours that can't help but love everyone, even when they fall short. That man I was would have married you and taken what he wanted. This one wouldn't."

Meg could hardly speak. "Why not?"

He leaned over her, trapping her with two braced arms, not touching though the distance between them seemed to halve every second.

"I would see you happy, Meg. I bought Blythe House because I wanted you to have a measure of freedom. If it's with Sam or some other—"

"Sam?" His face was so near that looking at it made her eyes almost cross and she jerked back to get a better look. "What has he to do with anything?"

"—man. If it's Sam, he won't make much money at first. Even if you marry after the apprenticeship—"

"What are you banging on about?" she ground out, shoving at his chest, feeling the granite-hard immovability under her glove. "I have no intention of marrying Sam Fletcher."

"You wouldn't marry a surgeon?"

"I would marry a surgeon if I loved a surgeon, but never in my life have I harbored tender feelings for that boy." She involuntarily gagged. "And it's not because he's training to be a surgeon. The idea. I don't have a jot of passion for the lad, and I assure you, I would not marry without it."

Nick's eyes narrowed suddenly, the golden lights blazing at her. The shift was barely perceptible, but it was the difference between the defeated lion in the London Tower and another in the wild grasslands, king of all he surveyed. Her breath caught.

His head dipped to her ear, his voice a soft growl, his breath tickling her ear. “You were willing to marry me, Meg.”

Her eyes shut as she savored this moment, and when she blinked them open again, hope blazed in her chest.

“Oh?” She gave what she supposed was a good imitation of innocent confusion. Fingers that appeared to move of their own volition walked up his chest. “I have no idea why that could be.”

“You are the worst liar,” he said, trapping her hand against his heart. “Do you think you might be able to discover a little passion for me?”

“Perhaps,” she whispered back. “If I apply myself to it.” She reached her other hand toward him, but he frowned and drew back.

“No more of this,” he said, tugging away her kid gloves, slipping them from her fingers. He tossed them aside where they hit the tile floor with a smack and laid her bare hand against his rough cheek, turning his head to kiss her palm and waiting for her to read him.

The man was ready for her, unfurling a memory like a bolt of fine Chinese silk. *He was coming back to Blythe House for the first time in six years. Old Mr Ross had invited him to take dinner and he felt an unaccountable excitement when he slipped the glass pebble into his evening waistcoat. She would be there. She must be. Were her eyes really the exact same color as this stone? Would they shine as brightly now as they did in his memory?*

Colors blurred and now he was bending over Isabelle's clammy hand, hoping for someone else, telling himself the lie that he wasn't. He wanted to ask after her, had almost resolved to, when her Grandfather said, "And Meg. We can't forget about Meg."

Nick's stomach dropped when he turned to her, fumbled for the stone, almost bringing it out for a comparison. Lord, he thought, memory had been a pale shadow.

Meg felt the wonder of his emotions pressing against her own throat. Relief that she had become more than he wished she would be, the first faint suspicions that he no longer belonged to himself.

Meg saved for another time the chance to dive deeply into his thoughts. It was enough—too much almost for her fragile emotions—to absorb the plain reality that he loved her, the heat of it sparking from their touch like a bead of water skipping off a hot pan.

Do you love me then?

The question filled his mind and she felt his longing as endless as the night sky for her to say the words.

"I do," she spoke. "I do love you."

A light came into his eyes and he dipped his head, bringing with his new assurance the half-pain of anticipation. Then he grasped her around the waist and closed the distance, settling his mouth on hers in a kiss that warmed her far better than the furnace in the center of the room. His hands were still filthy. Her frock would be ruined. These were her last coherent thoughts before she gave up trying to think at all.

"Tomorrow morning," he said at length, resting his forehead against hers, his heart thundering away under her hand. "I'll pay the vicar double to clear the church first thing in the morning and we'll drag everyone from their warm beds. There's no reason we need to put it off," he said, as though she had made him wait a decade already.

"Why not wait for better weather?" she laughed. "The church will be an icehouse." Each word was punctuated with a kiss.

"Then you'll have to dress from head to toe in flannel." He grinned, lifting her from the table and carrying her across the room like the lord of creation. There he settled with her in a deep armchair while his thumb made lazy circles on her arm.

"Do you remember that day when you suggested eloping to Scotland?" he asked, carrying on when she gave a nod. "It was all I could do to let you get out of the carriage. Please don't make me wait."

She wrapped her arms around his neck. "Tomorrow."

Long silent minutes followed when the only sound to be heard was of coal shifting in the furnace. A shuffling sound brought her head up to find Brooks standing inside the room, clearing his throat. Meg blinked and attempted to scramble off Nick's lap, horrifyingly certain that Brooks would see this sight in his mind's eye every time she asked him to bring wine from the cellar or organize the silver. She was sure of it.

Nick, however, was unconcerned, keeping her in place with the simple but effective method of clamping his arms around her waist. He kissed her on the tip of her nose and looked over her shoulder.

“What is it, Brooks?” he asked with such perfect mildness that Meg bit back a laugh.

“Araminta feared you would be waging a pitched battle, your worship. I came to see if you’d had enough of Miss Summers, and if she’d had enough of you.”

Nick reached for a cushion and threw it at the door, narrowly missing a pot of orchids as Brooks dodged.

Nick gave Meg a look far richer, as filled with fishing streams and childish mischief as it was of lover’s promises.

Tomorrow he would belong to her.

Tomorrow she would steal his banyan robe and make him tell her how he got that tattoo.

As the door closed, she tugged his head closer. They’d wasted enough time already.

Light sprung into those remarkable golden eyes that set her heart racing.

“Enough of you?” he said, a breath away from her mouth. “Never.”

ABOUT THE AUTHOR

Keira graduated from BYU with a B.A. in Humanities, and lives in Portland, Oregon with her husband and five children.

Over the last decade, she has co-authored *The Uncrushable Jersey Dress*, a blog and Facebook page dedicated to mid-century author, Betty Neels. Cultivating this corner of fandom confirmed the suspicion that people who like sweet romances are as smart, funny, and are as interesting as readers of any other genre.

When Keira is not busy avoiding volunteerism at her kids' schools like it is the literal plague, she enjoys scoring a deal at Goodwill, repainting her rooms an unnecessary amount of times, and being seized by sudden enthusiasms.

Take Tea with Keira at:
keiradominguez.com
facebook.com/keiradominguez8
twitter.com/keira_dominguez
instagram.com/keiradominguezwrites

Boroughs
Publishing Group

CPSIA information can be obtained
at www.ICGtesting.com
Printed in the USA
FSHW011953300421
81022FS